SCHRADER'S
CHORD

SCHRADER'S
CHORD

Scott Leeds

NIGHTFIRE

TOR PUBLISHING GROUP
NEW YORK

SCHRADER'S CHORD

A Nightfire Book
Published by Tom Doherty Associates / Tor Publishing Group
120 Broadway
New York, NY 10271

www.tornightfire.com

Nightfire™ is a trademark of Macmillan Publishing Group, LLC.

The Library of Congress Cataloging-in-Publication Data is available upon request.

ISBN 978-1-250-23207-6 (hardcover)
ISBN 978-1-250-23206-9 (ebook)

Our books may be purchased in bulk for promotional, educational, or business use. Please contact your local bookseller or the Macmillan Corporate and Premium Sales Department at 1-800-221-7945, extension 5442, or by email at MacmillanSpecialMarkets@macmillan.com.

First Edition: 2023

Printed in the United States of America

0 9 8 7 6 5 4 3 2 1

For Mom and Dad

Jim opened the door wider and stood in the music, as one stands in the rain.

—Ray Bradbury, *Something Wicked This Way Comes*

From the top of the mountain to the rotten sand
They dragged the dead farther west 'til they ran out of land.

—Wolf Parade, "It's a Curse"

SCHRADER'S
CHORD

The American businessman's eyes glowed brightly in the fading sunlight as he watched the shopkeeper pull the object from the shelf. It seemed indefensible to him that an item of such value should be gathering dust in such a place . . . lost amid a sea of worthless flotsam and cheesy tourist souvenirs.

Even with the shop windows open, the heat was thick. The stale air sat bitterly on the man's tongue, poisoned with decades of sweat and dust. Somewhere, buried in the mess of trinkets and baubles, a radio was on. Through its crackling speakers came the unmistakable sound of a baseball game, broadcast in broken English.

The shopkeeper grunted as he placed the object on the table, not because it was heavy, but because it wasn't. He smiled a false smile, one that was well rehearsed, and looked up at his customer, his brow slick with sweat.

"Tall tales, Mr. Remick. I believe this is what you called them, yes?"

The businessman nodded.

The shopkeeper traced the object lightly with his finger. "Stories that grow with the light of time?"

"I suppose so, yes."

"And what is it that grows in the light, yet disappears in the dark, Mr. Remick?"

The businessman was in no mood for riddles. The heat was unbearable, fraying his last nerve, and after all he'd been through—after the thousands of miles he'd put behind him over the past four months—his search was nearly at an end. All that remained was this transaction.

Thankfully, the riddle was easy enough to solve.

"A shadow."

The shopkeeper smiled, showing his teeth this time. They were small, packed tightly into large gums, and stained yellow. "Yes! A shadow. That is correct." His smile faded as he stared again at the object. "But the *taller the tale, the longer the shadow, Mr. Remick, and this tale casts a shadow so long and so black, it will swallow all of life . . . until there is only death."*

The businessman pulled out his wallet.

"How much?"

PROLOGUE

Louis Goodwin sat in his car and waited for the sun to go down.

Not that he needed to. The weather app on his phone told him that sunset was scheduled for 5:46 P.M., but here it was, only a few minutes past five, and it was already as dark as midnight. Through his windshield, he saw black clouds.

Black enough to blind a star, he thought, convinced he'd heard that line somewhere before. When he couldn't place it, he flipped on his wipers. It had stopped raining nearly twenty minutes ago, but there were still a few scattered patches of moisture on his windshield. He watched his wipers stutter embarrassingly across the window, all but missing the resilient raindrops.

That's what I get for buying the cheapies and installing them myself, he thought, staring balefully at the quiet street in front of him. Last spring, on a spur-of-the-moment drive up to British Columbia, Louis had stopped at a 7-Eleven in Bellingham to stock up on Corn Nuts and Diet Coke (his favorite travel combo) and had decided that he'd better switch out his tattered old wiper blades with some fresh ones. The Pacific Northwest was, after all, famously rainy, and it was one thing to putter around Seattle in his battered old Camry, but it was another thing entirely to putter around Vancouver (a city he barely knew) with a rain-sopped windshield and impaired vision. So, with the help of a YouTube tutorial on his phone, Louis stood in the parking lot of the 7-Eleven and switched out his old wiper blades with the new ones.

And they worked for a while. And then they didn't.

And he hadn't switched them out since. Why should he bother? They were the least of his worries.

The road to hell might be paved with good intentions, but Louis Goodwin's intentions (which, as far as he was concerned, were as honorable as intentions got) would never lead him to a place as interesting as hell. If anything, *his* good intentions would most likely land him in hell's waiting room.

He pictured spending eternity in a drab, windowless room with brown shag carpet, lifeless floral wallpaper, and corduroy couches with plastic covering.

And maybe that was what he deserved.

Louis had once overheard a colleague describe him over the phone. It had been a rare, after-hours occasion at work and his then officemate, Arlene Thompson, was making the obligatory call home to her husband. "At least I won't have to go through it alone," she had said wearily. "Louis is here." After a brief pause, Arlene cast a quick glance at Louis, then turned away. "You remember Louis," she said, then dropped her voice to a whisper, "he's the one you called *beige*."

Louis remembered feeling hurt by that, but as he sat in his car and gazed out into the shadows, he wasn't really sure that *beige* could be considered an insult. If anything, it was an accurate (and economical) description. It was not only the color of his car, his suits, and his hair (or what little hair was left), but also his personality.

Louis Goodwin was beige, inside and out. He had passed through life quietly, rarely left a lasting impression on anybody, and was—for lack of a better word—boring.

Until now, that is.

A bead of sweat crawled down Louis's forehead. He pawed at the airflow knob on his console and turned down the heat. There were no streetlights at this end of Wabash Street, and the house, which he'd been casing for nearly an hour, was as dark as the sky above.

Dark, and quiet, and waiting for him to make his move.

"I don't know why you're even bothering," said a voice from the passenger seat. "Even if you don't get caught, you'll fail."

Louis loosened his tie and gingerly rubbed his temples with his fingertips. A bolt of pain ping-ponged from one side of his head to the other. "I have to try."

"And what if—and we're talking a big *if*—you succeed? Then what?"

"I don't know," Louis replied, which was the truth. He chewed on his lower lip for a moment, then said, "I only know that if I sit here and do nothing, I'll die."

A snort came from the passenger seat. "I vote you do nothing, then."

Louis wheeled around and stared into the cloudy, gray eyes of his dead wife. She sat straight-backed and prim in the passenger seat, dressed in the same shawl-collared cardigan she'd been wearing when she died. That was almost two years ago now.

"I don't even know why you came, Deb."

"Not come?" Deb said, delicately placing a palm on her chest. "And miss your debut as a master criminal? I wouldn't dream of it."

"*Can* you even dream?" Louis asked, eyeing her up and down as if he were a wary customer examining a beat-up sedan at a used car lot.

"Wouldn't know," she said flatly, then primped her hair in the side-view mirror. "Don't need to sleep anymore."

"You never slept much when you were alive," Louis said, and thought about adding *wickedness is a powerful battery*, but thought better of it. When it came to the art of verbal fencing, Deb was maître, prévôt, and moniteur all wrapped up in one. Louis would only end up stabbing himself. "And anyway," he continued, "I'm not even sure it's technically a crime."

"Breaking and entering isn't a crime? *Burglary* isn't a crime?"

"Raymond was my *client*," Louis said firmly, then added, less firmly, "and my friend. He gave me the code to the garage door. Why would he do something like that if he didn't—"

"He may have given you permission to enter his house, but I'm sure he wouldn't like you taking what's inside."

"Whether or not he would like it doesn't really matter anymore, does it? He's dead."

Deb crossed her arms. "And for most people, that wouldn't be a problem, would it?"

Louis nodded soberly.

He didn't know if he would ever get used to the idea of seeing dead people.

More often than not, he couldn't tell who was dead and who was alive unless he was close enough to see their eyes. The eyes of the dead were vacant, emotionless, and oddly stormy, like little cups of black coffee dolloped with heavy cream. An unsettling image, to be sure, but not necessarily frightening. It was the violent or blood-soaked deaths that really frightened him. To see a man standing on a street corner with a shattered jaw, his teeth hanging by floss-thin tendrils of shredded muscle and gum tissue, waiting idly to cross the street as if his face hadn't been caved in, froze the very marrow in his bones.

"If Raymond is still in there," Louis said, nodding toward the house, "I'll just explain everything. If anybody would understand, he would."

"And what if he doesn't let you take it?"

"Then the original plan stands. I take it anyway."

Deb barked a laugh. "I don't know where you've found this sudden surge of confidence, but I'm not buying it for a second." She tilted the sun visor down and checked her smile in the mirror, giving the space between her front teeth a probing lick of her tongue. "You'll shit the bed—like you always do—and slink out with your tail between your legs. And when that happens, I'll have the delicious pleasure of saying I told you so."

Louis fell silent as her words—cruel, but accurate—echoed through his mind. He wanted to tell her she was wrong this time, but since he had never found the courage to stand up to his wife when she was alive, it only made sense that he would find no such courage now that she was dead.

"Your ear is bleeding again."

"I know that," Louis replied, and pawed at the warm ooze running down his neck. He wiped the blood absentmindedly on his pants, leaving a fresh streak next to the older, darker, drier ones.

"That's three times today. I'm guessing that's not good."

Louis frowned and opened the Camry's door. "And circle gets the square."

Outside, the air was crisp, appropriate for a December evening, and Louis watched his breath fog as he stepped gingerly onto the blacktop. Had there been a streetlight at this end of the block, he supposed he would have seen a curtain of fine mist descending beneath the glare of the lamp, but it was too dark for that. He could barely see his own shoes.

He closed the Camry's door gingerly, turned back toward the house, and nearly yelped when he turned around and saw his wife's face.

"Ready when you are," she said, wiping the wrinkles from her cardigan.

Louis studied her warily. It was still a mystery to him how the dead moved. He couldn't remember hearing Deb open the passenger door. Did she teleport onto the steet? Did she just step out *through* the car? If so, that would mean she wasn't solid, which brought into question her ability to sit in the passenger seat in the first place. Wouldn't she just fall through it?

"I really wish you'd stay here," Louis said, heart thumping. "I'll be faster if I'm alone."

"Not on your life, Winky," she said, then strode confidently across the street toward the dark house, heels clicking loudly along the wet pavement.

Louis followed her up the long stretch of damp lawn. After looking both ways to ensure the coast was clear, he hopped over a row of hedges and collapsed into a clumsy somersault. He shot to his feet, knees stained by the dewy grass, then spun into the shadows next to the garage door.

If Deb's eyes still had pupils, she would have made a show of rolling them. "Hope you remembered the code, Mr. Bond."

Louis shimmied over to a white keypad that had been installed on a brick column next to the garage door. He flipped up the cover to reveal a set of glowing green keys. With a shaky finger, he punched in the four-digit code as the dull-as-dry-crackers theme from *M*A*S*H* played in his head.

"Four . . . zero . . . seven . . . seven . . ."

The door growled to life and Louis ducked into the garage. He weaved his way quickly through darkness, hissing as he caught his hip on the edge of a table saw, then skittered over to the door.

Deb, on the other hand, took her time. She sauntered slowly through the shadows, pausing here and there as she inspected the contents of the space. "Hell of a car this guy had," she said, tracing the body of a 1953 Buick Skylark with her finger. The chrome arch that ran along its side glowed blue in the moonlight. "Takes some real heft between a man's legs to handle a car like this." She gazed up at Louis and grinned. "Not that you would know."

A bitter tang climbed up Louis's throat as he pushed her insult out of his mind. "No mistakes," he said quietly to himself, pulling a pair of blue nitrile gloves tightly over his fingers, "no fingerprints." He pressed a nearby button and watched the garage door rattle back down to the ground.

Deb smirked. "No fingerprints except for the ones you left on the keypad outside, you mean."

Realizing she was right, Louis swore loudly, which, for him, meant a deep-throated "Oh heck."

Deb snickered. "I love when you speak Minnesota. It gets me so hot."

Ignoring her, he opened the door to the house and switched on his phone light. Inside, snow boots, sandals, tennis shoes, and a weathered pair of Crocs lined the wall of a narrow hallway.

"What are we looking for again?" Deb asked, glowering at the dirt-caked Crocs.

"A black case," Louis said, and headed into the next room.

"About the size of a microwave. It's a bit beaten up, with two latch locks on it."

They passed into what appeared to be Raymond's office. Dozens of boxes lined the floor—some stacked as high as three or four— and formed a sort of maze. Louis moved his phone in an erratic zigzag pattern and watched as the thick beam of light climbed over the boxes, dove into the shadows, then resurfaced on a far wall.

"I don't see it."

He was disappointed, but not surprised. Finding it in the first room they'd entered would have been a lucky break, and Louis Goodwin had never been a lucky man.

And anyway, the treasure was *never* in the first room. As a boy, he'd read enough Doc Savage stories to know that much. X rarely ever marked the spot for Doc, and even if it did, it was never at the entrance of the catacombs. Doc had to hack his way through a cavalcade of gruesome creatures, deadly booby traps, and menacing henchmen to find the treasure.

Louis only hoped his quest would prove to be more uneventful.

He stepped softly into the hallway beyond, careful to keep the beam of his phone light low, especially around the windows. Deb followed him, heels clicking loudly. She made a point of commenting on anything that wasn't to her taste, which, as it turned out, was everything.

Over the next ten minutes, Louis searched the living room, the kitchen, the ground-floor bathroom, the laundry room, and the pantry. He left no cabinet door unopened; no closet unexcavated. He even checked Raymond's office a second time, just to be thorough.

The black case was nowhere to be found.

"Heck!" he said again, more forcefully this time.

"Came up short, huh?" Deb said as she watched Louis check the kitchen for the second time. "Why am I not surprised?"

"If it's not in the house there's only one other place it could be."

He took a chance and opened the oven door. Nothing. "And it'll be a lot harder to break in there than it was to break in here."

Deb, who had been somewhat amused by this boondoggle at first, had clearly grown bored. Had she still been alive, she would have yawned for effect, but since her brain no longer required oxygen, she chose instead to make her way back to the living room and take the ugly davenport near the front windows for a test drive. "You keep looking, Mugsy. I'll send up a signal if I see the fuzz."

Louis waved her off with an impatient hand and went back to the main hallway, cautious with his footing. The house was old and the floorboards were talkative, and even though they were alone and Raymond was dead, Louis had no desire to alert him of his presence.

Because Raymond was here somewhere. He had to be.

Over the last five days, Louis had encountered a number of things he had been unable to explain, but one thing that he *had* ascertained, with his wife's help, was that the dead seem to reappear at the location of their death. Like Raymond, Deb had died at home, but unlike Raymond, she had been taken by a heart attack while sleeping peacefully in bed.

Raymond did not die peacefully in his bed, and Louis had no desire to be reunited with his client if the reports of his death were even *half* true.

He reached the end of the hallway and came face-to-face with a large staircase. From his tiptoes, he could see the first few feet of the second-floor hallway. Two doors faced each other on either side.

And behind those doors . . .

He pictured Raymond—God knew what his death had done to his face—sitting in a chair, bathed in shadow, waiting for him.

It was a nightmare of a thought, but Raymond or no Raymond, Louis knew he couldn't leave until he'd checked every room. So, with an audible gulp, he placed his foot on the first step.

"Louis!"

He spun around with such force, his heel slipped off the edge of the bottom step. He grasped for the railing, but it was too late. Swiping at air, he landed with a thud on his backside and clapped a hand over his mouth to mask a shriek. He bent forward, reducing the pressure on the part of his undercarriage that had landed on his keys, then pulled himself up on his feet.

Deb came running through the foyer, cloudy eyes open wide, whisper-shouting something Louis couldn't understand. But Louis didn't need to understand. He already heard the noise.

It was the garage door.

"Somebody's home!" Deb said, giggling like a schoolgirl who'd been caught smoking in the bathroom. Her hair bounced with every syllable, and even though she was dead, Louis could have sworn he'd seen her cheeks flush.

Of course she's loving this, he thought resentfully.

"Come on!" Deb cried, and disappeared back into the foyer, almost skipping as she went. "If they see you, they'll call the cops!"

An image of spinning red and blue lights, barking dogs, and handcuffs flashed through Louis's mind. If he were to be arrested, his chance of finding the black case before it was too late would almost certainly vanish. And so, heart hammering, Louis bounded into the foyer after his wife.

They skidded into the living room and collided with the davenport, which screeched along the floorboards. Louis peered through the windows and saw a bright pair of headlights staring back at him.

There was a car in the driveway.

Louis ducked into the shadows under the main staircase and began to hyperventilate.

I'm dead, he thought, gazing up at the railing, which rose gracefully into the shadows and disappeared into the darkness of the second floor. Despair rolled over him like a thick fog. *This is where it ends.*

Deb flicked him on the bruised part of his temple. "Come on, Winky! Our goose isn't cooked yet!"

Louis clenched his teeth. The pain was almost unbearable, but it had done what his wife intended. It had provided enough of a distraction to quell his defeatist thoughts. He snapped back to reality, and gazed over at his wife.

"Through the backyard!" she cried, finger in the air like Custer. "We're gonna make it!"

Louis nodded, pausing to take one more peek out the window, then followed her.

When he got to the kitchen, the back door was already open and Deb was gone.

So she can't *pass through doors,* Louis thought, then slipped quietly onto the back steps. He crouched low and eased the door closed, hissing at the coldness of the brass knob. He tore the nitrile glove off his hand and checked his fingers for marks. He looked again at the knob, expecting to see thin vapors rising from the brass, as if it were made of dry ice.

Around front, one of the car's doors slammed shut, and Louis shoved his still-burning hand into his pocket. He crept down the steps and into the backyard, wincing as a snap of frigid air pinched his face.

Standing near a brittle rosebush, about five feet from him, was Deb.

She stood with her back to him, stone-still in the hazy moonlight. All of her excitement, all of her teenager-like vigor, had evaporated, and if it hadn't been for the light breeze that sent shallow ripples through her cardigan, Louis would have sworn she was a statue.

"Come on, Deb," he whispered, tugging at her sleeve. "Let's shake a leg."

But she wouldn't move.

Something in the yard had caught her attention.

"Deborah, *please,*" Louis moaned, "if we don't leave now, we'll be—"

And then Louis saw it.

Thirty feet away, across the frosty, barren stretch of dark grass, the lifeless, gray eyes of Louis's deceased client bored into his own.

Raymond's face, glowing white in the moonlight, seemed to float in midair. He stared down at Louis, his milky gaze both focused and not, as his bloated, purple lips curled into a knowing smile.

"Find what you were looking for, Louis?"

PART I

ONE

I've got bad news in my pocket, Charlie Remick thought.

He closed his eyes and steadied himself against the load-bearing beam next to the soundboard. When he opened them, the world had righted itself, or seemed to. It was hard to tell in the darkness.

Jimmy, the guy running the soundboard, must have noticed the sudden change in Charlie's weather and leaned over to clap a friendly hand on his shoulder. He asked Charlie if he was all right. *Shouted* it, really. The crowds at Brooklyn Steel never got big enough to achieve a chest-rattling roar, but tonight they were in fine form, whooping and hollering and clapping and whistling enough to beat the band . . . so to speak. The band wasn't onstage yet.

Charlie nodded at Jimmy, forced a lopsided smile, and said he was all right.

He gripped his phone through his pocket. It was still buzzing with incoming text messages. He ignored it—or tried to—and decided instead to applaud with the other concertgoers, but there was something *other* than the bad news that made him uneasy— something that crept up his arms and forced the hair on the back of his neck to attention.

Dread, Charlie figured.

Or maybe something more sinister.

He sensed it, only for a moment—the way someone will catch a whiff of an oncoming storm in the air on a cloudless day—and then it was gone. Something big had been set into motion and he had been dragged aboard, an unwitting passenger along for the ride. He only wished he knew where he was being taken.

His pocket buzzed again.

Onstage, the lights went up—a cool mixture of blue and green— and the crowd maxed out the dial. The band took the stage, smiling and waving sheepishly as the applause reached a fever pitch, and when Joey Banes—the rail-thin singer of the Mightier Ducks—grabbed the mic and said hello, he blushed openly as three hundred (and counting) smiling faces answered him.

Charlie stood in his little spot next to the soundboard, arms crossed coolly over his purple corduroy blazer, eyes trained on the stage, looking every bit like the A&R man he was. Seth Larson, the Ducks' drummer, gave the wing nuts on his cymbal stands a cursory—and entirely unnecessary—tightening. Charlie saw this and sighed. The wing nuts were already tight. Seth knew that. They had been tight at sound check and they were tight now. The kid simply didn't know what to *do* with himself while the other guys fished picks from their pockets and plugged in their guitars.

Soon Seth would learn what all drummers eventually learn: just sit there and do nothing until you're ready to play. Fidgeting with your cymbal stand doesn't make you look like a pro, it makes you look nervous. And Seth looked nervous. They all did.

Charlie wished he could smile. These were the moments he loved. But the bad news in his buzzing pocket wouldn't let him. With a decisive whip of his wrist, he pulled out his phone and powered it down. He hoped doing so would ease the invisible vise around his chest, but just before the screen went black, his eyes caught the text message that started this whole nightmare and the grip around his lungs tightened even more.

The text message.

The bad news.

Hey guys. Dad passed away last night.

His heart skipped a beat, then after a brief lull in his chest, hammered heavily on the return swing. He shook his head, trying to clear the words from his mind, but they remained—floating aimlessly behind his eyes, the way the sun will burn a ring into your closed eyelids on a bright day.

Hey guys. Dad passed away last night.

A loud squelch from the house speakers forced the crowd to cover their ears, and Charlie shot Jimmy the sound guy an icy glare. Jimmy merely responded with a *whaddya gonna do* shrug and dipped one of the faders on the mixer. Onstage, Joey Banes was having trouble plugging his cable into the output jack of his Strat. His hands were shaking badly.

"Jesus Christ, Joey," Charlie mumbled impatiently. "Act like you've been here before."

Jimmy the sound guy shot him a quizzical look. "You sure you're all right, man?"

Charlie didn't respond. He was embarrassed that he'd been heard. Joey Banes was a good kid. Seth, too. They were all good kids. And this was a big night for them.

So give them a minute for chrissakes, Charlie told himself. *You're just stressed. Stressed and worried and feeling guilty because it's been five years since—*

A wave of supportive cheers erupted. Joey had finally managed to plug his guitar in. He blushed again, giving them a bashful wave, and Jimmy the sound guy pushed the fader back up.

Charlie relaxed, but only for a moment.

Because the words were still there . . .

Hey guys. Dad passed away last night.

. . . hiding in his pocket . . .

Hey guys. Dad passed away last night.

. . . and with each subsequent buzz of his phone, more words were coming.

Which of his sisters had written the initial text? he wondered. He'd forgotten to look. Was it Susan or Ellie? And what's more—he felt a pinch of anger now—who broke that kind of news over a text message?

It could have been either of them, really. Susan had always been a bit robotic in the emotional department and would no doubt prefer to break such news impersonally. Eleanor, on the other hand, never would have been capable of relaying such terrible words out loud without breaking into incoherent sobs, so a text message would be the more sensible—and efficient—approach.

Where was Ellie now? he wondered. San Francisco? New Orleans? El Paso? Was she back home already?

Charlie had always gotten along with his older sister, Susan, but he and Ellie were thick as thieves, and had been since the day they were born eleven minutes apart. They not only looked alike and talked alike, they had nearly identical track records when it came to their dismal dating life. They had their fair share of differences, of course. Ellie was a nomad, having lived in ten different cities in the past seven years. Charlie had lived in only one, and hadn't planned on a second. Ellie was also a crier, and Charlie wasn't. He wasn't emotionally blocked or out of touch with himself. He felt his feelings like everyone else. He just didn't cry. In fact, he could only recall two moments in his life that had moved him to tears. The first occurred while watching *The NeverEnding Story* for the first time (the memory of Artax the horse sinking into the Swamps of Sadness still severely bummed him out), and the second occurred while his mother's casket was being lowered into the ground.

Two perfectly good reasons to cry as far as he was concerned.

And now here he was, presented with yet another perfectly good reason, and he couldn't manage a single tear.

In fact, he began to laugh.

He couldn't help it. It was too perfect.

Raymond Remick had died and people around him were cheering.

The timing was too on-the-money to ignore. If Charlie hadn't been certain that such a thing was impossible, he might have suspected that his father had planned the whole thing.

One last wink of the eye from the old man as he passed from this world into the next.

Up onstage, Joey turned to his buddies, shared a quick nod, and then kicked into their first song, a real scorcher called

"Olivia Quinn." Charlie's eyes drifted to the banner hanging above the stage. Emblazoned upon the vinyl in neat type were the words SONY BMG WELCOMES THE MIGHTIER DUCKS.

Charlie sighed. They would need to change their name before the record came out. It was a conversation he'd repeatedly kicked down the road for the last few months (he didn't like to ruffle feathers during the signing process, especially since he'd already lost too many would-be signees to Sub Pop and Hardly Art and 4AD—labels that offered less money but more credibility than his current employer).

If it was done tactfully, Charlie should have no trouble convincing the band that names like the Mightier Ducks never stood the test of time. They were meta and stupid and only funny the first time you encountered them (if they were ever really funny at all), to say nothing of the fact that Charlie was in no mood to spend the next two years sparring with the Walt Disney Company over parody law, only to suffer a public loss and have to change the name anyway.

None of that mattered now, of course. The name change was a problem for tomorrow.

Tonight, Charlie had his own problem to deal with.

He let his hand drift once more to his pocket. His phone had stopped buzzing.

That meant that Ellie and Susan had graduated from text messages to a phone call, and Charlie was now out of the loop.

And there was nothing worse than that.

He spun around and eyed the path to the bathroom, but knew there wouldn't be enough privacy in there. Brooklyn Steel had a bad habit of employing a bathroom attendant, and Charlie had no desire to read the details of his father's death while an aging hipster looked on, hoping to sell him a two-dollar pack of Juicy Fruit.

Instead, he made his way toward the stage. There would be plenty of privacy in the green room, and even if there wasn't, he could always kick people out. He hated power moves like that, but such were the perks of the A&R man.

The crowd was dense, but Charlie had perfected the art of the weaving walk, and as he approached the side of the stage, he flashed the laminate around his neck. This was more of a courtesy than it was a necessity, as the security team at Brooklyn Steel all knew him well by this point. Antoine, a beefy Belgian whose pectoral muscles tested the tensile strength of his black SECURITY shirt, shot him a brief smile and let him pass.

Once through the gate, Charlie turned and peeked out over the stage.

The view never ceased to exhilarate him. It was one thing to watch a band from the darkness of the crowd, packed and sweating in a throng of bodies. It was something else entirely to watch the crowd from the stage. A sea of faces, bathed in light, gazed up at the Mightier Ducks as they plowed their way through their soon-to-be first single, and although none of them were looking directly at Charlie—not that they could see him back there anyway—he still felt the rush of their eyes on him. And it felt good.

He allowed himself a few more seconds to sponge up a bit of vicarious glory, noted that the high E string on Joey's guitar was a little flat (nothing he could do about that now), then made his way through the VIP section, which was mostly populated by roadies and girlfriends at this point. The groupies wouldn't start showing up in earnest until the record had been out for a few months. After exchanging a few brief handshakes with the Sony brass, Charlie made his way into the green room and shut the door behind him.

The space was empty, and he was grateful. That meant he wouldn't have to kick anybody out.

Luke the Shithead loved kicking people out.

He probably kicked his own mother out of the delivery room 'cause she wasn't wearing a laminate, Charlie thought darkly, then switched on his phone.

He had thirty-eight missed messages.

With a flick of his finger, he scrolled back to the beginning of the thread.

Once again, he was met with the cataclysmic text.

Hey guys. Dad passed away last night.

It had been Susan who sent it.

Her next message—which Charlie was now seeing for the first time—did little to soften the blow.

I'm sorry.

Ellie had responded immediately.

WHAT?! Oh mu god Susan what happened???

Normally Ellie would have corrected such a glaring typo, but she let *Oh mu god* slide. Understandable, given the circumstances.

I just talked to him yesterday! He said he had taken some time off but when I asked him if anything was wrong he said no he felt fine!!!

Susan, ever the empath, simply replied: Yeah.

At this point, Ellie must have tried to call Susan, because Susan's next text message read:

Sorry, Ell, can't talk now. I'm at Maisy's play. It's almost over.

To which Ellie responded: YOU TOLD US DURING YOUR DAUGHTER'S PLAY?!?!

SUSAN: I only just found out. I wanted you to hear it from me instead of someone else.

ELEANOR: And you thought telling us over TEXT was the way
    to go??

There it was, Charlie thought. Twin-thinking. Ellie was right. Breaking the news over text was bad form, and Susan should have known better.

A shriek of laughter bolted past the door.

Charlie jumped, said "Fuck," then rushed over and flicked the lock. The band would be onstage for another forty-five minutes at least, but that wouldn't stop one of the girlfriends from popping into the green room to pass the time. He put his ear against the door and listened as the laughter drifted away. When he was satisfied his privacy wouldn't be interrupted any further, he returned to his phone.

ELEANOR: And you thought telling us over TEXT was the way to
    go??
SUSAN: It's not like I had a lot of time to think about it, Ell. I made
    a gut decision.
ELEANOR: Who told YOU?
SUSAN: Some girl who works at Dad's store. I can't remember her
    name.
ELEANOR: Was it Ana?
SUSAN: Can't remember.
ELEANOR: What about Dale?
SUSAN: It was Dale who found Dad, apparently.
ELEANOR: Dad died at the store??
SUSAN: No.
ELEANOR: Then where?
SUSAN: He was at home.
ELEANOR: What was it? Stroke?

Then . . .

ELEANOR: Heart attack?

Then . . .

ELEANOR: Susan what was it??

Charlie noted the time stamps on Ellie's last two texts. The first had been sent at 9:03 P.M. (6:03 P.M., technically, since both his sisters lived on the West Coast) and the second had been sent at 9:05 P.M. Ellie had waited a full two minutes for Susan to respond before following up. When no response came, Ellie tried again.

ELEANOR: Susan how did Dad die?
SUSAN: I really can't talk right now. The play's almost over. I'll call you when I'm out.
ELEANOR: Jesus Christ Susan how did Dad die??
SUSAN: I WILL CALL YOU IN A FEW MINUTES.

There was another two-minute break, and then . . .

ELEANOR: Jesus Christ Susan this is so fucked up.

Charlie gave his screen a frantic flick of his finger, desperate to know more, but Ellie's text merely bounced back into place.

The conversation had ended.

Out of nowhere, Charlie started to cry.

He turned toward the mirror and watched himself do it, although he didn't know why.

He traced his oval jawline, gazed vacantly at his messy crop of mahogany hair and his slim build that had been harder and harder to maintain now that he'd passed into his thirties, and watched—in a strange, voyeuristic fashion—the tears stream down his cheeks.

He reached for a loose roll of toilet paper near the mirror and dabbed at his eyes. It was dark enough backstage that no one should notice their puffiness.

When his face was suitably dry, he went for the door.

The next twenty minutes were a blur.

He half remembered saying "My dad is dead, I gotta go" to a small group of people backstage as he walked out, but who those people were (and why he chose to divulge that information in such a way) remained a mystery to him. He had a vague recollection of the cab ride home and the nausea he'd felt as the rain lashed violently against the windshield.

Thanksgiving had been three weeks ago and, even though the city streets had been decorated with the customary symbols of yuletide cheer, the temperature hadn't yet dropped below forty degrees. It looked like it was going to be another wet, snowless Christmas in New York.

It was still raining heavily when his cab turned north on Madison Avenue from Twenty-Third Street and Charlie told the driver to pull over. He had no desire to walk the remaining eight blocks in such a downpour, but his head was spinning violently and he knew if he stayed in the car he risked painting the plexiglass safety shield with the contents of his stomach.

By the time he reached the northeast corner of Madison Square Park, he was soaked to the bone. It didn't bother him. His stomach had settled a bit and the violent thrum of the rain against the sidewalk had done a good job of distracting him from his thoughts. So did the rest of his walk. So did the squeak of his shoes on the lobby floor of his building. So did the elevator ride up to the fourteenth floor.

Once he'd keyed his way into his apartment, however, he was met with oppressive silence, and his thoughts came thundering back into focus.

He flipped on a nearby lamp and made his way to the kitchen, caring nothing for the trail of watery footsteps he'd left in his wake, and upon opening the refrigerator was met with the choice between a six-pack of Pacifico or a single can of Schweppes ginger ale. He opted for the Schweppes. Ginger ale was supposed to calm the stomach, and while he was certain there was no actual ginger to be found in the soda, he knew he'd regret the Pacifico in the morning. In his experience, beer was a lonely beverage, not content to be consumed as a single bottle, and a full six-pack would get him into trouble.

He collapsed onto the couch and took two quick pulls of the Schweppes, allowing the fizz to make his eyes water. After a minute or so of slow breathing and steady sipping, he pulled himself back up to his feet and hobbled over to the corner of the living room where he'd dropped his jacket. He didn't remember taking it off. He shuddered at the squish of his wet socks inside his shoes, and bent low to retrieve his phone from the pocket.

He'd missed a call from Ellie.

He held his phone gingerly, as if it were a bomb about to explode.

There were now two timelines in his life: the time before the phone call he was about to make, and the time after it.

What horrors would the post–phone call Charlie know that the present one didn't?

His father was dead. That much he *did* know.

But there was something else. He read Ellie's text message again.

Jesus Christ Susan how did Dad die??

Susan never responded to that.

Why? If Raymond had died of a heart attack or a stroke, Susan surely would have said as much, wouldn't she? Heart attacks and strokes were awful ways to go, but they weren't exactly taboo. They were the number one and two dad-killers, common as colds, and Raymond Remick had lived sloppily enough to be prone to either, or even both.

So why not explain what happened over text?

Because this wasn't a heart attack or a stroke.

This was something darker, something too awful to type into a phone and make permanent, and as long as Charlie didn't make the phone call, he wouldn't have to know what that dark, awful thing was. He could stay in the gray space between *before the call* and *after the call* where it was safe. He could sit on his couch with squishy socks and sip from a cold can of Schweppes for all eternity, having no knowledge of the terrible thing he was seconds away from learning. The can of ginger ale wouldn't last for eternity, of course, so eventually he would be forced to go for the beer. And that was okay. If he was going to stay in the safe gray space, he would need something to do, and he sure as hell wasn't going to sit there and *not* drink something.

He settled into the couch, feeling good about his plan, when his phone rang.

It was Ellie.

So much for the safe gray space.

He answered on the first ring. She spoke first.

"Hey." Her voice was thick. She'd been crying. Heavily.

"Hey," Charlie said back.

"Dad's dead."

"I know."

"So you *did* see the messages." Charlie heard her wipe her nose. "Susan and I were wondering."

"Yeah, I was at a gig. Sorry."

"It's okay. We figured as much."

"Did you talk to Susan?"

"Yeah."

Charlie knew his next question would be to ask what Susan said, but he wasn't ready to hear it. Instead he asked, "Are you gonna head home soon?"

"Mm-hm." Another wipe of the nose. "I'm actually staying with a friend in Bellingham right now, so I'm close."

"Bellingham?" Charlie felt a sting of resentment. He'd spoken to Ellie two days ago and she never mentioned she was back in Washington.

"Yeah. I was couch-surfing for a while . . . spent a few months in Minneapolis, then Portland . . . but now I'm crashing at my friend Hugo's house. He goes to Western."

Charlie felt his protective brotherly instincts kick in and wanted to ask who the hell this Hugo guy was, but kept quiet. It would have been easy to blame Ellie's poor track record with men on her bohemian lifestyle, but that had nothing to do with it. The same way his corporate lifestyle had nothing to do with the rogues' gallery of women he'd been with. He and his sister were swill magnets. Plain and simple.

The last woman he'd dated, Stephanie, once kicked her colleague's dog at the park just because the little guy tried to lick her ankle.

A pearl of his father's floated into his head. *Any person who hates dogs never laughs for the right reasons.*

And in Stephanie's case, his father had been right on the money. Ten months ago, when they were still dating, the two of them had been walking home from a matinee showing of *To Kill a Mockingbird* and saw a woman snag her shoe on the curb in Times Square. She hit the concrete so hard her lip was bleeding, and as Charlie (and several other pedestrians) rushed to her aid, Stephanie hung back as tears of laughter streamed from her eyes.

"What about you?"

"Hm?"

Ellie breathed a quiet laugh. Spaciness was one of their shared traits. "When are you heading home?"

"Not sure," Charlie said, which was the truth. He knew he'd have to go home, of course. He just hadn't gotten that far yet. "I'll have to tie up a few loose ends at work tomorrow, but I'll probably start looking at flights tonight."

"Good. I don't know if I could face this with just me and Susan in the house, especially considering—"

The line went quiet.

Charlie sat forward. "You still there?"

Ellie's sniffles crackled through the speaker. She was crying again.

Here it comes, he thought, feeling his stomach lurch skyward. Here came the terrible thing that Susan wouldn't explain over text. He took another swig of his ginger ale, drained the can, and set it on the floor.

"It's okay, Ell."

"No . . . it's not . . ."

Her words came quietly between shallow breaths, and as Charlie waited for the hammer to fall, he felt a surge of nervous adrenaline. "Just tell me, Ell. Whatever it is, it can't be worse than what I'm imagining."

"I wouldn't be so sure about that."

"Just tell me."

She paused, took a breath, then said in an almost eerie calm, "Dad hung himself from the Grim Tree."

Charlie would only remember bits and pieces of the conversation that followed, but after he said goodbye and hung up the phone, he had no trouble remembering his trip back to the refrigerator.

He decided to have that beer.

And then, when that beer was finished, he decided to have five more.

TWO

Somewhere far away—farther than that, even—the Dixie Cups sang about their grandma and your grandma, sitting by the fire . . .

Ana Cortez opened her eyes. Pale light cut thin blades through her venetian blinds and spilled across her bedsheets in staggered lines. She yawned, her limbs quivering a little as she stretched, then pulled herself to her feet.

The Dixie Cups sang another line—this one being about a king all dressed in red—and Ana shuffled groggily into the living room of her two-bedroom Seattle apartment, searching for her phone. She passed by the window and stole a quick glance outside.

Gray and wet. Surprise, surprise.

She shivered. Her oversized Tears for Fears shirt and boxer shorts did little to protect her from the chill in the air, but she would see to the thermostat in a minute. She was on a quest, hunting the muffled sound of the Dixie Cups like a sleepy bloodhound.

All around the living room, stacks of records stood in uneven columns like wobbly Jenga towers ready to collapse at any moment. She staggered over to the couch, circumventing a stack of rare 45s that was one light breeze away from toppling, and plunged her hand between two cushions.

Her phone was wedged tightly, and as she pulled it free, she shuddered at the ringtone's change in volume.

Jock-a-mo fee-no ai na-ney, her phone sang loudly, pounding away at her ears. *Jock-a-mo fee na-ey.*

She swiped right on the little green phone icon. "Iko Iko" disappeared and was replaced by the sound of her mother's frantic voice.

"Ana? Are you there?"

"I'm here, Moochie."

"I've been calling for hours! Where have you been?"

Ana glanced at her watch. Mickey Mouse's hands told her it was just after 2 P.M. She swore loudly.

"Ana Cristina!"

"Sorry, Mama. I didn't realize how late it was."

"You only just woke up?"

"Uh-huh." She suspected her mother would disapprove of this, but Gloria Cortez was the sort of woman who knew when to pick her battles, and today was not that day.

"I suppose you have a right to sleep late."

Ana felt her shoulders relax. Her mother wasn't as hard-nosed and unbending as she seemed, but she wasn't a total pushover, either. After Ana's father died in a car accident in '92, circumstance had forced Gloria to be more like her *own* mother instead of the mother she'd planned on being. The sudden death proved to be an unpleasant echo for Gloria; a mirror image—although slightly distorted—of her own upbringing. An academic essayist turned political journalist, Gloria's father had been among the first to publicly voice his criticism of Marcos Pérez Jiménez's regime, and had spent the rest of his life in prison for doing so. And the rest of his life, it turned out, was a visible mark on the horizon. Six years into his sentence, he succumbed to a particularly violent bout of tuberculosis, and died on a Friday morning. Gloria still had the letter informing her and her mother of the news.

It seemed the women in her family were cursed. Cursed to lose their men.

Or perhaps it was the other way around. Maybe it was the men who bore the black mark.

Either way, Gloria feared for the poor soul Ana would eventually choose to love, whoever he might turn out to be.

The hardship of single parenthood had become something of a ghoulish tradition in their family, and had resulted in a no-nonsense, military-style approach to Gloria's parenting. Ana often wondered if her mother would have been so strict if she'd remarried, but the prospect of a stepfather was, to her knowledge, never considered; Gloria had been, and was to this day, still hopelessly in love with her deceased husband.

She still spoke to him when she thought Ana wasn't looking, and, for a lengthy period in the nineties, would watch Walter Mercado on TV next to an empty chair, arguing the validity of astrology as if he were sitting right next to her.

Ana might have only been six years old when her father died, but she had no trouble remembering the amused-slash-pained look on his face as her mother credited his everyday actions and decisions to a celestial crab.

In fact, when Ana considered all the evidence, it was a miracle she'd been born at all. As a young man, Diego Cortez had been a staunch pragmatist—a computer science and engineering professor at the University of Washington who had very little patience for anything that couldn't be reduced to a series of ones and zeros.

When he met Gloria Salguero, a young Venezuelan exchange student, he thought he'd found a kindred spirit. She was taking advantage of a Microsoft-funded program that taught MS-DOS to Spanish-speaking academics in the hope they'd return to their country of origin and spread the Gospel of Gates. But, as it turned out, Gloria cared nothing for computers. In fact, to Diego's horror, she believed computers would lead to the downfall of humanity, plunging Earth's populace into a morally bankrupt feedback loop that would be broken only once technology was abolished and every last microchip reduced to dust.

But the program *did* come with an all-expenses-paid stay in the United States, so she figured what the hell. She would stay in Seattle and engage in a battle of wits with the handsome Cuban Computer Boy for a few months, then head back to Venezuela and find a suitable man with a healthy distrust of technology. All she had to do was make sure she didn't fall in love. If she fell in love, she might never leave.

Nearly thirty years later, she still hadn't left Seattle.

"I'm happy you finally took a day off," she said to her daughter. "You work much too hard."

"It wasn't my decision to close the store. It was Dale's."

"That poor man . . . I can't imagine what he must be going through."

Ana bit her lip. "I'm going through something, too, Mama."

"Oh, I know, sweetheart, I know," her mother said quickly, sensing she'd just stepped in conversational horse shit. "I just can't stop thinking about what he saw in that backyard. Raymond hanging there like a rag doll. It's just . . ." She whispered a fragment of a prayer under her breath. "It's just terrible."

Ana's eyes moved again to her window. The rain was falling more heavily now. "Yes, it is."

"Why don't you come home? Just for a few days. I'll cook you whatever you want."

"I need to be at my own place."

"I don't think you should be alone right now. I can help you."

There was only one person that could truly help Ana, and Dale had just found him hanging from a tree in his backyard. "I'll come visit for a bit after the funeral, Mama. We're gonna open back up tomorrow and I'd rather stay on this side of town."

"Is it wise to open again so soon?"

"Christmas is just around the corner. We can't afford to shut the doors right now."

This was both true and convenient. If Raymond had died in, say, October, Dale probably would have closed the store for a week or two, but Christmas accounted for nearly twenty-five percent of their yearly earnings and, tragedy or no, it would be silly to risk losing the store out of respect for its dead proprietor. Even Raymond would have agreed with that.

She bandied a bit more with her mother, assured her for a second (and third) time that she would rather stay on her side of town, then made up a lie about an incoming call and hung up. After another minute or so of staring out the window, Ana made her way to the kitchen and whipped up a quick breakfast composed of a cold Pop-Tart and a reheated cup of coffee.

Once she'd eaten, she reentered the living room, a little more awake and a lot more frustrated. She might have been reeling from the news of Raymond's death, but sleeping past two in the afternoon wasn't like her. She'd always been an early riser, ever since she'd gotten her first job at fifteen.

The job that set her on a path to the Cuckoo's Nest and into the employ of Raymond Remick, and the pain she was now feeling.

After scouring the Northgate Mall and coming up short (Claire's and Sam Goody and Orange Julius had been fully staffed-up for the summer), she secured a position as a ticket-taker at the Varsity Theater, a small two-screener near the University of Washington. Her manager, a crusty old stoner named Rod, had hired Ana on the spot. She was young, but she was eager, which was more than could be said of his other employees. On top of that, she seemed to know her stuff (Bergman good, Michael Bay bad) and, because she was so young, she was willing to work for cash under the table. Lastly—and most importantly—when Rod shook her hand, he caught the distinct smell of pot on her jacket.

Ana liked her job at the theater. Because of its proximity to the University of Washington, it was always busy, owing mostly to the steady flow of students who were itching to see their favorite classics represented on the big screen, and it opened later in the afternoon, which meant her school schedule was never an issue. She could smoke pot when she wanted (usually with Rod, who was comically unaccustomed to the stronger modern strains), and take breaks whenever she wanted, and although the job didn't pay much, it paid enough to feed her one true obsession: music.

Having lived in the Fremont area of Seattle her entire life, Ana was no stranger to the Cuckoo's Nest, a local record store that had become a go-to destination for music-obsessives all across the Pacific Northwest. She'd popped into the store a few times during her youth to pick up the odd CD (Soda Stereo's *Canción Animal* and No Doubt's *Tragic Kingdom* among them), but it wasn't until the summer after her freshman year of high school that she became a regular staple among the store's clientele. It was the summer she stepped into the store not as a casual music fan, but as an addict in need of a fix.

And it all started at the lake.

Ana had been born pretty and grew up to be beautiful, a fact she pretended to never put a lot of stock in, at least publicly, but privately she was well aware that beauty had its perks—one of them being an uncontested induction into her high school's popular crowd, which, in turn, came with its own set of perks. During her youth, Ana spent the lion's share of her summers at her friend Ashley's lake cabin in Coeur d'Alene, Idaho. Ashley was as spoiled as they came—something Ana's mother brought up almost monthly—but she was nice where it counted, and even though Ana and Ashley had almost nothing in common, the idea of spending the summer months at a plush lakeside estate was too good to pass up. Even Gloria had to admit that.

Like most girls of fifteen, Ana spent her summer days lounging in the sun and her summer nights partying (and because Rod was the farthest thing from a tightfisted hand at the grindstone, he happily gave her June through August off). Most nights were spent in Rockford Bay or Arrow Point, with Ana shimmying away to local bar bands, smiling openly at cute boys who kept their sunglasses expertly perched atop their heads and smiling through gritted teeth as their mothers—clad in Ralph Lauren nautical wear and gripping sugary margaritas—casually remarked how jealous they were of her "natural tan." Most nights she would make a game of sneaking the odd beer around back with Ashley and her rotating stock of rich friends.

One night, while she was doing her best to discreetly pour a shot of rum into her Cherry Coke while Ashley kept lookout, a visiting bar band from Missoula broke into a rendition of Big Star's song

"September Gurls." It was a passable cover, a little sloppy during the verses, but everyone in the bar seemed to enjoy it. Some even took to the dance floor and tried to move their feet to it.

Ana Cortez, however, did not dance. She couldn't even bob her head. She was frozen, feet welded to the floor, eyes wide, Cherry Coke dribbling from the rim of her cup.

Simply put, she had fallen in love. Not with anyone in the band, who looked to be twenty-five going on fifty, but with the song.

Every word, every chord change, every hit of the snare filled her with a warmth no song had done before, and Ana knew that she had not only fallen in love with "September Gurls," she had taken possession of it. It was hers now.

When the song was over, Ana approached the stage and asked the band to play it again. They declined, stating they still had fifteen more songs to burn through before calling it a night, but were flattered that she liked the song so much. They told her the name of the song and who wrote it, and assured her that if she came back to Rockford Bay the following week, they'd play it for her again.

She nodded in thanks, then sprinted to the bar to scribble the name of the song (and the name of the band) onto a water-stained cocktail napkin.

That night, as the day's sunlight still worked its way through her skin, Ana Cortez sat in the guest room in Ashley's lake cabin and hummed the tune repeatedly to herself, committing it to memory. The following week, Ana returned to Rockford Bay and waited patiently as the band blazed through sloppy renditions of "Hang On Sloopy" and "Do Wah Diddy Diddy," rolled her eyes during "Rockin' Robin" and "Duke of Earl," and even began to lose hope as they weaved their way through a needlessly long cover of the Young Rascals' "Good Lovin'." Ten songs in, the band made moves to take a break, and Ana felt her heart sink, but when the lead singer whispered something to his cohorts and then turned to the mic and told the audience that this next tune was dedicated to a certain raven-haired beauty in the audience, she leapt to her feet, heart fit to burst.

They kicked into "September Gurls," and as the band played, Ana felt herself change.

She was no longer a passive listener of music, occasionally buying the odd CD and going to concerts only when there was an appropriately big enough group of friends to go with. She was now an active listener, and before the summer was over, she would become a record-store regular, forever scouring the world's sun-bleached shelves and dusty understocks for white-label 45s, first pressings, and rare imports.

But at that moment, she knew none of that. She was simply a girl who had found her song.

She flew back to Seattle the following week, which left her nearly a full month before her sophomore year started. And because she'd been at the lake all summer, nearly everything had been paid for by Ashley's family, so Ana returned home with a checking account that had been relatively unscathed. She dropped her bags off at home, gave her mother a quick kiss and an even quicker hello, then hightailed it over to the Cuckoo's Nest, ready to part with the money she'd been saving.

Standing behind the checkout counter, arm perched casually atop the cash register, was Raymond Remick. Ana had seen him before. His tangle of gray hair and bushy Mark Twain mustache were hard to miss. She gave him a little wave, made a beeline for the rock section, thumbed through a few CDs, and within seconds found what she'd spent the whole summer dreaming about.

She approached the counter and handed Raymond a crisp new copy of Big Star's *Radio City*.

His eyes twinkled behind his wire-rimmed glasses. "Excellent choice, kiddo. This is my favorite of theirs."

"Yeah . . ." Ana said absently, too lost in the success of her conquest to process what he'd just said. When she did, she gazed up at him and said, "Wait, they made more than one album?"

Raymond leaned forward over the counter, grinning. "They

made two more. Well, one and a half, if you want to be technical about it."

Ana didn't need to do the math in her head. She had more than enough money to cover the balance of two more CDs, and then some. "Do you have them here?"

"Tell you what," Raymond said, "come back after you've given that one a good spin. If you like it, I'll send you home with the other two. I'll even keep them under the counter for you so no one else can pinch 'em."

Ana's eyes lit up.

"And if you like *those* two," Raymond continued, "I'll take you around the store and show you some other stuff you might like."

Promising she would, Ana sprinted home, ripping the cellophane off her new CD. After another quick hello to her mother, she clomped heavily up the stairs to her room and spent the rest of the night parked in front of her boom box, drinking in Big Star's second album with the thirst of a desert-parched wanderer.

A week later, she bought the other two Big Star albums. A week after that, she strolled into the Cuckoo's Nest, a tote bag clutched in either hand, ready to drain what remained of her checking account.

Raymond was as good as his word. Better, even. He walked her through the store for a full hour and loaded her up with enough music to last her six months. Each selection was tied to Big Star in some way. Some were direct connections (the Box Tops), while others were influenced by Big Star (R.E.M.'s *Murmur*). Some even did the influencing (the Kinks' *Village Green Preservation Society*). When the time came for the total to be rung up, Ana frowned, knowing she'd have to put a third of the stack back, but Raymond wouldn't hear of it.

"Take them," he said, smiling.

Ana took a step back. "I can't, Mr. Remick. It's way too much."

"Whoa, whoa . . ." Raymond said, making a face. "First off, the *IRS* calls me 'Mr. Remick.' 'Raymond' will do just fine."

Ana nodded.

"And secondly, most of those records are desert-island necessities. All of my regulars already have them, so they pretty much never sell. Just promise me you won't let them gather dust on your shelf."

It was an easy promise to keep.

Over the next two years, she spent nearly every afternoon after school wandering the aisles of the Cuckoo's Nest and building up her collection. Raymond and his only employee, a British expat named Dale Cernin, had become the Virgils to her Dante, taking it upon themselves to guide her through the sprawling catacombs of recorded music and teaching her the art of collecting. On weekends, while her peers were haunting the shops at the Northgate Mall and attending keg parties, Ana spent her days arguing with Raymond and Dale over which Replacements album was the best (she pushed hard for *Pleased to Meet Me*), learning to love singers like Jim Croce and Andrew Gold (two artists she'd previously filed into the unlistenable category of Dad Rock), and making her case that "Take Me I'm Yours" by Mary Clark was the greatest dance song ever written.

Raymond was a seemingly endless font of information, and on the (very few) occasions where his knowledge fell short, Dale had no trouble picking up the slack.

Dale Cernin was the first British person Ana had ever met—a wiry, salt-and-pepper-haired beanpole from South Yorkshire whose conversational skills were strong only in one category: music. While most customers were lucky to get more than ten words out of Dale, even if they *were* talking music, Ana seemed to have the magic touch. Raymond always joked that Ana brought out the gadfly in Dale. She was a quick study and nonjudgmental, two qualities celebrated by Dale (and within the walls of the Cuckoo's Nest itself).

In three short years, the store had become her second home, and Raymond and Dale her second family. They'd even given her an endcap to fill with recommendations of her own, christening it with the punny name "Ana 1, Ana 2, Ana's Recs 4 U."

Feeling the store was lacking in *rock en español,* she filled the endcap with releases from Silvio Rodríguez, Caramelos de Cianuro, Zoé, Maná, and Los Enanitos Verdes. To no one's surprise, the endcap was a big hit, and with each passing day, Ana's emotional investment in the store seemed to blossom more and more. So it was inevitable, then, on the day of her eighteenth birthday, Ana saw fit to ask Raymond for a job.

Raymond, who had been expecting this for some time, shook his head. "You deserve better than this old shitheap, kiddo," he said, casting a weary glance across the store. "Go on and get yourself a real future and leave the stacks to old shrubs like Dale and me."

"Listen to him, Bangs," Dale told her, and Ana smiled at the nickname. She'd cut her hair into a bob two months before, leaving her with a razor-sharp curtain of bangs that fell neatly over her eyes. "This place is a bottomless well, and we've already let you fall too deep. Get out while you can still see daylight."

Not willing to take no for an answer, Ana persisted, and Raymond, who'd never been good at saying no for long, eventually caved.

After that, the Cuckoo's Nest became a house with three residents, and with Ana there, it had even begun to thrive. The resurgence in popularity of vinyl records certainly helped, but it was Ana's influence that transformed the Nest from an aging, dust-covered haven for sun-deprived record collectors into a sparklingly clean, refurbished Disneyland for music lovers of all disciplines.

Over the next six years, Ana dedicated every waking hour to the store. She even came in on Sundays when the store was closed and replaced blown-out lightbulbs, wiped down the banisters, gave the walls a fresh coat of paint, and oversaw a succession of contractors as they installed new tile flooring, repaired and refurbished the grand staircase that led to the upper level, gave the bathrooms a much-needed overhaul, and built all-new shelving that would more than account for the Nest's considerable stock.

As bosses go, Ana couldn't have hoped for better than Raymond

Remick, and even then, his title of boss was only a formality. She'd always bristled when someone used the expression "he's like a second father to me," having never known the sensation of having a *first* father, but Raymond had become exactly that.

Even Gloria Cortez, who had initially disapproved of her daughter's decision to waste her life in a record store, eventually warmed to Raymond and often bemoaned (jokingly, although Ana sometimes suspected her mother was only *half* joking) the fact that he was happily married.

In 2010, when Raymond's wife died of cancer, Ana, her mother, and Dale were given the honor of being seated in the second row during her funeral, behind Raymond and his children. She had met his two daughters at that point (and was even friendly with Ellie, who was something of a leaf on the wind, as her mother would say), but she hadn't yet met his son, Charlie.

And she wouldn't. Not for another five years. Not until Raymond hanged himself from a tree in his backyard and changed everything.

"Iko Iko" played again and she jumped, splashing a little coffee on her fingers.

She looked down at the mug in her hand. The coffee had gone cold. How long had she been sitting there?

She frowned, not recognizing the number on her phone, but answered anyway. The Dixie Cups were interrupted by a woman's voice.

"Hello?"

"Yes?" She wiped her coffee-stained fingers on her shirt. "Hello?"

"Can you hear me?" The reception was terrible. Whoever she was, she sounded distant, buried in pulsing waves of electric fuzz.

"I'm sorry, who's this?"

The woman told Ana her name, but it was lost in the static. She had an accent Ana couldn't quite place.

"I'm looking for Mr. Raymond Remick, please?"

Ana's heart sank. She'd forgotten she'd forwarded the store's phone to her cell the night before, when Dale told her he was planning on closing the store today. She supposed she would be getting a lot of these calls. The thought exhausted her.

"I'm sorry to tell you this," she said, her voice catching a little, "but Mr. Remick has passed away."

The line crackled silently for a moment; then the woman spoke again. "I'm sorry to hear that."

"Me too."

"When did this happen, miss?"

"Yesterday."

"I see . . ."

"If you were thinking of coming in to the store, you should know that we're closed today."

"No . . ." the woman with the accent said. ". . . no, I am not a patron of Mr. Remick's."

"A friend, then?"

"Yes," she replied, then paused. The crackle was starting to get on Ana's nerves. "Of a sort."

Because of her accent, "of a sort" sounded like *oven salt*.

"Is there anything else I can help you with?" Ana asked, trying her best to keep the annoyance out of her voice.

"No, miss. That will be all. Thank you."

There was a final stretch of static, then a sharp *click*, and the phone went silent. Once again, Ana stared out the window into the dreary afternoon sky. The gray light had sapped the room of color, giving her apartment an unfamiliar, sinister edge.

She switched on a few lamps in an effort to bring a little warmth and comfort to the place, but it was no use. The woman on the other end of the line had been perfectly polite—more polite than most customers who called the store, frankly; she couldn't remember anyone ever calling her "miss" before—but there was something about the call that had made her uneasy. And the woman wasn't a customer. She said so herself.

She was a friend, of a sort.

Oven salt.

Ana frowned. "Friend, of a sort" could have meant a lot of things—a client, perhaps, or even an accountant—but when she'd heard the news of Raymond's death, the sadness in her voice hinted at a certain level of intimacy between them that would have gone beyond a professional relationship.

An old lover, maybe?

She shook her head. Raymond had only ever loved one woman. His late wife, Joan.

Even after her death, he'd been true to her.

The Cuckoo's Nest wasn't exactly a babe magnet, but on the rare occasion an attractive woman found herself inside the store, Raymond would treat her like any other customer who walked through the doors: with an affable smile and a fatherly interest in their music taste.

In reality, the woman on the phone was probably just a creditor who had been caught off guard by the news of Raymond's death. That's all.

Ana pulled on her shoes and stuffed her arms into a large hooded sweatshirt. She paused in front of the mirror to tousle her bangs into formation and wondered if she should bother with any makeup. Deciding it couldn't hurt, she reached for a bottle of MAC foundation and brushed it into her caramel-colored cheeks, then, after searching for the appropriate hue, applied a thin layer of almond eye shadow to draw attention away from the bags under her eyes.

After a final check to make sure she'd adequately blended her foundation, she fished her car keys from the bowl next to her front door and ducked out into the drizzly afternoon.

Dale might have wanted to keep the store closed today, but she couldn't think of anywhere else she'd rather be. And anyway, he wouldn't mind if she opened up for a few hours. It wasn't like he was her boss. And even if he did mind, he would never say anything. When it came to Ana, Dale was a pushover.

She strolled down the driveway to where her car was parked on the street, knowing she should text Dale to let him know she was heading over to the store. It was the polite thing to do, after all.

Only, when she opened her phone, she saw that Dale had beaten her to it.

Hey Bangs, I know we said we should stay closed today but I don't think I can stand being home alone. I'm gonna go in and open up for a while. Feel free to come if you want. No pressure though. Cheers. D.

Ten minutes later, she was behind the checkout counter at the Cuckoo's Nest, watching a young punk rocker cast an embarrassed glance over his shoulder as he tucked a Barenaked Ladies record under his arm so his friends wouldn't see it.

Ana smiled.

It was good to be home.

THREE

Charlie strolled up to the Sony building at half past eleven the following morning. The rain had stopped a few hours earlier but now the wind was picking up, adding a layer of bone-crushing iciness that made his six-block journey feel like sixty. The hangover certainly didn't help matters, although Charlie supposed—begrudgingly—that the frigid air would do him good.

And not just for his hangover.

It had been a long time since Charlie had had a nightmare. Or, rather, it had been a long time since he'd had a nightmare worth remembering, and as he shuffled into the lobby of 25 Madison, the horrifying images his subconscious had whipped up the night before were still fresh in his mind.

"Morning, Mr. Remick!"

The heavily jowled face of Bill Neeley popped up from behind the front desk. Tufts of gray hair licked his temples, and even though it was freezing outside, his forehead glistened under a thin layer of sweat. He watched Charlie strip off his gloves and held up his own hands, showcasing a pair of comically large woolen mittens. "Decided to keep mine on, what with the doors opening every ten seconds. It's days like this I wonder if summer'll ever come again."

Charlie looked around the cavernous lobby with the dazed and slightly frightened expression of a lost child. He couldn't even remember walking through the door.

Bill leaned his considerable belly over the front desk and studied Charlie's face with friendly concern. "You all right, Mr. Remick? You're looking a little green."

"Hangover," Charlie croaked. The air from his walk had iced his throat and made him hoarse.

Not to mention all that screaming I did last night. That certainly didn't help matters.

"Ahhh . . ." Bill Neeley said with a knowing grin. He sat back down. "Too much eggnog, eh? Yeah, that's my downfall, too."

Charlie was about to contradict him when he spied the festive sprig of holly that had been pinned onto the lapel of Bill's security blazer. Above the front desk, three sparkling wreaths bathed the lobby in a warm yuletide glow. Each of them was decorated with a plump red bow that hung resplendently over the large stainless-steel SONY logo that had been mounted on the marble wall behind the front desk.

"I keep forgetting it's almost Christmas," Charlie said, then gazed up at the ceiling. "Carol of the Bells" spilled ominously from the lobby's PA speakers, its circular melody echoing across the walls.

Bill laughed. "I don't have the luxury of forgetting. Beth keeps saying she's gonna divorce me if I don't get my shopping done soon. I'm not gonna lie to you, Mr. Remick . . . I got half a mind to take her up on it."

"You've still got plenty of time," Charlie replied. "Ten days at least."

"Unless I find a way to knock over a Brink's truck, ten days ain't gonna make a difference." Bill sat forward again and lowered his voice. "Cindy—she's my youngest—wants an *iPhone*." He said this last bit with such gravity and parental horror, you'd think she was asking for a dildo instead of a smartphone. He threw up his mittened hands. "Who do I look like, Scrooge McDuck?"

Charlie grinned. "I've always seen you as more of a Launchpad McQuack."

"Yeah, but whose flying days are long over," Bill said, clapping a hand on his belly and chuckling. "She's a good kid, though, my Cindy. She may have to wait another year for the iPhone, but at least she gets to spend the full day with her pop on Christmas." He squared his shoulders proudly at the thought. "Never got to do that with *my* old man. He always had to work."

The mention of fathers stung a bit, and Charlie's smile faltered a little. Before Bill could take notice, Charlie tapped his watch to signal he was late and sped across the lobby toward the elevators. The carriage on the far left opened as he approached, and Charlie dove inside.

As the doors closed and silence pressed in on him, the bustling sounds of the lobby began to fade. The silence was comforting at first, but the building's elevators were on the slow side, and as the journey up to the twenty-third floor began to stretch out before him, the quiet of the carriage became suffocating. He felt his pulse quicken and closed his eyes to help steady his breathing, but it was no use. The nightmare came flooding back.

The sky came first, all gray with doomsday clouds that pulsated and writhed like angry celestial bodies. The grass came next—brown and haggard and sprawling, its dry blades quivering in the wind, too weak to remain upright but too strong to die off completely. Then there was the fence, each post shooting up from the ground, one after the other, refusing to stay buried. The fence boxed the yard in and kept him from running away. Beneath his feet, the ground began rolling in waves, forcing him forward toward the far side of the lawn; toward the thing he feared most.

The Grim Tree.

As a boy, he would stare at it from his bedroom window—eyes peeled open and alert, as if his vigilance were the only thing keeping that horrible tree from pulling its roots from the soil and charging at him. The Grim Tree, he'd called it. A twisted, ashen wraith with a reaching, clawing, unnatural branch that was both a bony arm and a scythe.

How many nights had he sat awake, staring into the yard, terrified the branch would crash through his bedroom window and pull him kicking and screaming from his sheets? How many times had he imagined himself dragged along the bumpy brown lawn for what seemed like miles, the sky thundering and roiling above, muffling his screams from his sleeping parents' ears, only to finally be dragged deep into the ground? To a place where no light could survive, where his throat would fill with dirt, collapsing his lungs and silencing him forever?

Too many times.

The nightmares slowed as he got older, as nightmares tend to do, and eventually stopped after he moved to New York. Perhaps it was the distraction of the city, or maybe it was the fact that he had put three thousand miles between himself and his childhood house, but he had gone almost seven years without dreaming of the Grim Tree until now. He had even forgotten about it. Or seemed to. But the tree obviously hadn't forgotten him. It had reached across those three thousand miles, slid its tendrils around his ankle, and was dragging him back home . . . back to the yard with the dead grass, where it could taunt him and torture him with the image of his father's hanging body.

The elevator carriage stopped with a shudder, and Charlie stumbled backward. The doors opened with a ding, and once again the sound of Christmas music returned, only now it was a distant echo.

The reception area—a sparse, Kubrickian stretch of antiseptic flooring and futuristic wall paneling—stretched out before him. Hoping his footing would hold, he stepped out of the carriage. His knees were shaking badly and his pulse was still racing.

Thirty feet ahead of him, a young receptionist clicked quietly at her computer. She hadn't noticed his arrival, which was strange considering the message that hung above her head.

Above the mounted RCA, Epic, and Columbia logos was a banner that read THE MAN WITH THE MAGIC EAR GOES TEN FOR TEN! CONGRATULATIONS, CHARLIE!

"Sorry about that, sweetheart," said a voice to his right.

Charlie turned and saw Jennifer Graham, all five-foot-five of her, clad in her trademark black pantsuit and thick tortoiseshell frames. "I wanted to get that taken down before you arrived, but I was only just able to shoo everyone out of here."

Charlie stared at her. "Everyone?"

"We had quite the shindig planned for your big day," Jennifer said, taking him by the arm and leading him across the lobby, "but then I saw your text about your dad and it was a mad dash to undo everything before you got here." She paused and gave his arm a little squeeze. "I figured you wouldn't be in the mood to celebrate."

"You're probably right, but I appreciate the gesture either way."

He gazed up at the banner behind the reception desk and bristled.

THE MAN WITH THE MAGIC EAR GOES TEN FOR TEN!

"*That*, however . . ."

"I know, I know," Jennifer said, grinning impishly, "but I couldn't resist. Ten signees all breaking the *Billboard* Top 20 in less than a year is nothing to spit at. I don't think *anyone's* done that. Not with *bands*. Not since I've been here."

Charlie's band-only ten-for-ten streak was no accident. He'd spent the last five years at Sony signing SoundCloud rappers and YouTube sensations (most of which had done relatively well and a few who had done *very* well), but he'd grown weary of signing talent he couldn't relate to. He missed the days when bands ruled the airwaves, and even though the airwaves were disappearing and streaming was now king, he saw no reason that up-and-coming bands should be relegated almost exclusively to boutique labels and DIY consortiums. Sony was a big label, and would be for the foreseeable future. They had the power to change the rules of the battle. All it took was a brave A&R rep to fire the first shot.

And if it weren't for Jennifer Graham, Charlie never would have had the chance to take that shot. It took all of her considerable negotiating skills to get Luke the Shithead to allow Charlie a full year to focus exclusively on bands, and even now, Charlie was still surprised that she'd managed to convince him.

He gazed up again at the banner. It was nearly eight feet long and three feet high, in what appeared to be seven-hundred-point font. "At least you were subtle."

Jennifer shrugged. "It would have been funny under different circumstances."

Charlie wasn't sure that was entirely true, but if there was one person he didn't mind taking the piss out of him, it was Jennifer Graham. She was a remarkable woman and a legend in the industry. She had been in the music business longer than anyone else in the building—her thirtieth-anniversary party the previous June had since become a thing of legend in certain circles—but aside from the shimmering silver streak that framed the front left side of her shiny black bob, she barely looked a year over forty.

In fact, it was Charlie who looked older than his age that morning. His face was lined and tired. He stared warily at the hallway beyond the reception desk.

"I don't think I can go back there," he said quietly. The distant sound of ringing phones and idle chitchat were making him queasy.

"Then go home," Jennifer said, giving his arm a squeeze. "I'm honestly surprised you came in at all."

"There are some loose ends that need tying up before I go. Luke wanted the Mightier Ducks to change their name before the launch last night, and I hadn't gotten around to it yet, so I was hoping to—"

Before he could finish, Jennifer waved his words away. "Leave that with me."

Charlie blinked. "Are you sure?""

"This ain't my first rodeo, Hoss."

"No, I know," Charlie said. "They're just *really* attached to that name."

"So were the Pendletones," Jennifer pointed out. "And if their label hadn't changed the name to the Beach Boys, we'd all be worse off."

Charlie squinted his eyes. "Would we, though?"

Jennifer took him by the arm again and directed him back to the elevators. "Have you booked your flight home yet?"

"No, but there are always plenty of flights to Seattle. I shouldn't have a problem getting out."

"Do you know when the funeral will be?"

"Soon, I imagine. Susan's already making calls to funeral homes."

"Do you want me to come? I would be happy to."

"Thank you, but no," Charlie said. "I'm hoping to get in and get out as quickly as possible. If you come, it'll make it harder for me to exit quietly."

"Listen," she said softly, "I know things between you and your dad were a little prickly, and I respect that, but I want you to seriously consider taking your time while you're out there, okay? There's no reason to hurry back."

"But—"

"Grief is a rotten thing, but there's no point in rushing through it. It's in the driver's seat now, so just sit back and let it tear down the highway until the tank is empty. That's the only way to get through it."

A shadow crossed Charlie's face. "I remember."

"I know you do," Jennifer said gravely. She reached for the elevator bank and gave the Down button a hard tap. "And you still haven't taken the time to grieve for your mother. Not properly."

"Everybody grieves in their own way, Jen."

"And that's fine. Just so long as you *do* grieve."

The elevator arrived with a ding, and Charlie stepped inside the carriage. As the doors slid closed, he spied a familiar door behind Jennifer.

"Before I go," he said, stopping the door with his hand, "you wouldn't be able to let me into the supply room, would you?"

Ten minutes later, as Charlie was making the six-block journey back up Madison Avenue toward his apartment building, Bill Neeley returned to the lobby after enjoying his noon coffee break. He straightened his black security blazer, gave the holly pinned to his lapel a cheerful little pinch, then took his seat behind the security desk. A quick flutter of yellow caught his gaze, and he sat forward. Next to the sign-in sheet was a brown Starbucks bag with a Post-it note stuck to the side. He peeled it free and read the message that had clearly been scribbled in a hurry.

Merry Christmas, Launchpad. Tell your daughter YOU bought them.

Bill reached into the bag and pulled out three brand-new iPhones, still in their packaging.

FOUR

I think we could make a go of it here," the voice said, and Charlie turned around.

He was alone.

Whoever had spoken to him had disappeared. Most likely through the open door on the other side of the warehouse. He thought about making his way across the space, but the door was too far (and the warehouse was too cold) for him to investigate. After all, he must have known the owner of the voice. How could he not? He certainly wouldn't have come to this place alone.

He was just tired. It had been a long flight and he hadn't slept a wink.

Or maybe he had slept and he was still groggy. It would certainly explain how he'd gotten from the airport to the warehouse without remembering the trip.

It didn't matter. He was here now.

He took a few steps, listening as the echoing click-clack of his footsteps filled the cavernous space, and looked around. It was empty.

This place was always empty.

And it was old. Thousands of feet of spiraling, diving, twisting, jerking, zigzagging rusty pipes lined the cathedral-high ceiling like a series of dark, dripping highways. Cracked, load-bearing columns lined the floor in twenty-foot intervals, and a thin layer of silt blanketed the ground. With each step, Charlie felt a slight crunch under his boots. His breath fogged the stagnant air in thick plumes, and every time he moved through it, he was reintroduced to the space all over again.

The light was strange, gray and flat and cold, which was somehow both too bright and not bright enough. His eyes traced the far wall, which had been lined with windows, all of them broken. Shattered glass sat neatly along the edge of the floor, as if someone had used a push broom to consolidate it but had forgotten to sweep it into a dustpan and discard it.

He stood on his toes, hoping to catch a glimpse of the view outside the windows, but they were too high. All he could see was that flat gray light.

It unnerved him, somehow making this familiar place seem unfamiliar, and gave him the impression that he was a stranger here, which he most certainly wasn't.

Or was he?

After all, how could he know a place so completely and, at the same time, feel like this was his first time seeing it?

"HEY, CHARLIE!"

His shoulders jumped. He turned (or maybe he didn't—he had lost his bearings in his own foggy soup) and glanced again at the door on the far side of the warehouse, but knew immediately that the voice had come from somewhere else. Somewhere far away, in another room, perhaps. Or one floor below, in the basement.

Did the warehouse have a basement? He should know that.

"HEY, CHARLIE! REMEMBER ME?"

The voice, like his footsteps, rang throughout the icy space, soaked in reverb.

He took a tentative step forward.

"HEY, CHARLIE! REMEMBER ME?"

Charlie spun around, eyes darting in every direction, searching for the source of the voice, and froze when he heard the distinct wail of a door opening.

He looked to his left. The sound hadn't come from the first door he'd seen, but a new door he hadn't noticed until now.

It stood upright and alert and alone, a tiny dark speck on a massive, white, water-stained wall. It was made of metal, or appeared to be, and was covered in patches of brassy rust. Charlie approached the door cautiously. It was open, but only slightly, providing him a sliver of a view of what lay on the other side. He gave it a firm push, and with *another wail, it swung open, sending up a cloud of swirling dust motes and flakes of rust.*

He stepped through, bracing for whatever waited for him on the other side, but found nothing more than another large space, nearly identical in dimension to the warehouse he'd just come from, and almost just as empty.

Almost.

At the center of the room, sitting on an old wooden table, was a gramophone. Its bell, which was battered and bent, hung to the side like an aging prizefighter, heaving up and down with every full rotation of the turntable as if it were a single lung, struggling for breath. Charlie moved closer for a better look. At first glance, the turntable seemed to be in fine working order—it spun without hiccup—although there was no record on it. It just turned silently, its needle having no groove, and sent wheezing breaths through the bell.

Ahead of him, large gossamer shapes moved slowly from left to right along the far wall, as if an invisible carousel had cast a parade of ominous shadows. He watched the shadows move, left to right, left to right, and looked down at the gramophone. They seemed to be moving at the same speed as the empty turntable.

And yet . . .

He looked again at the wall and frowned. There was no way the gramophone could be casting shadows that large. It was too small. No, the source of the shadows had to be behind him. It was the only logical explanation. And whatever it was, it was big.

He started to turn around, to see what it was, then stopped as a rush of chills spilled down his arms.

He didn't need to look. He already knew the thing that was casting these shadows, and it certainly wasn't a carousel.

Perhaps if he walked out of the room backward, he wouldn't have to see it at all. He would just leave. Easy as that. Pretend that he never set foot in this room in the first place and go on his merry way.

And yet it called to him over his shoulder. It begged him to turn around. It wanted to be seen.

No. That wasn't it.

It wanted to show *him something.*

Charlie felt himself begin to turn. He didn't have a choice. He knew now that this wasn't his story, and he didn't get to call the shots. He was merely a player on a board, and if the game required him to move, he moved.

So he turned around.

The Grim Tree towered over him like some cosmic leviathan, its highest branches scraping the ceiling and the pipes like fingernails. Charlie tried to see around it, but couldn't. It was too big. Bigger than he'd ever seen it.

And it was moving.

It turned slowly on the spot as if it were some frightful mobile.

Yes, a mobile, Charlie thought, but instead of little airplanes or ducks hanging from its branches, he saw bodies. They dangled limply by the neck from different heights like horrifying Christmas tree ornaments, all with frightful faces and leering eyes that burrowed into his own.

Faces he knew.

The faces of his family.

Of Ellie. Of Susan. Of his mother. Of his father.

And another figure, with its back to him.

As the tree continued to turn, Charlie watched with growing dread as the fifth body wound its way around to him. He knew instantly who it would be. Of course he did. How could it be otherwise?

As the fifth body slid out of the shadows and into view, Charlie found himself staring up at his own face.

He clapped a hand over his mouth to stifle a scream, but the scream still came. His own face smiled back.

"Hey, Charlie," the corpse said calmly, twisting slowly as the noose around his neck groaned under the strain of his weight. "Remember me?"

Thirty-five thousand feet above the ground, Alaska Airlines flight 2217 gave a little shudder as it began its descent into Seattle, and Charlie awoke with a yelp.

He lurched forward, felt the seat belt dig into his waist, then collapsed back into place. Becoming immediately aware of his surroundings, he swallowed his waking panic with a sputtering choke. The passenger seated to his right—a red-faced man in a business suit with a beer keg for a belly—gazed at Charlie over his reading glasses.

"You all right, son?"

Still facing the window, Charlie nodded.

There was a gauzy *ding* and the plane's PA system crackled to life.

"Flight attendants, please prepare for landing."

Charlie reached forward, grabbed the plastic cup on his tray, and sucked down the watery remains of his Jack and Coke. He crushed the ice nervously with his teeth, a sensation he both liked and hated simultaneously—like prodding a sore tooth with your tongue.

He sat back and closed his eyes, hoping the ice had soaked up enough Jack to calm his nerves.

The plane gave another shudder, and once again, the PA crackled. This time, it was the voice of a female flight attendant, requesting that everyone return their seats and tray tables to their upright and locked positions. For a moment, Charlie's eyes lingered on her neckerchief, which had been bloused neatly atop her collarbone, then moved up to her shock of red lipstick, which had been expertly applied.

The red-faced man sitting next to him clocked Charlie's lingering stare and grinned. "I've got something upright and locked for her," he said quietly, then added, "If you know what I mean."

Charlie, still too shaken by his dream to take offense, simply grimaced and turned back to the window.

As the plane continued its descent, he watched the darkness below break apart, scattering into a thin soup of wispy black clouds. All at once, Seattle appeared, glittering like a sequined dress that had been laid neatly across a stretch of black velvet.

Coming home had always felt strange. He had been born in

Seattle, had spent eighteen years of his life there, and yet he couldn't help feeling like a stranger whenever he returned. It was as if the city had taken on the characteristics of an ex-girlfriend; they were familiar with each other in ways only the two of them could understand, with a shared past unique to them and them alone. But now . . . now when he saw her again, it was an emotionless exchange. Yes, you had your first kiss here, and yes, you got busted smoking pot there, but that was all in the past.

The city had changed now.

I've changed now.

Twenty minutes later, Charlie strolled through the Avis parking lot, the key to his rental car in his left hand and a pack of Marlboros in his right. He hadn't smoked a cigarette in nearly a year, and as he wound his way through a labyrinth of rain-sopped sedans, he seriously considered chucking the pack over the chain-link fence that lined the perimeter of the lot.

Instead, he stuffed the cigarettes into his jacket pocket where they would be easily accessible. He had a feeling he would need them again before long. Avis would charge him a cleaning fee for smoking in the car, but he didn't care.

Something told him he'd be racking up steeper costs very soon.

FIVE

A little over fifteen miles from the Avis parking lot where Charlie Remick was now loading his bag into the back seat of his rental car, Ana Cortez flipped the laminated sign that hung from the front-door window of the Cuckoo's Nest with a practiced flick of her wrist. Out on the curb, leaning against the hood of a cream Mercedes 450-SL, a man in a tartan raincoat watched the sign switch from YES, WE'RE OPEN! to SORRY, WE'RE CLOSED with a mild sense of relief. Ana held up two fingers and mouthed the words *Two minutes. I promise!* The man responded with a cartoonish *I'll believe it when I see it* roll of his eyes.

Over at the checkout counter, Harold Meehan, dressed resplendently in a three-piece wool suit, absentmindedly swayed on the spot as the soft lilt of Frank Sinatra's "In the Wee Small Hours" spilled from the house speakers. Over the years, it had become the go-to record to signal closing time at the Cuckoo's Nest.

Ana slid behind the counter and planted a hand suggestively on the cash register. "How we doing, Harry?"

Harold Meehan laughed. Two neatly stacked columns of 45s sat on the counter in front of him. "I'm no closer than I was an hour ago, but I suppose I'll just have to bite the bullet and choose, won't I?"

Ana's eyes moved to the window. "If you still want to be happily married when you walk out of here tonight, you're gonna have to."

Outside, the man in the tartan raincoat had begun pacing back and forth.

Harold waved a dismissive hand. "Oh, let him pout. I had to sit through *Einstein on the Beach* for three hours with a smile on my face. He can stand to wait a few more minutes."

"Not a Philip Glass fan, I take it?"

"I loved him when I was younger. But I loved Kerouac, Salinger, and my straight neighbor Dennis when I was younger too, so what the fuck did I know?"

Ana let loose a good-natured *ahem* and pointed to the handwritten sign taped to the column behind her. Written in thick Sharpie were the words SNOBBERY WILL BE PROSECUTED TO THE FULLEST EXTENT OF THE LAW.

Harold genuflected playfully. "Sincere apologies, O great one."

"You're forgiven," Ana replied, then began listlessly sorting through a pile of the day's receipts. "Still, it's impressive you got tickets. I heard it sold out within hours."

"George got them through a gal he knows at work," Harold muttered, placing two records off to the side. He grabbed a third record, double-checked it, and held it up. "Is this mismarked?"

Ana inspected the price tag. "Nope, that's correct."

"Five dollars for 'Sleepy Lagoon'?"

"Fremont rent ain't cheap."

A hard *tap tap tap* came from the store's front windows. Ana looked up and saw George point urgently at his watch.

"Clock's running out, Harry," Ana said. "What's it gonna be?"

"Okay, *okay*," Harold mouthed breathlessly. He placed the Harry James record on top of the stack to his right and pushed them over to Ana, pouting a little. "Just these, I suppose."

Two minutes later, Harold and George were speeding up Asterion Avenue, and Ana closed up for good, giving the key in the door's lock a satisfying twist.

She placed Harold Meehan's receipt on a pile with the other day's takes, then reached beneath the register and flicked a series of switches. One by one, the ground-floor lights went out. She left the second-floor lighting on—a series of soft, recessed bulbs that traced the horseshoe-shaped balcony that lined the back and side walls of the store. There were no streetlights directly outside, so the upper-floor lights were always left on as a courtesy to whoever remained in the store after closing.

She switched off the house stereo, dousing the Sinatra, then surveyed the empty, dimly lit store. The Cuckoo's Nest looked strange when it was closed. Like a school at night, with no students to flood its hallways.

The pile of receipts clutched tightly in her hand, Ana hopped over the counter and made her way toward the grand staircase, the only original fixture left from the building's original floor plan. Like the exterior of the store, the staircase itself was a beautiful exercise in Art Deco design, with marble steps and wrought-iron railings. She took the steps two at a time, listening to her boots slap the marble, and reached the second floor a little out of breath. To her left, running along the west balcony, were five listening stations: small wooden tables that had been stocked with turntables, CD players, and tape decks for listening convenience. To her right, running the length of the east balcony, was the store's book selection. They carried a few novels (mostly Charles Beaumont and Richard Matheson titles Raymond had donated from his own collection), but the rest of the books were music-related.

Ten feet beyond the second-floor landing was the door to the main office. On its stippled, translucent window was a sign that read IF YOU MUST ENTER, PLEASE KNOCK FIRST.

Ignoring the sign, Ana pushed the door open and leaned against the frame.

Sitting at Raymond's desk, reading glasses perched crookedly at the end of his nose, was Dale Cernin. The dim light of the desk lamp cast deep shadows along Dale's face, making his slim, Ichabod Crane–like appearance more cartoonish than it really was.

He stared at the mess of loose papers on Raymond's desk, transfixed, almost as if he were trying to decipher a Magic Eye poster.

"I have today's receipts if you want them."

Dale yelped, nearly jumping out of his chair. "Fuckin' hell, Bangs!"

Ana smiled. Dale had lived in the States for more than twenty years, but his Yorkshire drawl was as strong as ever.

He tapped his chest with feathery fingers. "I think you made my heart stop."

"Most romantic thing a man has said to me in months," Ana replied, tossing the pile of receipts onto the desk.

Dale studied them for a moment. "Are we closed already?" He checked his watch and sighed. "Fuck me . . . I forgot to eat."

A loose sheet of paper covered in nearly illegible chicken scratch caught Ana's eye. She moved it under the lamp and immediately recognized Raymond Remick's signature scrawl.

> *Substance report came back from UW . . . Shellac, beetle shells, and bone. Not sure if bone is human or animal. Further study should confirm.*

Ana held up the note. "What's this?"

"Fuck if I know," Dale said, squinting against the light of the desk lamp. He prodded at the mountain of loose papers on Raymond's desk. "I've been at it for three hours and I can't make heads or tails of any of it."

"Where did it all come from?" Ana asked.

"It was all in the desk drawers."

"But those are locked."

"Raymond's attorney popped in earlier and dropped off a set of keys."

"When was this?"

"Around three. You'd stepped out for lunch, I think."

"What did he say?"

"Nothing really," Dale said, frowning. "He just said we might need the key since we'd be running the store in the meantime.

We're running low on Sub Pop apparel, and Christmas being around the corner, I wanted to get our order in now. Raymond usually kept the blank forms on the shelf above the light switch but there weren't any up there. So I used the key and found all *this*."

Ana sifted through a few loose documents, letting her gaze drift over patches of handwriting without actually reading it, then stopped when something caught her eye. She held it under the lamp to get a better look.

"Is this a travel visa?"

"Egyptian," Dale replied without looking.

Ana flipped it open. A glossy picture of Raymond Remick smiled back at her. "Why would he have an Egyptian travel visa?"

"To go to Egypt, I reckon," Dale replied, then reached for a stack of airline ticket stubs and held them up. "Amongst other places."

Ana shuffled through the stubs like a deck of cards, reading the names of the cities aloud as she did so. "Paris, London, Tokyo, Marrakesh, Lisbon, Cairo, Romania, Montreal . . . There have to be at least thirty tickets here."

"Did you see the duplicates? I put them at the end."

Ana shuffled down to the bottom of the stack. "Montreal . . . Montreal . . ." She looked up. "Why the hell did he go to Montreal so much?"

Dale handed her a leather-bound notebook. "This was all I could find on that."

A small sheet of stationery was stapled to one of the pages in the notebook. The heading read *Hôtel Place d'Armes* in muted blue ink. Below it, in Raymond's hand, were the words:

> *Aug 10*
> *4pm Université de Montréal*
> *Prof. Renée Toulon—Ethnography*
> *7:40pm—flight back to Seattle (Amer. Airlines no. 949)*

"I matched this note with one of the ticket stubs," Dale said. "He arrived in Montreal at noon that day. He went back to Seattle at 7:40 P.M. That means he was only in Canada for seven hours."

"Seems like a big hassle just to talk to a college professor," Ana said, frowning. "Maybe this Renée guy is an old friend?"

"Given the spelling, it's probably a woman's name."

Ana thought again of Raymond's undying love for Joan and shook her head. "I don't think so. Raymond wouldn't fly to Canada to meet some strange woman. It's not his style."

"I'm not saying they were fucking, Ana. It could be totally innocent."

"If it was innocent, why didn't he mention her?"

"Look at all this shit, Bangs," Dale said, holding up the plane ticket stubs. "Egypt? Morocco? Romania? He never said a word about *any* of this." He tossed the stubs onto the desk and chuckled. "I always figured when he went on holiday he went to Aruba or something . . . spent a week getting drunk at Trader Vic's and listening to old calypso records. Guess I was wrong."

Ana took a step back and studied the sum total of evidence before them. "He was searching for something."

"Yeah, records probably," Dale said indifferently. "Why else would he fly all the way to Montreal for a few hours? Maybe that Canadian professor had a good collection and Raymond was trying to get her to sell it."

Ana supposed it could be true. It wouldn't be the first time Raymond had traveled out of Seattle in search of rare records. Two years ago, he drove all the way to Memphis to buy a set of mint Sun 45s off a geriatric collector who had been looking to bankroll his dialysis treatments. But even then, a road trip to Memphis was a far cry from Egyptian travel visas and meetings with Canadian college professors. There was a story here, she knew that much, but she couldn't yet tell what it was.

Then something occurred to her—something that had flown,

unnoticed, past her ears when Dale first said it. "You said the lawyer dropped off Raymond's keys because we'd be running the store in the meantime, right?"

"Mm-hm."

"Well, what happens *after* the meantime?"

Dale looked up. The light from the desk lamp cast a reflective sheen across the lenses of his reading glasses, hiding his eyes. "I don't follow . . ."

Ana shifted uneasily on her heels. Until that moment, she'd never truly considered the question she was about to ask. Raymond was thirty years her senior, and yet she had never actually entertained the fact that he might die. He was like David Bowie in that way. Even though he was well into his sixties, Raymond never really seemed *old*. Sure, he had a shock of white hair and his skin was a bit leathery, but as far as Ana had been concerned, Raymond should have outlived her and Dale both, mainly because it was too ludicrous a concept that the Cuckoo's Nest could exist without him.

Raymond Remick *was* the Cuckoo's Nest.

"Dale . . ." Ana said, feeling her jaw tense as she asked the question she never thought she'd have to ask, "who owns the store *now*?"

SIX

Charlie pulled into the driveway of his childhood home at a quarter to midnight. All along Wabash Street, the houses were quiet; windows cast hazy reflections of the Christmas lights that had been strung up neatly along their frames.

The windows of the Remick household cast no such reflections. The eaves of its mansard roofs were bare. The house sat alone like a shadowy outlier, lacking any and all signs of yuletide cheer, but the windows still glowed brightly—all golden and orange, pulsing merrily in the evening mist as a crop of familiar silhouettes flitted from one room to the other.

There were people inside.

Charlie looked to his right. Parked next to his rental was Susan's Ford Explorer. Behind him, nestled up to the curb, was a navy-blue Honda Accord that had seen better days.

Ellie's, Charlie figured. Or, more likely, a beater that Ellie had borrowed for the trip to Seattle. The dreamcatcher dangling from the rearview mirror wasn't exactly Ellie's style. It no doubt belonged to one of her bohemian, candle-making friends.

He grabbed his bag, locked the rental car, and made his way up the lawn. As he reached the front steps, he smiled at the sight of a small wreath that had been hung from a lopsided nail on the door. Evidently the house wasn't a total pariah after all. He ran his fingers along the tips of the pine needles and smiled. This was no fake job that came out of a box. This was the real deal. An honest-to-God fresh wreath from an honest-to-God tree lot. Had his father hung it before he died? When he was growing up, the Christmas decorations had always fallen under the purview of Charlie, his mother, and his sisters. His father was only ever responsible for seeing that the exterior lights went up, and even then, he only submitted to such a responsibility after every other house on the block had been lit up for a full week and the Remick house started to resemble the Grinch's sad little shack at the top of Mount Crumpit.

After their mother died, Charlie's sisters had made a concerted effort to spend Christmas with their father—a tradition to which Charlie had been routinely invited but always elected to miss.

He leaned forward and let his nose hover next to the wreath. The smell of fresh pine filled his nostrils and made his head swoon a bit.

On the other side of the door, he heard the faint pitter-patter of tiny feet skittering from room to room.

"Slow down!"

The voice was muffled, but he knew it immediately.

Susan.

Charlie watched his sister's shadow flit across the frosted window next to the door, then pressed the brass button to his right. He heard the distant chime of the doorbell and saw Susan's shadow stop.

"You two had better hope that's not one of the neighbors complaining about the noise."

Charlie took a step back as the front door swung open. A woman stepped into the ring of light beneath the porch lamp and Charlie suddenly felt his muscles tense. His voice caught in his throat, cutting him off somewhere between *Hi* and *Susan.*

Because the woman standing in the doorway wasn't Susan.

The woman standing in the doorway was his mother.

Or, at least, she was for a second or two. She took a second step forward, allowing the light to spill more adequately across her features, and Charlie felt his shoulders relax.

"Charlie, hey!" Susan said through an exasperated smile. Behind her, a chocolate Labrador hoovered up a trail of potato chips that led into an adjacent room, its floppy ears bouncing with each erratic sweep of its snout.

"Susan . . . you look . . ."

"I know. I look like a mess." She tugged apologetically at the baggy Gonzaga sweatshirt that hung below her waist.

"No. You don't," Charlie said, still processing what he was seeing. "You look like . . ." He wanted to say *You look like Mom,* but it was more than that.

Susan's trademark bob—all sleek geometry, gunmetal dye, and angular bangs—was gone. In its place were sweeping curtains of mahogany hair that fell across her shoulders in loose waves. Her eyebrows were no longer tweezed into sleek blades; they were thick and natural. Her fingernails were short and colorless, painted only with a protective clear lacquer to keep them from breaking, and her cheeks, normally pale and evenly toned, were now flushed with color. She even appeared to have a tan. A fading tan, but a tan nonetheless.

Simply put, she looked like a Remick.

Charlie laughed nervously. "Shit, Susan, I didn't recognize you at first."

She crossed her arms and shot him a disapproving glare. "That's what happens when you go two years without seeing your big sister."

Charlie gave no reply. Instead, he stared at his shoes and ran a hand slowly through his hair—a gesture of guilt he'd inherited from his father.

"Oh, for God's sake," Susan said, and waved him inside. "Quit hugging the cactus and get in here."

Charlie did what he was told. He set his luggage down near the coatrack and took a look around. The house was warm but not stifling, dim but not dark, and something in the kitchen smelled so good and so inviting, he felt his stomach produce an envious growl.

Susan reached up and tousled his hair. "Gettin' pretty shaggy there, fella. You need a trim."

"Speak for yourself," he said, and motioned to her head. "What happened to the bob?"

"Too much work. Decided I'd try the Catherine Keener look for a while."

"It suits you," Charlie said, which was the truth, and although Catherine Keener wasn't a stretch, she looked so much like their mother he could hardly picture anyone else. Surely Susan must have noticed it, too. The resemblance was beyond uncanny.

He was about to say as much when Susan surprised him by pulling him into a tight hug.

Once again, Charlie felt himself tense up. He could remember hugging his older sister only once before in his life—at their mother's funeral—and it felt nothing like this. Whoever this new Susan was had obviously learned the art of the embrace since then. She'd even become a pro at it.

"How was your flight?" she asked, releasing him.

"Fine," he lied. The dream of the warehouse and the Grim Tree was still fresh in his mind, but he had no desire to talk about it, especially since Susan had been one of the bodies hanging from its branches. "How was the drive from Spokane?"

"With two kids and a dog? Eventful."

"Jeff didn't want to come?"

A pale shadow swept across Susan's face, but she blinked it away. "He offered. But I told him it would probably be better if he stayed put."

Charlie nodded. Ellie had filled him in on the details of Susan's recent divorce—including the part about Susan accidentally walking in on Jeff while he was getting a blow job from a client in his home office—and he decided if Susan didn't want to elaborate, he wouldn't push her. "How goes the interior-decoration business?"

"Good," she said. "Busy, but good. The South Hill is growing fast. Seems like every day a new house pops up. How about you?"

"Me? Oh, I gave up interior decorating years ago," Charlie joked. "If I see one more goddamned Eames recliner I'm gonna strap weights to my ankles and walk into the ocean."

"Uncle Charlie!"

Tiny feet careened frantically down the main staircase, and before he could brace for impact, a set of wild blond curls plowed into his stomach like a battering ram, nearly knocking the wind out of him.

"Maisy the Springtime Daisy!" he cried, hoisting his niece up into the air. She shrieked with laughter, hair bouncing like a bouquet of golden springs. "What's new, kiddo?"

"I'm a detective now!"

"You are?"

From her pocket, Maisy produced a comically large magnifying glass, the kind one would find at a joke shop or a costume store. "I'm looking for clues!"

"Have you found any?"

"Lots," Maisy said, absentmindedly wiping her nose with the entire length of her hand, the way children do. Charlie kept a watchful eye on the glistening, snot-covered hand that was now hovering dangerously close to his corduroy blazer. "But mostly I've just found a lot of dust."

"Well," he said, gently setting her down on the hardwood floor, "that's because Grandpa Raymond never learned how to use a broom."

Maisy's eyes went wide. "He *didn't*?"

Susan shot a covert glare at Charlie. "Of course he did, honey," she said, bending low and cleaning Maisy's hand with a wet wipe she had seemingly pulled out of thin air. "Big old houses like this make lots of dust. It's hard to keep up with the cleaning. Especially when you're old like Grandpa was."

Charlie smirked. Susan made their father out to be some shaky old codger whose spine would shatter into a million pieces under a light wind. She knew damn well Raymond Remick was a picture of health.

Had been a picture of health, he thought darkly, then involuntarily glanced in the direction of the backyard. His mind flashed to the image of his father's body as it hung from the Grim Tree: lifeless, alone, and in the dark.

Maisy gazed up at him, concerned. "Are you okay, Uncle Charlie?"

Charlie smiled. "Just a little tired, sweetheart." He took her magnifying glass and twisted the handle playfully in his fingers. "And your mom's right. Big houses get super dusty. But you know what that means, don't you?"

Maisy shook her head.

"That just means it'll be easier to find fingerprints!"

With a goofy toothless grin, Maisy took her oversized magnifying glass back and held it in front of her face, ballooning her right eye to the size of an orange. "They must be everywhere!"

"You can look for fingerprints tomorrow, okay?" Susan said, petting her daughter's head. "It's already way past your bedtime and we've got a long day tomorrow."

"Yep, got a long day tomorrow," Maisy echoed dutifully, then walked quietly up the stairs. "Better get to bed. *Loooong* day tomorrow."

"That's right," Susan called up, amused.

When Maisy reached the second-floor landing, she scampered off, giggling, feet clomping heavily, no doubt in search of more clues.

Susan dropped her shoulders, defeated.

"I'd get her a deerstalker for Christmas, but I don't think it'd fit over that hair," Charlie said, grinning.

A different voice entered the mix. "Mom, did you bring an extra charger? My phone's about to die."

Charlie whirled around and saw his nephew standing under the doorway to the living room.

"Miles," Susan said sternly, "can you say hello to Uncle Charlie?"

Miles raised his right arm and let it drop heavily to his side, figuring this was a perfectly acceptable wave. "Hey."

Charlie placed his hands on his hips and surveyed the young man standing before him. "Wow, Miles. Look at you. You've gotten so big!"

His nephew, whose lanky posture, rosy cheeks, and protruding Adam's apple placed him directly within the vicious throes of puberty, shrugged indifferently. "I guess so," he murmured, then shuffled up the stairs, shoes squeaking against the hardwood. "I'm gonna borrow your charger, Mom."

"That's fine," Susan said, sighing. "And please don't drag your feet, Miles. You begged me for months to buy you those skate shoes and you're going to ruin them."

When his nephew was out of earshot, Charlie grinned at Susan. "He skates?"

"He tries," she said. "His friends all got into it last summer but I don't really think he likes it. I think he just likes the fashion."

Nothing wrong with that, Charlie thought. Skaters were the least cringeworthy of the three teenage evils (the other two being Young Republicans and Mall Goths).

A sudden draft of cold air threaded itself through the room, and the chocolate Labrador reappeared, head bowed low, searching for a rogue potato chip or bread crumb he might have missed. Charlie bent down and gave the dog a lively pat on its head.

"He wouldn't pee," said a familiar voice from the other room. "I tried bribing him with an Altoid but he turned me down."

Charlie looked up and saw his twin sister shuffle into the main hallway, drowning in an oversized parka. Like the rest of the Remick children, Ellie had hair the color of rich mahogany, although instead of framing her face like it normally did, it was tucked lazily under a lumpy brown hat with a plastic daisy pinned to the front brim.

"Nice hat, Blossom," Charlie said, suppressing a laugh.

Ellie gave her brother the finger, then immediately pulled him into a hug.

Susan wrinkled her nose. "You smell like a head shop."

"A classy one, I hope," Ellie replied, slipping out of her parka. "That joint wasn't cheap."

Charlie took her jacket and hung it up. "You look frozen. Why didn't you just smoke it inside?"

"Absolutely not," Susan said sharply. "I don't want Maisy or Miles walking into the living room and seeing you passed out on the couch with a bong in one hand and a bag of chips in the other."

Ellie rolled her eyes. "Thank you for that image, Nancy Reagan."

"To be fair, they probably wouldn't even know what it is," Charlie reasoned. "When we were kids, Dad used to smell like pot all the time. I just figured it was bad cologne."

"Oh, they *know*," Susan said. "They learned all about pot in school. There's a cartoon and everything."

Ellie's eyes brightened. "McGruff?"

"Captain Wigglekins," Susan replied. "It's a panda bear dressed as a cop."

"Sounds like a fucking narc," Ellie said, then turned to her brother. "So what do you think of Susan's new look?"

"Uncanny."

"Right?"

"I swear I thought she was Mom when I first saw her."

"I did, too!"

"Hold on," Susan interjected, "I've always looked like Mom."

"You looked like *a* mom," Charlie said. "Not *our* mom."

Ellie nodded. "You fell somewhere between Uma Thurman in *Pulp Fiction* and the mom from *The Santa Clause*."

Susan stared silently at the two of them.

"The title has an *e* on the end, if that helps jog your memory," Ellie added. "It's a pretty important detail, plotwise."

"It does not," Susan said.

"This is actually on point," Charlie said. "The mom from *The Santa Clause* wouldn't have watched *The Santa Clause* either."

"You two are incorrigible," Susan said, glaring at them, then flinched as a series of sudden, high-pitched barks pierced the air. She sped into the living room, swearing under her breath. Charlie and Ellie followed her. The Labrador was standing on the davenport sofa, stiff-legged and tail arrow-straight, howling at the windows.

"Loud little guy, isn't he?" Ellie said, covering her ears.

"Bruiser, stop it!" Susan hissed. She grabbed him by the collar and moved him to the floor. "You're gonna wake up the whole neighborhood!"

Bruiser sat obediently and ceased barking, but refused to take his eyes off the perceived threat.

The three of them peered out the window just in time to see a beige Toyota Camry pull clumsily away from the curb and collide with a row of trash cans. All of them fell but one. It blew right past the stop sign at the corner of Wabash and Indigo and sped off into the night, taillights glowing in the fog.

"That was a solid hit," Ellie said, heading back to the foyer. "Maybe he'll circle round the block and come back to pick up the spare."

Charlie bent low and tousled Bruiser's ears. The dog puffed his lips out, muttering a final bark of warning, then trotted away after Ellie. "Bruiser the chocolate Lab," Charlie said, chuckling, "sworn enemy of the sensible four-door sedan."

"And everything else that moves, unfortunately," Susan said, annoyed.

Charlie followed her back to the foyer, but stopped when something caught his eye. He ambled over to a nearby bookshelf, on which sat a row of dusty picture frames. He picked up the frame closest to him and wiped the dust from the glass.

The Remick clan—twenty years younger—smiled at him from a small five-by-seven photo. Behind them loomed a large Bavarian lodge, half-timbered and appointed with diamond leaded glass windows. Charlie and his father were dressed head to toe in lederhosen. His mother and sisters wore matching dirndls.

"I keep meaning to make a copy of that one," said Susan, who had reappeared and was hovering over Charlie's shoulder. "Mom and Dad loved Leavenworth."

Charlie didn't respond. He'd spent the last five years so consumed with the bad memories of his father, he'd almost forgotten there had been some good ones, too. It was true, their parents had always loved their visits to the small German town nestled in the Cascade mountains of Washington, but so did Charlie. So did all of them. He set the photo back on the shelf and felt very heavy all of a sudden, as if his limbs had been filled with lead.

The sound of digital wind chimes floated up from Susan's back pocket. She pulled out her phone and swiped at the screen. "That's the timer for the oven. Are you hungry? I made Mom's Pasta Surprise."

Charlie felt his heart swell. "You did?"

"Enough to feed an army."

Five minutes later, the three Remick siblings took their places around the dinner table, their mother's signature dish loaded up on their plates. As they ate and laughed over old memories, Charlie couldn't remember being so grateful. It had been too long since he'd come home; too long since he'd spent any real time with his sisters.

To Ellie and Susan, he was not the Man with the Magic Ear, or the stooge who poisoned the musical well with insufferable YouTube sensations, or the rakish flirt who enthralled first and disappointed second. He was simply their brother. Little Charlie Remick.

And maybe, in the end, that was all he needed to be.

He smiled at the thought, knowing it wouldn't last.

But for now, it was enough.

SEVEN

Eleven miles away, across the frigid, ink-black surface of Lake Washington, in the small Seattle suburb of Kirkland, on a quiet street, in a little house set cozily between other little houses, Louis Goodwin burst through his front door and made tracks for the bathroom.

Deb followed him, throwing a series of I-told-you-sos at his back, but Louis paid her no attention. She was nothing more than an unpleasant side effect of what truly ailed him.

He slammed the bathroom door in her face, threw the lock, and reached blindly for a towel. He fell to the floor in a slump and pulled the towel tightly over his head, reducing Deb's voice to nothing more than a distant muffle.

She was right, of course. She *had* told him so. She'd warned him that going back to that house was a bad idea, that there were too many people there now, that if the case *was* in there, there'd be no way to break in and get it without being noticed.

But he didn't have a choice. He *had* to go back. And he'd go back again.

If he didn't get that case, he was a dead man.

Louis whimpered and collapsed into the fetal position. He focused on his breathing and tried to clear his mind of the awful thoughts that clawed their way out of the darkness and into his consciousness. Thoughts of the black case. Of Raymond's bloated, twisted face. Of his own inevitable and gruesome death.

And of *him*.

The man with no ears in a room full of machines. Machines that made horrible music.

Louis sobbed into the towel. He was exhausted. He couldn't remember the last time he'd slept. The more he tried to calm his thoughts, the more abstract (and terrifying) they became, crisscrossing dizzyingly and morphing into a tangled knot of screams, blood, and unavoidable death.

His pulse was racing. He buried two fingers under his jaw and checked his watch.

One hundred and sixty beats per minute, sitting still.

If he didn't slow his heart rate soon, finding the black case wouldn't matter.

He focused again on his breathing, counting steadily as he did so, and immediately felt his pulse begin to slow. It wasn't a significant drop, but the sensation of self-control, however small, gave him a small boost of confidence, and Louis doubled his efforts, inhaling slowly . . . and exhaling slowly.

Two minutes passed, and 160 became 120.

Two minutes later, 120 became 90.

When his pulse reached 78, Louis felt a wave of relaxation that would have buckled his knees if he'd been standing. His brain, whether by exhaustion or steady breathing, began to cloud over with the plush darkness of sleep, and his breathing slowed even more.

The horrible thoughts were still there, of course, only now they were in another room; faint and distant, like a loud party in an adjacent apartment. He counted his breaths . . . in and out . . . and finally, somewhere between his hundredth inhale and his hundredth exhale, he let sleep take him.

Minutes later (or maybe hours later; Louis didn't know how long), a knock woke him up.

"Nobody takes that long to shit, shower, or shave," Deb said through the door, "so I assume you're playing with that tiny pecker of yours."

Louis sat up and rubbed his eyes against the glare of the light. The towel lay in a clump to his left. It must have slipped off when he was sleeping.

Deb knocked again, harder this time, and Louis glared at the door. "Leave me alone, you—"

He thought about calling her a bitch, but Louis wasn't the type of man to ever use that word, even in anger. He considered substituting "witch," but knew that wasn't right either. To be honest, he didn't know *what* Deb was. She couldn't pass through doors without opening them, which meant that she wasn't a ghost (or, at least, a ghost defined by movies and books), but he was also the only person who could see her, which ruled out the zombie option.

Deb mumbled something on the other side of the door—another jab at his manhood, no doubt—then, receiving no response, stormed away in a huff.

Feeling a slight sense of relief now that his dead wife was no longer in proximity, Louis leaned against the bathtub and traced the bruise patterns on his temples with his fingertips.

They were still tender to the touch.

It had been almost two days since the man with no ears had grabbed him.

He had no trouble remembering it. He'd been in his kitchen, watching the microwave unevenly cook his Lean Cuisine dinner. Deb was in the living room, watching *Wheel of Fortune*. Dead or not, she never missed *Wheel*. The microwave went *ding*, he opened the door, and suddenly the kitchen was gone. And his Lean Cuisine dinner. And Deb. And *Wheel of Fortune*.

He'd found himself in the hallway first. The long, grimy hallway lined with dark doors. He remembered being drawn to the larger door at the end. The one surrounded by glowing light.

Oh God, why did he open it?

Louis forced himself to stand up. The idea of sleep was still too tempting a prospect, and he couldn't allow himself to falter again. His eyes zigzagged across his green-tiled bathroom, the way children's eyes do when searching the shadows of their bedrooms for any sign of the drooling, long-toothed thing that waited to devour them.

Because that's where the worst things hid. In the shadows.

He removed the hanging hand towels, tore down the shower curtain, closed every cabinet drawer, and chased every shadow in the bathroom away.

When the man with no ears came for him again, and he *would* come for him, Louis would not let it be a surprise.

He returned to his post by the bathtub, pinching his arm every few minutes to stay awake, and watched for any signs of trouble. As the minutes passed, his mind began to wander—not into the realm of a daydream, he was much too frightened to allow that, but into the open spaces where plans are formed.

He would go to Raymond's store and look for the case there.

There were too many people staying at his house now to attempt another break-in. And, now that he thought about it, it seemed unlikely that Raymond would have kept the case in his house in the first place. Its contents were much too dangerous. *Anyone* could stumble upon it.

Louis nodded.

Yes, the case was almost certainly at the store.

He would go there tomorrow. He'd slip in unnoticed and search the place while the staff attended to the other customers. And when he found the case, he'd just walk out with it. No stuttering, no bumbling. Just grab it and go. If the case proved to be his salvation, the theft would be justifiable. If it didn't, then Louis would be too dead to return it.

Either way, the horror would be over.

All he could do now was wait for the morning to come.

And so he sat. And waited. And refused to blink.

EIGHT

It was nearing 8 P.M., and Ellie Remick had just finished filling her siblings in on her candle-making exploits in Portland, which, due to insufficient capital and a flaky business partner, eventually fell through and landed her in Bellingham, where she'd been shacking up with a freelance graphic artist named Hugo, who, due to insufficient lovemaking skills, would be out of the picture as soon as she could afford her own place.

She hovered over the living room coffee table as she distributed the last drops of a cheap bottle of red wine among three glasses. "And with this final pour," she said, tipping the bottle over Susan's glass, "we say goodbye to Two-Buck Chuck."

"A bottle of Charles Shaw is more than two bucks now," Susan said.

"Fine, Adjusted-for-Inflation Chuck, then." Ellie giggled at her own joke and staggered sideways on unsteady feet. The bottle slipped from her hand and fell to the floor, resulting in a thin streak of red along the hardwood.

Bruiser, who'd been waiting in the wings for just such an occasion, happily dove in and lapped it up.

"Aw, Bruiser, *no,*" Susan said, slurring slightly. "You're turning my dog into a lush, Ellie."

"It'll make his coat shiny."

"That's fish oil."

"*You're* fish oil."

Susan shot a finger gun. "Good one."

At the other end of the davenport, Charlie was staring silently out the window.

Across the street, a garage door opened slowly and the Pearson family (whom Charlie had seen but never spoken to) spilled out onto the driveway. Their dog, a gorgeous Alaskan malamute, leapt erratically across the driveway in wide, sweeping arcs, barking amiable hellos to the neighboring Christmas lights. Mr. Pearson, who'd clearly been drafted into holding the leash, struggled to stay upright as the dog zigzagged across the slick asphalt.

"I'm glad to see they got a new dog," Ellie said, gazing out the window. "Their old one died last Christmas. Susan and I were here when it happened."

"Oh God," Susan said, taking a swig of her wine, "don't remind me."

"Wait a minute," Charlie said, slurring a little. "I remember that dog. The German shorthaired pointer, right?"

Ellie nodded. "Bandit."

"He died?"

"Hit by a delivery truck. Fourth of July weekend."

"Jesus . . ."

"Candace was on the front lawn when it happened. She saw the whole thing."

Charlie grimaced. "That's the little girl?"

"When the truck came down the road, Bandit probably thought it was going to hurt her, so he bolted out into the street to confront it."

Charlie turned back to the window. The malamute was now running circles around Mr. Pearson, wrapping his legs up in the leash like something out of an old Norman Rockwell postcard. Candace watched from the side of the driveway, doubled over with laughter as she cheered the new dog on.

Charlie smiled. "Looks like she's got a new pal."

Ellie glanced at an old clock on the mantel. "It's only eight?"

"Eleven my time, technically," Charlie said.

"*Fuck,* we're getting old," she replied, yawning. "I can barely keep my eyes open."

Susan leaned forward and began stacking plates. "We should

get some sleep. We've got a meeting with Dad's attorney and the cremation at two."

"We're cremating him?" Charlie asked. "Already?"

"Dad didn't want a funeral," Susan said, "so I didn't see any reason to draw it out."

This was news to Charlie. "I thought Dad would have loved the idea of a bunch of people blubbering and crying over him."

"He nixed the idea a few years ago," Ellie said, staring at her wineglass. "After Mom's funeral, he said he didn't want us going through that kind of pain twice. So he told us to hold a wake instead."

Charlie fell silent. He felt the urge to curse his father as a phony martyr, but that would mean divulging information about Raymond that his sisters were, to date, unaware of, and Charlie wanted to keep it that way. Now that he was gone, there was no sense in spoiling their image of him.

"Which reminds me," Susan said, "it's gonna be too difficult to find a venue short notice, especially with Christmas around the corner, so I was thinking we could just have the wake here."

Ellie's jaw went slack. "Here? In the house?"

Susan shrugged. "It's as good a place as any."

"But . . ." Ellie shifted uncomfortably and lowered her voice. "Dad *died* here."

Outside, the wind had begun to pick up, and Charlie stared vacantly into space, his gaze aimed in the direction of the backyard. The more he stared, the more the intervening walls seemed to dissolve into molecules, giving him an unimpeded view of

the Grim Tree, which towered over him, turned on the spot like a mobile, the five bodies dangling limply by the neck from different branches, all with frightful faces and leering eyes that burrowed into his own.

The faces of his family. Of Ellie. Of Susan. Of his mother. Of his father.

And himself.

"Charlie?"

"HEY, CHARLIE!" his own hanging corpse screamed, mouth flapping open and engulfing the whole room in darkness. "REMEM-BER ME?"

A hand grabbed his shoulder and gave it a brisk shake. "You fall asleep?"

He blinked a few times, forcing his gaze to rack-focus back to the living room. Both of his sisters were staring at him, amused.

"Are we that boring?" Susan asked.

"Sorry," he said, averting his eyes. He could still see their life-less faces. The image made him feel sick. "What were we talking about?"

"What do you think about holding the wake here at the house?"

He forced a smile. "Sure. Whatever you think is best."

Ellie still wasn't crazy about the idea, but she could see she'd been outvoted. Of the three Remick children, her pocketbook was the lightest, which meant that Susan and Charlie would most likely be splitting whatever bills their father's death accrued. "Let's just make sure it's not a long wake," she said, setting her empty wineglass down. "I don't want people prowling around the house for six hours."

Susan and Charlie both agreed, and, having settled matters, dropped their dishes in the kitchen sink to soak for a few hours and said good night to each other.

Susan and Ellie disappeared up the stairs (the two of them were staying in their respective childhood bedrooms) but Charlie stalled for a bit, electing to have a cigarette out by his rental car while his sisters prepared for bed. He was in no mood to explain the reason why he wanted to sleep in the living room that first night. He was too tired and too tipsy (and still too rattled by his nightmare) to stay in his own childhood bedroom, with its horrible window that looked directly into the backyard.

He would confront the Grim Tree when he was good and ready.

And if it turned out he never got around to being ready, then that was absolutely fine by him.

Two cigarettes later, he snuck back inside, careful not to wake Bruiser, who was snoring peacefully in his crate upstairs. He stole a pillow from a nearby love seat, pulled a quilt around his shoulders, kicked off his boots, and collapsed onto the davenport.

Through the windows, the neighboring houses twinkled warmly in the darkness. He fished his phone from his pocket, went to place it on the nearby coffee table, and saw that he'd missed a text message. It was from Jennifer Graham.

Thinking about you and your family, honey. Take all the time you need. I'll see to it that all the ships make it to sea.

He tapped a quick response (thanks JG), pressed Send, and rolled back onto the couch.

Outside, a car passed.

Charlie watched the echoes of its headlights sweep across the ceiling.

Sleep was still a ways off. He could feel it. Tired as he was, his limbs were restless and his mind was still humming. He thought about his sisters: Susan, now happily divorced and with two children she loved, just as sharp and yet ten times softer than she'd been growing up. Then there was Ellie, a freewheeling bohemian pothead with a failing candle business who was shacking up with a freelance graphic designer named Hugo. Then he pictured them both and smiled, feeling a sudden rush of love and gratitude for the two of them. He promised himself that he would make a concerted effort to see more of them.

Another car passed outside, its wheels sloshing peacefully along the street, and Charlie was overtaken by a second feeling, this one much more unpleasant than the last. It was a feeling of reluctant certainty; of dreadful inevitability. A feeling that the backyard was closer to him now than it had been all night.

No matter how much he tried to distract his mind with pleasant thoughts, he knew he wouldn't be able to sleep until he saw it.

With a jerk of his leg and an audible grunt, he kicked the quilt from his body and got to his feet. The floor was cold, but he had no interest in pulling on his boots. In the time it took to lace them up, he might change his mind, and this whole process would start all over again. And so, he made his way across the darkened living room, stepping lightly and avoiding the creaking floorboards he remembered. Upon entering the kitchen, he risked a brief glance at the window over the stove, but the curtains were drawn. He could pull one of the curtains back, of course; take a look at the tree, then go back to bed; but something told him a quick peek through the window wouldn't pass muster. He would need the full dose if he was ever going to sleep.

It's not enough to know the closet door is closed. You have to throw it open and flip on the lights to be absolutely sure the monster isn't there.

And that's exactly what he would do.

Breath held, Charlie opened the door and stepped confidently into the backyard.

There was no big reveal. No swirling layer of ground fog that obscured his view and then dissipated in a strong gust of wind, unveiling his monster with a dramatic flourish.

It was just standing there. Without fanfare. As if it weren't a thing of nightmares.

Charlie traced the Grim Tree's gruesome shape with his eyes. The canopy that resembled a wraith's hood, the jagged trunk, the crooked branches—all brittle and bone and skeletal white.

He took a few steps forward to get a better look, hoping his closer proximity to the tree would chase the shadows away and make it appear less menacing, but getting a better look only made it scarier. With each step, another horrible memory flooded his mind; memories of screams in the night, of panicked scrambles into his parents' room.

Dry pine needles buried themselves into the pads of his feet, and more than once he felt something tickle the space between his toes.

Probably loose blades of grass, he told himself. *It's too cold for bugs.*

When he was halfway across the lawn, he forced himself to stop. The Grim Tree was only ten feet away, now, and Charlie couldn't bring himself to take another step.

Halfway was close enough.

Close enough to feel the negative energy surrounding it.

Close enough to see the worn strip of bark on the Grim Tree's longest gnarled branch.

Charlie stared for a long while at the spot where his father's noose had been. He didn't know how long exactly, but by the time he went back inside, his feet were numb from the cold. Somehow that thin strip of branch—worn down to tan wood where the weight of the noose had rubbed it raw—had changed the narrative. As he made his way back through the kitchen, fear dripped from his body, leaving a trail of diluted nightmares behind him in small puddles. He felt like a paint-covered canvas that had been splashed with thinner.

That small noose-shaped strip of worn branch was not a souvenir of the Grim Tree's triumph, but a wound.

Charlie felt a sudden pity for the tree. He imagined its wounded limb reaching out—not to grab him, but to beg for forgiveness; to curse its own fate for being used as a means for suicide.

The Grim Tree was nothing but an innocent bystander, involuntarily used as a tool for a grisly, lonely death.

It was no monster. Just a tree that had been born in the shape of one.

He thought of the nightmare he'd had on the plane and laughed; laughed at how ridiculous it all was—how ridiculous *he'd* been— then grabbed a bottle of water from the refrigerator and drained it in one go. It was cold and made his eyes water, but it was cleansing. His own private little baptism. Right there in the kitchen.

Eyes still streaming, he padded his way over to the davenport and sank heavily into its worn cushions. He pulled the quilt over his shoulders and rubbed his feet together, dislodging a few pine needles that had managed to hang on, then gazed out the window, sparing half a second to note that the Christmas lights on Wabash Street were no longer on before falling asleep instantly.

NINE

It had been a slow morning at the Cuckoo's Nest.

It was nearly noon and Ana had counted only seven customers so far. That was probably for the best, considering her mood, but if the slow trickle of paying customers was any indication of how the rest of the month was going to go, the store was in big trouble.

She knew who to blame, of course. The streaming services had finally begun to eat into their revenue. For a nominal fee, they had made it too easy, too convenient, to access any song or any album at any time. Well, *almost* any.

The biggest hit, though, was the steady decline of the "blind buy." One-hundred-and-eighty-gram repros of the Beatles' or Stones' catalogue would never stop selling. Even a novice vinyl-head knew that a collection without *Sgt. Pepper's Lonely Hearts Club Band* or *Exile on Main St.* wasn't really a collection at all. It was everything else. The little records on little labels that no one had ever heard of. Exclusive seven-inches on Captured Tracks or Hardly Art, new releases on Sub Pop or Stones Throw; *those* were the records that weren't selling like they used to. Who took the chance on a blind buy anymore when you could simply pull it up on your phone and test-drive three tracks without ever getting off the toilet? And that wasn't even the biggest problem. The true insidious nature of the streaming services was what happened *after* the test-drive. When the album was already on your phone, why buy it?

It was all just too easy.

And so, as Ana rang up the Cuckoo's Nest's seventh customer of the day, she twisted her lips into an amiable smile and thanked him ardently for his purchase, trying her best to ignore the fact that the only thing he'd purchased was a used copy of the *Grosse Pointe Blank* soundtrack for a whopping $3.80 (which, after applying the storewide holiday discount of 20 percent, came to $3.04).

She placed the CD into a bag and encouraged him to tell his friends about all the holiday deals going on.

And to spend more than three fucking bucks, she thought sourly.

She leaned forward, propping her elbows on the counter, and watched him go, then shifted her gaze to the blurry red taillights of the parked Camry.

"Yearning for the outside world, Bangs?"

Dale Cernin descended the main staircase, the tassels on his brown suede vest shimmying with each step.

"That car's been parked outside the store for almost two hours," she said, motioning to the street.

Dale sidled up to the counter and looked out the window. "Which one?"

"The Toyota."

"That means nothing to me. I don't know cars."

"The beige one. The sedan."

Dale studied the car for a moment. "Maybe they're waiting for someone."

"The driver keeps looking at the store every couple of minutes," Ana said, squinting to see if she could read the faded sticker on the Camry's bumper. The only thing she could make out was the name *SAM* in big block letters.

"Maybe he's casing the joint," Dale joked.

Ana tapped the No Sale button on the register, and the cash box opened with a *ca-chunk*. "We got three bucks and a Quiznos punch card that expired during the Clinton administration. He's welcome to it."

Dale grinned. "Maybe he just wants to buy a copy of the Eagles' *Greatest Hits* but he's too embarrassed to come in and do it."

"Why be embarrassed? Everyone likes the Eagles."

"No one likes the Eagles," Dale replied.

Ana shrugged. "Same difference."

The man in the driver's seat cast a furtive glance at the store. Even from thirty feet away, it was clear that he was sweating.

"Guy's putting off some real George Costanza energy."

"Not to mention he's talking to himself," Dale said. "That's always a good sign."

Ana leaned forward. Dale was right. The man's mouth was animated.

"He could be on the phone," she reasoned.

"I don't think so," Dale said. "Watch. Every time he talks, he turns to face the passenger seat, but there's no one there." He chuckled and shook his head. "What a nut."

Perhaps it was her bad mood, or the fact that they'd only had seven customers that day, but Ana felt a sudden surge of devil-may-care waggishness that sent her sliding over the checkout counter feetfirst. She strolled confidently over to the door, threw it open, and shouted into the street, "We got plenty of Eagles CDs, baldy! Don't be shy!"

Panic flashed across the face of the man in the Camry. His eyes went wide, his mouth a perfect oval of surprise, and instead of responding to Ana, he turned to the empty passenger seat next to him and cried, "I told you they'd see me!"

He threw the car into drive and sped away, tires screeching, tailpipe belching a thick gray cloud of exhaust.

Ana watched, dumbstruck, as the car hung a woozy right turn and disappeared around the corner.

"Guess he wasn't an Eagles fan after all," Dale said to Ana as she made her way back to the front counter.

"I feel bad," she said, slightly rattled. "He seemed really spooked."

"You cut an imposing presence, Bangs. I hope you never yell at *me* like that."

"I hope he was okay. Mentally, I mean." Ana glanced back at the empty spot where the Camry had been.

"Like I said, he's a nut," Dale said almost too reasonably. He groped blindly for the pair of eyeglasses that hung from his neck on a thin braided cord and set them gingerly on the tip of his nose. He held a small piece of paper up to his eyes. "By the way, Ellie Remick called. She says Raymond's wake is tomorrow."

Ana felt a nauseating squeeze behind her navel. All thoughts of the strange man in the beige Camry dissolved into mist. "Where?"

"At the house," Dale said darkly. He studied the piece of paper in his hand. "I wish they'd chosen a different venue, if I'm honest."

Ana saw his hand begin to shake. If it had been she who found Raymond hanging from that tree instead of Dale, she wouldn't have been able to get out of bed, let alone crack jokes about the Eagles. "That's fucking ghoulish. They should know better."

"No, I get it," Dale said, waving her words away. "They're his kids. They'll want to have it in a familiar place."

Ana's eyes became stormy. "That'd be like Danny Torrance holding his dad's wake at the Overlook. It's creepy, Dale."

Dale smiled weakly and patted her hand. "Don't dig too deep into it, Bangs. I'll just avoid the backyard."

She nodded, then felt a question crawl up her throat so quickly she didn't have time to stop herself from asking it.

"Is he gonna close the store?"

"Who, Charlie?"

"Yeah," she said, then added, "Sorry, I know it's not the best time to ask."

Dale's weary eyes moved across the store.

They only had one customer at the moment, and she was up on the balcony, test-driving a bargain-bin audiobook at one of the listening stations. If she decided to pull the trigger and buy it, the store would be two dollars and ninety-nine cents richer.

He sighed heavily.

"Maybe he should."

TEN

I'm sorry. Can you say that again?"

Charlie Remick leaned forward in his chair. It slid a little on the slick concrete. He quickly threw out his right leg to keep the chair (and himself) from going ass over teakettle.

Frank Critzer lurched forward, then, seeing that Charlie was all right, sat back down. "Sorry about that, Charlie. I'll make sure to get an area rug put in."

The law offices of Critzer, Powell, and Gray had recently leased two floors in a newly renovated building on Fifth and Union and were clearly still getting settled. Frank's office, which sat at the end of a long hallway and boasted five floor-to-ceiling windows that looked out onto a resplendent swath of downtown Seattle, was particularly spartan. There were no law books spined neatly on shelves, no file cabinets parked dutifully in the corners, no diplomas spaced along the walls. Just a desk, four chairs, and a lonely (but well-made) replica of a Rothko that hung next to the door.

"Did I hear you right?" Charlie asked.

"You did indeed," Frank Critzer said, then tapped a document on his desk. "The Cuckoo's Nest. He's left it to you."

Charlie turned to his sisters, his expression cold and hard. "Did *you* know about this?"

"Not officially," Ellie said. "Dad may have mentioned something about it in passing, but that was a while ago."

"And you never thought to say anything about it to *me*?"

The attorney, whose salt-and-pepper coiffure and square head gave him the appearance of a game-show host rather than an attorney, smiled a well-rehearsed smile. "Mr. Remick, if I may proceed?"

Charlie cleared his throat and recalibrated his posture. A slight ringing in his ears had surfaced, and as the attorney resumed reading Raymond's will aloud, all Charlie seemed to hear was a series of hollow, muffled squawks from a toothy, grinning mannequin in an expensive suit.

"I don't want it," Charlie said, cutting him off.

Frank looked up. "Pardon me?"

"The store. I don't want it."

Ellie placed a hand on Charlie's arm. "This isn't a decision you have to make now."

"She's right," Susan added. "Take a few days to think it over."

"I don't need a few days," Charlie said. "I don't want it."

"It can often be difficult for people to process this moment," Frank said, threading his fingers together thoughtfully. "Many people feel like they're not worthy of the gifts that have been left to them, but I assure you, your father wanted you to have—"

"This isn't a *gift*," Charlie said. "It's a prank."

The attorney's eyes narrowed. "I'm sorry?"

"The store was his legacy, Charlie," Ellie said. "He wanted you to have it."

Charlie spat laughter. "It's not his legacy, it's a fucking joke." He turned to Frank. "What happens if I refuse?"

"Normally it would pass to an alternate beneficiary, but since Raymond didn't name one, it returns to the estate."

"And then what?"

"Well, from there, we have several ways forward. As executor of Raymond's will, I can name an alternate beneficiary, or, if no other party wants it, I can liquidate the store's inventory and sell the property."

"And what happens to the money you make from that?"

"It goes to the estate, where it would be distributed to the beneficiaries."

"Meaning us."

The attorney nodded. "Yes. You three were the sole beneficiaries in Raymond's will."

Ellie opened her mouth to speak, but Charlie powered forward. "How would the money be distributed?"

"Once the inventory of the store has been liquidated and the property sold, the three of you would each receive a percentage of the earnings based on the value of the store. After fees and taxes had been taken out, of course."

"Swell," Charlie said, fishing a pen out of a cup on Frank's desk. "Let's get started."

Frank placed his hands delicately on his desk. "Mr. Remick, this is a big decision. A decision you may come to regret."

"I won't."

Ellie and Susan exchanged a brief look of disappointment.

"Nevertheless," Frank conceded, "I would urge you not to make any big commitments today. Legally, you have nine months to disclaim your inheritance. I'm not saying you need to wait *that* long, but taking a few nights to sleep on it would be wise. If you still feel this strongly about it by the end of the week, then at least you can move forward knowing you didn't make a rash decision. Surely that must count for something."

It didn't.

What Ellie said next, however, *did*.

"Charlie," she said softly, brushing her hair back from her face and pinning it behind her ears, "you're not the only one affected by this decision. There's Ana to consider. And Dale. He's been working there for over twenty years. If you sell the store, they're both toast."

Charlie had never met Ana, but he'd known Dale since he was a boy. Good old Dale Cernin, the goofy Brit, with his suede vest and lanky arms, always going on about the Ornette Coleman Trio and why *they* were the unsung heroes of modern jazz . . . or Klaatu, an obscure Canadian rock band that, according to him, was as good as the Beatles.

How would *he* handle the closing of the store?

The Cuckoo's Nest had been his home for over two decades, and while Dale was a nice guy (and practically a savant when it came to music trivia), Charlie doubted that he would have luck finding gainful employment anywhere else. There were plenty of other independent record stores in Seattle, but the Cuckoo's Nest was the biggest—not in name, but square footage—and while Jive Time or Sonic Boom would certainly benefit from Dale's expertise, they wouldn't profit much from his customer service acumen.

"Your sister makes an excellent point, Mr. Remick," Frank said. "There are livelihoods at stake here, to say nothing of the cultural impact of such a loss to the Seattle community."

Charlie rolled his eyes. A "cultural loss" was laying it on pretty thick, but Ellie's words *had* made an impact. Not just the words themselves, but the way she'd said them. Maybe it was a twin thing, or maybe Ellie just knew how to pull his strings, but after a nice pregnant pause to show that cooler heads had prevailed, Charlie promised he would take a few days to consider his decision.

Frank smiled. "Very good, Mr. Remick." He motioned back to the documents on his desk. "Now . . . that just leaves the matter of the house." He cleared his throat nervously, hoping he wasn't about to open another wound. "Your father has given the house to Susan and Eleanor. Split evenly. Including all its contents."

A quiet feeling of relief fell upon the room, almost as if the air had thinned out.

Susan took Ellie's hand and offered her sister a brief, melancholy smile. "You okay with that?"

A tear fell neatly down Ellie's cheek. "I'm okay with it if you are."

"I'm glad to hear it," Frank said, relieved. "Raymond was very fond of that house. He would be delighted to know it was staying in the family."

Charlie was delighted, too. He was fond of his childhood home, and while he had no desire to live there or maintain it, he would have been genuinely sad to see it sold, or worse, reduced to being the knot in a game of legal tug-of-war between his sisters.

A fifty-fifty split was clean.

The deal wasn't all daisies, of course. The house was old—*built between the death of the locomotive and the birth of the automobile*, his father used to boast—and required a fair amount of upkeep.

Ellie couldn't be counted on to keep the house tidy. She would be the first to admit it. Susan, however, *could* be counted on. Susan wasn't a sentimentalist like her sister, and would have probably had no problem selling the house, but as long as she legally couldn't do so without Ellie's cooperation (which she would almost certainly never get), she would make sure it didn't fall into disrepair. She was much too proud to let that happen.

Charlie hated the thought of giving his father credit for a good idea, but he had to admit, the fifty-fifty split between Ellie and Susan was a clever plan to ensure that the house both stayed in the family *and* didn't deteriorate.

The look on his sisters' faces told Charlie they had realized the same thing.

"As for the remainder of Raymond's estate," Frank said with a breezy note of finality, "I'm afraid there isn't much left to disperse. He had no bonds, no trusts, and no other assets."

Ellie grinned sheepishly. "Dad wasn't much of a planner."

"What about the car?" Susan asked.

"Ah, yes," Frank said, pointing a finger skyward and referencing his notes. "The Skylark."

Shit, Charlie thought. *I forgot about the car.*

"Since it resides in the garage," Frank said to Susan, "it's technically part of the house, so you and Eleanor each own half of it." He chuckled. "If you can't decide who gets it, suppose you could always take a chainsaw and slice it right down the middle, headlights to taillights."

Susan nodded darkly and avoided Ellie's gaze. This was going to be a prickly subject.

Raymond's car, a 1953 Buick Skylark, had been their father's one and only flashy possession, and it was a beauty.

Back in '86, he'd won the car by calling in to KCMU-FM (now KEXP, one of Seattle's most well-known alternative rock stations) and providing the correct answer to DJ Roddy Rodman's Million-Dollar Question. The questions were always absurdly easy, and certainly never won anyone a million dollars, but on the day Raymond called in and answered the Million-Dollar Question correctly ("David Bowie's real name is David Jones"), his prize had been the station manager's pride and joy: a Matador Red over Majestic White convertible set off by mirror-finish chrome and whitewall tires with deluxe wheel covers.

In the end, Raymond almost didn't take the Skylark, given that the insurance was a lot pricier than what he'd been paying for his Datsun, but after a night of dramatic pleading from his kids (and even a little sexual cajoling from his wife), Raymond went down to the station and signed his name to the title of the car.

In the end, he decided to hold on to the Datsun as his daily driver and took the Skylark out only when the weather was agreeable. This being Seattle, those days were few and far between, but on the days the Skylark was allowed to see daylight, it was an occasion on par with a visit to Disneyland, and, as the years passed and each of the Remick children approached sixteen, they had made a tradition of begging their father to let them take the convertible out for a spin. In turn, Raymond had made a tradition of telling them to dream smaller.

When it came to the Skylark, Raymond Remick was a Dickensian landlord: unbending, humorless, and unforgiving to anyone who crossed him.

No one drove the Skylark but him.

And now, as the three Remick children sat silently in the cold, museum-like office of Frank Critzer, they each secretly dreamed of taking the car for themselves and spiriting it away into the sunset. Even Charlie, who had no legal right to it.

"As for the rest," Frank said, threading his fingers together again, "meaning whatever remains of Raymond's checking and savings accounts, it'll be divided evenly between the three of you. After fees and taxes have been accounted for, of course."

"And how much is that?" Susan asked.

Frank referenced a separate sheet of paper to his right. "Not much, I'm afraid. After all is said and done, it looks like it'll be around three thousand dollars. Give or take a couple hundred."

The three Remicks stared at him, dumbstruck. Even Charlie.

"That's *it*?" Ellie said.

Frank nodded solemnly. "I'm afraid so."

Susan took the wheel. "Please understand, Mr. Critzer, this isn't a reaction of greed. We're just shocked. Dad never let on that things were this bad."

"Until very recently, they weren't," Frank said. "Your father was normally a prudent man."

"I wouldn't go that far," Ellie said, softening a little. "He did once spend a month's mortgage on Little Richard tickets."

"Front row," Charlie pointed out, as if that would justify it.

"He never let us go broke, though," Susan said, then looked at Frank. "What happened?"

Frank's eyes darted between the three Remick children. Had Raymond not mentioned any of this to them? "Your father spent the last few years traveling," he said, then cleared his throat and added, "extensively."

Ellie frowned. "Traveling? Traveling where?"

"Your father and I never really discussed it, and his bank statements only list the airlines where he purchased his tickets, not the destinations."

Susan leaned forward. "What about the purchases he made once he was *at* the destinations? The statements should list those, shouldn't they?"

"Normally they would," Frank conceded, "but your father paid cash whenever he traveled."

Again, Ellie frowned. "Why would he do that?"

"Hard to know, really. There are several reasons someone might choose to pay cash while traveling. Avoiding sales tax, for one. Especially if he'd made some particularly spendy purchases."

Charlie looked knowingly at his sisters. "Records."

"I don't think so," Susan said slowly, working some quick math in her head. "Dad had quite a bit squirreled away. I can't imagine he spent all of it on records."

Charlie had no problem imagining it. But then again, his sisters never really saw the *other* side of their father. His true side. The Hyde to his Jekyll. The man who once left his ten-year-old son stranded and scared and alone in the ER with a broken ankle so he could flit across town and purchase a rare misprint of the Suburbs' 1984 LP *Love Is the Law* from a fellow collector. Charlie could still picture the pitying stares of the nurses as the doctor reset the bones in his ankle and prepared the cast. Two hours later, when Raymond finally returned to the hospital, out of breath and in possession of his prize, he slipped Charlie a crisp twenty-dollar bill and begged him not to say a word about what had happened.

And to this day, he hadn't.

Although he certainly wanted to *now*.

"I'm not your father's accountant," Frank said. "The only reason I have access to his bank statements is because I'm the executor of his estate. I only know what the statements tell me, and it's not much."

Susan pointed to a number that hadn't been highlighted. "What about this? It's in a different column."

"That's not a payment," Frank said. "It's a deposit."

Charlie turned the piece of paper around. Upon reading the number, he almost swallowed his tongue. "*Three hundred thousand dollars?*"

"Who the hell gave him that much money?" Ellie said.

Frank pointed to the letters *CC* in the description line. "You see this code here? That could either be a certified check or a cashier's check. Either way, there's no way to know where the funds came from. Not without jumping through some complicated hoops."

Ellie stared at the statement as if it were in another language. "I don't understand . . ."

"Your father had a sizable collection of rare records," Frank said. "Some of them extremely valuable. Perhaps he found a buyer."

"Dad only sold the rare records when he had a good reason," Ellie said. "Like when I needed braces or when Mom got sick. He paid off a big chunk of her hospital bills with only three shelves' worth."

After I spent weeks begging him to do it, Charlie thought bitterly.

Frank's watch beeped. He pushed his chair back from his desk and prepared to stand. "I'd hate for you to think I was pushing you out, but I've got another appointment in a few minutes." His toothy game-show-host grin had returned. Charlie supposed it was more for his next appointment's benefit than theirs. "If you have any questions, you know how to reach me. And Charlie, whichever side you land on your inheritance, I'll be here to help you every step of the way, okay?"

Charlie nodded and followed Frank and his sisters to the door, where Frank placed his hand on the knob, ready to turn it, but didn't. He snapped his fingers, suddenly remembering something, then went to his desk. "Right. I almost forgot."

He returned holding a large, dark object, and handed it to Charlie. "It's a lot lighter than it looks, trust me."

It was a black case, made of hard, vacuum-formed plastic. The kind of case musicians used to store gear during transport. Charlie gave it a little bounce in his hands. Frank was right. It wasn't heavy at all. In fact, it felt empty. He looked up, confused. "What's in it?"

"No idea," Frank said.

"Is it locked?"

"Don't think so. There's a note taped to the top, though. Your dad wanted me to make sure you read it."

Charlie set the case down and removed the slip of paper. On it was a short message, written in his father's distinct scrawl.

Ellie stood on her toes. "What's it say?"

Charlie grimaced as he read the message a second time, then handed the note to Ellie. She held it between her and Susan so they could both read it. Written in Raymond's small, nearly illegible handwriting were the words:

I told you they were real.

Charlie opened the case. The bottom half was lined with charcoal-colored foamcore, normally used to protect mixing equipment or microphones from being jostled around and damaged. There was no gear in this case, however. Instead, Charlie was presented with four old records—*very* old, by the look of them; 78 rpm, scratched heavily, and without labels. They were housed snugly into four parallel slits that had been cut into the foamcore.

On the underside of the lid was a strip of cream-colored masking tape that bore two words in black marker. As Charlie read them, his lips grew thin.

Ellie craned her neck forward. "What's in it?"

With a knowing glare, Charlie spun the case around and watched his sisters read the two words written on the masking tape.

SCHRADER'S CHORD

ELEVEN

Ana Cortez closed the register with a grateful sigh. The rest of the day hadn't been nearly as bad as it had started (unloading two crates of recently tagged records to a few of the regulars had certainly made up for the slow morning), but she was tired.

In fact, she could hardly remember feeling so tired.

She flipped the sign on the front door so it read SORRY, WE'RE CLOSED and turned to face the darkened store. Her eyes swept the dim linoleum—POP/ROCK to her left, CLASSICAL/JAZZ to her right—and she drew in a quiet, shuddering breath.

Her heart ached. Stomach, too. A hollow sense of loss squeezed at her insides and she felt the sudden—and alarming—sensation one feels when the ground beneath them begins to shift. Ground that, only a few days before, had seemed so steady and so solid.

A foundation on which to build a future.

She wanted to cry but forced herself not to. It had been bad enough losing Raymond, but the thought of losing the store as well was almost too much to take.

And that's what would happen. She was sure of it. Whether or not Charlie Remick chose to close the store or not didn't matter. She would still lose it.

The Cuckoo's Nest had been her home for almost six years. And now some shit-eating A&R prick she'd never met was going to take it away from her. Not because he loved the store. Not because he'd poured his blood, sweat, and tears into making this place what it now was. Simply because—*only* because—he was Raymond's son.

She glared through the glass doors at the lower half of Asterion Avenue. It was past eleven, but there were still a few stragglers breezing up and down the sidewalk—mostly people taking their dogs on a late-night stroll to the nearby park. No shoppers, though. The little boutique across the street had closed hours ago. Her eyes moved to the boutique's window, where a mannequin was sporting a sleek-looking leather jacket. Supple leather, and soft. No doubt lambskin. A classic silhouette, with wide lapels, and a pair of epaulettes that provided the shoulders with geometric stability and a hint of military style. She sighed wistfully. She was just about the mannequin's size, and if the shearling collar was detachable, she'd be able to wear the jacket well into spring and maybe even early summer. It had been ages since she'd purchased something for herself that wasn't records, and a nice jacket might be just the thing to break that cycle.

Her mother's voice floated into her ears.

Oh, Ana Cristina, yes. Now this *is a smart use of your money. You can wear a jacket like that forever and it'll never go out of style.*

Like most baby boomers, Gloria Cortez considered vinyl a nostalgic, but useless, remnant of the past. As far as she was concerned, pouring money into a vinyl record collection was about as idiotic as investing in a typewriter.

Which was exactly why Ana chose to stow her Adler J4 in the closet when her mother came to visit.

In this case, however, her mother's spectral voice was right. The leather jacket *would* be a smart purchase, and Ana was in dire need of good outerwear.

She made a mental note to pop over there in the morning, possibly on her lunch break, but suddenly felt her shoulders sink when she remembered what tomorrow was.

Raymond's wake.

She and Dale had already made the decision to close the store for the day. The wake was sure to be an emotionally draining affair, and both of them agreed it would be too depressing to come back to the store and hook a smile over their ears while a group of acne-ridden teenagers asked them which Joy Division album was better.

Both of them, she thought paradoxically. *Both of them are better.*

Dale ambled into the room, his arms full of Christmas lights. When he reached the checkout counter, he let the bundle of lights fall to the floor. "I know it's wasteful, but I'm thinking I might just chuck these in the bin and buy some new ones." He picked up a badly tangled strand of lights and scowled. "Look at this fucking thing. It's like a yuletide Rubik's Cube for idiots."

Ana smiled, although the expression was merely a formality. Seeing the lights only added to her hollow feeling of loss. Preparing the store for Christmas had always been one of her favorite times of the year. Raymond would heat up a jug of apple cider and throw on a Vince Guaraldi record, and the three of them would work through the night, stringing up lights, hanging wreaths, and dressing the battered cardboard standup of Elvis Costello in a Santa suit.

She appreciated Dale's initiative, but holiday decorations seemed like a luxury afforded to stores whose futures were set, and Ana felt like she could no longer see the future.

"Do you need any help?" she asked, hoping he would refuse. When he did, Ana made her way back to the counter and counted the day's receipts. By the time she finished, Dale had already traced the NEW RELEASES display with a string of lights and plugged them in. They glowed warmly in the dimly lit store, casting a web of hazy golden sprites along the linoleum.

"Well?" Dale said, standing proudly next to his work. "What do you think?"

Ana shrugged, turned the stack of receipts over, and began plugging the numbers into a nearby calculator. She hit the buttons with such force, the calculator hopped along the countertop, as if trying to escape the needless abuse it was being subjected to.

"Easy, Bangs," Dale said. "It's a friendly machine, not Skynet."

"I just want to make sure our books are correct," Ana said tersely, plunging her finger into the Equals button. "I don't want to give Mr. Madison Avenue any reason to think we're not responsible employees."

Dale studied Ana over the lenses of his circular glasses. "He's not the villain you're making him out to be, you know."

Ana ceased torturing the calculator and crossed her arms.

"He's a good guy," Dale said gently. "And more like Raymond

than he knows." He paused, pondering this, then added, "Or willing to admit."

"Then how come he never *once* visited Raymond after Joan died? Ellie's been here dozens of times. Even *Susan* stopped by once."

"They had a complicated relationship."

"That's bullshit."

"It's not."

"I find it hard to believe that anyone could have had a complicated relationship with Raymond. The guy was a teddy bear."

Dale exhaled slowly, a long and thoughtful breath. "No, he wasn't."

Ana felt her next words choke themselves into silence. In all her time at the Cuckoo's Nest, she'd never heard Dale speak so much as a syllable against Raymond's character.

"Don't get me wrong," Dale continued, "I admired Raymond. I loved him, really. He was a good employer and a better friend, but the man had his demons like anyone else. He was good at hiding them, of course, but when you know a man for twenty years, you get to experience every flavor of his personality. And Raymond definitely had a sour side to him, especially when he was younger and the kids were growing up."

Ana shifted uneasily on her heels. She felt like she was standing in the center of a beautiful room and the wallpaper was starting to peel.

"He treated the girls like gold," Dale said. "Joanie, too. But Charlie was a different story. He was *rough* on that boy."

Seeing Ana's pained expression, Dale quickly tempered her thoughts.

"He never got physical with Charlie, I want to make that clear. Raymond was not a violent man. But he could be cruel when he wanted to be. And dismissive. And fiercely competitive."

Ana narrowed her eyes. "Competitive? Raymond?"

"Did you ever hear those audio tapes of Murry Wilson?" Dale asked.

"You're saying Raymond was as bad as Brian Wilson's dad?"

"No, he never smacked Charlie across the ear and made him deaf or anything. Joan would have kicked his ass to the curb if he'd done that. But Raymond saw something in Charlie early on, something Raymond never really had himself. Although, he never would have admitted that out loud."

"Which was?"

"When Charlie was a toddler, still walking around in nappies, he would stand at the piano, hum a note, then play it. Then he'd hum a different note in a different octave and play *that*. He'd do this for hours, note after note after note. And he was dead on. Every time."

Ana was impressed. "He had perfect pitch?"

"Little bugger couldn't even talk yet but he could sing a perfect B-flat or G-sharp without even thinking. He did the piano thing for a while, but then he got bored with that and he took to waddling around the house humming tunes to himself. At first, he'd just mimic whatever was playing on the stereo. Some days it was Brahms, other days it was the Beatles, but eventually, Charlie started humming tunes no one recognized. He'd hum them over and over, adding a little more each time, until, after a day or two, he'd composed an entire song. And when I tell you they were good . . ." Dale's eyes bored into Ana's. ". . . they were *good*. Kid had an amazing ear for melody. And that's when a lightbulb switched on over Raymond's head.

"On Charlie's fifth birthday, Raymond shoved a guitar in his hands, and Charlie, being a kid, thought the guitar was nothing more than a cool gift. He was too young at that point to see the hunger behind Raymond's eyes, and by the time he was old enough to wise up to his dad's motives, Charlie was too far down the path to change course. By the time he was sixteen, he'd recorded hundreds—literally hundreds—of songs on a little tape recorder."

"Jesus," Ana said. "You make him sound like Daniel Johnston."

"Raymond sent the tapes into a bunch of labels without Charlie's permission," Dale continued. "And every one of them called back, chomping at the bit. EMI, apparently, chomped the hardest."

"He got signed?"

"Three-record deal," Dale said, then snapped his fingers. "Just like that."

"How is it possible Raymond never mentioned this?"

Dale's face darkened. "When Charlie found out about the deal, he was furious. Those tapes were never meant to be heard by anybody except him. He felt betrayed. He stopped eating, he stopped going to school. He was so embarrassed he didn't leave his room for days.

"Joan was furious, as you can imagine. I thought she was gonna divorce Raymond right then and there, and I wouldn't have blamed her for it. But Raymond must have worked his magic on Charlie, because a few weeks later, he signed with EMI."

"What finally convinced him?" Ana asked.

"At the end of the day, all Charlie cared about was making music. I think he figured if he got paid to do it, he'd never have to stop."

"Sound logic right there."

"They booked him two weeks of studio time and set him up with a band, and things were going all right for a while. They'd tracked a few songs, and Charlie was a natural in the studio, but it all fell apart when Raymond started meddling."

A dull ache bloomed behind Ana's eyes as Dale pressed on.

"It was little things, at first. Charlie would give a note to the drummer or the bass player and Raymond would contradict him from the mixing booth. Fight him, really. Whenever Charlie would push back, Raymond got up on his hind legs. 'I'm a songwriter too, Charlie. . . . You wouldn't even be in here if it weren't for me.' That kind of stuff.

"Eventually it got so bad, they almost came to blows, and Charlie kicked him out of the studio. Raymond was furious, and that night, he broke into the control room and started changing all the mixes."

Ana couldn't believe what she was hearing. How could this be the same Raymond she'd come to know and love? The same Raymond who'd been like a father to her? Raymond Remick wasn't a jealous stage dad with delusions of grandeur. He was the most trusting, lenient, funny, charismatic, and caring person she'd ever known.

And secretive, a voice said from somewhere deep in her mind. *Don't forget secretive.*

Raymond's mysterious collection of boarding passes floated past her thoughts, all of them bearing the name of a faraway destination.

. . . *Paris, London, Tokyo, Marrakesh, Lisbon, Cairo, Romania, Montreal . . .*

What the hell had he been doing in all those places? And why hadn't he trusted her enough to tell her?

"So what happened next?"

Dale sighed. "It didn't end well, of course. When Charlie found out what Raymond had done, he destroyed all the masters and backed out of his record deal."

"He backed out?"

"And hasn't written a song since," Dale said. "At least, not publicly." He picked up another strand of lights and began untangling them. "When Joan found out what Raymond did, she kicked him out of the house and filed for divorce. He didn't fight her on it, and almost ended up signing the divorce papers, but before he could, Joan stopped him. It was clear by that point that he'd had a come-to-Jesus moment. He was a totally different guy when Joan let him back in the house, as if he'd snapped out of a fugue state or something, but his relationship with Charlie never fully recovered. The damage was done. Charlie sold his guitar and threw all his recordings in the trash."

Ana groaned.

"They got along all right after a while, though, or pretended to," Dale said. "Charlie made an effort to be civil. Mostly as a way of placating his mom, I'd guess. She even convinced him to work here at the store for a bit."

"She did?"

"I think she hoped it would mend the wound, but in the end, it only made them drift further apart."

"Well, sure," Ana said, motioning to the nearest bin of CDs. "Every square inch of this place is a reminder of what went down between them."

"Bingo," Dale said, and tossed the tangled string of lights on the counter, surrendering to its unbreakable knots. "The fact of the matter is, Bangs, the store is Charlie's now. Not yours. Not mine. *His.* And this place doesn't mean to him what it means to us."

"So you're saying he'll close it down."

"He *may* close it down. And if he did, I wouldn't hold it against him."

"But the store looks completely different now. Look around. It's barely recognizable from the way it used to be."

Dale leaned an elbow on the counter and surveyed the dimly lit store. It had taken nearly four years of backbreaking work, but it really did look magnificent. And it was all her. Every inch of it had been renovated, replastered, repainted, relit, and redesigned at her own hand.

And she was proud of that.

Mostly because she had no trouble remembering what the store looked like before. Nor, as it happened, did the man sitting in the rental car parked across the street.

The smoke of Charlie Remick's cigarette curled up into the air next to him. He strained his eyes and tried to get a good look through the store's windows, but it was too dark. All he could make out was the blurry glow of Christmas lights and the familiar suede vest of Dale Cernin.

His eyes drifted up to the sign above the entrance. The cracked painting of the dazed-looking bird wearing headphones had been touched up. Maybe even repainted from scratch.

It looked good.

He heard a faint sound—*tsss*—and raised his left hand. The tip of his cigarette was soggy and black. Something had put it out. He leaned out the driver's-side window and gazed up at the sky.

It had started to snow.

Charlie looked again at the store and felt his vision blur upon seeing the glow of the Christmas lights. A sudden warmth flooded his chest, and he closed his eyes to keep it from fading. He sniffed lightly, then wrinkled his nose at the arrival of a familiar scent.

Apple cider.

He knew it wasn't real, just a memory manifesting itself, but he didn't care.

He kept his eyes closed and basked in the sweet sting of the phantom scent, letting his head drift slowly from side to side. Without thinking, a Vince Guaraldi tune hummed itself from deep within his throat.

Every note was perfect.

TWELVE

The Woodbury Funeral Home was lit like a soap opera—soft and gauzy—and had the distinct, sickly odor of freshly cut flowers and Pledge, the latter of which had been used liberally on the wood furniture in the sitting room. The end table next to Charlie had been so saturated with polish, he could see his reflection.

The seafoam-green carpet (and matching wallpaper) did little to quell the nausea-inducing smell. Nor, for that matter, did the temperature. The air was thick and heavy and stale, and Charlie was quickly regretting his decision to wear a sweater and corduroy pants.

The whole place had such a cartoonish, grandmotherly atmosphere, he half expected to see an old woman dragging Sylvester the cat through the waiting room by the nape of his neck as Tweety Bird laughed and jeered and bobbed up and down through the air.

He passed the time by nibbling on a piece of hard candy he'd taken from the bowl on the Pledge-sopped table. He stared absently out the window into the parking lot and felt his hand drift toward his pocket, where the note Raymond left him was folded neatly inside.

I told you they were real.

His gaze drifted to Susan's SUV, where he'd left the black case sitting on the back seat. Part of him wished he'd just left it with the lawyer, but that would have meant refusing a *second* bequest from his father, and he didn't have the energy to do that, especially since he would have felt an obligation to provide an explanation why.

Which would mean explaining what Schrader's Chord was in the first place.

He imagined how Frank Critzer would have responded to *that*.

Probably with an amused chuckle, a shake of the head, and then something like: *"I'll bet your dad was real fun around the campfire."*

And he wouldn't have been wrong. Raymond Remick had many faults, but he'd always been an excellent storyteller, especially when those stories were scary.

As children, Charlie and his sisters spent many a night sitting in a semicircle on the living room floor, fascinated, as their father weaved yarns about the Wendigo, the Bermuda Triangle, and the Loch Ness Monster. As they got older, Raymond's tales intensified accordingly. They learned all about Bloody Mary, the escaped lunatic with a hook for a hand, and the call that came from inside the house, but Raymond's favorite story, the story he told so many times his children (and his wife) knew every word by heart, was the story of Ivan Schrader, the insane composer who opened a gateway to the land of the dead.

And now Charlie had a bona fide artifact of that very story, sitting in the back of his sister's SUV. A case that held four records. Records that, when played simultaneously, were supposed to play a chord that opened Schrader's grisly gateway.

He felt a sudden urge to run out to the parking lot and chuck the damn thing into the woods. Not because he thought the story was true, or that the records were real . . .

I told you they were real

. . . but because he didn't want to give his late father the satisfaction of even entertaining the idea that the story was true.

Because that's all it was. A story . . . passed down through generations by crusty old music geeks whose thirst for rare collectibles had gone beyond the boundaries of reason and into the realm of delusion.

Horseshit, Charlie thought. *Every word of it.* He crossed his arms tightly and turned back to the funeral parlor.

At the far end of the room, Susan's children sat at a small table, busily ignoring their surroundings. Maisy, blue crayon clutched tightly in hand, concentrated hard on a coloring book. It was clear from her furrowed brow and her protruding tongue—pinched tightly between her lips—that she was having trouble staying inside the lines. Miles, on the other hand, was slumped low in his seat, like a towel that had been draped unceremoniously over a chair, and watched a video on his phone through heavily lidded eyes.

Ellie sat in a nearby chair, perusing a pamphlet that said, in big block letters, THE END IS JUST A NEW BEGINNING IN DISGUISE.

Over at the front desk, Susan spoke quietly to Gordon Woodbury, the owner of the establishment. Gordon, who was forty-five going on seventy, wore an impeccably pressed suit and an expertly applied smile that was both sympathetic and somber, but not cloying.

Ellie, having exhausted the information in her pamphlet, set it down and joined Charlie on the couch. Her expression was pained.

"It's a joke, right?" she whispered. "The Schrader records?"

Charlie smiled. Twin-telepathy strikes again. "If it's a joke, it's a weird one. You always liked that story more than I did. Why would he leave the records to me?"

"Maybe it's not a joke, then."

Charlie made a face. "You're saying the records are *real*?"

"Of course not," she said. "But maybe this was his way of bury-ing the hatchet. Of reminding you of a better time . . . when you weren't so pissed at him."

"If that was his goal, he didn't succeed."

At the front desk, Susan and Gordon Woodbury solemnized their transaction with a gentle handshake. Woodbury disappeared through an ornate door and Susan crossed the room and joined her siblings.

"Okay," she said, clapping her hands together, "apparently they get pretty backed up during the holidays. They weren't gonna be able to cremate Dad for another two days, but I got them to move him to the top of the list. He'll be ready in about an hour."

"How'd you manage that?" Charlie asked.

"I paid double the normal fee."

Ellie's eyebrows shot up. "That must've set you back a couple bucks."

"I was happy to do it," Susan said, waving her hand dismissively.

"Is that really fair, though?" Charlie said. "To the other families on the list, I mean?"

"The owner assured me it wouldn't affect their schedule too badly. And this way, we don't have to postpone the wake and we can all get back to our lives."

Ellie laughed humorlessly. "Because God forbid you have to stay in Seattle two more days, right?"

"Excuse me?" Susan replied, narrowing her eyes to thin slits. For a brief moment, Charlie saw a flash of the old Susan. He'd forgotten how intimidating she was.

"We've *all* had to put our lives on hold, you know," Ellie said. "Not just you."

"I don't think Susan meant it that way," Charlie said.

"Don't defend her," Ellie said. "She's always like this."

Susan crossed her arms and stared daggers at her little sister. "What the hell's wrong with you?"

Ellie shot to her feet. "You've barely been here for two days and you already want to leave. That's what's wrong with me."

In the corner of the room, Maisy and Miles ceased their respective activities and were now watching the tense exchange with a mixture of fascination and unease.

"It's been a long time since the three of us have been in the same place," Ellie continued, "and now that Mom and Dad are *both* gone, we're all that's left. I wanted us to . . . I don't know . . . play games and watch movies and spend some real time together. *After* the cremation. *After* the wake." She threw her hands up. "But I guess two days was enough for you. Sorry this has been such an inconvenience."

"Ellie," Susan said softly. "I don't want to leave; I *have* to. The kids are missing school and I've got clients who are waiting on me. Important clients."

Charlie winced. That last part was a grenade and Susan just unknowingly pulled the pin.

"Oh, *excuse me*," Ellie said, dramatically clutching a set of invisible pearls. "I didn't realize you had *important* clients waiting. What *will* the Kensingtons do without their interior decorator for a few days? Panic and put a flowerpot in the fireplace?"

"Ellie . . ."

"Install linoleum instead of hardwood?"

"Ellie."

"Oh *God* . . ." Ellie said, raking her teeth with worried fingers. ". . . go to *Ikea*?"

"Knock it *off*," Susan snapped. "You're being a child."

"I'd rather be a child than someone who just throws a bunch of money at every problem that crosses their path."

"Being self-reliant isn't a bad thing, Eleanor. You should try it sometime."

"Paying off the mortician to move Dad up to the front of the line isn't self-reliant, Susan. It's spoiled. Charlie was right. There are other families, other *grieving* families involved here. And you just cut in front of them like a fucking soccer mom who's too impatient to wait for her kombucha. What you did was sick. It was worse than sick, it was ghoulish."

Charlie stood up and peaceably raised the palms of his hands. "Hey, guys. Why don't we take a quick breather? Let's just—"

"You're calling *me* spoiled?" Susan spat. "Everything I have, I've worked for. Can you say the same?"

Ellie's jaw tensed. "I work."

"You have *hobbies*," Susan shot back. "Monday it's candle-making, Tuesday it's an Etsy store for your pottery. The next week it's that stupid CBD locator app which, after four months and a couple thousand dollars dumped into R&D, turned out to do exactly what Google Maps does already . . . except a million times worse. And who *paid* for that app? Who has bankrolled every single one of your harebrained fucking ideas? Mom and Dad. Every time."

"Mom and Dad helped you too," Ellie said weakly.

"Oh, *did* they? When I was fifteen, I needed a sewing machine to fix my cheerleader's uniform. I asked Mom and Dad if we could get one and you know what they told me? Get a job. When my first car—that *I* paid for—blew its alternator, I called them from a pay phone in Aberdeen and asked them to pick me up. Know what they said? Take a cab. When Miles was in first grade and Jeff and I didn't have two nickels to rub together, I called Mom and Dad and asked if they'd loan me some money to pay for his glasses. Know what they said? Tell him to sit at the front of the class."

Charlie glanced at Miles, who, by the look on his face, had never heard this particular story.

"He was *six years old*," Susan said. "Their fucking *grandson*, and they still couldn't resist teaching me the lesson of *self-reliance*. But you? You could have told them you were making quilts out of ass hair and they'd back up a Brink's truck. Anything for their precious baby girl. They gave *everything* to you and I never saw one red cent. So you wanna call *me* spoiled? Go fuck yourself, Ellie."

Silence descended upon the room like a lead blanket. Susan's chest heaved soundlessly. Miles and Maisy stared at their mother, dumbstruck. They'd never seen her so mad. Not even when she was going through her divorce with their dad, and Susan *hated* their dad.

Charlie, who'd been standing far back enough to avoid the blast zone, shifted his gaze back and forth between his sisters, who were now facing each other like gunfighters. He opened his mouth to say something, but no words came. Was this a regular point of contention between them or was this merely an argument that had finally exploded after being bottled up for years? He didn't know. And it was the not knowing that made him feel guilty. If he had just spent more time with them—more time with them *together*, rather—maybe he could have helped. At the very least, he wouldn't have felt so out of the loop.

On the bright side—if such things *could* have a bright side—he suddenly felt closer to Susan than he ever had. He was sad to hear that their mother had been so withholding, but at least he wasn't the only Remick sibling that had a bone to pick with their father anymore.

The silence was finally broken when Ellie pulled out her phone and opened the Venmo app. "How much?"

Susan blinked. "Excuse me?"

"How much did you pay to have Dad bumped up to first class? I'll split it with you."

"Put your phone away, Ellie. It's done. It was my treat."

Ellie scoffed. "You're not buying us a round of drinks, Susan. You're paying to burn Dad's body. How much?"

Susan hesitated, looked to the side, then said quietly, "Four thousand."

Ellie's mouth fell open. "*Dollars?*"

"I told you, I need to get back home."

"That's insane," Charlie said, finally cutting in. "For Christ's sake, Susan, *we* could have burned him if you were in that much of a rush."

Defeated, Ellie slipped her phone back into her pocket.

"You win."

She shuffled over to the couch and let her full weight fall into the cushions. With a heavy sigh, she turned her head and stared out the window, ashen-faced and drained of energy.

Susan took a half step toward the couch, as if to say something, but hesitated and instead crossed the room and took a seat next to her children. She leaned over the table and feigned interest in the coloring book Maisy had been working on.

Charlie felt for his cigarettes and made tracks for the front door. As he passed the front desk, Gordon Woodbury emerged through the ornate door he'd disappeared through five minutes before. He shot Charlie his well-rehearsed sympathetic smile. "Your father's remains will be ready in about an hour."

Charlie thanked him, told him they'd just wait there, then went outside and had a cigarette.

An hour and a half later, Charlie made his way through the

parking lot, urn in hand. It was heavy; heavier than he expected it
to be, and housed in the finest receptacle Woodbury Funeral Home
offered. Free of charge, Mr. Woodbury was happy to point out.

For four thousand dollars, I should fucking hope so, Charlie thought.

Ellie sped past him, eyes low, and climbed into the back seat
of Susan's car. Figuring he was riding shotgun, Charlie removed
the case from the back seat and brought it round front. For a brief
moment, he thought he felt a pair of eyes watching him, but a quick
glance around the parking lot alleviated his suspicion.

Susan's car was the only one there.

Shaking off his discomfort, he climbed into the front seat and
peered behind him. Miles and Maisy sat quietly in the back next to
Ellie, both of them engrossed in their phones.

Without a word, Susan fired up the Explorer and pulled out of
the parking lot. Two blocks later, Charlie was forced to roll down
his window. They all reeked so badly of potpourri and Pledge, the
car smelled like a miniature funeral home on wheels. He only hoped
they'd have enough time before the wake to change.

As Susan made her way across town, she made a conscious effort
to avoid looking at the back seat. Seeing Ellie's tear-streaked cheeks
would only make her feel worse than she already felt, so she tilted
the rearview mirror up and refused to look behind her.

If she had, she would have noticed the beige Camry that had
been tailing them since they left the funeral home.

THIRTEEN

Your father was a hell of a guy, Charlie. Hell of a guy."

Charlie stared into the face of a man he didn't recognize and nodded politely. "Yes he was."

"Did he ever tell you about the time he got a flat tire on I-90 and got a tow into town by the Allman Brothers' tour bus?"

Charlie's face hurt. He'd been grinning stupidly for nearly an hour, and had endured so many hearty claps to the back from gruff old music junkies, he was sure a large bruise was already blooming between his shoulder blades. "He did tell me that story, yes."

"Betcha thought he was pullin' your leg, huh?"

"Well, you knew Dad . . ."

"Turns out he was only pullin' *half* your leg," the big man said, then slung a beefy arm around Charlie's neck and leaned in close. "He actually got a tow from Dan Fogelberg's bus!" He leaned back and shotgunned a laugh from his throat that was so loud, it rattled the china in the cabinet next to him. "He was just too embarrassed to tell anyone! Can you believe that?"

Charlie, who'd known the true side of this story since he was a boy, ballooned his eyes and said, "You're kidding!" then excused himself to refill his glass, which was still full.

He weaved his way through a smattering of low-talking mourners and searched for his sisters. The wake was supposed to end at 5 P.M., but here it was, only two, and he was already eager to pull the plug. Because it was a wake and not a party, he supposed it wouldn't have been socially acceptable to ask everyone to leave early.

Well, maybe not acceptable, he thought, *but certainly forgivable.*

He entered the living room and saw Ellie nestled between the beverage table she had set up near the foot of the staircase and the cast-iron fireplace tool set Susan had asked her move earlier that day in order to provide more sitting room near the hearth. She swayed lightly on her feet as she ran a finger absentmindedly across the tip of the fireplace poker, observing with a mixture of pride and sadness the people who had turned up to pay tribute to their father. Her mood had improved a bit since the funeral home— improved but not brightened, he amended, considering their current surroundings—and Charlie was hoping she'd join him out back while he snuck a cigarette. He knew for a fact that she'd rolled three fresh joints that morning, and judging by the unblemished ivory sheen of her eyes, she hadn't had the chance to light one up yet.

He'd made it halfway to the staircase when the doorbell rang.

"It's open," he said, ducking his head into the foyer. "You can just come right in."

The door swung open slowly and Dale Cernin stepped inside.

"Charlie, hi."

Chah-lee.

It had been a long time since Charlie had heard his name pronounced in that lazy Yorkshire accent. He jogged into the foyer and extended his hand. Dale shook it.

"We're a bit late," Dale said apologetically. "Finding a parking space was a bit of an issue."

"We?"

"Yeah, Ana and I."

Aner-and-eye.

Charlie tilted his head to the side and watched Ana Cortez step through the door. Her hands were stuffed firmly into the pockets of her sweater, and her eyes searched the entryway for a moment before finally landing on him.

She was pretty. Very pretty.

He felt guilty for thinking so, especially since it was the first thought that came to him, but such thoughts were beyond anyone's control. Even at a wake.

She and Dale made a funny-looking pair, standing in the foyer. Like some old Chuck Jones cartoon about a lanky, graying stork and a sleek, witchy raven.

Charlie offered Ana his hand and introduced himself.

"Ana Cortez," she said, slowly shaking his hand. She was struck by how much he resembled Raymond. Only, Charlie was taller. Much taller, with thicker eyebrows and a stronger jaw. "Your dad hired me," she said warily, wondering if mentioning Raymond would prompt a spike in his emotional EKG. It didn't appear to. "Six years ago."

"Yikes," Charlie replied, laughing nervously. "Six years. That's a lot of time to form an opinion of me. I hope Dad didn't paint too bad a picture."

"Of course he didn't," Dale cut in, patting Charlie on the shoulder.

It was a lie, of course. But a generous one, and Charlie was grateful for it.

Ana felt extremely uncomfortable standing there, face-to-face with Charlie. There was uneven weight between them. She could practically feel it bearing down on her. There was so much about him she already knew, and all he knew about her was her name. As he reminisced with Dale, she stared at his face and reran the conversation she'd had with Dale the night before. All at once, she saw Charlie the toddler, standing at the piano in his diapers and humming pitch-perfect notes; Charlie the boy, alone in his room, playing songs into his tape recorder; Charlie the teenager, darting around the recording studio while his father stood in the mixing booth, plotting his late-night sabotage of the masters; and Charlie the man, back home to sweep up the broken pieces of his past.

And possibly close the store, she reminded herself. *Don't forget that.*

"Nice to meet you, Ana," Charlie said after finishing up his brief niceties with Dale. "Why don't you guys make yourselves comfortable? There are drinks over by the—"

A white-hot bubble of panic rose up Ana's throat, and before she could stop herself, the bubble burst.

"Are you gonna close it down?"

"—stair . . . case . . ." Charlie said, his words unspooling like loose thread. He cocked his head to the side. "I'm sorry?"

Dale, clearly embarrassed, nudged Ana with his elbow. "I don't think this is the best time to talk about this."

"I'm sorry," Ana said, clearly ashamed that she'd been so tactless. But now that she'd jumped into the deep end, she figured she'd might as well swim. "It's just . . . I need to know if I'm still gonna have a job in a few days, that's all. Dale, too."

"Nothing's . . . been decided yet," Charlie said clumsily. He was so thrown off by her bluntness, he struggled to form clear sentences. "But, there's, uh . . . some . . . well, there's some stuff with Dad's lawyer that I . . . that we need to look over."

"Of *course* there is," Dale said, eyes burning into Ana. "And I'm sure whatever he decides will be the best course."

Charlie smiled awkwardly. "But nothing will happen immediately. I promise."

"Good," Ana said, brightening a little. "That means there's still time for me to change your mind. Is Ellie here?"

"I . . . Yeah . . ." Charlie motioned blindly to the doorway behind him, still a bit flummoxed. "She's in the . . . she's over there I think . . ."

Ana shot him a quick grin and disappeared into the living room. The scent of her perfume hung in the air for a second or two, and Charlie paused to drink it in. Sycomore by Chanel. She didn't seem the type.

"Sorry about that, mate," Dale said. "She's just worried. We both are."

"I'm sorry you got dragged in the middle of this mess," Charlie replied heavily.

"Oh, don't worry about me. I've got enough stashed away to keep me warm until something new comes along. Ana's the one you got to keep your eye on. She'll go ten rounds without breaking a sweat if it means keeping the store's lights on. She wasn't kidding about trying to change your mind, you know."

Charlie watched Ana make her way to the beverage table, where she pulled Ellie into a tight hug. "Think she has a chance of succeeding?"

"I'd bet money on it," Dale said. "I tried for years to get your Dad to renovate that dump, and my sole victory was finally convincing him to buy a plunger for the loo. And even then, I think he bought it secondhand."

Charlie smiled.

"But Ana? She wasn't there two months before her and Raymond were drawing up plans for renovations."

"I passed by the store last night just after closing," Charlie said. "I saw the new paint job on the sign. It looked good."

"Wait till you see the inside. Ana poured everything she had into it. Your dad was so excited when it was all finished, he held a grand reopening. It was even in the paper. Big picture of him and Ana in front of the jazz section, grinning like a couple of Mormon missionaries."

Charlie watched as Ana and Ellie spoke in hushed tones, dotted by the occasional laugh. "She and Dad were pretty close, huh?"

Dale nodded. "Thick as thieves."

Charlie bit his lip, considering this, then said, "I'm not sure if that casts Dad in a good light or her in a bad one."

"Your dad wasn't the same man after you left, Charlie. He was softer. Kinder, too. It was like all his hard edges got sanded away." He looked over at Ana again. "I think she was his chance for a do-over."

As Ana joked quietly with his sister across the room, Charlie felt a sudden coldness grip his chest.

"Lucky her."

FOURTEEN

By the time four o'clock rolled around, the wake was still in full swing. It was less crowded now, but those who chose to stay had thrown decorum to the wind and were now lounging on the furniture like lazy cats. Titters of laughter erupted all around the living room as people recited well-worn stories about the late Raymond Remick.

The alcohol was flowing more freely now, and Susan decided to put Maisy down for a nap. Miles was already upstairs, fiddling around with his new Nintendo system.

Charlie wandered noncommittally from group to group for a while, eventually parking himself on a chair by the window to talk jazz with Harold Meehan.

After a solid hour of jazz talk (which was mostly focused on the big band era of the thirties), Harold's husband, who reminded Charlie vaguely of Rob Lowe's character from *Wayne's World*, came over and asked Harold to excuse himself. There was someone he wanted Harold to meet. Harold made his apologies and went with George, leaving Charlie alone to look around the room. There were a few familiar faces—lifelong customers he'd known since he was a boy and a smattering of family friends he hadn't seen in ages—and a few unfamiliar ones.

Ana, who had been tied at the hip with Ellie since she'd arrived, was now on her own, studying a row of framed photographs on a nearby bookshelf.

Charlie had been looking for an opportunity to strike up a conversation with her since their first exchange, but had struggled to drum up the courage. The truth was, she intimidated him. Not just because she was pretty (and carried with her the distinct smell of Sycomore by Chanel, which had always rendered Charlie powerless in its presence), but because she appeared to have an intimate relationship with the Remick family that, until now, he'd been unaware of. It felt as if he'd left a band to pursue a solo career, and instead of breaking up, the band hired someone else to replace him . . . and somehow, six years had passed without him knowing about it.

She stood alone by the bookshelf (Ellie had gone out back to finally smoke one of her joints), and Charlie figured now was as good a time as any. He brushed the wrinkles from his pants and straightened his jacket, having no clue what he was going to say to her but figuring he'd find the words when he got there. After all, this wasn't flirting, it was diplomacy.

He only had one mission: to not make a fool of himself.

He approached her cautiously. She was examining a photograph of Charlie as a young boy. In it, he was holding his first guitar, a powder-blue Fender Stratocaster. The Strat was nearly twice his size.

Sensing his presence, Ana set the photo down and turned around.

Charlie waved sheepishly and said with a goofy smile, "Come here often?"

Before the words had even left his mouth, he grimaced painfully. Mission failed.

Ana scrutinized him for a moment, and Charlie was so mortified he was prepared to pull the rip cord and fling himself down the basement stairs, but before he could, her face softened and she laughed. Charlie didn't know if she was simply being charitable, but when she winked jokingly and said, "Good one, junior," his shoulders immediately relaxed.

"Wanna take a mulligan on that one?" she said, taking another sip of her drink.

"Yes I do," Charlie replied gratefully. "And, if it's possible, I'd like to strike any memory you may have of my first attempt."

"Can't promise that," she said, then took a step back, like a spectator waiting for a magic trick to happen. "Okay, let's go. Take two."

"The truth is, I wanted to come over here and apologize."

"Apologize for what?" Another sip.

"This thing with the store. It's unfair that you and Dale are caught in the middle of it."

Ana's smile faded. "We're not children in a custody battle, Charlie. We're employees at a record store. *Your* record store, now. In the end, it doesn't really matter whether you decide to keep the store open or not. We get the crap end of the deal either way."

"How do you figure that?"

Ana drained what remained of her drink, eyes watering a little as she forced down the final gulp. "I haven't had many bosses in my life," she said, "but of the few I've had, none of them compared to your dad. None of them even came close. And no offense, but if you decide to keep the store open, you're gonna be the boss now, and that, frankly, sucks."

"That's not very fair. You don't even know me." He saw Ana about to reply, then quickly added, "And please don't take into account whatever shitty things my dad may have said about me. I'd appreciate it if you came to your own conclusion."

Ana glared at him. "Well, I would have to, wouldn't I?"

"What do you mean?"

"I mean your dad never said *anything* about you."

Somewhere above them—upstairs and to the left to be exact—came a loud thump. The other guests cast a brief glance up at the ceiling, then returned to their conversations.

Charlie, still absorbing the hit of Ana's verbal missile, looked up too. "Susan," he called out to the room, "is Bruiser upstairs?"

"He's in the backyard," Susan replied. She was standing near the fireplace, engaged in a pleasant catch-up with an elderly woman in a heavy coat. "I just fed him a few minutes ago. Why?"

Charlie looked again at the ceiling. It had probably just been Miles and Maisy horsing around. When he looked back at Ana, she was staring vacantly into her empty glass.

"Charlie," she said quietly, "what I said . . . I didn't mean—"

"It's okay," Charlie said. "To be honest, I'm not surprised Dad didn't mention me. It's just a bummer to hear it out loud."

"But it's not true." She set her empty glass down and rubbed her face with her hands, as if doing so would erase the embarrassment she felt. "Look," she said, removing her hands to reveal a set of rosy cheeks. "When I first started working at the store, you were all he talked about. Everything was my-son-Charlie-this and my-son-Charlie-that and oh-Charlie-would-love-this-record and oh-I-can't-wait-for-you-to-meet-my-Charlie . . ." She paused, staring at her own shoes, then said, "After a while, I got a little jealous."

Charlie laughed dryly. "Don't be, trust me."

"It was hard not to be. He would talk about how important your job was and how any day now, you were coming to visit. He'd spend months setting aside records he thought you'd like. Little curated piles for Charlie Remick. A seven-inch here, a first pressing there . . . sorted by mood, or by theme." Ana gazed vacantly into the middle distance. "But you never came. And the stacks of records began to pile up. They filled an entire wall in his office. Dale and I would dust them occasionally, just so they didn't look so pathetic, but one day, we came in, and the stacks were gone. He'd sorted all of them back onto the floor." She took a long breath then exhaled slowly. "After that, he stopped talking about you."

Her words hung heavily in the air between them. Charlie felt a lump form in his throat. Why hadn't his sisters ever mentioned any of this? Why hadn't Raymond, for that matter?

And then he remembered why.

The last words he'd ever said to his father, on the day of his mother's funeral, echoed through his head.

Don't call me. Don't visit me. Forget I exist. From now on, you no longer have a son.

He could still taste the bitter tang of the words in his throat.

He wanted to tell Ana why he'd never visited, but that would mean telling her about the fight, which would prompt Ana to ask why the fight happened in the first place.

Not even his sisters knew the reason behind the fight.

Not the real one, anyway.

For the second time, he heard a loud thump above him. He looked over at Susan again, but she was still deep in conversation with the woman in the heavy coat.

"I'm gonna go check on my niece and nephew," Charlie said, and Ana nodded silently.

Halfway up the stairs, he cast a quick glance over his shoulder at Ana. She'd resumed looking at the framed photos. He smiled gently and continued his trip up to the second floor. As he did, Ana turned and watched him go.

When he reached the landing, he heard another loud thump. He made his way to Susan's door and knocked before opening it. He expected to see his niece and nephew standing among hastily rearranged furniture, jumping from a crooked dresser to an overturned chair, all in the name of avoiding that most common of childhood hazards, carpet lava, but all he saw was darkness, lit only by the glow of Miles's handheld Nintendo device. It washed over his face in flickering bursts of LED illumination and cast a dim blush of pale light over the bed where Maisy lay sound asleep.

Miles looked up and removed his earbuds.

"Is Bruiser up here with you guys?" Charlie asked, scanning the room a second time.

"No, Mom always keeps him outside when guests are around."

"Have you seen anyone else up here?"

Miles shrugged, then said, "Is everything okay?"

"Of course it is, buddy. I just thought I heard something and—"

The thump came again, this time accompanied by a second noise. It was muffled but Charlie recognized it immediately. It was a voice. An angry voice.

Miles stared at his uncle, face swimming in the glow of the Nintendo screen. "Who was that?"

"Probably just a guest trying to find the bathroom," Charlie lied. "Just stay in here with Maisy, okay? I'm gonna go see if they need any help."

Miles nodded and returned to his game, although he didn't put his earbuds back in. Charlie closed the door and heard the thump for the fourth time. Once again, the muffled voice followed it, but this time Charlie could make out the words.

"*I'm trying, you miserable witch! Don't you think I'm trying?*"

It was coming from his childhood bedroom.

Charlie crossed the hallway and flung the door open.

He didn't know what to expect upon opening it—a couple engaged in a marital spat would have been the obvious guess—but he never would have imagined what he *did* see.

Standing near the window was a man holding a box.

Only that wasn't entirely correct.

The man wasn't standing near the window, he was climbing *out* of it—one leg inside, one leg outside. And he wasn't holding a box. He was holding the black case his father left him. The case containing Schrader's Chord.

Charlie stepped forcefully into the room, finger pointing accusatorily.

"Put that down."

He wished he'd said something more forceful, like "Get the fuck out of my room," but when he saw the man's face, any sense of authority had drained out of him.

The man was pale, and clearly ill. His face was drawn, his cheeks were hollow. What little hair he had left stuck out at odd angles, like the fur of a mangy cat. He wasn't a thin man, yet his posture was that of a starving wretch. And his ears . . .

His ears were caked in several coats of dark blood, crusted into little crimson barnacles that trailed down the side of his neck. Charlie could smell the blood from across the room. It smelled faintly of rust and buttery decay, an odor exclusive to a festering wound.

"Are you all right?" Charlie asked, covering his nose. "Do you need a doctor?"

"I *told* you this would happen," the man said, hissing to the air beside him. His eyes were wild and unfocused, as if the entire room were a Magic Eye poster and he was struggling to see the hidden image. "We should have waited until the house was empty!"

Charlie took a cautious step back. "Listen," he said, raising his palms to show he wasn't a threat, "I think you're in the wrong house."

"You don't understand," the man said weakly, clutching the case tightly to his chest. "I n-need this."

"That's fine," Charlie said calmly. "That's absolutely fine. But why don't you climb back through the window? The case will survive the fall. I'm not sure you will."

The man's eyes darted briefly to the right. "My wife told me I should jump. That people would notice if I left with the case, so I should go out the window."

"No offense to your wife, but that was a stupid plan. I jumped out of that very window when I was ten years old. Broke both my ankles."

For the first time, the man smiled. "No offense taken," he said, then shot an icy glare into the air next to him. "You hear that, Deb?"

Charlie risked a small step forward. "Listen, why don't you come back into the room and we'll talk—"

Immediately, the man reared back, hugging the case even tighter. "No! I'm sorry, I can't. You'll just try and take it from me."

Charlie took another small step forward. "I'm not sure what you think is in that thing, but I promise you, it's worthless."

"No," the man said darkly. "They're not."

Charlie stopped.

They're.

He knew what was inside the case.

"You're a collector?" Charlie asked.

The man shook his head.

"Well, I am, and I can assure you, *the case* is worth more than the records inside it."

"Then you won't mind if I take them."

On any other day, the man would have been correct. Charlie

didn't give two shits about his dad's little parting joke, and, truth be told, he was probably just going to throw the records in the trash anyway. But now that someone else wanted them—someone who was bold enough to sneak into a crowded house full of mourners and steal them—Charlie felt the sudden urge to keep them.

It was childish, but there you go.

"Why do you need them so badly?"

The man laughed a defeated, breathless laugh. "You'd just think I'm crazy."

"Who isn't?" Charlie said, shrugging. "I almost didn't come back to Seattle because I was scared of a *tree,* okay? We all have our issues."

The man considered this for a moment, then turned back to the window and ducked his shoulders, preparing to jump.

Charlie lunged forward. "Wait, wait!"

"Stay back!" the man cried. He gazed down at the ground below him. It was a twenty-foot drop into the backyard. Maybe more. "It's too far, Deb," he said, panicking. "It's too far." He turned back around and searched the room for an alternate exit.

The only way out was past Charlie.

"Please . . ." the man said, holding the case as if it were his own child. "I *need* this."

"I can't let you take it," Charlie said quietly. Any fear he had regarding his own safety had vanished. The man was barely strong enough to stay upright, and if their exchange happened to become physical, Charlie would have no problem taking him. "Now, I think I've been pretty cool about all this so far," he continued, "but if you don't give me the case and leave, I'll have to call the police."

"The police can't help me." He dropped his chin and closed his eyes. "No one can help me."

"Charlie?" a voice called from the bottom of the staircase. "Are you up there?"

Panic flashed across the man's face.

Charlie held up a cautionary finger. "Easy . . . that's just my sister."

Susan's voice came again.

"Charlie, Harold is leaving and he wanted to say goodbye!"

"Be right down!" Charlie called back, then he took another step forward and said, "Look, I'll just let you leave, okay? I won't call the police, but you have to go. *Now.*"

Spilling tears, the man shook his head. "You have to let me take the case. If you don't, I'm a dead man."

"Look, if you owe someone money or something—"

"He's angry with me. So angry."

"Who's angry?"

Before the man could respond, the top half of the window came sliding down like a guillotine and snapped his collarbone in half. He shrieked, immediately releasing his grip on the case, and flailed about as he tried to free himself from the grip of the window.

Charlie watched the case tumble into the backyard and out of sight, then scrambled to help the man free himself. He reached out to pull the window up, but someone . . . or something . . . beat him to it.

It was as if someone had pressed the rewind button on life. With a racking screech, the window flew back up into the top jamb and the man was pulled violently into the room by an unseen force. He landed on the floor with a hard thud, gasping pitifully as he clutched his chest. The air had been knocked clean out of him.

Charlie hovered over him, mouth open in shock. If he hadn't seen what had just happened with his own eyes, he never would have believed it.

He wasn't sure he believed it even now. He stared at the open window as if it were the mouth of some horrible beast, half expecting it to come down again and chew them both up.

"P-please . . ."

Charlie looked again at the man on the floor. His tear-streaked eyes stared desperately at the air over Charlie's shoulder. To another invisible presence in the room. "Please don't do this. . . ."

Charlie turned to his left and saw nothing. There was no one else there. Hands trembling, he pulled his phone from his pocket. "I'm gonna call an ambulance, okay? Just hold on."

He was only two digits into 911 when the man was dragged violently across the floor by his leg. It whipped him back and forth along the carpet with such force, Charlie leapt into the corner to avoid being hit.

The man wailed like a wounded animal. Loose, foamy strands of saliva spilled from his lips. His desperate cries for help were unintelligible, each word nothing more than a guttural croak. He dug his fingers into the floorboards and tried to pull himself forward, but the force that held him was too strong. With a swift, singular movement, it dragged him, legs flailing, out into the hallway, leaving streaks of bloodied, splintered fingernail buried in the floor.

Charlie scrambled into the hallway, where Miles and Maisy cowered in the corner, their cheeks streaked with tears. They watched in silent horror as the strange, bloody-eared man in a beige suit was hoisted onto his feet by a set of invisible arms.

"Stay away from them!" Charlie cried.

But the man had already moved past the children. He thrashed and bucked and bore his heels into the ground as the invisible force dragged him to the edge of the staircase.

Below them came the sound of Susan's furious voice.

"WHO ARE YOU? WHAT HAVE YOU DONE TO MY CHILDREN?"

Charlie stumbled over to the banister and peered down.

Susan was standing halfway up the stairs, her face a mask of murderous resolve as she faced off with the bloody, sobbing stranger. A sea of confused, terrified faces looked up from the ground floor.

Charlie approached the man from behind, careful to keep his

distance. "Susan," he called over the banister, "the kids are fine. He didn't hurt them."

"Who is he?" Susan cried back. "Who *are* you?"

Giving no reply, the man turned around and and placed his hands calmly on the banister, as if he were a doomed defendant awaiting a jury's decision. Blood oozed steadily from his ears, staining his already-stained shirt collar. "*Please, Charlie . . .*" he whispered between steady shuddering breaths. "Whatever you do, don't pl—"

There was a percussive crack, and the man's body was propelled violently forward. His back bent like a tightly-strung bow, and for a split second, Charlie saw what appeared to be the impression of a boot between the man's shoulder blades.

Charlie lunged forward to keep the man from going over the railing, but he wasn't quick enough. He winced, closing his eyes, and heard the collective gasp of his father's mourners as they watched the man fall headfirst into the fireplace poker Ellie had moved earlier that day.

FIFTEEN

That night, after the police had concluded their business and the final guests had gone home, Charlie ran through the sequence of events in his head again.

He could still hear the stifled gasps and horrified murmurs of the guests as he descended the staircase and surveyed the damage.

The man, who the police would later tell him was named Louis Goodwin, lay sprawled across the beverage table on his stomach like a suction-cup Garfield doll, his foot twitching.

Splinters of glass glittered like diamonds along the floor.

Charlie could still feel the crunch under his shoes as he approached the beverage table. One of the guests—he still wasn't sure who—dove out the front door and vomited into the hedges.

Even now, with the house empty and the body removed by the coroner, Charlie could still trace, in his mind, the path of the fireplace poker as it bored through the underside of Louis Goodwin's jaw, up through his mouth, and out the top of his head, its blackened point oozing with red blood.

It was an image he didn't expect to forget anytime soon, and as he sat on the front porch and lit up his fourth cigarette in a row, he tried to come up with a logical explanation for how (and why) Louis Goodwin went over the railing.

Because it wasn't suicide, no matter what the police said. Louis Goodwin spent the final minutes of his life trying to stay alive. He pleaded for his life. He begged for it.

Charlie chose to keep that particular detail from police, just like he chose to stay quiet about the set of invisible hands that sent Louis to his doom.

Just like he chose not to mention the black case, which was the reason Louis was in the house in the first place.

These were details that would raise too many questions. Questions he didn't have answers to.

And so Charlie played ignorant, and the police ruled Louis Goodwin's death a suicide.

But it definitely wasn't suicide. Charlie was certain of it.

What he wasn't certain of was anything else.

SIXTEEN

Sometimes a week feels like a day, and other times, a day feels like a week.

In Charlie's case, it felt like the latter. Here it was, Wednesday, two days after the wake, and it seemed like a month ago that the Seattle Police Department's cleanup crew had tried (and failed) to sponge Louis Goodwin's blood out of the floorboards. Wanting to hide the stain from her children's eyes, Susan dragged an old rug out of the attic and laid it over the spot where the man in the beige suit met his grisly end, but it didn't stop Miles from occasionally sneaking a peek.

Charlie still chose to sleep on the davenport in the living room instead of his old bedroom, only now it was for a different reason. The Grim Tree had suddenly become the lesser of two fears. He went back to his bedroom, only once, after the police had gone, to close the window. He could still smell the faint, rust-tinged odor of Louis Goodwin's bloody ears. He figured his mind was probably playing a trick on him—a phantom sensation brought on by the trauma of what transpired there—but trick or no trick, Charlie had no interest in sleeping in that bedroom. And probably wouldn't for a while.

Not that he slept particularly well in the living room. Every time he closed his eyes he saw Louis Goodwin's mouth, a distended, misshapen black hole, skewered clean through by the fire poker.

The police had made a return visit earlier that day. Now that the emotional dust had settled a bit, they were hoping Charlie and his sisters would have more information for them, some newly re-membered detail they forgot to mention on the day of the incident: if they'd ever seen Louis before, what his connection to Raymond could be, if he gave any reason as to why he wanted to kill himself.

Standard stuff. The officers assured them they wouldn't be in trouble if they'd accidentally left something out. Shock has a tendency to fill the brain with cement.

Susan and Ellie shook their heads. Charlie did, too. He hated to lie, but the truth wasn't something he was ready to deal with yet, and as far as he was concerned, the police could wait their turn.

As he watched their squad car pull away, Charlie wondered if the Cuckoo's Nest would be their next stop. While the police had been busy snapping pictures of Louis's mangled body, he distinctly remembered hearing Ana whisper something to Dale about a car.

A Corolla. Or maybe it was a Camry.

Had she mentioned it to the police? In all the hubbub, he couldn't remember if Ana had been questioned or not.

He decided he would ask her about it when he saw her next. Which would be soon. The incident with Louis Goodwin might have tacked on a few unexpected days to his trip, but now that the police had finished with him, it was time to get back to the task at hand.

He had to deal with the matter of the store.

And this, he thought, staring at the dented black case. It took a hell of a fall when Louis dropped it out the window, but the case served its purpose. The records inside hadn't sustained so much as a chip. He read the strip of masking tape on the underside of the lid for the hundredth time.

SCHRADER'S CHORD

With his fingertip, he traced the edge of one of the records, then pulled it out and examined it under the light.

It was old. Very old. And only one side held grooves. The other side was blank, except for a small ornate etching near the center hole he couldn't quite make out. He held the blank side closer to the light.

The etching appeared to be a word of some kind. A foreign word. He tilted the record back and forth under the light, trying to read it, but the etching was so florid the word was practically indecipherable.

Morvolantia? Mirvoluminous?

Outside, he heard the sound of a car door closing. Fearing the police had returned to ask more questions, he slipped the record stealthily back in its case and peered out the window.

Susan was hoisting two suitcases into the back of her Explorer.

"So you're finally heading out, huh?" he asked Susan an hour later as the family sat down to dinner. No one had volunteered to cook, so Ellie ordered Chinese.

"Tomorrow morning," Susan replied, twirling a sizable helping of lo mein onto her fork. "Bright and early."

Charlie nodded. Susan had been uncommonly quiet since Louis Goodwin's death. She'd even taken to sneaking the occasional cigarette out back, which Charlie hadn't seen her do since she was a teenager. She'd also become extremely preoccupied with the safety of her children over the past couple of days, which he figured was understandable. After all, Louis could have just as easily gone into the kids' room instead of Charlie's, a thought she'd expressed repeatedly over the last forty-eight hours.

Charlie wished he could set her mind at ease and tell her that Goodwin never had any interest in the children, but if he couldn't explain that to the police, he certainly couldn't explain it to Susan. She intimidated him more than any police officer ever could.

Especially when she was this tense. So tense, in fact, that she nearly jumped out of her chair when Bruiser started barking in the other room.

She dropped her fork onto her plate with a clatter and shot Miles a stern look. "Will you go tell that dog to calm down, please?"

Miles did as he was told.

"What the hell was he barking at?" she asked when he returned.

Miles chuckled. Bruiser cantered into the dining room after

him, tail wagging eagerly. "He was barking at one of Uncle Charlie's suitcases. I think he's kind of slow."

Maisy reared back, indignant. "No he's *not*! Mom, tell Miles Bruiser isn't slow."

"Which suitcase?" Charlie asked.

"The small black one."

"He was barking *at* it?"

"Uh-huh. And scratching at the latch-things. Like he was trying to open it."

Ellie grinned knowingly. "Bruiser might be smarter than you give him credit for, Miles. Dogs are supposed to be pretty in tune with the supernatural. They can often sense things humans can't."

Miles, who, as a rule, rarely showed interest in things, brightened suddenly. "What do you mean?"

"*Nothing*," Susan interjected, staring icily at her sister. "She's just messing around."

"No I'm not," Ellie said, annoyed. "They did a study on it. I read about it in *The New York Times*. Dogs can sense all kinds of stuff we can't. Like, when an earthquake is going to strike, or when there's going to be a storm. And yes, even the supernatural."

"Sure it wasn't the *Weekly World News* you were reading?" Charlie said teasingly.

Maisy looked up, cheeks stuffed with orange chicken. "What's 'supernatural' mean?"

"It means *ghosts*," Miles said, spookily wiggling his fingers.

"That's enough," Susan said tersely.

Ellie rolled her eyes. "Oh, lighten up, Susan. Kids love this kind of shit."

Maisy gasped: "You said *shit*."

Susan threw her fork down. "*Maisy!*"

Miles looked around the table, confused. "I don't get it. What's in the case?"

"Just some stuff that your grandfather left behind," Charlie said. "Nothing that interesting, trust me."

"Then why did Aunt Ellie say it was supernatural?"

Charlie looked to Susan for support, but she merely sighed and went back to her food. She was clearly outnumbered, and she didn't have the strength to battle it out.

Charlie turned to his niece and nephew. "Your grandfather left me that case as a joke."

"Like an inside joke?" Miles said.

"Exactly. There was a story he used to tell us when we were kids . . . a scary story . . . and that case has something to do with it."

"What was the story?"

"For your mom's sake I won't go into too many details, but it involves four records. And when you play those records at the same time, something—" He paused, thinking of the best way to continue without scaring Maisy. "—something bad happens."

"Scary-bad?" she asked quietly.

Charlie nodded. "That's right."

"The story wasn't *all* scary, though, sweetheart," Ellie said comfortingly. "Grandma Joan actually thought it was romantic."

"So what happens when you play them?" Miles asked.

"I'll tell you when you're older," Charlie said.

"What? I'm almost fourteen!"

"When your sister's older, then."

Miles dropped his shoulders, defeated. "Aren't you at least gonna play them?"

Charlie smiled. "No. I'll probably just throw them away."

"But what if there's something cool on them?"

"There won't be," Charlie assured him. "Like I said, Grandpa Raymond was just playing a joke on me, that's all."

"What if you're wrong? What if they have, like, secret messages on them?"

"Like the identity of the Zodiac Killer," Ellie offered. "Or where they hid Jimmy Hoffa."

Charlie made a face. "Knowing Dad, it's probably just four copies of 'Kokomo.'"

Miles shook his head in disbelief. "This is insane."

"Insane or not," Susan said, rejoining the conversation, "they're your uncle Charlie's records, and if he wants to throw them away, that's his prerogative. Now, can we please talk about something else?"

They all said they could.

At the other end of the table, Maisy stared inquiringly at a strange-looking vegetable she'd speared onto her fork. "I like 'Kokomo.'"

Charlie fired a playful glare at his niece. "Eat your chicken, squirt."

He awoke the next morning to a cold wet nose on his cheek.

Bruiser pawed encouragingly at his arm, hoping to induce a farewell scratch behind the ears, and Charlie was all too happy to oblige. The dog licked him on the chin then trotted away happily, tail wagging and paws clacking against the floorboards.

Charlie checked his phone.

5:08 A.M.

Susan wasn't kidding. She was hitting the road bright and early. Miles and Maisy were already slumped over in the back seat of the Explorer, fast asleep. Charlie wondered if they ever really woke up. He pictured the scene: Miles, dozily dragging his feet down the driveway, hair askew, and Maisy, limp as a rag doll in her mom's arms, stirring just long enough to mutter "Where are we going?" before falling asleep again.

The sun wouldn't be up for another ninety minutes or so, which meant Susan would be taking Snoqualmie Pass in the dark. Charlie brought up a weather report on his phone. The pass saw an inch of snow through the night, but, according to the report, the plows had already driven it away. That was good. Visibility was clear and traffic was all but nonexistent. Also good.

He got up and shuffled out the front door.

Ellie and Susan were speaking quietly near the hood of Susan's car. The tailpipe belched pale smoke into the gray air, and there was a slight rattling sound under the hood, obscuring his sister's voices.

Charlie hung back and let them talk privately, hissing at the cold concrete under his bare feet. He had no intention of eavesdropping, but after years of spending his evenings in loud venues, he'd gotten pretty good at reading lips. He saw Ellie mouth the words *Are you sure?* and Susan reply with a nod, smiling. They hugged each other tightly, then Ellie made her way back over to the front door, her face frozen in a state of amused shock.

Charlie sped past her, his bare feet dancing along the freezing driveway, and gave Susan a quick hug. He told her he'd visit soon. She promised she'd do the same.

After a final check to see that her children were safe and secure, she backed out of the driveway and trundled slowly down Wabash Street, the Explorer's red brake lights bleary in the low morning fog. Charlie spotted the sudden appearance of an icy blue glow in the back seat.

Miles's handheld Nintendo system. Guess he was awake.

When the car turned the corner and disappeared from sight, Charlie turned to Ellie. Her face was still frozen, buried behind the curtains of her hair. "Everything all right?"

"She's giving me the house," she replied softly. "All of it. She called Dad's lawyer this morning and left a message."

"Are you serious?"

Ellie nodded. "Yep."

Charlie smiled, then wrapped his arm around Ellie's shoulder and gave it a squeeze.

Susan, who had only just recently come to resemble their mother, had now embodied her spirit as well. As he made his way back inside, he doubled down on his promise to visit her soon. He would even buy a plane ticket so he wouldn't back out. As soon as he got back to New York.

If he got back to New York.

He laughed at the thought. If the last few days were any indication of his luck, he wasn't so sure fate would *let* him go back.

Very soon, that thought would cross his mind again.

He wouldn't find it as funny.

PART II

SEVENTEEN

The snow started to fall around 10 A.M.

By noon, the entire city of Seattle had been coated in three inches of sparkling white; by 3 P.M., another two inches had accumulated. If the weather reports continued to be as accurate as they had been, by nightfall the plows would be pushing away a whopping eight inches of fresh powder.

The wind whipped violently through the Fremont shopping district, and the few stores that remained open at the southern end of Asterion Avenue served as both commerce for Christmas shoppers and refuge for anyone looking to escape the cruel weather.

The small boutique across the street from the Cuckoo's Nest had been serving free cups of hot cocoa to snow-pelted customers. One of them was Ana Cortez, who had spent the bulk of the afternoon wrestling with her desire to claim the leather jacket she'd seen in the window of the boutique a few days ago. It was nearly three hundred dollars, more than Ana had ever spent on an article of clothing. She rarely bought something new off the rack. She'd spent the last ten years diving through secondhand shops and had found some real gems, but the thought of wearing something that hadn't been worn before—hadn't been sweated in or spilled on before—was more enticing than she allowed herself to admit. Especially since the jacket would look spectacular on her frame. She didn't need to try it on to know that.

She waffled around the Cuckoo's Nest for a bit and weighed her remaining funds against her desire to wear something that was truly her own. Her next paycheck was two weeks away and she hadn't even started her Christmas shopping. Buying the jacket would clean her out, but her bills were all paid up and her freezer was freshly stocked with a wide variety of Lean Cuisines, so after a minute or two more of playing mental tug-of-war, she figured *fuck it* and told

Dale she was heading out for a bit. There were no customers to sell records to anyway. And judging by how fast the snow was piling up outside (it had already sunk the store's front door by a foot), there probably wouldn't be any until the plows reached Asterion Avenue, and God knew when that would be. So, she flipped the store's OPEN sign to CLOSED and trudged across the street to buy the jacket as an early Christmas present for herself.

The jacket fit beautifully. Better than she had expected. Even the proprietor of the boutique, a lithe forty-something with aggressively stylish eyeglasses named Bernice, was impressed.

"Maybe I should trash the mannequin and stick *you* in the window," Bernice joked as she rung Ana up.

Ana smiled at the compliment but grimaced when Bernice ran her card. Even though she'd spent the better part of the day justifying her purchase, three hundred dollars was three hundred dollars.

Good thing the jacket's fucking warm, she thought, helping herself to a cup of complimentary hot cocoa and watching the snow swirl outside.

She was halfway through her first sip when a dark blue rental car came sliding down Asterion Avenue, its tail end swerving drunkenly from side to side. The car spun its front tires angrily as it tried to regain its grip on the pavement, only, there was no pavement. The street had been buried under a solid sheet of hardpack. Ana watched the car through the boutique's windows, coffee cup held absently at her lower lip.

Bernice, who still held Ana's debit card in her hand, groaned as she watched the car slip into a wobbly skid and slalom dangerously close to her brand-new Volvo.

"Out-of-state plates," Bernice said darkly as the car finally came to a stop in the middle of the street. "Bet he didn't pump the brakes. They never pump the brakes." She tore the receipt from the feeder and handed it to Ana. "Want me to bag it up or do you want to wear it out?"

Ana didn't respond. She crept toward the window to get a better look at the car and felt her heart gave an acrobatic little thump when she spied a tangled mess of hair in the driver's seat.

"Honey?" Bernice said, and held up the jacket.

Ana turned.

"I'll wear it out," she said, and left the store.

She'd been outside only five seconds and already her new jacket was justifying its hefty price tag. She could barely feel the icy whip of the wind on her arms and torso. The rest of her body was a different story. Her jeans were still wet from the first time she'd crossed the street.

Thirty yards away, the driver wrestled the rental into submission and parked it in front of the Cuckoo's Nest, albeit at an angle that would almost certainly have earned him a ticket had the parking lines been visible.

The car's door opened with an icy crunch, and Ana watched Charlie Remick exit the vehicle in a less-than-graceful manner, shoes sliding and limbs flailing as he struggled to stay upright on the icy sidewalk. He clapped a hand on a nearby parking meter to steady himself and shot Ana a goofy smile.

"Cars are hard."

"My friend said you should pump the brakes."

"I did!"

She took a few cautious steps toward him. It was getting dangerously slick outside. "So, where've you been? You went radio silent after that shitshow on Monday."

"Yeah, I'm sorry about that," Charlie said. "I almost texted you a few times, but then . . . I didn't."

"Riveting," Ana said flatly.

Charlie winced. Had the cold weather rendered his brain useless?

"What were you going to text me about?" she said, heading toward the entrance of the Cuckoo's Nest. "And how did you get my number?"

Charlie waddled over to the door. "Ellie gave it to me. I hope you don't mind."

"Even if I did mind, which I don't, I guess it doesn't really matter. You never got around to using it." When Charlie didn't answer, she said, "So why are you here?"

There was a tinge of concern in her voice.

"It isn't bad news," Charlie said. "I was just thinking about you—" He paused, blushing a little, then added, "—and Dale, of course . . . and I wanted to see if you guys were okay after what happened on Monday. You know, with that Goodwin guy."

Ana smiled at Charlie's pitiful attempt at a save. "Well, I think it's gonna be a while until I can have kebabs again . . ."

"Right," Charlie said, laughing dryly. "Yikes."

"But now that you mentioned it, there was something I wanted to show you."

Now it was Charlie's turn to smile. "There is?"

Ana grabbed his hand. It was warm. Even after being in the cold. She led him through the door and into the store.

"Come on."

EIGHTEEN

Do you want some coffee?"

Ana's voice was little more than an echo.

Charlie could hardly believe his own eyes. He turned slowly and took it all in.

Dale was right. Ellie, too. The Cuckoo's Nest as he'd remembered it was gone. He marveled at the wrought-iron railings that belted both sides of the grand staircase. Had they always been there? He couldn't remember. If so, they had never been polished. Now they practically gleamed under the ceiling lights. The floor, a black-and-white linoleum checkerboard tile, gleamed too, in its own way. Aside from a few barely visible scuffs, it looked as if it had been laid down that morning.

Strands of thick Christmas bulbs lined the perimeter of the ceiling, burning warmly against the red velvet curtains that flanked the store's sixteen-foot-high windows. Walnut room dividers had been placed strategically around the floor, mounted by tension rods on either end. The alcove near the supply closet had been neatly pasted with grass cloth, on which a double-coned brass sconce had been mounted, spraying dim halos of light in both directions. Even the checkout counter had been renovated. Gone was the chipped linoleum countertop, replaced by a slab of rich butcher's block.

Every square inch of the store had been rewritten. And not little edits here and there. It had been a page-one rewrite.

"What do you think?" Ana asked nervously.

Charlie laughed. "Are you kidding me? It's incredible. I mean, truly incredible."

"Incredible enough to keep the store open?"

He smiled. "To be honest, I haven't had a lot of time to think

about what I'm going to do, but I will admit, whatever I was expecting to see when I walked in here, it wasn't this."

"And that's a good thing?"

"It's definitely not a bad thing. Is this what you wanted to show
me? The store?"

"Oh," Ana said, her eyes darkening a bit. "No. That's upstairs."
She gestured to the office at the top of the grand staircase. "After you."

Unlike the store, Raymond's office hadn't changed a bit. It even
smelled the same. As he stepped inside, Charlie's nose extracted the
subtle notes of his father's Old Spice aftershave from the base coat
of dusty wood and stale air.

Dale Cernin hovered over Raymond's desk, studying a mountain of loose documents. He looked up when he heard approaching
footsteps. "All right, Charlie?"

Charlie stared at the mess, frowning. "What the hell is all this?"

Dale looked at Ana over his glasses, then back at Charlie.

"You might want to sit down."

Ten minutes later, Charlie's head was reeling.

Dale and Ana had done their best to string together a coherent
presentation of the pandemonium on his father's desk, and had
done a decent job of it, but it was still a lot to take in. The plane
ticket stubs, the travel visas, the meetings in Montreal . . .

. . . not to mention a piece of paper on which three xeroxed
images of corporate checks were neatly stacked. All of them made
out to his father for a hundred thousand dollars each. All of them
signed by Louis Goodwin.

A business card had been stapled to the paper showing the
checks. Charlie picked it up and held it under his father's desk lamp.
"Louis Goodwin," he read aloud. "Director, Department of Rare
Antiquities at the Seattle Art Museum."

"SAM," Ana said. "There was a bumper sticker on Louis's car

that had those initials. It was parked in front of the store the day before the wake."

Charlie felt as if he'd suddenly been dropped in the middle of a John le Carré novel; that his father wasn't a record store proprietor at all, but was instead a globe-trotting spy who had died before he had the chance to come in from the cold.

He'd have a hell of a story to tell Frank Critzer when he saw him next.

"The only thing we still don't know," Ana said, resting her arms on the desk like a wartime officer, "is what the Seattle Art Museum paid Raymond a king's ransom to find. Whatever it was, it clearly drove that Goodwin guy insane. Dale looked him up. He was a pretty well-respected guy at the museum."

Charlie pictured this well-respected man's jaw, shattered and bleeding all over Susan's refreshments table. He stood slowly, brushing the wrinkles from his jacket, and stared across the desk at Ana and Dale, knowing he'd have to tell them what he hadn't been able to tell the police or his sisters. He just wished there were an easy way to do it.

"I know what Goodwin paid Dad to find," he said slowly.

Ana and Dale froze, mouths drawn in a thin line, staring at him eagerly.

Charlie sighed.

"It's Schrader's Chord."

Under the pale halogen lights, Dale's face went white. He was silent for what seemed like a full minute before finally reaching for his jacket and saying:

"I think I need a drink."

NINETEEN

El Camino on North Thirty-Fifth Street and Evanston Avenue was not a place one would go for a quiet conversation, but the snow-storm had all but nullified any sidewalk patrons, leaving the bar sparsely attended and a little sleepy. One of the bartenders there, Clarice López, had become a regular at the Cuckoo's Nest over the past year after a similarly quiet evening wherein Ana and Clarice (who was still on the clock) went shot for shot reciting music trivia. Since then, El Camino had become Ana's go-to spot.

That afternoon, Clarice was the restaurant's sole employee. The waitstaff had been given the day off. There were only two customers: an elderly man enjoying a plate of tacos in the back, and a mother and her two children, seated at a table by the window.

The mother ate quietly while the children marveled at the swirling snow outside. Clarice saw Ana enter and threw up a wave from behind the bar.

"Three Modelos?"

Ana nodded as she, Charlie, and Dale took a seat. They remained quiet until Clarice brought over the beers. She stayed for a minute and shot the breeze with Ana, but, sensing the ever-growing orb of tension that surrounded their little four-top, she excused herself and returned to the bar.

Over in the corner, Charlie watched an old Rock-Ola jukebox cue up a dusty 45 of "Forever in Blue Jeans" by Neil Diamond. The Rock-Ola's speakers were clearly in need of refurbishment. It was all bass and midtones. No treble. Neil sounded as if he were singing from the basement one building over.

Dale stared absently at the table, caressing his sweating pint glass with his fingertips and drawing vertical stripes in the condensation.

Ana looked from Dale to Charlie and back again, waiting for

either one of them to break the silence. When neither of them did, she took the wheel. "So what's this 'Chord' thing?"

"Schrader's Chord," Charlie said. "My dad really never told you the story?"

"Nope. Should he have?"

Charlie shrugged.

She looked at Dale. "He told you?"

"Heard about it back in London when I was a kid," Dale said, still stroking his glass. "Raymond's version differed a bit from the one I heard, but that's urban legends for you."

"This isn't fair," Ana said. "How come you both know it and I don't?"

"Not many do anymore. It's a bit of an old dog."

"Well, are you going to tell me or not?" she asked.

Charlie sighed, trying to remember how his dad always began the story. He watched the bubbles in his glass bob and whiz up through the amber liquid. They reminded him a bit of the snow-flakes that were falling outside—only they were moving in the wrong direction. "Supposedly," he said finally, "in the late nine-teenth century, there was a composer named Ivan Schrader."

"I always heard his name pronounced 'Eye-van,' not 'Ee-von,'" Dale said, but fell silent when Ana shot him a look.

"I think it's 'Ee-von,'" Charlie said. "He was supposed to be Eastern European."

Ana crossed her arms. "You know what I think? I think I don't give a shit. Let's move on."

"As the story goes," Charlie continued, "Schrader came to America during the late nineteenth century and settled in upstate New York. He got work as a composer for a while, and did pretty well, but then he met this woman . . . the daughter of a wealthy landowner or something—"

"He was a railroad tycoon," Dale interjected.

"Right. Her dad was a rich railroad guy. So Schrader meets her, they fall in love, and get married. The wedding was a big deal. Apparently, Teddy Roosevelt was there."

"So Schrader was a real person?" Ana asked.

Charlie nodded. "You can find his name in a few books, but he's never really been anything more than a footnote."

"He wrote a few good symphonies, though," Dale added. "Good enough to put him up there with the greats."

"Allegedly," Charlie noted. "No one's ever heard any of them. He burned all his sheet music."

"He was nuts," Dale said, before Ana could ask why. "Big into the occult."

"Anyway," Charlie continued, "at some point, Schrader's wife commits suicide. Pretty violently. And Schrader, being the occultist he is, was convinced he could bring her back from the dead so they could be together again."

Ana was hooked. She loved a good ghost story. "And did he?"

"He spent a year or two trying all the usual methods: séances, rituals, spells . . . but nothing seemed to work. He began to lose hope, until a priest in some underground Satanic order gets in touch with him. The priest heard about what Schrader was trying to do and tells him about another way to see his wife. It's way more dangerous than a séance or a spell, but, if done correctly, it's surefire. All Schrader has to do is find the right combination of musical notes to sonically open a pathway to the land of the dead."

"A chord," Ana said, grinning.

Charlie nodded again. "Exactly. After that, he locked himself away and tried every combination of notes he could think of. The people in town began hearing strange noises coming from his house. Not just music, but screams and stuff. Unholy sounds."

Ana was not just leaning forward now. She was practically salivating.

"They felt sorry for him at first," Charlie said, relishing his audience of one. "Here was this guy on the verge of a sparkling career, and he'd been driven to madness by the death of his wife."

"That's actually kind of romantic," Ana said. "In a weird way."

Charlie smiled. "That's what my mom used to say." He and Ana locked eyes then, and it wasn't until Dale surreptitiously cleared his throat that Charlie pressed on. "Anyway, things came to a head when Schrader's housekeeper showed up in town one night and started talking about what he was doing up there."

Ana smirked. "Loose lips sink dipshits."

"She never had the chance to sink," Charlie said. "The townspeople—being an open-minded bunch who were completely tolerant of the occult—formed a mob to draw Schrader out of his house, except when they got there, he was gone. *Vanished.* House empty."

"Some people thought he skipped town," Dale added. "Others thought he killed himself. But the legend says Schrader really *did* succeed in finding the chord; that he opened the gateway and crossed over to the other side where he could be with his wife."

"And the only thing remaining in his house," Charlie said ominously, "was the chord. Pressed onto four records."

Ana narrowed her eyes. "Why did he make four copies?"

"They weren't copies. The four records were a fail-safe; a way of stopping anyone from accidentally playing the chord and opening the gateway. The chord itself was made up of four notes, so Schrader pressed one note onto each record. And when you play all four records simultaneously—"

"Hello, dead people."

"Exactly. And the townspeople were so spooked, they packed each record up and shipped it to a different corner of the world so they could never be played together."

"And Raymond went and found them," Ana said, then drained the rest of her beer.

"What he *found*," Charlie said firmly, "was four moldy old records. Nothing more. It's just a story, Ana."

She shrugged. "The museum didn't seem to think so. And neither did Raymond."

Charlie pulled a slip of paper from his pocket and laid it on the table. "You're not wrong about that."

Ana leaned forward and read Raymond's handwriting. "I told you they were real."

"That note was taped to the case with the records in it. Dad's lawyer gave them to me."

Dale stared hollowly at Charlie. "You actually *have* them? In your possession?"

Charlie nodded. "They're back at the house."

A surge of electric light crackled across Ana's eyes. "Fuck *yes* they're back at the house. Let's go get them!"

Dale reared back, offended. "Excuse me?"

"So we can listen to them!" She turned to Charlie. "We've got more than enough turntables at the store. Let's hook them up to the house speakers and meet John Lennon!"

Dale's face drained of color. "Ana, the two people that found those records are now dead. I don't know about you, but that doesn't exactly make me want to reach for the stylus."

"Dale—"

"Ana, listen to me. I knew Raymond for twenty years. He never *once* showed signs of being suicidal. He was terrified of death. When Joanie got sick . . ."

Upon his mother's name, the music from the jukebox disappeared, and Charlie gazed blankly at Dale, almost *through* him, as he remembered his mother's face—lifeless and yellowing as the heart monitor chirped listlessly. Her eyes, weighed down by four months of chemotherapy, stared into his own, dried of the tears they could no longer produce. He remembered his sisters' faces, too, on the other side of the bed, wrung out and exhausted as they stared at the wreckage that was once their mother. And Raymond? Where was Raymond? Not here. Not holding her hand.

He was at a fucking basketball game.

She died that night, while his father was cheering on the Sonics, and when his mother pulled her last breath over a dry tongue and asked Charlie where his father was—where her husband was—he had to lie to her.

He had to lie to her about the basketball game.

Which meant lying to her about the other thing. The thing he'd never told anyone.

The jukebox came blaring back, and Charlie blinked away the memory.

"Suicide just wasn't in your father's nature, Charlie," Dale said quietly. "He had no reason to do it."

A rigid scowl formed on Charlie's face. "He might have."

Ana, feeling a change of tone was desperately in order, signaled Clarice for another round. "Look, the point is, Raymond *left* Charlie those records. He could have just destroyed them or given them to the museum, but he didn't. He left them with his lawyer so he could be *sure* that Charlie got them. Not Goodwin. Not anybody else. Charlie." She gazed around the table, face pleading. "Don't you want to know why?"

Neither Charlie nor Dale responded. It was a good point, and one neither of them had considered.

"It'll be easiest if we do it at the store," Ana said. "The listening stations are already wired up and amplified. All we have to do is splice them together."

"Those turntables are six feet apart and bolted down," Dale pointed out. "How are the three of us going to play four records at the same time?"

Ana smiled. "Does this mean you're in?"

Dale sighed and drained his beer. "Fuck me. I guess it does. But if we set loose a bunch of Cenobites or something, I'm gonna slap you two across the face and say 'I told you so' all the way down to hell."

Ana said that was fair.

"It'll be fine, Dale," Charlie said. "Didn't you ever play with a Ouija board or a Magic 8 Ball when you were a kid?"

"No, I didn't," Dale said flatly. "And I never fucked with tarot cards, neither."

"Well, you're gonna fuck with this," Ana replied, holding up her glass. "Because they're rare as shit and I want to hear them and we can't play them without you."

"Fine," Dale said repetitive. "But you still need a fourth, and I ain't volunteering anyone."

"Already got that covered," Charlie said, fishing his phone from his pocket.

He tapped a quick text to Ellie that read: Come to the store. Bring the records.

TWENTY

By the time Ellie's navy-blue Honda wheezed and sputtered its way down to the southern end of Asterion Avenue, Charlie and Ana were putting the finishing touches on the daisy-chained turntables. Dale remained on the ground floor, sitting moodily behind the checkout counter with his arms crossed. He might have been drafted into this battle, but he certainly wasn't going to help load the rifles. The five listening stations had been installed on the east end of the U-shaped balcony, bolted onto a series of wall-mounted shelves that sat six feet apart from each other. To free the turntables from their restraints would have been too much of a headache, so Ana dug through the Cuckoo's Nest's storage closet and returned with a tangled assortment of cords, cables, and input jacks.

After a series of trial and error, she and Charlie were able to route four of the five turntables through two preamps and into the master PA system on the ground floor. They were working so quietly and so diligently that they nearly jumped when Ellie knocked on the door.

With a quiet sigh, Dale hoisted himself over the checkout counter and let Ellie in.

"Why is it so dark in here?" she asked, stamping the snow off her feet. She held the case in her arms, hands pink from the cold. "Are we having a séance?"

"Something like that," said a voice from above.

Ellie looked up and saw her brother up on the balcony, both hands on the railing like a king overseeing his subjects. Long, looping strands of black cable hung from the edge of the balcony like black vines. "Why was the door locked?"

Ana grinned mischievously. "We don't want any interruptions."

Ellie stared at the two of them, amused but wary. "You look like the cats that ate the canary. Or are *about* to eat the canary. What's going on?"

"We're gonna play the records," Charlie said. "We've got four turntables all set up and ready to go."

Ellie's mouth dropped open, a half smile curling the corners of her lips. "You're kidding."

"Is that okay?" Ana asked. She realized she hadn't yet considered Ellie's feelings about all this.

"Fine by me," Ellie said, then looked over at Charlie. "But your nephew's gonna be pissed that we did this without him."

"Miles would have gotten his hopes up too high. Ten bucks it's just four separate recordings of Dad saying 'I can't believe you fell for it, you dope.'"

Ellie climbed the grand staircase and stole a glance over her shoulder to ensure she wouldn't be overheard. When she reached the balcony, she ducked down next to Charlie, who was busy double-checking the connections of the cables, and whispered, "Okay, really, why the sudden change of heart? Yesterday you were ready to throw the records in the trash."

"Ana made a good point," Charlie said. "Dad could have sent the records to anybody, but he sent him to me. There must be a reason why."

Ellie regarded her brother suspiciously. "Kind of a flimsy point, if I'm honest." She glanced down onto the floor below, where Ana was currently futzing with the levels on the store's PA system, then looked back at Charlie, slyly. "Are you doing this to impress her?"

"What? No!"

"If you are, I get it. She's a babe. And I think she actually kind of likes you. But this is a weird way to get into her pants, man."

Choosing to ignore the *get into her pants* part, Charlie said, "Look, you're always harping on me for being so hard on Dad. This is clearly what he wanted me to do. For *us* to do. You saw his note. He was basically daring us to play them."

"Dad was a fool."

Charlie sat back, impressed. He'd never heard Ellie speak ill of their father. That was normally *his* job.

"Don't get me wrong, I loved him," Ellie said, "but he was a fool." She sat down cross-legged and ran her hair behind her ears. "And after Mom died, he got really weird, Charlie."

"I hate to tell you this, but Dad was already w—"

"Just let me finish, okay?"

Charlie nodded.

"You never visited him after Mom's funeral, so you never saw what he was like after that. He changed."

"Changed how?"

"He started spending hours in the garage. He'd go in there after breakfast and only come out when dinner was ready. Susan asked him about it once, and he said he was working on the Skylark."

"So? Lots of dads do that kind of thing."

"Yeah, but not *our* dad. He'd send the car to the shop if the air freshener needed changing."

Charlie shrugged. "Maybe he finally wanted to get under the hood and repair it for himself. New hobbies are good. They keep the mind sharp."

"And I'd agree with you," Ellie said. "Except Dad didn't do shit to that car. I snuck in there once, just to see what he was doing, and he was sitting in the driver's seat, listening to the radio. A few hours later, I snuck in again, and he hadn't moved."

Charlie blinked. "A few *hours* later?"

"Dawn to dusk. For days at a time."

"Why didn't you tell me any of this when it was going on?"

"Would you have cared?"

Charlie opened his mouth, ready to protest, then closed it again. She was right.

"Yes, Dad was always weird but he was funny-weird. Like, kooky. But once he lost Mom, he got *weird*-weird. Concerning-weird. It wasn't really noticeable at first, but it got noticeable fast. I caught him talking to Mom. A lot."

Charlie shrugged. "That's not unusual. People often talk to their dead spouses."

"This wasn't mundane chitchat, Charlie. This wasn't 'How was your day, honey? . . . Oh, mine was good.' He was talking to her like she was still alive. He was calling out to her, like she was at the bottom of a well or something. Said he was coming to rescue her." Her face fell and she sniffed lightly. "When he realized he couldn't, I think the guilt was too much for him and he . . . gave up."

"Maybe he would have felt less guilty if he'd actually been there for her when she died," Charlie said hotly.

"I'm not gonna rake over those coals again, Charlie. I only brought it up to say that I think he went searching for the Schrader records because he thought they might help him see Mom again."

"Ellie, for Christ's sake, it's just a *story*. It's not real."

Ellie's face darkened. "I'm not so sure Dad could tell the difference anymore."

"Look, you have to admit Dad would have gotten a kick out of this whole thing. The four of us, here in the store, *actually* playing Schrader's Chord? He would have eaten this up."

Ellie's face softened. "Maybe . . . but I still think you're doing this just to impress Ana."

"I think you need to reassess what counts as impressive. We're playing records here; I'm not competing in the Olympics."

"But you *are* doing it to spend more time with her."

"Only partly," he said, then gave her a good-natured shove.

Ana ambled over, paging noncommittally through an old issue of *DIW* magazine. "So, how was the caucus? Are we go for launch?"

Ellie smiled. "Let's talk to some dead people."

Coaxing Dale upstairs was difficult, but after a series of negotiations that culminated in Charlie, Ana, and Ellie promising to cover his bar tab for the next week, they were finally able to draw him out from behind the front desk.

"You lot better pay up," he said. "'Cause I'm picking from the top shelf."

He followed them over to the listening stations. Four turntables sat with their dust covers propped open, like sentries saluting their commanding officers. On each platter was one of the four records Raymond had found.

"They've taken a bit of a beating," Dale observed, inspecting the record nearest him. "Are we sure they'll even play?"

"Nope," Charlie said. "In which case, you'll be knocking back your drinks a lot sooner than expected."

"From your lips to God's ears," Dale murmured.

Ana placed her hands on her hips. "So one person per turntable, obviously, but how exact do we have to be when we place the needles on them?"

"Not sure," Charlie said. "There isn't really an instruction manual for these things."

"Well, let's see if the setup even works." She pressed Play on her turntable.

The platter began to spin and she placed the needle gently on her record. A loud *boom* sounded over the store's PA system, followed by a skeletal crackle.

The four of them listened.

After several seconds of silence, there was nothing coming from the speakers but the crackle of the needle in an empty groove. Ana frowned and moved the needle to the center of the record, ignoring Dale's fussy plea to use the tone-arm lever instead of manhandling it.

Again, there was nothing but crackle.

"Stupid question," Ellie said, "but is the volume turned up?"

"It's nearly maxed out," Ana said. She bent over the spinning record to get a better look. "Why would there be grooves on it if nothing was recorded?"

"Maybe it's a John Cage record," Charlie said.

Ana ignored his joke. "Try yours."

Charlie placed the needle on his record just as Ana was lifting the needle off hers. For the half second the records played at the same time, they heard something. However, once Ana's needle lost contact, there was nothing but crackle coming from Charlie's record.

"Did you hear that?" he said, face lighting up. "Put your needle back on it."

Ana did. The moment it made contact, the sound returned. From the PA speakers came an ethereal hum. It warbled and pulsed fluidly, filling every square inch of the store as if it were a viscous substance, oozing and rising toward the ceiling.

"How is that possible?" Charlie said, staring wide-eyed at his spinning record. "On their own, they produce no sound, but together . . ." He swept his hand through the air, as if caressing the noise. ". . . they make this."

"I feel like I'm in a classy spa," Ellie said dreamily, her eyes closed.

"Put your needle on, El," Charlie said.

Ellie opened her eyes and lowered her needle. Upon contact, she felt a sudden rush of giddiness. A moan of ecstasy spilled from her lips, and her hand shot to her mouth. She glanced at the others, bashfully.

"That was involuntary, I swear."

But Charlie and Ana barely heard her. They were experiencing their own spasms of euphoria. For Ana, it began as hot breath on the back of her neck. Breath became liquid warmth, which spilled down her shoulders, slithered between her shoulder blades, then changed course and washed over her chest and stomach, massaging her skin like a pair of ghostly, invisible hands. She closed her eyes and purred serenely, running the tips of her fingers over her lips.

Next to her, Charlie stood bolt still, riding the razor's edge between childlike exhilaration and orgasmic ecstasy. Every nerve hummed like a tuning fork, and he was certain that even the smallest movement would set off a total corporeal collapse, forcing his body to dissolve into molecules. All at once, his mind was a dazzling, baroque web of crisscrossing emotions—all of them spectacular. He felt the electric excitement of a child who'd just woken up and realized it was Christmas morning; the fluttering sense of vertigo a teenager experiences upon receiving their first kiss; the comfort and coziness of a boy up past his bedtime, sitting at the top of the stairs as he listened to the adults down in the living room talk and clink glasses and play cards; the intoxicating rush of climbing out the window and spiriting away into the darkness with his friends, the night ahead of them filled with laughter and discovery and endless possibilities.

"Dale . . ." he said in a voice that was both his and not his as euphoria crashed over him in metronomic waves, "Dale, drop your needle. You have to feel this."

Dale stared at the other three, bemused and a little nervous. A few seconds ago, they were properly functioning human beings, articulate and in control of their faculties. Now they looked more like those inflatable-tube figures that lined the freeway in front of used car lots—twisting and bobbing on the spot like drunks on a street corner.

In his youth, Dale had enjoyed a brief summer romance with heroin—a result of his days as a young punk rocker in the Thatcher-run London of the eighties—but kicked it when his older cousin, Neil, who'd introduced him to the leather-jacket-and-safety-pins scene, OD'd on his aunt's doorstep. He had many unpleasant memories of his spat with the needle, but the memory that was arguably the least pleasant was the sickening atmosphere surrounding the foul stuff. To sit on a dingy, soiled couch in a shoddy, dimly lit room, surrounded by strung-out zombified cretins whose eyelids flickered and hiccupped while their jaws ran slack—almost made sticking a needle in your arm worth it. Just to escape from it all.

And here were Ana and two of Raymond's kids, looking and acting exactly like those slack-jawed cretins, only now there was no heroin. There were no drugs at all. They had simply placed a needle on a record.

And yet . . . he felt a pull, somewhere deep inside him. A sudden yearning to feel what the others were feeling. Of sticking that needle in (or, rather, *on*) one more time.

With a trembling hand, he set the tone arm on his turntable, watched the fourth record start turning, and dropped the needle. There was a soft boom on the PA speakers, followed by a dull crackle, and Dale closed his eyes, bracing himself for what he assumed would be a rush of ecstasy, but when no such rush came, he opened them again.

He felt nothing.

In fact, he heard nothing, too.

The store was silent.

"Hey, what happened?" Ellie said, gazing at Dale and wiping her hair—which she'd been whipping around in a large oval motion—away from her face. "Why did you stop it?"

"I didn't," Dale said, then pointed to the four turntables. "See? The records are still turning."

The air around them felt suddenly thick and suffocating, and yet the store wasn't warm. It was cold. So cold that each of them could see the fog of their breath on the dimly lit balcony.

Charlie, aggravated that he'd been ripped from his repetitive trance, stepped forward on the balcony and looked down at the main floor. "Did we overload the preamps or something?"

"Don't know," Ana said, shivering. "But it got fucking cold in here. Did we leave the front door open?" She bent forward to take a look, but turned back when she heard Ellie moan again, only this time, it was not a moan of euphoria.

A thin sheen of sweat greased Ellie's brow. Her eyes were wild with fear. "Do you hear that? That sound?"

"I don't hear anything," Charlie said. "I think we fried the system. I'll run downstairs and—"

And then he heard it.

He looked at Ana and Dale, who clearly heard it too.

"What is that?" Dale said, not noticing the sweat on his own brow. "It sounds like voices."

"Not voices," Charlie said, tilting his ear toward the house speakers. The sound was low—almost imperceptibly low—but still audible enough to be recognizable. "It's a note." He leaned his head over the balcony to hear better. "It's so deep that the tone is breaking up, like when a bow moves slowly across a low string. It stutters. That's why it sounds like voices."

"It's getting louder," Ana said.

"Shh, listen." Charlie held up a hand and shut his eyes. More notes had been added, higher ones this time, although he couldn't pick them out. "Those notes are microtonal."

"Meaning?"

"If you look at a piano, the space between two keys is called a semitone. Like if you moved your finger from a C to a C-sharp. But the tones *between* those notes are microtones."

"Whatever it is, I don't like it," Ellie said, holding her stomach. "It's making me feel sick."

Ana felt it, too. The notes were vibrating with such force, it felt like the contents of her stomach had been poured into a paint shaker.

Charlie leaned over his turntable. "Maybe if we just reset the needles, we can get back to the first sound we—" He stopped, hand hovering over the spinning record, confused.

"What is it?" Ana said. "What's wrong?"

"It's a locked groove."

Ana and Dale both looked at their turntables.

"These are seventy-eight-rpm records," Charlie said. "The needle should be at least a quarter of the way through the play cycle by now, but it hasn't moved. See? It's still sitting on the far edge of the record. It's a locked groove."

"But the sounds are constantly changing," Ellie said uneasily. "How is that possible if the needles aren't moving across the record?"

"Ana's is," Dale said, pointing to Ana's turntable. "Her needle's almost reached the dead wax in the center. Look."

Ana bent low, studying her record as if she were surveying an archeological site. "After we didn't hear anything when I first cued it up, I dropped the needle in a random spot, remember? Maybe that's why mine is playing through."

"Which would mean only the outside grooves are locked?" Charlie said.

Ana shrugged and lifted the tone arm from her record. "Only one way to find out."

Dale threw his hand out in front of him. "Ana, wait. What if—"

Before he could finish, Ana dropped the needle on her record's starter groove and stood back.

All of them watched tensely as Ana's needle slid into place. It was like watching the spark trail on a fuse and bracing for an explosion. After a brief stretch of silence, the crackly sound of Ana's record once again joined the others.

Dale dropped his hand to his side, relaxed his shoulders, and chuckled. "For a second there, I thought—"

And then the explosion came.

A sound unlike anything any of them had ever heard bloomed through the air like black ink on wet paper. It no longer came from the PA speakers; it came from everywhere. It came from the floor, the ceiling, from the air itself; a terrible sound—inhuman, ancient, and unholy.

Charlie felt a sob escape his lips. His ears burned horribly, as if his eardrums had been singed by a pair of branding irons, and for the first time, fear took him.

Ellie stumbled back and fell to the ground, arms flailing. Dale braced himself on the railing, unwilling—or unable—to open his eyes for fear of getting sick. Ana and Charlie clapped their hands over their ears, but it did them no good. The sound was coming from within as well as from without. Charlie's head throbbed painfully. Each wave was like a hammer blow to his temples. Ana gritted her teeth and tried to lift the tone arm from her record, but it wouldn't budge. It was as if the needle had been welded into the groove. She ripped the power cord from the wall, but the record continued to spin uninterrupted.

The sound grew and grew, and with it, the awful sensation that accompanied it.

The already dimly lit store cloaked itself in silky darkness, and a hollow wail coursed through the air like an angry wind.

Charlie's hands moved to his stomach. The sound tore at his insides like a spoon scraping the inner rind of a pumpkin. He staggered back and leaned his weight against the wall. His senses seared with the bitterness of a thousand sensations, each one more overpowering than the next. The perfume of decay snaked its way into his nostrils. His tongue ached at the metallic twinge of blood, the sickly tang of sweat, the rotten taste of shit. Sorrow overtook him, stunning his faculties, and as he strained his eyes to verify his surroundings—to provide himself some sort of bearing—his eyes were not met with the familiarity of the store's upper balcony. Instead, there was only oblivion.

Emptiness.

He stood on the edge of Nothing, eyes watering and heart breaking. He closed his eyes to stop himself from seeing it, but it was no use. Eyes open or closed, he saw it anyway. It pulled at him with a thousand invisible arms, called to him with a thousand bodiless voices. Somewhere far off, a horn blew a low, guttural note that echoed endlessly across the space. All around him, the voices cowered and wailed, flitting past his ears as they hid from the horn's sinister call. A powerful wind threaded itself through Charlie's legs, threatening to pull him from his feet and send him headfirst into the abyss. His stomach continued to churn, to be scraped clean of his insides, and as the spectral voices continued to scream, his throbbing head reached a fever pitch and Charlie felt his legs give out beneath him.

He collapsed in a pitiful heap, hacking and gagging and sputtering; his mind a wild blue fire that burned and popped like decaying wood . . . until every sound, every smell, every sensation finally fizzled away into nothingness.

And then he was alone.

Alone, cold, and shaking in a dark room. He listened for his own breathing but heard nothing. He spoke to hear his own voice and again heard nothing. He reached blindly into the darkness, hands grasping for anything that might be familiar, but felt only the cold ground beneath him.

And then the voices came.

Or was it a single voice?

He felt a presence but could not see it. He was both surrounded by shrouded figures and totally alone.

A deep, grating voice whispered into his ear. The voice was so close, he could feel the hot pulse of breath that punctuated the two words it spoke.

"Mors occidendum . . ."

And then . . . he was back.

Charlie sat at the edge of the balcony, limbs shaking as his hands tried to support his weight. He pried his eyes open and looked at the turntable to his left. The record had stopped spinning and the tone arm had been returned to its clasp.

"Is everyone . . ." he said, chest heaving, "is everyone all right?"

"I . . . I think so," said a voice nearby. Charlie had trouble identifying its owner. His ears were ringing fiercely.

Behind him came the frantic squeak of rubber on linoleum. Charlie turned, blinking away a gooey slick of tears, and watched Dale scramble onto all fours, the soles of his shoes grinding against the floor. A thin wet croak escaped his lips, and with a heave of his chest, he emptied the contents of his stomach onto the ground.

The others turned their heads to give him some privacy. Ellie shuddered at the noise and held her breath to keep the smell out of her nose, resisting the pangs of her sympathetic stomach.

Eventually, Dale managed to pull himself to his feet. Hands shaking badly, he stared down at the puddle of sick that oozed around his shoes and shook his head in disgust.

"Dale . . ." a voice said.

He looked up and saw Ana, pale as the rest of them, slumped against the back wall. Dark shadows circled her eyes.

She opened her mouth to speak, but closed it again and swallowed. Her tongue felt like sandpaper.

Dale stared at her, his expression a mixture of pain and disappointment.

She felt her heart sink. She wished she could say something to comfort him, to let him know how awful she felt about dragging him into this, but all she managed to say was "I'm sorry."

Dale wiped his mouth with the sleeve of his shirt and headed for the staircase, arms hanging heavily at his sides.

"I'm going home," he muttered, then hobbled down the stairs.

"Dale," Ana called down. "Please don't go. I'm sorry."

He crossed the ground floor silently, then stepped through the door and disappeared out onto the dark sidewalk.

A few stray snowflakes swirled inside as the door swung closed.

The three of them sat in silence for what seemed like an hour, unsure of what to say or do next. Outside, the wind picked up again, but it appeared that the worst of the storm was over. The sky was clearing up.

When the moon finally peeked its way through the thinning clouds, Charlie pulled himself to his feet and checked his watch. It was nearly 7 P.M.

He looked again at the four records.

They seemed so innocent now that they weren't spinning.

One by one, he placed them back in the case, glad to see the last of them.

He closed the lid with a definitive thud, then placed his hands on his hips. "Remember that giant warehouse in 'Indiana Jones' where they stored the ark? That's where this needs to go."

"Let's get a drink first," Ana said. Her color was returning, but her eyes were still wide with fright. "I don't really want to be alone right now."

Charlie and Ellie told her they couldn't agree more.

TWENTY-ONE

The walk to El Camino was a silent one, broken only by a dry, raspy voice that called to them from the shadows behind a tree in front of the restaurant.

"Spare change, me brothers? It's a cold'un out t'night and the red twirlies'll be after me if my skin don't warm soon."

"Sorry, Del," Ana said, pulling the pockets of her jeans inside out.

Ellie fished for change, but had none. Charlie, who had been volunteered to carry the case, shrugged apologetically.

Under the cold moonlight, Del's leathery skin had taken on a grayish hue. He thanked them anyway in his thick Irish brogue, gave them a polite nod, and made his way back over to the tree. The wind continued to blow bitterly and the tree seemed to be the only cover Del could find.

Ana stepped into the warmth of El Camino's dining area and searched for a place to sit. The restaurant was livelier than it had been earlier that day, but was still far from rollicking. Several patrons were peppered along the bar, and a few of the tables along the wall had been taken, but the tables by the window were empty.

Probably too cold, Ana figured, and made a beeline for the windows. Given the conversation they were about to have, she figured it would be best if they weren't overheard. She also had no desire to compete with the volume of the Rock-Ola. Her voice was still hoarse and the jukebox was currently thumping out a bassy version of "Jimmy Mack" by Martha Reeves and the Vandellas.

Once Ana and the others were seated, Clarice strolled over to their table and set down three glasses of ice water. "Couldn't stay away, huh?" she said, smiling wearily. She was clearly working her way through the back nine of a double shift.

Ana didn't have the energy to smile back. Neither did Ellie or Charlie.

"Jesus," Clarice said, staring at the three hangdog faces around the table, "you guys look like wet shit."

Ana looked up, eyes heavy. "We're in need of well-made drinks at a friendly price, Clarice."

Clarice told her she could oblige, then shimmied away while Ana, Charlie, and Ellie stared out the window and watched the cars trundling by on North Thirty-Fifth Street. There weren't many. Over near the tree they'd passed, Del danced in the shadows, swaying dreamily from foot to foot. They couldn't hear him through the windows, but it was clear he was singing.

"He should come inside," Charlie said. "It's freezing out there." He placed the case on the seat next to him, where he could keep an eye on it.

"He won't," Ana said. "He never does. Clarice has tried a thousand times, but he just tips his cap and says he'll be fine right where he is."

Charlie shrugged. It seemed futile to try and engage in small talk while they waited for their drinks. Anything they could say would seem absurd considering the experience they'd just had. So they stayed quiet, still shaken—it would be a while until their systems returned to normal—but happy not to be alone.

When Clarice returned, she doled out the drinks and slipped a little umbrella into each of their glasses. "Because you three look like you could use a little vacation."

Ana looked up, holding her glass. "Pineapple juice and—?"

"Rum."

The three of them moaned gratefully and took a sip. Clarice chuckled and returned to her post behind the bar, where a rowdy trio decked out in UW purple were chatting loudly.

Charlie took another sip. Although the drink was cold, warmth flooded his body and he felt himself start to perk up. The rum and pineapple juice seemed to have the same effect on Ana and Ellie. Their cheeks blushed with color and their posture no longer bore an invisible weight. Charlie felt a laugh coming on, the same way someone laughs after a near-miss car accident, but stopped himself when Ana cleared her throat.

"We fucked up, guys."

Charlie and Ellie exchanged a brief glance, then nodded.

"First thing tomorrow morning," Ana continued, "I'm gonna sage the fuck out of that store, and then we're gonna drive out to the sawmill in Snoqualmie and throw those records into a fucking woodchipper."

"Hold on," Charlie said. "Let's just take a second and think about this before we do anything rash."

"What the hell is there to think about? It would take me a year to describe what I felt back there, Charlie, and if the two of you felt even a *sliver* of what I felt—and I'm pretty sure both of you got the full dose like I did—you know we have to get rid of those records."

"But we don't even know what really happened back there."

"It was death," Ellie said quietly. The light from the red ceiling lamp above the table spilled ominously across her features.

"Maybe," Charlie said. "But there was life, too. Remember how good it felt in the beginning?"

"All I care about is how it felt at the end," Ana said. "Ellie had it right the first time. It was death. And we opened the gates, just like that stupid Schrader story said would happen."

Charlie scoffed, mainly because he was at a loss as to how to respond. He couldn't very well say that the Schrader story wasn't real, especially after what they'd experienced, but he couldn't agree with them either. There was no proof that Ivan Schrader had anything to do with what happened. "Maybe it was just the power of suggestion," he said, finally. "Or a group trance or something."

Ana glared at him. "Please don't tell me you're gonna try and *logic* your way through this."

Charlie held his hands up. "All I'm saying is maybe, deep down, all of us *wanted* the Schrader story to be real, so we manifested some sort of shared hallucination."

"But it wasn't all of us. Dale definitely didn't want it to be real, and he felt the same thing we did. The poor guy practically puked up his own body weight."

"I know," Charlie said, ashamed. He and Ana had bullied Dale into this whole mess, and that somehow made him feel worse than whatever the records had done to them.

Ana leaned forward and took Charlie's hand. "I'll tell you what happened, Charlie. We fucked up. We capital-F fucked up. We thought the records were a joke, so we played them, and all hell broke loose. Maybe literally." She let go of his hand and sat back in her chair. "So we can sit here and whip up theories to explain away what we felt, but you know as well as we do that those records brought some serious shit down on our heads. And frankly, we're lucky that's *all* they did."

"What about the voice?" Ellie said, quietly. "Did either of you hear that? Someone spoke to me."

Charlie deflated. He'd forgotten about the voice. He and Ana both nodded.

"Did either of you catch what it said?" Ellie asked.

Charlie shook his head. "It was probably buried deep in the mix. That's why we couldn't understand it."

Ana sighed. "It wasn't on the records. The needles were in locked grooves. If the voice was on the recording, we would have heard it speak every time the record made a full turn. But we didn't. We only heard it once."

Charlie frowned; she was right. "None of this makes any sense."

"And why should it?" Ana said. "After all, 'There are more things in heaven and earth, Horatio . . .'"

Charlie grinned. "Look, all I'm saying is that there used to be a time when people didn't know why a high-pitched note could break glass . . . or how Beethoven could compose his ninth symphony while deaf . . . or who let the fucking *dogs* out, but, in the end, there was *always* a logical explanation.

"Whatever Dad found, it was clearly some kind of musical phenomenon that hasn't been explained yet. Maybe we heard sounds the human mind hasn't ever heard before, so it caused a sort of mental freakout."

Ellie glared at him. "The Man with the Magic Ear strikes again."

Charlie ignored her. "I'll bet if we set up a camera and film ourselves listening to the records, we'll get a clearer picture of what happens wh—"

"You're fucking high," Ellie said, cutting him off. Her face burned with disbelief. "After what happened to Dad?"

Charlie closed his eyes and rubbed the bridge of his nose. "Ellie, Dad killed himself. It had nothing to do with the records."

"But what if it did? What if he listened to the records so many times it drove him to commit suicide? I only listened to them once and I wanted to die."

"We don't know that Dad listened to them more than once," he said.

"And we don't know that he didn't. But Dad *wasn't* insane and he *wasn't* suicidal. Something drove him to kill himself."

"You said yourself that Dad was acting strange after Mom died," he reasoned.

"What about Louis Goodwin?" Ana asked Charlie pointedly. "He's the only other person besides Raymond that had anything to do with those records and look what happened to him."

"Wait, the guy who died at our house?" Ellie said.

"He's the one who paid Dad to find the records," Charlie said. "That's why Dad was traveling so much, and that's why he had so much money."

Ellie wanted to ask him how he knew all of this, and more important, why he was only telling her now, but she moved past it.

"If the records were meant for exhibition," she said, "then that Goodwin guy would have wanted proof they were legitimate. Dad would have, too, to make sure he'd found the real McCoy. And the only way to do that would be to play them."

"Probably multiple times," Ana added. "To check for inconsistencies or alternate results."

"And now they're both dead," Ellie said, boring her words into Charlie's eyes.

Having no counterargument, Charlie nodded. Their logic was sound.

"So we all agree, then," Ellie said. "We never play those records again."

"Why not just destroy them?" Charlie asked. "That way *no one* can play them."

Ana shook her head. "That might be a bad idea. We still don't know anything about them. How they actually do what they do. Destroying them might be like setting off a bomb or something."

"So we lock them up and throw away the key," Ellie said. "Agreed?"

"Agreed," Ana said.

Charlie still felt a nagging tug to listen to the records one more time, to learn more about them, but knew they were right. One time through the gates of hell was enough.

He held up his glass. "Deal."

Now that the deal had been struck, the tone of the evening lightened considerably. With each minute that passed, the darkness they'd experienced while listening to the records faded a little more, until finally, they were laughing and joking around like the whole terrible ordeal never happened. They especially had a good chuckle after Ellie returned from a trip to the bathroom with a soaked phone. She'd been checking her email while peeing and accidentally dropped it in the toilet.

"My favorite picture was on there," she said, tossing the ruined phone on the table.

Charlie snorted into his drink. "The one with you and Marvin Hamlisch?"

"Uh-huh."

Ana scrunched up her face. "Marvin Hamlisch? The guy who did the music for *The Sting*?"

Ellie nodded, tears in her eyes. "I met him at Walgreens."

"*That's* your favorite picture?"

Ellie glared at her. "Hey, fuck you. Marvin Hamlisch is the total package."

At this, they all burst into laughter. Even Ellie.

Ana called Clarice over and ordered another round of drinks. When they came, Ana solemnly raised her glass and toasted the memory of the Marvin Hamlisch picture.

They stayed at El Camino for nearly three hours and downed five more rounds of drinks. They took turns plugging quarters into the jukebox and singing along to the selections, and at one point, feeling they were adequately lubricated enough to comply, Ellie nudged Ana and Charlie into the center of the dining area. It wasn't a dance floor in the traditional sense, but neither Charlie nor Ana seemed to mind. They fell into each other's arms and bobbed and swayed drunkenly to a particularly boomy rendition of Hubert Kah's "The Picture." Clarice, a consummate professional, dimmed the lights, bathing the two of them in a dim red halo.

As they turned on the spot, Charlie caught a whiff of Ana's perfume and involuntarily closed the gap between them. He blushed a little when he realized he'd shifted from a friendly gear to an intimate one, but was elated when she took hold of his arms and pulled him even closer. He placed a hand on her lower back and smiled serenely at the cool, buttery feel of her leather jacket.

"I love this song," she said into his shoulder, her voice muffled.

"Me too," Charlie said.

And then, in unison: "Way better than the German version."

They pulled away from each other and laughed.

"I would say 'Jinx,'" Ana said, moving back into his body and resting her chin on the crook of his neck, "but the Coke here is basically just sugar water with day-old syrup in it, so I'll let it slide."

"Fair deal. Next time we Jinx, the payment'll be two Cokes. To make up for this one."

Ana gave him a little squeeze then. She wasn't sure if it was because he was being playful or because he said there would be a next time or because the song was putting her in a romantic mood, but she was grateful for all three.

She wasn't sure what moved her to say what she said next, but she hoped it wouldn't break the spell of the moment.

"Dale told me about your record deal and how you destroyed all your tapes."

She felt his arms tense a little.

"That was a long time ago," he said softly. "It almost seems like it happened to a different person."

"But it *is* true?"

"I'm afraid so."

"Even the part about Raymond breaking into the studio and changing your mixes?"

A pause, then: "Dale told you that too, huh?"

"I'm sorry if he shared too much."

"No, it's okay," he said, then twirled her into a surprisingly agile dip, considering his blood-alcohol level. She was elated, not only by his dancing abilities, but by his willingness to talk about his past. "It wasn't all bad, you know," he said, guiding her arms back around his neck. "Getting to work in a real recording studio was pretty mind-blowing. Up until then, I'd only ever used this four-track mixer that recorded to tape."

"Dale said you made hundreds of them."

"Tapes?"

She nodded.

Charlie laughed. "He might have oversold it a bit. But there were a lot. Almost twelve years' worth."

"And you really destroyed all of them?"

"Mm-hm."

"That's too bad," she said quietly. "I wish I could listen to them."

He smiled. "I wish that too, sometimes."

Ana felt the full weight of him—the warmth and comfort of him—against her body then. She scolded herself for wanting him in that moment; told herself silently that he lived in New York, and that he was Raymond's son, which was weird, even though there was no reason it should be. But most important, he held the future of the Cuckoo's Nest in his hands. Yes, he'd been impressed with the changes she'd made to the store, but he could still close it down if he wanted to.

And that was what troubled her. She had no idea what he wanted.

She only knew what *she* wanted. And in spite of all the reasons not to, she wanted him.

At the far end of the bar, the jukebox cued up another record. The song was coming to an end, and Ana felt the sudden urge to make a move before that happened.

Charlie felt the same urge. He pulled his head back and gazed into her eyes. The corners of her lips curled up, hinting at a smile that dared him to kiss her.

He moved in closer, the hair on his neck standing on end as her warm breath spilled from her lips and mixed with his own.

She closed her eyes.

He closed his.

And then—

"Hate the Police" by Mudhoney came blaring out of the jukebox, obliterating the moment and scattering the ashes into the wind. Charlie and Ana both blinked as if suddenly waking from a deep sleep and laughed at the timing of it all. When they returned to the table, Ellie was there, drink clutched in hand, frowning at the missed opportunity she just watched unfold. She wanted to find the fucker who put Mudhoney on the juke and smack him upside the head.

They ordered a final round of drinks and spent the next twenty minutes nursing them, a little light-headed and a little giggly. Ellie attempted to facilitate a second magic moment between Charlie and Ana, but didn't succeed.

No matter, she thought, satisfied. *The flame's been lit. That's what counts.*

At ten o'clock, the sound of a police siren blared past the windows, and Ellie prodded her brother, saying, "Name the note." Charlie, who normally would have protested his sister's provocation of what she called his "parlor trick," was just liquored up enough to reply.

"C-sharp bending into an E."

"Fucking *hell*," Ana said, laughing. "Who are you? Rain Man?"

By ten thirty, the conversation had fizzled down to embers, and Ellie decided it was time to call it quits. Charlie and Ana agreed. They had Clarice split the bill three ways and called themselves an Uber. They would come back to the store in the morning and pick up the cars.

On their way out the door, Ana spied Del out by his tree, still swaying on the spot and serenading the night wind.

"Hey, Clarice," she said, holding the door open with her elbow. Clarice looked up. "Give Del a drink, will ya? It's fucking freezing outside."

She slipped through the door and chased the others to the Uber, where they all piled into the back seat.

Clarice watched them go, her expression a mixture of confusion and regret. She wanted to call out to Ana and correct her, but it would be useless to do so. She had clearly let Ana drink too much. A good bartender should know her regulars, and if Ana was liquored up to the point of hallucinating, Clarice had done her a great disservice.

She peered out the window at the spot where Del died, two days ago.

She could still remember the way the ambulance lights cut through the evening air and strobed the bar counter in a red wash.

Red twirlies, Del had always called them. *The red twirlies'll be after me if my skin don't warm soon.*

TWENTY-TWO

Charlie and Ellie said goodbye to Ana and made their way up to the dark house on Wabash Street. Ana watched with a crooked smile as Charlie, black case clutched tightly to his chest, stumbled over a particularly small bush near the front door. As the Uber driver pulled away from the curb, she heard his voice cry out, "I'm alright!" and she laughed, relaxing into the back seat as the car turned the corner.

Even the Uber driver seemed to relax a bit. His car, a pretty black Mustang (a recent model and a total gas-guzzler, Ana observed with both disgust and envy), had been lovingly kept, and it was clear that he hadn't exactly loved the idea of three people crammed in his back seat with their feet up on the leather and their alcohol-soaked breath fogging his windows.

He was young, most likely a student at UW (the hypnotic dance of the purple GO DAWGS! air freshener hanging from the mirror had captured Ana's attention for a few blocks), and had a face so fresh and so unmarred by life's slings and arrows, he practically looked like unbaked dough.

A freshman, Ana figured. Probably no older than nineteen.

He wasn't a chatty driver, which she was grateful for, but he was also clearly an introvert, which never made for comfortable transportation. Don't be chatty, but don't be a weird stiff, either. It was a fine line to walk, but a good driver knew how to walk it.

She thought about saying something to ease the tension, but instead fixed her gaze out the window. Shadowy clusters of trees and houses swept smoothly by. Dirty, pebble-flecked banks of snow had been plowed to the side of the road. They rose and fell in dizzying parabolas as the Mustang breezed past them.

Having nothing better to think about (other than Charlie, of course, but she wasn't ready to unpack those feelings just yet), she walked herself through the listening of the records, making mental notes about who placed the needle on the groove first (herself) and who did it last (Dale). Charlie had done it second. That's when the beautiful sound (and sensation) first came. When her and Charlie's records were playing at the same time.

Her and Charlie.

No, she thought, stopping her mind from chasing that thread. *Back to the records.*

She closed her eyes and remembered the sudden rush of euphoria brought on by the sound; the feeling of warm hands on her body and the protective sensation it had given her. She wished she could feel it again. No squeezing, no massaging, just . . . holding. The pressure of another warm body pressed up against her own. It was a feeling she'd always loved, and one she'd routinely asked past boyfriends to indulge.

Most of them were never any good at it. They'd hold her for a little while, but inevitably they would tire or become bored and roll away from her.

Eventually she tried to produce the sensation on her own, but doing something like that is like trying to tickle yourself. You know the right spot and the correct amount of pressure to use, but somehow your brain knows it's you and won't let itself indulge in the fantasy, no matter how badly it wants it.

And worse, trying to do it by herself made her feel that much more alone.

Alone.

The word clouded her mind, and she suddenly wished Charlie were still with her in the back seat.

Up ahead, the climbing treetops of North Beach Park approached. She was only a few blocks from home.

The Mustang crawled to a soft stop in front of the traffic light at Ninetieth Street and Twenty-Fourth Avenue. The engine purred quietly as it waited for the light to change. Outside, a kid walked his bike slowly along the crosswalk.

Very slowly.

Ana checked her watch. It was just past eleven.

"A little late for a bike ride, don't you think?" she said to the driver. When he didn't respond, she looked back out the window.

The kid was still taking his sweet time crossing the street.

The light would be green in a second and Ana had to pee. She thought about rolling down the window and asking him to pick up the pace, but gasped when the bike's front tire came into view. It had been bent in two places and was wobbling between the forks as it rolled across the street.

"Shit," she said quietly. "That's a bummer."

The driver's eyes shot up to the rearview mirror then returned to their forward position.

Ana continued watching the boy through her own window.

He wasn't walking slowly. He was limping.

He passed under the antiseptic glow of the streetlamp and Ana was able to get a better look at him. His left pant leg had been torn to shreds and the side of his face and neck were smeared with blood. Even from twenty feet away, Ana could make out the little pebbles and shards of asphalt embedded in the boy's shin.

He'd been in an accident, and recently.

She rolled down the window and leaned her face out into the cold night air. "Hey, kid, are you okay?"

The boy nearly jumped out of his skin when he heard Ana's voice.

"I'm sorry," she said quickly. "I didn't mean to scare you. But I think you need to see a doc—*hey!*"

The boy scrambled through the dense thicket that lined the perimeter of North Beach Park and disappeared into the shadow of the woods beyond.

Ana wheeled around and faced the driver. "We need to go after him. He looked really bad."

The light turned green and the Mustang lurched forward, blazing through the intersection.

"Hey!" she shouted, gripping her door handle for balance. "Slow down! It was probably some fucker like you that *hit* that kid!"

Seconds later, they pulled up to Ana's apartment building.

She got out of the car without a word and gave the back door a defiant slam.

The driver sped away, leaving Ana in a swirling blanket of ground fog that that bloomed red in the Mustang's taillights. She flipped him the bird, then made her way up the stairs to her apartment on the second floor, cursing him under her breath.

An hour later, she would be asleep on her couch, a pair of cockeyed headphones clamped over her ears. She would wake in the morning, a little hungover and with a bad ringing in her ears, but feeling relatively okay after the strange events of the previous night.

At 6:12 A.M., she would put on a fresh pot of coffee.

At 6:15 A.M., she would take two Advil to quell the rum-soaked headache that hammered her temples.

At 6:18 A.M., she would call Charlie in a panic, staring wild-eyed at her television as a toothy news anchor reported the death of fourteen-year-old Tyler Lawson, killed in a hit-and-run accident on his bicycle the previous night at the intersection of Ninetieth Street and Twenty-Fourth Avenue, next to North Beach Park.

TWENTY-THREE

By the time Charlie showered and toweled off, it was nearly 6:45 A.M. He slipped on his underwear and slid into yesterday's jeans, then lay on the davenport for a while. His ears had been ringing badly ever since he woke up. He thought a hot shower might help a bit—he was no stranger to the effects of tinnitus, having spent most of his life in concert venues—but the ringing this morning had been particularly aggressive, like the steady squeal of a microphone that had been placed too close to an amplifier. Before he stepped into the shower, he fumbled through his suitcase for a bottle of Advil and took three.

Now, as he lay sprawled on the davenport and watched the sporadic car pass by the windows, the ringing began to subside. He tried to replay the incident with the records in his mind, but his thoughts seemed to be stuck in a repeat pattern that refreshed every couple of seconds, always showing him the same image: Ana Cortez.

She floated there, in and out of focus, blocking the view of any other thought that tried to push its way forward. His thoughts of her weren't anything specific. There was no intricate scenario that played itself out, no narrative he could follow. She was just simply *there*.

He rolled over and stared at the ceiling. He hadn't heard a peep from Ellie all morning. He figured she was still asleep, working off her hangover.

His eyes moved to the coffee table, where his phone sat, fully charged, next to his keys and wallet. He thought about calling Ana, to see if she was okay, but remembered how early it was and tabled it. It wasn't even 8 A.M. yet. She was probably still sleeping, too. He figured sending a text was less intrusive, but still ran the risk of waking her up, and the last thing Charlie wanted to be was an annoyance.

He decided to make a coffee run to kill some time. Ellie probably wouldn't be up for a while. He pulled on a pair of socks and began lacing up his shoes, wondering what kind of pastry would best soak up the hangover juices that were currently splashing around his stomach, then paused when he heard a buzzing sound nearby.

It was quiet and intermittent. A faulty wire perhaps, somewhere behind one of the walls.

Just what we need, he thought sourly. *A house in flames.*

He walked the perimeter of the living room silently as he attempted to track the noise. The ringing in his ears might have tapered off a bit, but it was still loud enough to mess with his sense of aural detection. He ran his hands along the walls and felt for hot spots, worried about what would happen if he actually found one. He was hungover enough that the idea of calling the fire department seemed like more of a hassle than the house was worth.

The buzzing grew louder as he approached the window in the corner. He slowed his pace, inspecting every inch of space, from the crown molding to the baseboards, then stopped when his eyes moved to the windowsill.

His stomach gave a lurch.

The buzzing was coming from an old strip of flypaper. Very old, by the look of it. No doubt installed and subsequently forgotten by his father months—or even years—ago. It was coated end to end with dead flies.

And the flies were moving.

To someone only an inch tall, the scene would have looked like the aftermath of a battle; a barren stretch of field, strewn with quivering, helpless bodies, fighting and gasping for life. The flies struggled and twitched, buzzing wildly as the adhesive stuck to their wings, heads, antennae, and legs.

Charlie counted fourteen of them. All of them still alive.

One of them pulled so hard in an effort to free itself, it tore its thorax in half. The bisected fly collapsed back into the dust-caked adhesive. To Charlie's astonishment, it didn't remain still. Like the others, it resumed its struggle to free itself.

"That's impossible," Charlie whispered aloud. He gave the bottom half of the bisected fly a delicate prod with his forefinger and nearly jumped out of his skin when it responded to his touch, aggressively batting at the tip of his finger with its free leg.

Head swimming, he backed away from the window. All fourteen flies continued to struggle; wings whirring wildly, legs trying to push their way out of the tacky yellowing muck.

It didn't make sense. It was December. Flies weren't an issue this time of year.

He supposed it was possible that a few flies had survived the weather change, and that yesterday's snowstorm could have driven them inside, but fourteen of them? He'd never seen more than two or three flies buzzing around a room at any given time. Fourteen was practically an infestation.

There was only one explanation for what he was seeing.

The flies had come back to life.

They were dead and now they were alive. Alive and buzzing angrily at their sticky fate.

Over on the coffee table, his phone bleated a chipper text alert. He hopped across the room and picked it up.

Three missed calls and a text message.

The calls had been from Ana. He read the time stamps. 6:18, 6:22, and 6:31 A.M.

Shit. He'd been in the shower when she called.

The text message was from his father's attorney.

Charlie, it's Frank Critzer. Sorry to bother you so early, but I've got to leave town for a few days and wanted to give you some documents to look over re: your ownership of the store.

Before Charlie could type a response, a second message from Frank came through.

My flight leaves at noon. Can I interest you in breakfast? On the firm's dime!

Sure, Charlie replied. He was in no mood to dine with a lawyer, especially so early in the morning, but he wanted to put as much room between him and the dead flies as possible.

They're not dead, he assured himself. *They were wintertime stragglers, driven in by the storm. That's all.*

His phone bleated again.

How about Shuckers at the Fairmont Olympic? Frank replied. Say 7:30?

Charlie checked his watch, then typed: See you then.

He went to the kitchen and dashed off a quick note to Ellie to tell her where he'd gone, then scrambled out the door. He would call Ana back while he drove.

And then he remembered he'd left his car down at the store.

"Fucking hell," he said, and brought up the Uber app. Luckily, a car was only two blocks away.

As he made his way down to the Cuckoo's Nest to pick up his car, he wondered why Ana had called him three times.

Three calls all within an hour spelled emergency.

Or she was calling me to put an end to things before they start, he thought. *Something about how we live in different cities and also it's weird because I own the store now and it would probably be best for all parties concerned if we just remained friends.*

He certainly wouldn't have held such a call against her. He would be disappointed, sure, but he would understand.

Then again, all three calls came in before 7 A.M. The *let's just be friends* call wasn't normally so urgent a matter that it had to precede breakfast.

The Uber pulled up to the Cuckoo's Nest at 7:14 A.M.

He was going to be late.

He thanked the driver and hopped into his rental car. He high-tailed it to the Olympic Hotel, smoking as he drove.

As he sped through a yellow light, he wondered if the dead flies were still buzzing in the living room.

He supposed they were.

Just like a tree that falls in the woods, he assumed dead flies still buzzed even when there was no one there to hear them.

TWENTY-FOUR

Charlie Remick didn't often think about death. At least, no more than the average person does. When he did, he pictured death in the abstract way most people do: an unpleasant thing that was inevitable but also hopefully a long way off. When he thought of death specifically, his mind conjured up images of hospital beds, morgues, mausoleums, and weather-worn gravestones under a desaturated, gray sky—all images cemented in his youth, when death was a new concept.

Shuckers Restaurant and Oyster Bar—a pleasant, warmly lit space with cozy leather seating and dark mahogany woodwork—was not the sort of place Charlie would have thought of when he thought about death.

He stepped through the doors, bringing a brisk nip of winter wind in with him, and felt an immediate sense of relaxation at the sight of the place. Glasses clinked, silverware scraped quietly along plates, and the low murmur of morning conversation trickled from table to table.

The maître d', a fussy little man in a crisp suit who looked like a character from a *New Yorker* cartoon, turned a judgmental eye at Charlie's clothes and asked if it was just him this morning.

"I'm actually meeting someone here," Charlie said, then found Frank's face and gestured to the back of the restaurant: "He's over there."

The maître d' smiled sourly. "Enjoy."

Charlie weaved his way through the dining area, catching the occasional snippet of conversation as he went. He brushed by a large man in an expensive suit holding court over an enormous plate of rock shrimp as two other men in suits looked on, captivated.

". . . and then the sonofabitch went berserk! He came out of the bathroom, nearly in tears, and stormed over to Sally's desk and said . . ."

Charlie held his breath as he passed the table, hoping to hear what the sonofabitch said to Sally, but reluctantly kept moving so as not to be accused of eavesdropping.

In the back corner, Frank Critzer had posted up in a chair/booth combination table, and was nursing a cup of coffee as he perused an article on his iPad. Another man sat beside him; tall, with graying temples, and dressed in an impeccably tailored suit. No doubt an associate from the same firm, Charlie assumed. The man gazed absently across the dining area with an expression that seemed to telegraph an air of disinterest and superiority.

Charlie suppressed a laugh. Here were two men that could not have looked more like lawyers if they tried. "Sorry I'm a bit late," he said, pulling out a chair and taking a seat. "I had to pick up my car at the store. I hope I'm not holding you guys up."

Frank set his iPad down and looked briefly from side to side, as if searching for something, then stared at Charlie, an amused smile on his lips. "Late night?"

"You could say that. I think my blood type is now Bacardi Positive."

Frank chuckled. "When you start seeing double, it's time to hang up your spurs, cowboy."

"I woke up with a bad ringing in my ears. Have you ever had that?"

"I stopped keeping track of my hangovers during college, but I'm sure ringing ears is somewhere on my dance card." He gave his coffee a gentle stir with a small spoon. "Did you at least get something for all your pain?"

Once again, Ana floated into Charlie's thoughts. He saw her face, bathed in the red light of El Camino as Hubert Kah's "The Picture" poured through the Rock-Ola's battered speakers. He remembered the nearness of her, the heat of her, and, in spite of himself, smiled.

Frank smiled back, eyebrows arching cartoonishly. "Attaboy."

Ana's face vanished from his thoughts, leaving in its place not her warm smile but Frank's sly grin. He gestured to the slim green folder on the table between them. "Is that what you wanted to see me about?"

"Ah," Frank said, suddenly all business. He picked up the folder and handed it to Charlie. "I know you probably haven't had a whole lot of time to think it over—especially after that nasty business at the wake"—Frank gave a campy shudder of his shoulders—"but since I'll be gone for a few days, I figured I'd give these to you now so you have a chance to look them over."

Charlie opened the folder. At first glance, the documents appeared to have been written in a language other than English. He always hated reading legalese. It made him feel like a first grader, sounding out a Berenstain Bears book syllable by syllable. He frowned and looked up at Frank. "Can you give me the gist?"

"All it really says is that, by signing it, you consent to forfeit your inheritance."

"And if I do that, I have no say in what happens to the store?"

"No. For that to happen, you would need to retain ownership."

Once again, Ana's face floated into Charlie's mind. Only now, she wasn't smiling. "What about the employees that work there?"

"They would receive severance packages. I can't say how handsome they'd be without looking at the books, but they certainly wouldn't leave empty-handed. Is the store in debt?"

"I don't think so," Charlie replied, although he didn't have the foggiest idea about the store's financial situation. It looked a lot nicer than it used to, but that didn't really mean anything. Lots of businesses pump a bunch of money into renovation in the hopes that it will reinvigorate their brand, only to fold anyway.

"That's good!" Frank said, signaling the waiter for a refill on his coffee. "That makes either scenario easier to swallow. If you decide to keep the store, you're the owner of a successful business. If not, you can sleep well knowing the employees won't be left with nothing but moths in their pockets."

The waiter, a slim man with platinum-blond hair, approached the table and refilled Frank's cup. "Can I interest you gentlemen in some breakfast?"

"Two eggs," Frank said. "Sunny-side up. Two strips of bacon."

The waiter nodded, then looked to Charlie, who hadn't yet had the chance to look at a menu. In the interest of expediency, he ordered the same.

"Coffee?"

"Sure," Charlie said. "Decaf."

The waiter nodded again and turned swiftly on his heel. When he was gone, Charlie turned to the man sitting next to Frank. "You didn't want anything?"

For the first time, the man spoke.

"I already ate."

His voice was hoarse, with a hint of liquidity that pointed to an oncoming cold or a flu.

Charlie moved his chair back a few inches, hoping it wouldn't be seen as rude.

"Hm?" Frank said, looking again at his phone.

"I just asked your colleague if he wanted any food."

Frank looked up. "Colleague?"

"Yeah," Charlie said, then pointed to the man with graying temples. "I'm sorry, I didn't catch your name."

"It's Sam," the man replied, all smiles.

Charlie felt himself recoil. The man's teeth were stained red. The inside of his lips, too. It looked as if he'd mistakenly reached for a bottle of Merlot instead of Listerine that morning.

Frank stared at Charlie with the blank, expectant face of someone awaiting the punch line to a joke.

"*Sam,*" Charlie said firmly, pointing at the man sitting next to Frank. "Your colleague. Or maybe your friend?"

Frank shook his head and chuckled. "I don't know what the hell you're talking about, Charlie, but you've certainly got your pop's sense of humor. I never really understood *his* jokes, either."

Charlie stared back across the table, his own face waiting for the curtain to fall.

Next to Frank, Sam smiled again. Blood trickled down his upper gumline and pooled between his teeth in dark lines. "I had a quick breakfast," he said, each word bubbling up through his throat like thick soap.

Charlie glared angrily at his father's lawyer.

Frank blinked, confused.

"It was real quick," Sam continued. A thick ebb of blood oozed slowly from his teeth and settled into the crevices of his chapped lips. "Barely even tasted it . . ."

For the first time, Charlie noticed his eyes. They were clouded over. Almost milky.

"Frank, what the hell . . ."

"Maybe I should help myself to another taste," the dead man said, and produced a handgun from underneath the table. "Whaddya think?"

He stuffed the barrel of the gun in his mouth and pulled the trigger, painting the wall behind him with blood and bits of brain matter.

Charlie shot to his feet, knocking his chair over with a loud, percussive rattle. The dining area fell to a hush. The other patrons stared, quizzically. He backed away from the table, leaving Frank absolutely flabbergasted.

"Charlie, what the hell—?"

The dead man bit down on the barrel, laughing hysterically, and pulled the trigger four more times.

BLAM BLAM BLAM BLAM

Each time, his skull acted like a paint cannon, spraying the wall behind him.

Charlie staggered back, knees colliding with a bar cart, and ducked into the dimly lit hallway at the back of the restaurant, leaving Frank alone and stunned into silence.

Ears still ringing from the gunshots, Charlie traced the wall of the hallway with his fingers. Bright flashes of pale red exploded before his eyes. His head throbbed painfully, and Charlie half wondered if this was what an aneurism felt like.

He stumbled over to a small coatroom at the end of the hallway and dove inside, colliding with a rack of floor-length overcoats that swung lazily back and forth like a set of wool wind chimes.

Struggling to breathe, Charlie clutched his chest and pulled air slowly through his nose, counting as he did so. In for seven, out for five. His heart raced, skipping every few beats as it struggled to pump oxygen to his brain. He closed his eyes for ten seconds and opened them again, forcing them to adjust to the dim light of the coat closet . . .

. . . only there was no coat closet.

He was in another hallway. Not the hallway at the back of the restaurant, but a different hallway. A corridor of doors.

He bristled at the taste in his mouth. The air rolled over his tongue like the sour sting of a battery terminal. His nose filled itself with the hot stench of blood and metal.

Above him, or maybe behind him—he couldn't really tell—he could hear the voices of the restaurant patrons. Their whispers skittered along the walls like panicked mice.

". . . probably a seizure . . ."

". . . prop his neck up? I think I read that somewhere . . ."

Charlie wanted to respond, to assure them that he was fine, but even if he could find a way to communicate with them, he knew he could assure them of no such thing.

Because he wasn't fine.

He was in real trouble.

A lone candle, nearly expired, flickered dully in a sconce to his left. The wallpaper, a faded red damask pattern, hung from the walls in loose folds, torn and withering like the dying petals of a flower.

He took a step forward, and another, and the walls seemed to breathe with him, inflating then deflating with each step. The carpet that lined the hallway was crimson; shredded by time and streaked with dirt and decay.

Ahead of him, at the far end of a hallway, was a door. It was bigger than the others that lined the walls, and from behind it came the faint hiss of steam and the dull whine of poorly oiled machinery.

And tones; ghostly, resonant tones that pulsed and played continuously, like melodic wails of grief.

Charlie tried to pick apart the tones and identify them, but he couldn't. Like the sounds that emanated from the records, the notes were microtonal.

Thin blades of light traced the perimeter of the door, and Charlie knew just by looking at it that it was not locked. How he knew such a thing he could not say, but he knew nonetheless.

He raised his hand, ready to push the door open, then didn't.

Fear took him then, and every part of him wanted to run.

But what good would it do? Even if he could find an exit, where would it lead? The hallway had no windows. Only doors. And what would happen if he walked through one of them? Would he set himself loose in a world to which he was a complete stranger? And what if there *was* no world? What if through those dark, smaller doors there was just another hallway waiting for him? Another hallway, identical to the one he was in now, with decaying wallpaper and crimson carpet that led to the same big door with light around its edges? What if the big door was inevitable?

He felt a lump form in his throat.

As a boy, he had always been drawn to the story of the Minotaur—the abomination born of Pasiphae and Poseidon's white bull, doomed to wander the endless halls of Daedalus's labyrinth. Using couch cushions and spare pillows, he would build a maze and pretend he was Theseus, the brave Athenian who had been sent to slay the terrible beast. Yet now, as he faced the door at the end of this strange and terrifying hallway, he knew he was not Theseus.

He had neither the enchanted ball of thread to help him find his way out, nor the love of Ariadne to give him courage. He was the Minotaur itself.

He was trapped.

With a shuddering breath, he whispered, "The way out is through," and pushed the door open.

Warm light spilled over his eyes. The door opened on a room filled with a dizzying array of clutter. Dozens of pipes jutted out at odd angles, belching thick clouds of steam. Rods of wood and metal had been fashioned into mechanical arms, all of them bent sharply at their joints. Their appendages, which had been fashioned out of rusty springs and clamps, held bows, paddles, and sticks that moved from side to side with a strange—almost absurd—jerking motion. The one holding the bow played a weathered cello. It sawed the strings back and forth, while four smaller arms (made from small brass rods) twisted the tuning knobs clockwise, then counterclockwise.

The sound it produced was nauseating.

Another set of mechanical arms moved a series of thin rubber paddles around the rims of several glass bowls. Each of the bowls, which varied in size, had been half filled with water and produced a wailing hum as the rubber paddle circled its rim. Charlie had once produced a similar effect with his fingertip and a wineglass, but nothing on this scale. He counted eleven bowls in all, and the cumulative sound they made was so loud, he could feel the vibrations in his teeth.

He searched the room for a master power source, but there was none. The mechanical arms were exactly that. Mechanical. Like an old clock, they operated under the power of their own locomotion, helped along by a series of cogs and catches that jerked and rotated with a metronomic tick.

He wiped a slick of sweat from his forehead. The heat was almost unbearable now, and as he searched for a way to turn the machines off, something in the corner of the room caught his eye.

It was a man, crouched low and facing the wall. He was fidgeting and shaking, like a leaf caught in the intake of a vacuum tube, and he seemed to be mumbling something, although, over the sound of the machinery, Charlie couldn't hear what it was.

The man was frail, skin and bones really, and as he shook and quivered, so too did his tangled shock of gray hair. His clothes were old. A century out of date, by the look of them. A stained collar, which Charlie surmised had once been white, stood high against the back of the man's neck. His shoulders, slim and heavily curved, shuddered beneath a brownish moth-eaten frock coat, the tails of which jutted out over his knees. His feet were bare and grimy, and his toenails were long and yellowed.

Before he got any closer, it occurred to Charlie that he might be required to defend himself. He reached for a small length of pipe on a nearby table, careful not to disturb the sheets of rust-colored paper it sat on, and made his approach.

When he was close enough to land a hit, Charlie brandished the pipe and hissed, "Hey!"

The man whirled around on crouched legs and hissed back.

Charlie heard the steely *clang* of the pipe hitting the floor before realizing he'd dropped it.

"Oh, Jesus *Christ* . . ."

The man's eyes burned like a scorched sky, furious and red, his irises clouds of roiling smoke. His cheeks were gaunt and sunken, and his skin was stretched so tightly over his cheekbones, Charlie was certain the smallest amount of movement would force it to snap. His upper lip and chin were covered in badly manicured hair, a wiry and untamed Vandyke that had gone to ruin. His hair—long, graying, and caked with grime—was slicked back over his head and tied off in the back, forming a thin rat's tail.

And his ears . . .

Charlie felt his bowels turn to water.

The man's ears had been melted off his skull. The lobes and cartilage had been sheared away, and the areas where the sockets had once been were now scabbed over, their cavities filled with molten, rubbery flesh that pulsed with an angry heartbeat.

In his right hand, he held an old chisel. Thin strips of pale skin dangled from its rusted tip in loose, bloody ringlets. His sleeve had been rolled up to the elbow, and the underside of his forearm had been flayed wide open. Reluctant, but unable to stop himself, Charlie peered into the gash and saw that the man's bone bore a series of long, jagged scrapes.

That was why he was shaking and fidgeting. He'd been carving away strips of his own bone.

Charlie leapt back, screaming. He turned to run, but he wasn't fast enough. Without warning, the man lunged at him and clapped his hands hard over his temples.

Charlie felt his body go limp. The moldering hands squeezed his head like a vise, and all at once, every memory he'd ever made came crashing into his mind like a thunderous rogue wave. Images of his own life, his own experiences, whipped past his eyes at a dizzying speed like demon-possessed microfiche. Every face he'd ever met, every voice he'd ever heard, spoke at once. Every feeling he'd ever experienced, he now experienced simultaneously. His limbs bobbed and jumped, his eyelids fluttered like hummingbird wings, and as the storm in his head reached its agonizing apex, the man pulled Charlie's face close to his own and smiled. From between his cracked lips spilled three words:

"You opened it . . ."

And then Charlie saw something new. Some place he'd never seen before. It flashed before his eyes in blinding images. Gravestones choked by decades of growth under a gray sky. The dull crunch of a shovel breaking ground.

And then, a sign, ashy and wooden, with two wind-chapped words branded into its grain.

BOLERO HILL

The flashes came quicker now: a circle of ash on the floor; the silhouette of a woman, throwing herself from a cliff; a powerful wind extinguishing the flames of staggered candles; the sound of the chord itself—and a voice, pleading into the shadows, begging for its life. Then, in the center of a room made of what appeared to be black tile, three tall figures sat calmly on square thrones, listening to the voice's pitiful request for salvation with cold indifference.

Charlie staggered backward, releasing his head from the man's grip. "I . . . I know . . . you," he said, breathing heavily between words. "I know . . . who you are . . ."

Ivan Schrader gazed placidly at Charlie, his furious eyes now calm. An eerie emptiness had settled into his horrible features. He raised his flayed arm slowly and reached again for Charlie, but Charlie began to fall.

He fell to the ground, then fell *through* it. He fell through the space beneath the floor, beneath the cold earth. Somewhere where he felt nothing at all, and that was—

"Charlie!"

Frank Critzer's face floated into view. His hair hung limply across his forehead. The scent of sweat and cologne spilled from his dress shirt, which had been loosened at the collar.

"Charlie, you all right?"

Other faces began to take shape. They swam lazily above him, all concerned eyes and furrowed brows. A waiter stood to his left, a sweating pitcher of ice water and a damp napkin clutched in his hands.

Charlie reached up and touched his forehead. Cold water on hot skin. The waiter had been dabbing him.

With a thick grunt, he sat up. Frank lurched forward, bracing his left arm. "Whoa . . . slow down, man. Just rest a bit."

"Did I—" Charlie swallowed. His throat was bone dry. "What happened?"

"You hit the floor like a sack of bricks," Frank said, a relieved smile forming on his face. He took Charlie's chin in his hands and moved his head gently from side to side. "I'm not sure how you managed it, but you've got two pretty nasty welts on your temples.

It looks like somebody took a baseball bat to both sides of your punch bowl there."

"How long was I out?"

"Not sure. Twenty seconds. Maybe thirty."

"It felt like a lot longer than that," Charlie muttered gravely. He planted his palms on the floor and tried to hoist himself to his feet.

"Sit tight," Frank said, placing his hand on his shoulder. "An ambulance is on its way."

Charlie pushed his hand away. "I don't need an ambulance. I need to go home."

Now that he was back in the real world—or, what he assumed was the real world; reality had suddenly taken on a worrying malleability—he came to the conclusion that whatever it was that he'd just experienced, it stood to reason that the others were in danger of experiencing it too. That is, if they hadn't already.

Three phone calls . . .

He groaned. That's why Ana had called him that morning. She was trying to warn him.

His thoughts then turned to Ellie. She was alone at the house. If the same thing happened to her and no one was there . . .

Charlie whimpered and got to his feet. His head swam dizzyingly and he felt his knees start to buckle.

"Charlie," Frank said. "Listen to me. You need to see a doctor. It's not up for debate."

"Just email me those inheritance forms, okay?"

"The ambulance will be here in a minute. I really think you should—"

"Just do it! Okay?"

After a beat, Frank nodded. He watched with trepidation as Charlie stumbled his way across the restaurant, banging his hip on one of the tables and sending a fork clattering to the floor.

The maître d' rushed ahead of him and opened the door.

"Sorry about the all the commotion," Charlie said, and paid no attention to the maître d's response. Whatever it was, it sounded polite enough.

Before he left, he turned around and faced the restaurant. Not because he had any great wish to get one last look at the strange scene he'd just caused or the sea of concerned faces staring back him, but because he had to double-check something.

He had to be certain.

Sure enough, Sam was still sitting in the back corner booth, flashing his bloody smile at him.

TWENTY-FIVE

He made the drive home in fifteen minutes. As he turned onto Wabash Street, Charlie was shocked that he hadn't been pulled over for speeding or reckless driving. He vaguely remembered running two red lights, one of which resulted in a close call with a blue sedan.

Or maybe it was a gray sedan. Either way, Charlie had no trouble remembering the blare of the sedan's horn. His temples were still throbbing painfully.

He keyed his way into the front door and called for Ellie.

The house was quiet. He made his way up to Ellie's room and peeked inside.

Judging by the messy bedspread and the faint smell of pot, she'd been there recently.

"Ellie?"

He made his way back downstairs and checked the living room and the dining room. Both were empty.

Maybe she's in the bathroom, he thought, *and went to the kitchen for a glass of water.*

That's where he found her.

She was on the floor, back pressed up against the cabinets, hugging her knees to her chest. She rocked slowly back and forth, eyes closed and humming to herself.

Charlie rushed to her side and dropped to one knee.

"Ellie, are you all right?"

She stopped rocking and looked up at him. Her cheeks were streaked with dried tears and her lower lip began to tremble.

"Charlie . . . ?"

She released the grip on her knees and pulled her brother into a powerful hug, spilling deep, wrenching sobs into his shoulder.

"It's okay," he said, patting her back. "It's okay, I've got you."

"He . . . he's here, Charlie . . . I saw him . . ."

"I know," he said soothingly. "I saw him, too."

Ellie pulled back. Her face was red and splotchy and her hair clung to her forehead like wet reeds. "You d-did?"

Charlie turned his head from side to side. "He gave me these."

"Oh, my God!" she cried, staring at the welts on his temples. "He did that to you?"

He nodded.

"How did he—?" she said, then paused. "Wait, I don't understand. He grabbed you?"

"Uh-huh."

"Physically?"

"Yeah."

"How?"

"No idea. I'm just lucky I got away. The important thing is, I made it out of there, and I'm going to make sure neither of us ever go back."

Again, his sister looked confused. "Back where?"

"To the room with all the machines. The place where he grabbed me."

"He brought you somewhere?"

"Yeah. He didn't do that to you?"

"No. He was here."

Charlie shot to his feet. "He was in the *house*?"

She gestured to the door leading to the backyard, which Charlie now realized was slightly open. "He's still here."

A rejuvenating anger coursed through Charlie. He pulled a large knife from the cutlery block and gripped the hilt tightly. Last time, the bastard startled him, and Charlie dropped the pipe. That wasn't going to happen this time.

He brandished the knife and gave the air a few deadly swipes.

"Charlie," Ellie said nervously, "don't."

"Just stay here," Charlie said, and flung the back door open. He leapt into the backyard like an action hero, ready to drive a stainless-steel blade deep into the belly of Ivan Schrader.

But there was no Schrader.

There was only the body of his father, hanging from the Grim Tree.

Raymond Remick opened his eyes. Like the man with the bloody teeth, his eyes were clouded over with the milky fog of death. His lips, ballooning with stagnant blood, curled into a clownish grin. He pried them apart, the dry saliva smacking like glue, and waved a cheerful hand. "Hey, kiddo!"

Once again, Charlie dropped his weapon.

PART III

TWENTY-SIX

It had been nearly five days since the terrible phone call, and Renée Toulon was finally beginning to shake that awful feeling.

Hanging the Christmas lights helped, as did the two hot toddies she sucked down to stave off the frigid cold that came off the St. Lawrence River, but even now, now that the lights were strung up around the living room, now that Bing was wishing her days be merry and bright from the old hi-fi she'd inherited from her father, that awful feeling remained, just a little, just enough to push her toward that third toddy.

"I'm sorry to tell you this," the voice on the other line had said, *"but Mr. Remick has passed away."*

She remembered the hurt in the woman's voice when she said it. It was the kind of hurt that comes when death is a surprise. Acute and raw with shock.

She shuffled over to the window and drew up the blinds.

Outside, the wind sent a ribbon of snowflakes dancing up the Boulevard LaSalle. She batted away a few flakes that tried to push their way through her window and sighed.

Through the wall, she heard her father's hi-fi switch from Bing Crosby's "White Christmas" to Frank Sinatra's rendition of "Jingle Bells."

Dashing through the snow, indeed, Renée thought wearily, then looked up at the sky. Flat white, with a soupçon of gray that hinted at the oncoming shroud of night.

She loved Montreal, but the winters were exhausting.

Every now and then she'd dream of moving back to Marseille. She'd only gone back twice since her family moved to Canada when she was a little girl and she missed it dearly, but her life was in Montreal. Her friends were here. Her students were here. Her job was here. And it was a job she loved.

She never entertained the idea of returning to France for long. She'd browse a few sites and look at apartments, and even get as far as the payment screen for an airline ticket, but in the end, she'd always back out. She missed Marseille, but she suspected that she missed the memory of Marseille more. And after all, wasn't that the magic of adulthood? Romanticizing our formative years? She could have grown up anywhere—the town where dancing was outlawed in *Footloose,* for example—and the memory of her childhood would rewrite itself as a halcyon dream.

Her closest brush with moving back home came when she spent her final year of university abroad in England. She shared a room with another French student, Camille Baudin, from Nice, who was so homesick, her constant talk of France seemed to infect Renée's subconscious, and at one point, she actually *did* book a ticket for Marseille.

Her time in Cambridge *not* spent with Camille, however, was much more pleasant. She quite liked the English sense of humor, and the friends she'd made on campus were the lifelong kind. She didn't see them much in person anymore, but they still spoke regularly via video chat.

Renée pictured their faces and grinned.

What would *they* think of the phone call?

Nothing, she thought. *They would say it was just a phone call. A sad phone call, yes, but a perfectly normal one. A man had died. Like people do. And to read anything more into it would just be old Renée putting stock in her ancient French hokum again.*

Her college friends never truly understood Renée's somber respect for the supernatural. They were never rude about it, or even dismissive. On the contrary. Like many good university students, they welcomed differing perspectives with open arms. Renée could remember spending countless nights over drinks endeavoring to persuade them that science and the supernatural were not the opposing forces everyone had convinced themselves they were. The supernatural was, as her grandmother had always called it, "the blind science."

The "cause" lives in the unknown, she would say, *and the "effect" is only visible to those who respect the privacy of the unknowable.*

Was that what caused Raymond's death? The unknowable? And if it did, wasn't Renée partly responsible?

She *had* helped Raymond, after all. She'd assisted in locating the records. She performed the rituals. She summoned the spirits while Raymond looked on, not because she wanted to prove to Raymond she could find the records—she knew she could find them; her grandmother had taught her the craft well—but because . . .

Because . . .

Because you were greedy, she heard her grandmother's voice say. *You knew perfectly well that Schrader's abominations were real, and yet you couldn't resist pulling them out of the shadows and into the light. You couldn't resist the foolish glory in finding what wasn't meant to be found.*

"I did warn him," Renée reasoned out loud. "I told him the records were dangerous, that no good would come from listening to them. That has to count for something."

She paused, waiting for the spectral memory of her grandmother's voice to reply. When she didn't, Renée went to the kitchen, satisfied, and prepared toddy number three. After an initial sip to check the flavor, she bit her lip and stared absently into space.

Okay, yes. She had played a part in Raymond's fate, but Raymond was an adult. He was responsible for his own choices. And if it hadn't been for Renée, Raymond would still be searching for those damn records. He never would have stopped. Because Raymond was a believer. And what was it her grandmother always said about believers?

They will walk through fire just to see the face of God with their own eyes.

Renée sighed and clutched her toddy to warm her hands.

She went back to the window and stared up at the pale sky; the sky that spat snowflakes onto the streets faster than the plows could clear them away. Somewhere nearby, carolers were singing.

"I'm sorry you died, Raymond," she said somberly, letting the icy wind carry her words out to the river. "Wherever you are, I hope you're at peace."

TWENTY-SEVEN

Two thoughts ran through Charlie's mind as the sound of his scream expired along the distant treetops.

The first thought—easier to explain than the second—was that his father looked old. Much older than he would have expected. His hair, which, five years ago, had been a salt-and-pepper mixture of dusty gray and rich brown, was now fully white. The skin on his face no longer had its tanned, rugged, leathery texture. It was now delicate and soft, deeply set by wrinkles in all the expected places, and pale. Very pale.

Except for the yellowing bruises on his temples.

The second thought—much harder to explain than the first— was that his father was dead. And not just dead. Cremated. Expensively so.

And yet here he was, hanging from a tree. Definitively *not* ashes. He swung gently in the wind, shoes four feet above the ground, and waved at his son.

Charlie felt the air leave his lungs. Every nightmare he'd ever had about the Grim Tree paled in comparison to the grisly scene before him.

Reality, which had been teetering on the brink of ruin since the night before, finally came crashing down around him, and Charlie came crashing down with it. He landed on the ground with a dull thud, the wet cold of the midwinter grass soaking into the seat of his jeans.

From his dangling perch, Raymond stared down at his son, his milky eyes drinking in the sight of his boy.

They looked so much alike.

More than he'd ever noticed while he was alive.

A harsh snap of wind whipped across the backyard, and Raymond's body began to turn. He gave the air a swift kick of his shoes, then slowly began turning back the other way. The rope he'd used to kill himself groaned under his weight. It dug itself further into his bulging, purple neck and sent a shock of blue veins up his cheeks. As he spun back into view, he chuckled self-consciously.

"I feel like a piñata."

The faint rumble of thunder rolled across the sky.

Charlie continued to stare up at his father, mouth agape. He hadn't noticed that Ellie was standing beside him.

She was crying.

"How is this—" Charlie said quietly. "It's really you . . ."

"Gonna have to speak up, kiddo," Raymond replied. The rope dug into his vocal cords, compressing his voice. "I'm a top-shelf toy now."

Charlie got to his feet. Ellie held his arm tightly. He didn't know if she was helping him stay upright or keeping *herself* from collapsing.

"I said, it's really you," he repeated, louder this time.

Raymond raised his arms like Beetlejuice and smiled. "In the flesh."

"But . . ." Charlie shook his head. "This isn't possible."

Raymond's smile vanished. "Of course it's possible, and I think you know how." His already cloudy eyes became stormy. "That was a foolish thing, playing those records."

A sudden blast of aggravation shot through Charlie. He took a step forward and pointed an accusing finger at his father. "Don't start with me, Dad. You knew exactly what you were doing when you wrote me that note."

"I was *warning* you," Raymond said, each word squeezed under the strain of the rope. "'*I told you they were real.*' What more did you need?"

"How about an additional fucking sentence? You weren't writing me a telegram, for chrissakes. There was no need to keep it short. You should have specifically said *not* to play them."

"And that would have stopped you?"

Charlie shook his head. He wasn't playing this game. "You

handed me a giant red button with a blinking sign that said 'Don't Push.' You were practically begging me to do it. Why else would the message be so cryptic and short?"

"I thought it would be enough."

Charlie laughed humorlessly. "Don't give me that shit. If you really didn't want me to play them, you would have left me a set of detailed instructions explaining what they truly are and how to handle them carefully."

"I was running out of time," Raymond said. "What would *you* have done?"

"I WOULDN'T HAVE GONE LOOKING FOR THEM IN THE FIRST PLACE, ASSHOLE!"

Raymond fell silent. He had never seen his son scream like that.

"What you should have done was *nothing*," Charlie said, a little quieter now. "Lord knows you were a fucking pro at it."

Raymond's blackened lips drew into a sad frown. His voice was soft, almost inaudible under the light breeze. "I'm sorry, kiddo."

Somewhere nearby, a car sloshed along the road and Charlie couldn't help but wonder what an outside observer would think of this ghoulish tableau.

They wouldn't think anything, of course.

He wasn't totally clear on the rules, but Charlie was fairly certain that only he and Ellie could see their father. To an outside observer, Charlie was simply a strange man yelling at a tree.

And Ana and Dale, of course. They would be able to see him, too.

(Ana!)

He'd completely forgotten about her. He pulled his phone from his pocket to see if she'd tried reaching him again.

Eight missed calls. All of them from Ana Cortez.

She'd sent text messages, too. A lot of them.

The light from his phone spilled across his face, illuminating the bruises on his temples.

Ellie moved closer to get a better look. "Those look really bad,

Charlie." She reached out to touch one of them and he recoiled. "What happened to you?"

It was Raymond who answered.

"You saw him, didn't you?"

Charlie's eyes shot back to his father.

The wind began to pick up. Above them, a blanket of dark clouds rolled in.

From one of the neighboring houses came the faint tinkling of wind chimes.

Raymond's body swayed more regularly now, putting more tension on the tree branch. "Look, the three of us need to talk," he said. The rope around his neck moaned with each slow swing. "I'm sure you've got lots of questions and I'll do my best to answer them. But, in the meantime, I wonder if you'd be kind enough to help me down so we can discuss it inside." He looked down at his dangling feet and sighed. "This isn't a very dignified way to have a conversation."

TWENTY-EIGHT

Two thoughts ran through Ana's mind as she held her phone in her hand.

The first thought—a disagreeable one—was how pathetic she felt. She read the number of attempted calls on her screen.

Eight.

Eight attempted calls to Charlie. Not one of them answered. She didn't even factor in the unanswered text messages. The number was too mortifying to count.

Never in her life had she tried so hard to talk to someone who obviously didn't want to talk to her.

The second thought—more agreeable but also more worrying—was that maybe Charlie had been *unable* to answer her. She'd spent the whole morning trying to tell him about the dead boy she'd spoken to the night before—*Tyler Lawson,* the newscaster's voice said on an endless loop in her head, *fourteen, killed in a hit-and-run accident on his bicycle*—but only now she wondered if she hadn't been lucky. The dead boy might have been dead, but he was harmless. He even seemed to be frightened of her, which Ana found curious, especially considering how fucked up the boy's face was. She could still picture the tattered flesh on his cheek and the bits of asphalt lodged in his skin.

The dead boy was scary, yes, but only after she found out he was dead. Before that, he was just a boy who'd been in a bad accident. Nothing more.

And for that reason, she was lucky.

After all, what if she had run into someone she knew? Someone who was supposed to be dead and wasn't? What would her reaction have been then?

The thought hit her like a thick fist.

Raymond died at the house.

She grabbed her phone and tapped Charlie's name for the ninth time, and for the ninth time, there was no answer. Knowing it was fruitless, she tried Ellie's number again. No dice. Her phone must have never recovered from its accidental toilet bath at El Camino.

She tore the earbuds from her ears.

It was a horrible feeling, being stranded and alone, and more horrible still that she couldn't pull herself out of it.

Even Dale was ignoring her. Not that she blamed him. It was she who bullied him into listening to the records in the first place, and after what had happened (and was still happening), she wouldn't be surprised if he never spoke to her again.

She swiped over to the FAVORITES section of her contacts list.

MAMA CELL sat in the top slot, accompanied by a picture of her mother that was so pixelated, she would have been unrecognizable if not for her trademark aquamarine earrings. She thought about calling her, but before she could make a decision, her mother made it for her.

In her quiet apartment, the Dixie Cups' rendition of "Iko Iko" seemed to scream from her phone's speaker, making her jump. Ana swiped the Call button, dousing the song.

"Hey, Mama."

There was a pause, then her mother spoke.

"You sound stressed."

Ana chuckled dryly. "You got that from two words?"

"Am I wrong?"

She wasn't, of course, but Ana knew that if she confirmed her mother's suspicion, she'd feel duty bound to tell her about what had happened the night before. And if she did that, she'd never hear the end of it.

It wasn't a matter of her mother not believing her. Gloria Cortez would believe every word Ana told her about the records. She'd spent decades receiving an earful about Jesus and astrology and Santería and Los Diablos Danzantes and Epiphany and altars to every kind of saint that had ever been sainted; not only had her mother been primed to believe the supernatural, but for her it was practically a science. The problem was, Gloria Cortez was no Egon Spengler. Ana needed help. *Real* help. Not the kind of help that came from lighting *veladoras* and gripping a faded set of rosary beads.

"I'm fine, Mama."

"If that were true, you would have visited me by now."

"I will come and visit, I promise. I just need a few days to sort some things out."

"What do you mean, 'sort some things out'? What kind of things would a girl your age have to sort out? That sounds like a line from a bad movie."

"Maybe it does, but it's the truth."

"It's not the truth if you're hiding something. Your father would never say what was wrong, either. He'd keep everything locked up until it made him physically ill."

The dull sting of tears bloomed over Ana's eyes.

"I would always tell him, 'A problem shared is a problem halved,' but did he listen? Of course not. He would just sulk and brood and say everything was fine when the one person he *should* have been able to talk to was kept in the dark." Gloria sighed, sending a crackle through the speaker. "Or maybe I simply pushed too hard. Maybe I spent too many years watching my mother write letters to my father and receive nothing back."

Now it was Gloria's eyes that began to burn with oncoming tears. Ana could hear the catch in her voice.

"I suppose he thought he was being gallant. If he didn't write to her, she'd never have to know what prison was like and she wouldn't worry. But she worried anyway. She worried every morning when she opened her eyes and every night when she closed them and every minute in between. And when he finally died in that horrible place, her worry turned to anger . . . and that's how she spent the rest of her life. Angry that he never communicated with her. Angry that he never trusted her to be strong enough to tell her the truth about what was happening to him. I don't want that for us."

"It's not like that, Mama," Ana said quietly. "I do trust you."

"Not enough to tell me what's troubling you."

"I wouldn't know how to begin," Ana replied. "I'm not even sure if there's a word for what's troubling me. But I promise you, when I've figured it out, I'll tell you everything."

"And then you'll come home?"

"Yes, then I'll come home."

"Before Christmas?"

Ana laughed in spite of herself. "I'll do my best."

She said goodbye to her mother, blowing her a kiss, then ended the call.

The truth was, she wanted to go home, but more than that, she wanted to go to the Cuckoo's Nest. She wanted to make sure that Dale was all right; that he hadn't been nabbed by some blood-soaked ghoul in the supermarket or held up in an alleyway by some resurrected goon from the twenties with a tommy gun.

She glanced reluctantly at her windows. What sort of madness was waiting for her out there? Seattle was a big city. How many people had died here? Millions? Tens of millions? How many people had died on her block alone? She probably wouldn't make it ten feet without seeing a walking corpse. And while she suspected most of them would probably just leave her alone like the boy with the bike did, not all who die are harmless. It was this thought that had kept her from going straight to Charlie and Ellie's house hours ago.

No, she would stay put. For the time being, at least. Her cupboards were well stocked with two weeks' worth of food and she'd always been a compulsive hoarder of toilet paper, so she was well prepared.

The thought of food made her stomach growl.

She hadn't eaten since the previous night at El Camino, and even then, her dinner had mostly been liquid. A few handfuls of mixed nuts didn't count.

She walked to the kitchen, debating whether or not she wanted to toast a Pop-Tart or just eat it straight out of the wrapper, and stopped when she heard the sound of running water.

She cast a glance down the hallway toward the bathroom door.

Had she accidentally left the sink running?

She couldn't even remember going to the bathroom.

She made her way down the hallway and slowed as she approached the far end, frowning. A giant water stain bloomed outward over the carpet from beneath the bathroom door. She lifted a foot and grimaced. Her socks were wet. She hated that.

Swearing under her breath, she opened the door and switched on the light.

The floor was completely flooded. Water spilled from the edge of the tub in a thin sheet. The tail of the shower curtain, a blue and gray number that hung along the outside rim of the tub, floated dreamily along the flooded tile floor.

"*Shit,*" Ana hissed, tiptoeing toward the tub.

This much water was going to be a pain in the ass to soak up. She only hoped it hadn't made its way to the apartment below her. Mrs. Rasmussen, her downstairs neighbor, wasn't exactly the type to forgive and forget.

She slid the shower curtain to the side and screamed as the woman in the tub stared up at her through a set of milky, vacant eyes.

The corpse floated weightlessly, almost above the water. Her black, gelatinous hair clung to her head like seaweed, and she was incredibly thin—with skin like soiled tissue paper that stretched itself across her bones. Blue varicose veins crawled up her thighs like earthworms, and the skin around her lips was red and patchy.

She turned her head toward Ana and opened her mouth to speak, but was choked off when a spurt of brown water dribbled from her lips and spilled onto her chin.

"Please . . ." she croaked as water filled her throat. "Please help me. . . ."

Ana turned to run, but her feet slipped on the flooded tile, and before she could register what had happened, she was falling toward the tub. With a thunderous splash, she landed face-first onto the woman. The bones in the corpse's legs cracked like charcoaled wood under Ana's weight, and they both sank beneath the surface of the water.

Ana reemerged, spewing water onto the tiled floor and wiping her hair away from her eyes. She grappled for the shower curtain, hoping against hope that the cheap curtain rings she'd bought at Ikea would bear her weight.

The dead woman rose from the water, her milky eyes wild and round with fear. Bloody tears streamed down her gaunt cheeks.

"Pleeeeease . . ." She grabbed hold of Ana's wrist and squeezed. The flesh on her fingers was spongy and cold. "Please don't leave me alone. . . ."

Ana howled, clawing at the shower curtain like a trapped animal. It was too slick. She reached for the curtain rod, but couldn't free herself from the dead woman's hands. The woman pawed at Ana's skin, shirt, and hair; tried to drag her back down into the water, and for a brief moment succeeded. Ana closed her mouth and thrashed around, spraying brown water all over the white tile that lined the wall. She buried her fists into the dead woman's gut and hoisted herself out of the water. She reached blindly above her, swiping at thin air, and as she began to descend, was able to grab a fistful of dry shower curtain.

She pulled with all her strength and felt the curtain rod sag under her weight. Two of the Ikea rings popped off and landed in the tub, but the curtain was strong enough for Ana to pull herself to her feet. She leapt clumsily from the tub, hitting her shin on the rim, and collapsed onto the floor with a splash.

The dead woman thrashed wildly, sending frothy claps of brown water into the air above her, then lunged over the side of the tub. She grabbed hold of Ana's face with both hands and pulled it toward her own. Her mouth hung open in a silent, desperate wail, baring two rows of small teeth, set crookedly into dark gums.

"Pleeeeease . . ." she sobbed quietly. "Don't leave me alone . . . no one knows I'm here . . ."

Ana, soaked and shaking, pried the dead woman's hands from her face and dragged herself across the flooded floor toward the hallway. She wanted to cry, wanted to scream again, but was too exhausted to do either.

The dead woman reached for Ana, her lifeless eyes pleading, her chapped lips trembling, her long seaweed-like hair clinging to her face. Bloody teardrops fell from her chin into the floodwater, blooming into pale red clouds. Thick saliva fell from her mouth in loose ribbons.

"Please . . . *please* don't leave me by myself . . . no one knows I died here . . ."

Ana turned and crawled clumsily into the hallway, slamming the door behind her.

The dead woman's muffled voice still followed her.

"I didn't mean to frighten you . . . please stay with me . . ."

Ana leaned her head against the door and cried. "I'm sorry . . ." she whispered breathlessly. "I'm so sorry." She got to her feet and stumbled down the hallway, using the wall as leverage. The farther she got from the bathroom door, the softer the woman's voice became, and by the time she turned the corner and entered the living room, she could no longer hear it.

Exhausted and shaking, she doubled over, clutching her stomach. Racking sobs hollowed her throat, straining the muscles in her neck.

Tears streamed across her eyes, blurring her vision. She reached blindly for her phone.

Her hands shook badly, but that didn't matter. Her text message was a simple one.

comingg over

She tapped Send, then collapsed onto her couch and continued to cry until it stopped hurting.

TWENTY-NINE

Two thoughts ran through Dale's mind.

The first thought—clearheaded and practical—was to remember to lock the doors behind him. The lower half of Asterion Avenue was now teeming with Christmas shoppers, and he didn't want to see any customers today. Or Ana. Or Charlie.

The store was dark and it was going to stay that way.

Besides, the darkness meant he couldn't see his reflection in any of the store's mirrors.

The bruises on his temples hurt badly, but they hurt more when he looked at them. He knew they were getting worse. He didn't need to see them to know that.

The second thought, which came to him as he climbed the grand staircase, was: *I'm going to die tonight.*

And so he stepped inside Raymond's old office, closed the door, and waited for that to happen.

THIRTY

Two thoughts ran through Ellie's mind as she sat on the couch with her father.

The first thought—obvious but shocking—was the realization that she was holding her dead father's hand.

The second thought—which she tried desperately to ignore—was that he looked awful. After she and Charlie cut him down from the tree, she offered to run a comb through his hair, but knew the gesture would be about as effective as throwing a water balloon on a house fire.

When he spoke, she did her best to focus on his forehead. His eyes, cloudy like overcreamed coffee, were hard to look at. His lips, blackened and plump with congealed blood, were even harder.

A part of her didn't even want to touch him, but she resisted that urge and continued to hold her father's hand.

It was cold. Colder than she realized skin could be.

She asked if he'd like her to turn up the heat, or light a fire.

"It wouldn't make any difference, honey," he said with a crooked smile.

"But you're freezing."

"Can't feel a thing." He gave his cheek a hard pinch with his free hand. Ellie expected to see his skin go red, but it didn't. It retained its pale, grayish hue. "See? My nerves are as dead as I am."

Ellie scowled. "That's not funny, Daddy."

"True," he said, nodding slowly, "but then, I wasn't ever that funny, was I?"

"Mom thought you were hilarious," she said, and gave his hand a squeeze. "That's what counted."

Raymond broke into a serene smile. "She was a great laugher, your mom. She laughed loud and she laughed often."

A guttural scoff came from the other side of the room.

They turned to see Charlie, sitting with his arms crossed near the windows.

"What was *that* for?" Raymond asked.

"Take a fucking guess."

Raymond drew himself up. "If you've got something to say to me, kiddo, let's hear it."

Ellie shifted uncomfortably. The tension made the air thick. She stood and offered in a cheery voice to make tea.

"Do you . . ." she said, staring warily at Raymond. "That is, *can* you drink tea?"

"I'm not sure," he replied. "Why don't we give it a shot?"

She nodded and left.

While she waited for the kettle to boil, she listened for the sound of voices. She heard none. Either Charlie and Raymond were speaking quietly or they weren't speaking at all. Ellie placed the odds on the latter.

When the tea was ready, she pasted a smile on her face and made her way back to the living room, three steaming mugs in hand.

The tension in the room remained unchanged. Raymond and Charlie stayed silently on opposite sides of the room, avoiding each other's eyes. She handed Charlie his tea first, then returned to her seat next to Raymond. He took the mug with a smile.

"Here goes nothing," he said, and brought the mug to his bloated lips. He took a small, exploratory sip, and swallowed. Immediately, a viscous, squelching sound rose up his throat and the tea spilled back out of his mouth and into the mug.

Ellie did her best to mask the look of disgust on her face, but knew she hadn't been very convincing.

Raymond studied the mug as if it were a transistor radio on the blink. "Huh."

"Did it hurt?" she asked.

"No, but it didn't feel good, either. It was a struggle to swallow. Like I'd forgotten how."

"I suppose you wouldn't need to swallow," she said, deflated. "Not anymore."

"Afraid not."

Ellie sighed. "I guess there was a part of me that hoped you were . . . that what *happened* to you, I mean . . . had been undone."

"I didn't come back to life, honey," he said, placing a hand on her knee. "I'm still dead."

Ellie felt a surge of tears coming. A thick stone had lodged itself in her throat, making it difficult to speak.

She spoke anyway.

"Why did you do it, Daddy?"

He smiled tenderly. "I didn't really have a say in the matter. If I had, I would have chosen a more dignified way to go, believe me."

"Maybe like a fire poker through the face?" Charlie said moodily.

Raymond cocked his head to the side. "Excuse me?"

"That's how your buddy Goodwin went out. Happened right here, during your wake. He came here looking for the records and ended up being dragged across my bedroom floor like something out of a Freddy Krueger movie and thrown over the banister. Skewered his head on Mom's fireplace poker. That dignified enough for you?"

Raymond buried his face in his hands. "Oh my God . . ."

"What do you mean he was thrown?" Ellie said, wiping her tears away. "The police said it was a suicide."

"Nope," Charlie said. "Murdered. And now that I've got these little beauties . . ." He brushed his hair back and revealed the splotchy purple marks on his temples. "I know who did it. And seeing as you and Louis both had the same bruises, I guess my question is . . . how long do I have?"

Raymond stared vacantly into the middle distance, his pearly eyes flushing red. "I don't know. Schrader got me after only a few days. Obviously, Louis was able to last a little longer."

Ellie straightened up. "Schrader?"

Raymond nodded.

"So, he's real? The records really *were* his?"

"Still are," Charlie said pointedly.

"You saw him?"

"With both barrels, I saw him." He pictured Schrader's sunken cheeks, the grimy hair, the wiry goatee, the moth-eaten clothes. And his arm, flayed open with the bone exposed.

"When he grabbed you," Raymond asked him, noting Ellie's unease at the thought that Schrader was not only real, but had the power to grab, "what did you see?"

"I can't remember," Charlie said. "It happened too fast. Like trying to read a billboard at a hundred miles an hour."

This was clearly not the response Raymond was hoping for.

"What about you?" Charlie asked.

Raymond shook his head. "I remember seeing candles, and there was something about a sign, but the rest is a blur."

Like a bolt of lightning, the image of a sign under a gray sky flashed through his mind and disappeared, leaving an impression behind his eyelids.

"There *was* a sign. I do remember that."

"Can you remember what it said?"

It was at this point that Ellie sprang to her feet. "Who gives a shit about a fucking sign?" She paced the room erratically. "What are we gonna do about Schrader?"

"I don't think there's anything we *can* do, honey," Raymond said.

"That Goodwin guy didn't seem to think so," Ellie said, then turned to Charlie. "You said yourself he came here looking for the records, right?"

Charlie nodded.

"So maybe he knew something we didn't. Maybe he knew a way to stop Schrader."

"He did seem to think the records could save him," Charlie conceded.

"He was a desperate man," Raymond said softly. "Desperate and scared. A cornered animal who would have done anything to survive. I wouldn't take anything he said to heart."

Charlie's face went still. He looked upon his father with disgust.

"So you're saying we should just give up; that we should just hand Schrader the rope now and let him hang us, too."

Raymond reached for Ellie's hand and squeezed it tightly. A crimson tear crawled down his bloated cheek. "You were right, Charlie," he said, head bowed. "I should have never gone looking for those damn records in the first place. And I *never* should have left them to you. I was a foolish old man. I *am* a foolish old man."

A bloody teardrop dotted the hardwood at his feet.

"And now I've doomed you both."

THIRTY-ONE

You've reached the Cuckoo's Nest. Our store hours are ten A.M. to eleven P.M., Monday through Friday. Open to midnight on weekends. If you wish to place a record on hold, leave a message."

Ana waited for the beep, then whisper-shouted into her phone. "Dale! If you're there, I need you to pick up, okay?"

Above her, Phil Collins's "Another Day in Paradise" oozed out of the PA system.

She cringed at the idea that Dale might hear the song on the answering machine and think she'd elected to listen to Phil Collins at home, so she quickly added, "I'm at Rite Aid. I had to get out of my apartment. There was this—"

Please don't leave me by myself . . . no one knows I died here . . .

"—this woman. In my apartment . . . or maybe it was *her* apartment before mine . . . I don't know . . . but, Dale, she was *dead*. She was naked and dead and she was in my *bathtub*."

She peered into the neighboring aisle to ensure she was alone. If someone were to overhear the shit she was saying, they'd call for the whitecoats to collect her.

Wouldn't that be a pretty picture? Feet scraping along the linoleum tile as two burly men in antiseptic smocks loaded her into a van destined for the loony bin? Blue-vested Rite Aid employees watching the scene unfold with dropped jaws, tweeting and Instagramming the whole thing?

She lowered her voice and cupped her hand over the receiver. "She was *dead*, Dale. It was horrifying, and so fucking sad. And then there was this boy last night. He was killed in a bicycle accident. It was on the news this morning. And then, when I was on my way here, there was this body on the sidewalk. He turned over and smiled at me. His face was all smashed in, like he'd been hit by a falling piano or something. And now . . ." She lowered her voice to the point where could barely hear herself. ". . . now there's this old man . . ."

She popped her head up like a meerkat and glanced over at the pharmacy. The old man was still sitting there, hand placed gently on the crook of his cane, tweed cap still sitting snugly on his head.

She ducked back down into the aisle. "I went to the pharmacy to see if they could recommend something for anxiety, you know, so I could calm down, but there was this old man sitting there. I asked him if he wanted to go before me and he practically jumped out of his skin when I talked to him. He told me to 'go right ahead,' so I turned to the pharmacist and she was looking at me like I was fucking nuts. She asked me who I was talking to." She bent low and whispered louder. "Who I was *talking* to, Dale."

The rattle of a shopping cart approached. Ana dropped her phone by her hip and pretended to read the instructions on a box of gauze. At the far end of the aisle, a woman breezed by, pushing a shopping cart in front of her. When she was gone, Ana put the phone back to her mouth.

"The old man is fucking dead, Dale, and I'm the only one who can see him. I don't know how he died. I didn't ask. Maybe a heart attack or a diabetic episode or something?" She shook her head. "Doesn't matter. The point is, the records are real. I can see the dead, and I'm pretty sure the rest of you guys can too, so I'm heading over to Raymond's house. I suggest you do the same. Charlie and Ellie are probably there, and . . ." She swallowed. ". . . and Raymond probably is, too. If there's anyone who can tell us how to stop what's going on, it would be him. So please, Dale. Please go there. And if you're already there, then congratulations, you're smarter and braver than me. I hope I'll see you soon."

She was about to hang up, then brought the phone back to her mouth. "I'm really sorry, Dale. For everything." She gazed up at the white speaker embedded into the ceiling tile. "Especially the Phil Collins."

With that, she hung up and made her way to the exit, careful to avoid looking in the direction of the pharmacy.

THIRTY-TWO

There was no mirror in the basement.

That was good. Louis Goodwin had no desire to see his own face.

He'd read (or heard somewhere) that chickens can live several minutes—even hours—after their heads have been cut off. When the fireplace poker went through his head, he remembered feeling it. He remembered the electric jolt behind his eyes, the metallic taste on his tongue. He remembered feeling the pressure of the iron rod on his brain and the pulse of his heartbeat in his teeth.

What he couldn't remember was how it looked when it happened. He was grateful for that.

The poor souls who *did* see it happen would remember it forever, and for that he was sorry.

When he came back—back from wherever he'd been after he died—the living room was no longer filled with the shocked faces of mourners. It was dark, and the mess he'd made from his fall had been cleaned up. Even the refreshments table had been cleared away.

He was alone. In a house that wasn't his.

Living but still dead.

He didn't have to wonder how it happened. He knew how it happened. Someone had played the records.

He strolled quietly through the living room and wondered who'd done it. Raymond's son was the most likely candidate, of course. He was the last person to know where the case was when Louis died.

I dropped it out the window, Louis remembered. *When I saw Schrader in the room.*

He supposed the police could have collected the records as evidence, but it was doubtful they'd played them. Even more doubtful that they'd play all four of them at the same time.

He sat on the davenport and stared out the windows, pondering his new existence. By the time the black Mustang pulled up to the house, it was nearly midnight. He watched Charlie and a dark-haired woman (his girlfriend? his sister?) get out of the car.

If they were the ones who listened to the records, they would be able to see him, and Louis didn't want to be seen. He was embarrassed. He'd inflicted a gruesome death on a houseful of unsuspecting people. Innocent people. Two of them little children!

Raymond's grandchildren, no doubt.

How scared they must have been.

Louis ran a hand across the nightmarish damage to his face. He wasn't going to scare anybody else.

He would stay in Raymond's basement. He would remain alone.

Somewhere in the city, his wife—reanimated once again by the records—was probably searching for him. That was fine. Let her look. He owed Deb nothing now. His survivor's guilt had been cured. All it took was no longer being a survivor himself.

He had earned a little peace and quiet.

He pressed his ear to the basement door and listened to the muffled voices of Raymond and his children on the other side.

It was nice to be around a family. Even if it wasn't his own.

His time was limited. He knew that. Sooner or later, Schrader would come for those who played the records, and once he'd taken them, Louis would return to the nothingness of death, but as long as he was here, he was going to remain in the basement and enjoy his spot on the sidelines.

And so he listened, and smiled, and continued watching the light under the door.

THIRTY-THREE

It was nearly dark by the time the Mercedes pulled up to the Cuckoo's Nest.

Harold Meehan, dressed luminously for a Christmas party he and his husband George were now an hour late to ("We're pushing past fashionably late and entering the zone of rude, Harold," George had said tersely when Harold asked him to make a quick detour), looked up at the store's dark windows and frowned.

"That's weird," he said. He peeked at the clock on the Mercedes' dashboard. "It's only five o'clock."

"I hate that it gets dark this early," George grumbled. He gripped the steering wheel and checked his watch, hoping that somehow the car's dashboard clock was off by an hour. His watch, however, agreed with the Mercedes. It was almost five. "By the time we get there, it'll be nearly six."

Harold wasn't listening. He just continued to stare at the windows, as if doing so might make the lights inside the store magically come on. The neon ribbon that traced the shape of the store's sign was dark, too. "They should be open now," he said, then checked to see if any of the other stores on Asterion Avenue were dark.

They weren't. The Cuckoo's Nest was a shadowy blemish on an otherwise twinkling block of warmly lit windows and breath-fogging, coffee-clutching Christmastime foot traffic.

"Maybe they blew a fuse or something," George offered. "We can come back tomorrow."

Harold gestured at the dark windows. "That won't work. The Tomlinsons' gift is in there. I ordered it a few days ago. Dale promised me it would be here in time."

George grumbled again, although this time Harold couldn't make out any actual words. The Tomlinsons were good friends. Best friends, really—if such a thing existed for adults in their late thirties.

Brad Tomlinson and his wife, Jacquie (Reynolds in the old days; Harold still had trouble thinking of her as Jacquie Tomlinson), had been friends since college.

It had been Jacquie who'd introduced him to George.

And now here he and George were: almost twenty years later and still together. They'd never been a perfect match (what couple was?), but there was a comfort between them that was undeniable. Both Harold and George knew that as you get older, comfort is what counts in the end. They had built a home together and a life together, and even though it wasn't always obvious to third-party observers, they loved each other very much.

George reminded himself of that when he saw the concern in Harold's eyes.

"Honey, I'm sure everything's fine," he said, running his hand along the back of Harold's neck. "They're just closed."

Harold bit his lip, brow furrowed. "I'm just gonna go check that everything's all right."

George resisted the urge to tell him he was overreacting. Harold was clearly worried, and when Harold was worried, it usually meant that there was something to be worried about. His husband had always been a little witchy that way.

"Okay, just please be quick," he said.

Harold promised he would be and opened the passenger door. A blast of wind sailed across the dashboard. George dove for the center console and cranked up the heat.

Harold trotted up to the store's front door and gave the handle a good tug. It didn't budge. Cupping his hands over his eyes, he pressed his face up against the window. There appeared to be a light on at the top of the stairs. Was that the office? He pressed the crescents of his palms harder against the window, forming a seal.

He couldn't tell if the light was coming from the inside of the store or if it was just the ambient streetlight reflecting itself in the glass. He turned back to the car, shrugging, then shuffled back to the curb, shoulders hunched against the wind.

George, happy their momentary detour had reached its conclusion, put the car in drive.

Harold reached for the passenger door but stopped before grabbing the handle.

George checked to see that the car was unlocked. It was. He looked up at Harold, who was staring at the car's window, and laughed. "Did you fall in love with your own reflection?" When Harold didn't respond, he added, "That's how Narcissus met his end, you know!"

Again, Harold didn't respond.

Genuinely aggravated now, George threw the car back into park and got out. "Enough is enough, Harold," he said, glaring at his husband from across the hood. "We're already late enough as it—"

There was something in Harold's hand. It looked like a bit of street garbage.

"What is that?"

Harold rolled the object between the tips of his fingers. "It's a suede tassel," he said. "It fell on the car."

"Well, throw it away!"

"It fell from the sky," Harold said, studying the tassel. It was old, and soft, and soiled by time.

"Harold, I mean it. If we don't leave now, we might as well not go."

But Harold wasn't listening. As he rolled the tassel between his fingertips, a horrifying thought dawned on him. He hopped into the street and stared up at the sky.

No, not the sky.

The roof of the Cuckoo's Nest.

What he saw sent a flash of panic across his eyes.

"George, call 911. Now."

THIRTY-FOUR

The walls of the Remick living room danced under the spell of a crackling fire.

Ellie crumpled up a few sheets of old newspaper and stuffed them under the charred logs. Satisfied that the reinvigorated flames would burn for a while, she slid the grate in front of the fireplace and joined her father over by the bookshelves.

"I always loved this one," Raymond said, handing her a framed photograph of the entire Remick family in front of the Haunted Mansion at Disneyland. In the picture, Joan and the girls made spooky faces while a five-year-old Charlie, sporting a pair of slightly askew Mickey ears, sat on Raymond's shoulders, grinning ear to ear.

"Oh, *God*," Ellie said, smiling. "Charlie made us ride that mansion, like, ten times."

Raymond chuckled. "He was so scared the first time. When the lights went out in the stretching room, he squeezed my hand so tight, I thought he was gonna pulverize my knuckles into dust." He glanced at Charlie, who was sitting on the davenport and staring out the window. "Remember that, kiddo?"

"Yep," Charlie murmured, eyes fixed on the neighbor's house.

Raymond shrugged at Ellie as if to say, *I'm trying*.

Across the street, a garage door opened, and once again the Pearson family spilled out onto the driveway, dressed in their wintry best. Their new dog, the Alaskan malamute, cantered happily across their yard, his nose cutting a path through the snow.

They set off into the night with the malamute leading the front of the pack while their little girl, Candace, brought up the tail end.

An additional shadow cut across the streetlight behind Candace, and Charlie felt himself bolt upright. He leaned forward to get a better look, ready to sound the alarm, then felt his heart sink when he saw what it was.

Limping next to Candace was a badly injured German short-haired pointer.

Bandit, he thought. *Of course.*

The dog's back leg, which had been separated at the hip joint, dragged behind its body like a broken muffler. Its fur was matted with thick blood, and the right side of its head had been caved in.

Charlie scowled. *Fucking delivery truck.*

Lagging behind a little, Candace sped up, calling after her family. Bandit did, too, matching her pace and eagerly hobbling along beside her, not wanting to be left behind.

Even though Candace couldn't feel it, Bandit lifted his shattered snout and licked her hand, a promise that, even in death, he would always stay by her side.

A pair of headlights splashed across the window, pulling Charlie from his reverie, and a car he didn't recognize rolled drunkenly up onto the driveway, almost taking out the mailbox.

"What was that?" Ellie said, turning away from the bookshelf.

Seeing a familiar face emerge from the car, Charlie leapt from the couch and scrambled into the foyer, stopped momentarily to check his reflection in the mirror.

He ran his hands through his hair, but it was pointless. Even if he could tame his wild mane (which he couldn't), his clothes were so rumpled, he looked as if he'd just tumbled out of a hamper.

Five seconds later the doorbell rang, and Raymond looked up. "Are we expecting anyone?"

Charlie opened the door and Ana Cortez flung herself into his arms. Her leather jacket was so cold it felt wet, but he didn't care. He squeezed her tightly then stood back, drinking her in.

Seeing the bruises on his face, she reached up and grazed his cheek with her fingers. He flushed at her touch. "What happened?" she said, frowning. "Are you hurt?"

"It's nothing," Charlie said dismissively. "How are *you* doing?"

At this, Ana's eyes grew cold. "Not good, Charles!" she said, placing her hands firmly on her hips. "Where the fuck have you *been* all day? I called you, like, a hundred times!"

"I know, I'm so sorry. It's been an unbelievably weird fucking day."

Ana pictured the dead woman in her tub; the cold, spongy hands reaching for her. "Wanna compare notes?" she replied flatly.

"Sorry to tell you this, champ . . ." a voice said, and Ana turned. Raymond Remick stood under the archway, smiling guiltily. ". . . but your day's about to get a lot weirder."

Hot tears spilled onto her cheeks. She rushed over to him, seemingly unconcerned with his corpsified appearance, and pulled him into a tight bear hug. She held him for a moment, then pulled away and slapped him across the arm. "And *you*, you miserable old bastard! With all the secrets and the globe-trotting and the museum money. If you would have just *told* me what you were up to, I could have talked you out of it, and then we could have avoided this whole shitshow!"

"I know," Raymond said, eyebrows sagging sheepishly. "I'm sorry you had to find out this way, kiddo."

Charlie felt a momentary pang of jealousy. He liked Ana. *Really* liked her. But "kiddo" was *his* nickname, not hers.

Ana rounded on Ellie, looking like she was going to unload for a third time, but didn't. "You I have no problem with," she said. "You were incommunicado on account of Toilet Phone, so you're in the clear."

Ellie grinned. "If it helps, Charlie *did* want to call you. But today's been one freak show after the other. We've barely had a minute to get our heads straight."

"Let's pull up a few chairs, then," Ana replied. "Maybe by the time we're done trading stories, we'll be singing 'Show Me the Way to Go Home.'"

Charlie, Ellie, and Raymond sat quietly on the couch as Ana told them about the boy on the bicycle, the naked woman in her bathtub, and the man at the pharmacy. When she finished, she exhaled forcefully and slumped into her seat.

Ellie was ashen-faced. "That poor woman . . ."

"I can't get her voice out of my head," Ana said. "She was so alone and so *scared*. She kept saying 'No one knows I'm here.'"

Upon hearing this, Ellie stirred in her seat. "After high school, I moved down to LA for a while," she said. "I didn't know a single person there, and sometimes, at night, I would lie awake and think about what would happen if I died there."

Raymond reached for his daughter's hand. "You never told me that, honey."

"It's not something I think about much anymore, but I thought about it a lot then. I lived alone in a shitty apartment in East Hollywood, and no one really knew me. I'd made a few friends, but they weren't the type of friends that would check up on you if you'd been off the radar for a few days. Most of them didn't even know my address. So, I would lie there at night and wonder how long it would take for anyone to notice I'd died." She gave Raymond's hand a little squeeze. "It wasn't the thought of dying that scared me. It was dying anonymously."

Ana shook her head. Her eyes were heavily lidded, weighed down by guilt. "I should have asked her her name."

"Wendy Blythe."

Charlie held up his phone. On its screen was a badly xeroxed image of an obituary. The headline read MISSING ELEMENTARY SCHOOL TEACHER FOUND DEAD.

Beneath the headline was a black-and-white photograph. The photocopier had all but obliterated her features, but Ana recognized her face immediately.

"That's her."

"'Winifred Blythe,'" Charlie read, "'a third-grade teacher at Manito Elementary School in Spokane, Washington, was found dead in a Seattle apartment. Her body was discovered after a neighbor filed a complaint with the apartment building's superintendent. According to the neighbor, Ms. Blythe's unit, which was rented under the name Jane Carter, had been the source of an unpleasant smell for nearly a week. Once police were notified, they were permitted access into Ms. Blythe's unit, a second-floor walk-up with a street view of Galen Boulevard and North Beach Park.'"

"Yep, that's my apartment," Ana said, nauseated. "Lovely."

Charlie read on. "'The discovery of Ms. Blythe's body put to rest a "missing persons" case that had flummoxed the Spokane Police Department for nearly twenty-three weeks.

"'"It was unlike Wendy to be absent without any heads-up," notes Diana Burgess, Manito Elementary's vice principal and a close personal friend to the deceased. "She was as responsible and dependable as they come." Ms. Blythe was first reported missing last October' . . ." Charlie scrolled back to the top of the article. "This was back in '92."

"Does it really matter when it happened?" Ana said. "It happened."

"At least it was a while ago," Charlie reasoned. "It's not like it happened right before you moved in."

"Since she's literally lying in my bathtub at this very moment, I don't see how any of this applies."

"Does it say anything about *how* she died?" Ellie asked. "Or what she was doing in Seattle if she was supposed to be a teacher from Spokane?"

Charlie continued reading. "'Ms. Blythe, a diabetic, was not married and had no children. Cause of death is unknown, but police have ruled out foul play.'" He scrolled a bit more, then looked up from his phone. "That's basically it. No follow-up articles."

Ana couldn't help but roll her eyes. "That's some crackerjack reporting right there. Why spill any extra ink on a woman who died scared and alone? They've got Mariners games to recap."

"Speaking of alone," Raymond said, "what's going on with Dale? Have you heard from him?"

"Radio silence," Ana replied. "I Ubered to the store to pick up my car, but the windows were dark, so I tried his house. I rang the doorbell a few times. He didn't answer."

"I don't like the sound of that," Raymond said.

"I'm sure he's fine," Ellie said. "Maybe he just went someplace to hide out for a bit. Until this whole thing blows over."

"Not likely," Ana said. "Other than the market and the movie theater, there are only two places Dale ever goes. His house and the store."

Raymond stared gravely at Charlie. "Neither of which protects him from Schrader."

Ana nearly choked. "Ivan Schrader?"

"Yep," Charlie said.

"He's actually real?"

"Actually real, and very pissed off." He gestured to his bruises.

"He *touched* you?" Ana said, more shocked by the idea than frightened. "Where?"

"I just showed you."

"No I mean where *were* you when he touched you?"

Charlie told her about what had happened that morning at Shuckers. The bit about the man with the gun and the bloody smile was gruesome, but wasn't particularly shocking. Not after what she'd seen in her tub. When he got to the part about the corridor of doors and the room full of machinery, she started to tense up.

"That's when I saw him," Charlie said. "He was over in the corner, using a chisel to scrape shards of bone out of his arm."

"God . . ." Ana said queasily. "Why would he do that?"

Over by the fireplace, Raymond stared into the flames, his bloated lips drawn in a thin line. "He was making the records."

The others looked at him.

"We had a study done, me and Louis—" Raymond said, then stopped, suddenly startled by the feeling of a dull thump under his right foot. "I think something just fell over in the basement."

"Stay on track, Dad," Ellie said.

"Sorry. We had a study of the records done at UW. The lab found traces of shellac and beetle shells, both of which are common ingredients in old records, but when the reports also showed traces of blood, dirt, and bone, that raised a few red flags."

Ellie shuddered. "I wonder why."

Ana turned to Charlie, her face all eyes. "How did you get away?"

"Not sure," he said. He tried replaying the event in his head, but like a dream upon waking, the memory was fading fast. "One second, Schrader had me, then the next, I'm back in Shuckers and everyone is looking at me like I was the jester that fainted at the king's coronation."

Ana eyed Raymond's matching bruises. "That's what happened to you too, I'm guessing?"

Raymond nodded somberly.

If there was a hell, he deserved to spend eternity in its deepest circle for getting them involved in this madness.

Ana felt her throat tighten. "And . . . is that what's gonna happen to the rest of us?"

"I'm afraid so, champ."

That was when Ana's phone rang the first time.

THIRTY-FIVE

Do you need to get that?" Charlie asked.

Ana looked at her phone. It was Harold Meehan, no doubt calling to see why the store was closed. She liked Harry, but there was a time for haggling over the price of old jazz 45s, and that time was certainly not now. "It's nothing," she said, stuffing the phone back into her pocket. "So what happens next? Schrader comes for me? Ellie?"

"Yes," Raymond said solemnly. "And Dale, too. If he hasn't already."

"But why? All we did was play the records. Isn't that why he made them? So they can be played?"

"That's a good point," Ellie said. "He succeeded. Why would he care if we played them, too?"

"I have no idea," Raymond said.

Charlie scoffed. "You're the one who *told* us the story, Dad. How can you not know?"

"That's just it," Raymond said. "It's a story. Passed down through the years like a game of telephone. Who knows how many of the details changed over time, or how many were lost entirely? Yes, Schrader is real, and yes, he succeeded in creating the chord, but beyond that, I can't be sure of anything. I didn't even know about the four deaths until I saw the records in person."

Ana blinked. "The what?"

"The four deaths," Raymond said. "They were engraved on the records. Didn't you see them?"

Ana and Ellie shook their heads.

Charlie sighed. The day Frank gave him the records, he had removed one from the case and inspected it. The engraving had been on the back side of the record, the side without the grooves.

It was so faded and timeworn, Charlie figured it was merely a floral embellishment. A maker's mark of some kind.

"I may have noticed something like that," he said, suddenly angry with himself.

Two minutes later, Raymond splayed the records across the coffee table, surveying them like a dealer at a blackjack table. Charlie, Ellie, and Ana looked on from the couch.

"Each record was inscribed with a different type of death," Raymond said, pointing to a series of ornate engravings along the inside edges.

"Looks like writing," Ana observed.

"It's Latin," Raymond said. He reached over to a nearby end table and produced a small pad of paper and a pen. He scribbled down four phrases and tossed the pad over to the others. It landed on the coffee table with a dull *smack.*

The others leaned over and read what he wrote.

> *Mors Naturalis*
> *Mors Accidente*
> *Mors Occidendum*
> *Mors Voluntaria*

"Four records, four types of death."

With his pen, he pointed to the first term: *Mors Naturalis.*

"Natural."

Then to *Mors Accidente.*

"Accidental."

Then to *Mors Occidendum.*

"Murder."

And finally, to *Mors Voluntaria.*

"Suicide."

He gazed up at them, his cloudy eyes unmoving. "Whatever record you played, that's the death you get."

Charlie recognized the third term down. "*Mors Occidendum,*" he said, tapping the paper. "When we played the records, we heard a voice, remember? That's what it said."

Ellie pointed to *Mors Naturalis.* "Mine said that one."

Ana studied the list as if it were a difficult math problem.

"What about you?" Raymond asked her.

"I'm not sure," she replied, a fluttering note of panic in her voice. "I can't remember."

Charlie read the third phrase again, unblinking. Realization had turned to panic and his eyes were suddenly blurry. "*Mors Occidendum* . . . that means—"

"You've been marked for murder, kiddo," Raymond said. His voice was heavy and full. "I'm so sorry."

Before Charlie could stop it, a hot tear burned a path down his cheek. He wiped it away with his sleeve.

Ellie and Ana remained silent.

Having been a lifelong fan of legal procedurals, Ana often wondered how she would react in a courtroom if she'd received the death sentence. Would she remain calm and dignified, or would she freak out, clawing and howling in fear as the bailiff dragged her out?

Now, here she was, handed her very own death sentence, and all she could think about was nothing.

Her mind was a blank. Any thought that tried to rise to the surface immediately burst like a bubble of soap and disappeared back into the cognitive ether. She struggled to remember the simplest things. Things that should have come easy to her. Her mother's face, her favorite rainy-day record, the name of that famous Seattle coffee chain, but there was nothing.

Just an empty void where thoughts used to be.

And then her phone rang a second time.

It was Harold Meehan again.

She refused the call, but before she could place the phone back in her pocket, it rang a third time.

"Jesus fucking Christ, Harry, we're *closed*!" she howled, and stabbed the End Call button with her finger.

Raymond's lips slanted into a weary smile. "Harry Meehan?"

Ana nodded, flustered.

"Guy's desperate as a Catholic on a dry cruise."

"I know this seems like the obvious question to ask," Charlie said, "but can't we just destroy the records?"

Raymond shook his head. "I already tried that."

"Well, maybe you didn't try hard enough."

"I tried breaking them, burning them, melting them, and crushing them. I even tried running them over with my car. Nothing worked."

"Wow," Ana said, eyebrows raised. "What are they made of, vibranium?"

"No, you don't understand," Raymond said. "I *tried* all that stuff. I didn't actually do them. The records wouldn't let me. The second I doused them in gasoline, my ears felt like they were on fire. It hurt so bad I couldn't even light the match. When I put them in the oven, my ears felt like they were melting before I even turned the knob. Every method of destruction I thought of trying, my ears would mirror it."

Ana considered this for a moment, then said, "It's a safeguard."

The others stared at her.

"Schrader somehow made it so the records can't be destroyed. I don't know how . . . magic, for all I know." She turned to Raymond. "Did you find out anything else from the tests at UDub? When the records were made? Or where?"

"They couldn't give me an exact date, but they placed the records' origin somewhere around the beginning of the twentieth century."

"Which keeps in line with the legend," Charlie said.

"They also pointed out a few witness marks Schrader must have left when he was making them, as well as traces of soil in the grooves that are indigenous to North America."

"Also confirming the legend," Charlie said. "The townspeople shipped the records to different corners of the world, but Schrader supposedly made them here."

Ana's phone rang again. She growled, silencing it. "Where *did* you find them?" she asked Raymond. "There were all those plane-ticket stubs in your office."

"I found the first one in Marrakesh," Raymond replied. "The others were in Cairo, Portugal, and Romania."

Charlie smirked. "Guess those townspeople kind of biffed with the whole 'different corners of the world' thing, huh?"

"There's no telling how many times the records were found and relocated since Schrader originally created them," Raymond said.

"You became quite the world traveler, Dad," Ellie said. "The food alone must have been amazing."

"They weren't exactly vacation hot spots, honey. And I wasn't what you would call a welcome presence. Finding someone who'd even *heard* of the records was difficult enough. Getting them to talk was a different ball game entirely. And that was if they knew any English. If they didn't, I was shit out of luck."

"I was in Romania for two months before I found a guy who both knew English and knew the supposed location for one of the records. I offered him ten thousand dollars to take me, and he turned it down."

"Too dangerous?" Ana asked.

"Too scary. According to him, the record was supposed to be in a cave somewhere deep in the Hoia Forest. I knew I couldn't navigate it on my own, but the locals were too scared of the forest to go anywhere near it."

"What do they think's in there, Cthulhu?"

"Some believe the forest is an entrance to hell. Others believe anyone who steps foot there is cursed with an ancient evil that will be passed down through your family like a virus. There was even one woman who said she'd seen an image of the devil in the bark of a tree. He was pissing blood and grinning, and the blood poured from the trunk like sap."

"Sounds like a nice place," Ellie said, frowning.

"So how did you finally convince him to take you?" Charlie asked.

"I didn't," Raymond said. "I never even made it to the forest. I found the record in a small market nearby. An old man was using it as part of a display for a vintage phonograph."

Ana stared at him unblinkingly. "You're shitting me."

"Not even a little bit."

"It was just sitting in a shop? Where anyone could take it?"

Raymond nodded.

"Jesus," Charlie said soberly. "That's like using the Staff of Ra as a walking stick."

"I offered the guy five hundred bucks for the record," Raymond said, "but the only way he'd sell it to me is if I bought the phonograph, too. So, a thousand bucks later, I had the fourth record in hand and was winging my way back home."

"But how did you come up with Romania in the first place?" Ana asked. "Or Egypt? Or the other places? Did you just throw a dart at a globe and get lucky?"

"I have a friend. A college professor in Canada. I met her selling records on eBay a few years ago. She specializes in this kind of stuff."

Charlie narrowed his eyes. "And by 'stuff,' you mean . . ."

Raymond paused, then said, "She has a way of finding things that can't be found."

"You didn't do anything illegal, did you?" Ellie asked warily.

"No, sweetie. Renée is part of a long line of . . ." He hesitated, trying to find the right words. ". . . people who trade in the mystical arts."

Ellie was delighted. "Like witchcraft?"

"Kind of. Her family descends from the Cathars."

"And Cathars were witches?" Charlie asked.

"No," Ellie said flatly.

"Okay, maybe it wasn't the Cathars," Raymond said, "but her family comes from a long line of mystics. That's how she knew how to perform the rituals."

The others stared at him, amused. Even Charlie.

"It's not like it was an exact science," Raymond said sheepishly. "Renée misfired a few times, but eventually she hit the nail on the head, and that's how I found the records."

Charlie laughed dryly. "Sure, Dad."

Raymond turned and faced his son, annoyed. "Charlie, last night you played a cursed record and now you're sitting here talking to your dead father. You're telling me French magic is where you draw the line?"

Once again, Ana's phone interrupted the proceedings. Only this time, it beeped with an incoming text message. She swore loudly and ripped it from her pocket, vowing to everyone in the room that if she survived this whole Schrader ordeal, Harold Meehan would be banned from the Cuckoo's Nest for life.

As she read the text message, her face drained of color.

"We need to get to the store. Right now."

THIRTY-SIX

Jake Quigley's day was full of unexpected things.

For starters, he hadn't expected to find his sixteen-year-old daughter sneaking back into his house at nine o'clock that morning. She'd only recently started dating, and he had hoped her days of shimmying up the drainpipe and unlatching her bedroom window before sunup were still a few years ahead of her.

He also hadn't expected to find a foot of snow in his driveway. The blizzard had tired itself out before the sun came up, but living out near Snoqualmie Pass—while beautiful—certainly had its drawbacks. It took him forty-five minutes to shovel away the tightly packed powder on his driveway, and another fifteen minutes to excavate his police cruiser.

He also hadn't expected to spill coffee all over his uniform that afternoon (staining his crisply pressed shirt with what looked like dried baby diarrhea), nor had he expected to find his eight-year-old son's retainer in his jacket pocket; and he certainly hadn't planned on writing Father Wyatt a speeding ticket at the corner of Barham and Maine. Normally he let the early-morning speedsters off with a warning, but Father Wyatt was doing sixty-five in a thirty. No one got away with that. Not even a man of the cloth. The priest took it well, pocketing the ticket with a smile, but as Jake pulled back onto the road and trundled slowly down Barham Avenue, he said a few Hail Marys just to be on the safe side.

And then he said a few more.

Seattle was a big city, and in big cities, the spattered blood comes more regularly than it does in smaller towns. When he was still cutting his teeth as a deputy in Wenatchee, he could go six months without seeing blood, and when he did, it was often the result of a hunting accident or an unfortunate run-in with a table saw.

When he got the transfer to Seattle, he expected things to get a bit grislier. True, compared to other big cities, Seattle was a fairly well-behaved metropolis, but big cities bring the big bleeding, and during his ten years on the force, he'd seen some pretty heavy stuff.

And yet, he'd always been able to sleep at night. Up until that week.

He'd been the first officer on the scene at the big brown house on Wabash Street. As he approached the front door, he had to side-step a middle-aged woman who'd burst onto the front steps and emptied the contents of her stomach.

When he went inside and saw what had happened, he was surprised that more of them hadn't puked.

The way the Goodwin fellow's face looked with the fireplace poker running through it had haunted his dreams every night since he'd seen it.

Human faces are supposed to look a certain way. When the mouth opens, it opens on the hinge of the jaw. The eyes are supposed to move in unison, blink in unison, and, traditionally, sit symmetrically in their sockets.

As he strung up the yellow tape, all he could think about was how wrong Goodwin's face looked.

It was incorrect.

The mouth, pried open by fire-blackened iron, sat distended in a ghoulish yawn, the jaw knocked to the left by the force of the blow it had taken on impact. The eyes bulged like bubbles ready to pop. The pupils stared in opposite directions, as if Foghorn Leghorn had taken a giant mallet to the side of Goodwin's head, knocking the irises out of place.

In his ten years on the force, Jake had been no stranger to carnage, both physical and emotional, but there was something about Goodwin's face that frightened him.

It frightened him badly.

His captain offered him a few weeks' paid leave, but he turned it down. After all, seeing the things most people shouldn't see was part of the job.

And besides, what were the odds he'd see another violent death again so soon?

Jake Quigley's day was full of unexpected things. And when darkness fell, and the day gave way to the first blushes of night, he was sitting in his cruiser at the northern end of Asterion Avenue, choking down a dry Cajun sandwich, when his radio crackled to life and a voice said two words.

"Jumper up."

Jake set down his sandwich and got out his notepad, but had no need to jot down the address.

He knew the place. He'd gone there a year ago looking for a John Prine record for his brother's birthday.

It was only half a mile away.

With a practiced flick of his wrist, he switched on his lights and his siren, reported officer responding, and made his way down to the Cuckoo's Nest.

THIRTY-SEVEN

Bright phantoms of red and blue skated along the wet pavement next to the Cuckoo's Nest. Concerned murmurs and horrified voices swirled through the air, and as Jake Quigley asked the crowd to "stand back and give us some room" for what seemed like the hundredth time, his stomach lurched with the notion that Louis Goodwin's mangled face wasn't the only gruesome thing he was going to see this week.

Crowd control was one of Jake's least favorite aspects of the job. In cases like this, where there was a possible jumper, it was difficult to keep their attention directed at him for more than a few seconds at a time. Barking orders like "Stand back" and "Give us some room" did a good job of drawing their eyes back to the ground for a second or two, but like a spectacular fireworks show, the story was in the sky, and that's where the eyes wanted to be.

That's all this is, Jake thought. *A fireworks show.* Eyes to the sky. Mouths open. Faces bathed in bright, swirling colors.

Jake's shoulder-mounted walkie-talkie crackled to life. It was dispatch. The crisis negotiator was two minutes away.

Beverly Reese had been with the force almost a year now. She was brought up from Portland on a recommendation from the precinct's previous CN, Richard Hayes, now retired. She was younger than most CNs Jake had met, but crisis negotiation didn't hinge on the negotiator's age, it hinged on their ability to empathize and to adapt, and Beverly had earned her stripes after defusing a hostage situation in Portland that was, by anyone's estimation, headed for certain disaster.

Jake once asked her which scenario was easier to talk her way through: suicide or hostage situation. He never forgot her answer.

"Despair is a fingerprint," she said. "From a distance, it all looks the same. But up close, no two cases are alike. The one common factor is hope. And hope, once lost, is harder to get back than trust. All I can do is try to find their particular cocktail of hope and pour them a big enough glass to avoid disaster."

Jake wondered what the man standing on the top of the record store's cocktail of hope was.

He'd been up there nearly twenty minutes already, according to the guy who called it in, and by the look of it, he had no interest in moving any time soon, either toward life or death. He just stood there, staring out into the darkness over Salmon Bay, the fringe of his vest dancing in the breeze. Jake supposed it was a good thing the breeze was so soft. The jumper was standing so close to the edge, the toes of his shoes were visible from the ground. If the wind had been any stronger, it might have made his decision for him.

To his left, a panicked voice spoke to one of the other officers.

"Yes, his name is Dale. I'm not sure what his last name is, but he's an employee of this store."

"And your name is?"

"Harold Meehan."

"Do you know the owner, Harold?"

"Yes. Or, actually . . . no. The owner died recently."

"How recently?"

"A few days. Maybe a week. I'm not sure."

"Now, the man on the roof; you said you know him?"

"Yes."

"Is he a friend of yours?"

"Not really a friend," Harold said, feeling guilty for saying so, especially considering Dale's current predicament. He looked up and strained his eyes, almost as if to send Dale a telepathic apology. "But I'm a regular at this store. I've talked to him a million times. He's a really sweet guy."

"Does he have any family we can notify? Anyone that might be able to give us any information that can help us?"

"I'm not sure. He's from England, so I don't know." Harold looked up again. Dale still hadn't moved. "Why isn't anyone talking to him? Aren't you guys supposed to have someone here trying to talk him down or something?"

"They're on their way, sir," the officer said, then asked, "Is he married?"

Harold suspected the questions were performing double duty: to extract and distract. He wasn't sure either was working. "I don't know."

"Girlfriend? Boyfriend? Someone he's seeing?"

"I don't know! I tried calling one of his coworkers, but she hasn't responded!"

"What's the coworker's name?"

"Ana," Harold murmured, suddenly on the verge of tears. "I don't know her last name, either."

The wind picked up a bit, nothing forceful enough to knock Dale from his death-defying perch, but cold enough now that Harold turned his collar up to stop his neck from freezing.

He turned to George and took his hand and gave it a short, reassuring squeeze.

"You all right, sweetheart?"

George didn't reply. The spinning red and blue lights whisked across the whites of his eyes over and over again, like some endlessly spinning zoetrope.

It was unsettling to see his husband's face, usually so steely and composed—infuriatingly so, on occasion—reduced to a mask of vacant shock. George Meehan was a tree that no wind shook, and tonight, he'd been shaken.

The officer cleared his throat. "Mr. Meehan, if you wouldn't mind . . ."

Harold's face snapped back into position. "Yes. Sorry."

"You said one of his coworkers' name was Ana?"

"Yes. Are you sure someone's coming to help?"

"As I said, they're on their way."

Harold rolled his eyes. "No rush."

The officer's face tightened. "I'm sorry?"

Harold was about to apologize for his snark, but a voice from the crowd cut him off.

"Someone's up there with him!"

Harold's eyes shot up. The officer's did, too.

Murmurs in the crowd rose like a wave.

"Look, he's talking to someone!" Harold cried, pointing. "Is the negotiator up there with him?"

Jake Quigley weaved his way through the onlookers, eyes locked on the rooftop. He squeezed his shoulder-mounted walkie and spoke as quietly as he could.

"This is Quigley. Is Bev Reese here? I didn't see her pull up."

"Eight blocks away," a crackly voice replied.

Shit.

Someone was on the roof with the jumper.

How was that possible? Four officers had been stationed on the sidewalk in front of the store and two were around back.

No one could have gotten in there without them knowing.

Which meant that either the potential jumper was talking to himself, or someone had been hiding inside the store since the 911 call had been placed.

Jake grabbed his shoulder-mounted walkie. "We need eyes on the roof. Now."

THIRTY-EIGHT

Slow down, Charlie!"

The blare of the Mazda's horn was still audible as Charlie prepared to plow through another stoplight. He checked his rearview mirror to see that his close call was okay. The Mazda had skidded to a stop in the middle of the intersection. As it faded into the distance, he thought he could make out the image of a middle finger being thrown his way.

Totally justified.

The next intersection appeared clear. Charlie plunged his foot onto the gas pedal and sailed through the red light.

"Charlie, come on. Slow down."

"If Dale jumps, it's on us."

"I know that."

It was a knee-jerk reply, but as the dust settled onto her words, Ana knew they were true. They had pushed Dale into listening to the records. Whatever happened to him next was their fault.

Up ahead, a green light switched to yellow, then to red. She leaned forward to see if any cars were in danger of crossing their path. There was only one: a small sedan with a thin crust of snow on its hood. If they punched it, they would beat the sedan to the intersection with a second or two to spare.

She checked her watch. How long had Dale been up on the roof before she finally answered Harold's text message? If he jumped, she'd not only be responsible for his death, she'd also never be able to look Harold in the eye again.

Feeling her guilt stacking up, she said, "Go faster."

Charlie complied.

The rental's engine roared, and Ana watched the driver of the sedan's eyes go wide as they flew by. Up ahead, the street was clear, and Charlie ate up every inch of road before hanging a right on North Thirty-Ninth Street.

"Fuck!"

Charlie laid on the horn and screeched to a stop. His and Ana's heads both lurched forward then bounced back.

A sea of red brake lights lay ahead of them.

They searched for a way to get around the jam, but the street was packed. Charlie flirted momentarily with running the car up onto the sidewalk, but there were too many pedestrians.

"What the hell . . . ?"

"Look," Ana said, pointing to a wash of swirling lights ahead of them. "The police are diverting traffic."

"We're still about a half a mile away. We don't have time for this." Charlie ducked his head and peered through the passenger-side window. "I need to find a place to ditch the car."

Ana pulled out her phone, tapped a name in her contacts list, then placed the phone on speaker. After a single ring, a voice answered.

"Ana? Jesus Christ, where are you?" Harold Meehan sounded out of breath.

"Half a mile away, but the traffic's jammed up. What's happening?"

"The police negotiator finally got here, but there's someone else up on the roof with Dale."

Charlie and Ana looked at each other. "A cop?"

"I don't think so," Harold said, then got quiet as he seemed to be speaking to someone nearby. When his voice returned full-force, he was reciting what he'd just heard. "They sent cops up to the neighboring rooftops to see who was up there with him, but—"

Harold went quiet again. Another voice spoke, but it was too far away from Harold's phone to be distinct.

"But *what,* Harry?" Ana said.

"Sorry," Harold said, returning. "They're saying no one else is up there. That he's alone. But he was talking to someone, Ana, I swear. I saw it with my own eyes. We all did."

Ana gazed knowingly at Charlie. "Schrader."

"Who?" Harold said loudly.

"Nothing. Is the negotiator up there with him now?"

"Not yet. Since there's no one else inside, the fire department is breaking the door down."

This sent a twinge of sadness into Ana's gut. The Cuckoo's Nest had become a fifth appendage, a part of her identity, a favorite T-shirt that refused to give up—and now it was surrounded by police tape and flashing lights, and firefighters were breaking the doors in. Crowds were gathering under its darkened neon sign, not because they were there to rake through the stacks or buy the latest Chromatics album, but because there was a man on the roof threatening to jump.

A man she knew. A man she had come to love as family.

"Can you see him, Harry?" she said, tears welling in her eyes. "What's he doing?"

"No," Harold replied, breathing heavily. "He was standing near the edge for a while, but he stepped back and now we can't see him."

"What are the police saying?"

"Nothing, really. They're just trying to keep the crowd back far enough so that—" Harold cut himself off, but Ana knew what he was going to say.

—so that when he jumps, people won't see him hit the ground.

Even though he didn't need to, it was decent of Harold to censor himself. Ana loved him for that.

"Look," she said, pointing to a darkened alley. "Can you make that?"

"I'll have to run up onto the curb," Charlie said. "Do you see any parking meters?"

"No, you're clear."

Up in the sky, a helicopter with KING-5 emblazoned on the hull floated above them, its rotors cutting through the frosty night air with a guttural *chocka chocka chocka . . .*

"Harold?" Ana said into her phone. "Keep talking to me, okay? What's going on?"

"The firefighters just broke through," Harold replied, followed by a rash of static swishes. He was moving through the crowd. "A few cops just went in."

"Did the negotiator go with them?"

"I think so. She had a different kind of police jacket on."

"Okay, good," Ana said. "That's good."

Charlie gripped the steering wheel with both hands. "Ana, I'm gonna hop the curb. Hold on."

"*Wait, what?*"

The voice came from neither of them. They looked down at Ana's phone.

"Harry, what happened?"

Commotion spilled through the phone's tiny speaker.

"Harry!"

"They can't get up to the roof," Harold said. "Dale barricaded the door."

A heavy shadow passed over Ana's face. "He's gonna jump." She reached for the door handle, then looked back. Her eyes asked the question before her mouth could, and Charlie said, "Go."

She went off like a shot, sprinting down the sidewalk and disappearing around the corner.

Charlie gauged the distance between the curb and the alleyway. It couldn't have been more than ten feet.

Keeping his eyes peeled for pedestrians, he gunned the engine.

Ana's lungs burned in protest. She ran full-tilt for nearly half a mile before pausing to catch her breath. She bent low and coughed uncontrollably, promising herself that when all this was over—if she survived—she would run through North Beach Park every morning, rain or shine.

Harold, still on speaker, heard her hitched breathing. "Ana, are you okay?"

"Fine," she said, pawing at a stitch in her side, "what's happening now?"

"I'm not sure. I can't tell if they're up on the roof yet or not. It's hard to see from down here."

"Okay . . . keep . . . me updated . . ."

Ana's heart hammered her rib cage. Her face was flushed and her entire body was coated in a thin layer of icy sweat. She sucked in a deep gulp of air, then another, then broke back into a full sprint.

She was still a quarter of a mile from the waterfront. Her heart continued to thud a stomping beat, not only in her chest, but in her ears. Every muscle in her body cried out in agony, pleading with her to collapse, to give up, but that wasn't an option. She bent low, reducing drag, and rounded the corner onto Asterion Avenue.

She saw the flashing lights at the bottom of the hill.

Only four more blocks.

"Something's happening," Harold's voice said, and Ana lifted her phone to her mouth. It was as heavy as a brick.

"Wha—what is it?"

"I think the firemen got through. I think they're up on the roof."

"How do you know?"

"I heard one of the policemen's radios, and—OH, JESUS!"

Through the small speaker on her phone, she heard a collective gasp, followed by a chorus of screams and stolen breath.

After that, all she heard was the percussive slap of her shoes on wet pavement.

"Harry?"

Ana held her phone to her ear.

"*Harry!*"

No response. Just the low hiss of wind passing over the speaker. If her heart was still beating, she could no longer feel it.

It took nearly thirty seconds for Harold Meehan to regain control of his vocal cords, and when he said Ana's name, it went unheard.

Her phone was stuffed into her back pocket, and she was running.

MOVE!"

Heads whipped around. Faces were wrung out. Hands covered mouths. Ana pushed her way through all of it. Adrenaline coursed through her system. She wasn't even sure she was breathing.

"Get out of the way!" she wheezed. "I work here!"

The crowd cut a path and let Ana pass.

She ducked beneath a line of yellow police tape and zigzagged her way through a dizzying patchwork of flashing squad cars. A policeman tried to stop her, to warn her that it wasn't a pretty sight, but she slapped his hands away and stumbled onto the sidewalk.

A small cluster of police officers and firefighters stood in a semicircle in front of the Cuckoo's Nest's battered door. The way their heads were bowed low made Ana wonder briefly if they were praying.

No, she thought. *Not praying.*

They were looking at something on the ground.

One of the firefighters broke formation when he saw her coming. He held his hand up and said something, but she didn't hear him.

She heard nothing now.

Dale Cernin lay facedown, nose burrowed into the pavement. His eyeglass lenses lay on either side of his head, shattered into a mosaic pattern. His neck was compressed like a set of accordion bellows.

Ana tried to scream, but her lungs were like sandpaper, and whatever noise she did make in that moment, it did not contain words.

She staggered backward and felt her knees give out.

As she fell, she caught a glimpse of the bruises on Dale's temples just before everything went black.

"Is that what you did to Dale?"

"What do you want from us?"

"Stay away from me!"

"STAY THE FUCK AWAY FROM ME!"

THIRTY-NINE

W ake up, honey."

Ellie's hair clung to her cheeks and her pillowcase was soaked with sweat. Raymond grabbed her ankle and shook it.

"Ellie, wake up."

Her eyes shot open. A slurred scream spilled from her lips as she searched the room, eyes wide, and clawed at her bedsheets. It wasn't until Raymond switched on a lamp that Ellie began to realize she was awake.

He sat down gingerly at the foot of her bed. "Are you all right, sweetheart? You were screaming."

Ellie buried her face in her hands. Her cheeks were red hot. "It . . . it was just a dream. A bad dream."

"Do you remember what it was about?"

Ellie shook her head. Her hands were trembling. "I got tired of waiting to hear from Charlie and Ana, so I smoked a joint and lay down for a minute. I didn't mean to fall asleep."

Raymond sighed knowingly. "Indica?"

"It's all I had on me."

"That's nightmare fuel for us Remicks."

"You're tellin' me," Ellie said. Her heart was still pounding. "Are they back yet?"

"Not yet."

She fell back onto her pillows with a dull thump. "I feel so useless waiting here at the house. I wish I could help."

"That's actually why I came up here," Raymond said. "I could use some."

T he light was already on in Raymond's study. A laptop sat perched on his desk, and Ellie saw her reflection in the monitor as she entered the room. FaceTime was open.

"I need to make a call," Raymond said, pulling the chair out from the desk. "But the person I'm calling hasn't played the records, so he won't be able to see me. I need you to be my voice."

Ellie took a seat in front of the laptop. "Who is it?"

"Renée Toulon."

"The professor from Montreal?"

"Exactly. Tell her that I'm next to you, and that I need her help."

"And she'll believe that? That you're next to me?"

"She will."

He placed the call. The FaceTime app rang three times, glitched for a brief second, then connected.

Renée Toulon sat in a wood-paneled room. A fifties-style fan blew in one corner. Palm fronds hung in the other. Her eyes, which were initially wide with shock, relaxed. She spoke softly in a lilting French accent Ellie found instantly soothing. "Oh . . . I'm sorry, miss. I was expecting to see someone else."

"Hello, Miss Toulon," Ellie said. "My name is Eleanor Remick, I'm Raymond Remick's daughter."

Renée's eyes fell. "Yes, of course you are. Please, allow me to express my most sincere condolences regarding your father's—"

"Tell her it's fine," Raymond said. "She doesn't have to do all that."

"I'm not gonna tell her that," Ellie whispered from the side of her mouth. "She's being nice."

Renée tilted her ear to the screen. "I'm sorry?"

"I hope this isn't an inconvenient time, Miss Toulon."

"Renée, if you please. No need for formalities."

Ellie nodded. "You see, the thing is . . . I . . ." She stopped, then started again. "The reason I'm calling—"

"Just tell her," Raymond said. "She'll believe you, I promise."

"She's gonna think I'm crazy!"

"Just say it."

Before she could, Renée leaned forward and stared knowingly at the screen. "Raymond?"

Raymond elbowed his daughter's arm. "Told you."

Renée's face was hard, but not unkind. She gazed intently at the air over Ellie's shoulder. "How did it happen? Murder? Accidental death?"

"Suicide," Ellie replied, stunned that Renée had not only guessed what was going on, but was clearly unfazed by it. "He hung himself from a tree in the backyard."

"*Hanged,*" Raymond corrected her, and Ellie shooshed him.

Renée closed her eyes. "Mon Dieu, Raymond."

"It wasn't my choice, Ren," Raymond said. "I would have happily taken a stroke or an aneurism or a bottle of pills and saved my kids the shitshow of having to look at this face." He turned to Ellie. "Tell her what I said."

Ellie did her best to recite her father's words.

Renée listened, fingers interlocked in front of her lips. When Ellie finished, Renée sat back in her chair and said, "I'm sorry to hear it. I tried calling him about a week ago. When he didn't answer, I called the record store. A girl answered and told me the news. Was that you?"

Ellie shook her head.

Ana, Raymond thought guiltily.

He'd been so preoccupied with how his death had affected his children, he hadn't even considered how it must have affected her. Dale, too.

"I never should have gone looking for those records, Ren," he said solemnly. "I should have listened to you. I'm sorry I didn't."

Ellie relayed his words.

"It's in our nature to search for that which destroys us," Renée said plainly. "Ever since Prometheus showed us how to make fire, we seem to be intent on burning ourselves. You are not alone in this, Raymond."

"I wish I was. Now my kids are tangled up in this shit and I don't know what to do."

Ellie felt a slight snag in her throat as she repeated this part.

"I'm sorry to hear that, Miss Eleanor," Renée said softly. "When did you listen to them?"

"Two days ago."

"Ask your father if he knows of any sort of timeline. Between listening to the records and . . ." Renée's brow furrowed. ". . . what comes after."

"Not that he knows," Ellie said, relaying Raymond's response. "He lasted three days. Goodwin lasted longer."

Renée's eyebrows shot up. "Louis Goodwin? The man from the museum?"

Ellie nodded. "He broke into the house to steal the records, but Schrader got him before he could."

"I see. . . ."

"Can you think of any reason why Louis would have wanted them?"

"My guess is he wanted to destroy them."

Raymond shook his head.

"I don't think so," Ellie replied. "Dad said they can't be destroyed."

"No," Renée said, rocking back and forth as she contemplated this. "No, I wouldn't think so. The records contain tremendous power; enough power to open a gate between the realm of the living and the realm of the dead. Destroying them could mean destroying the power they contain, and that could have serious consequences."

"What kind of consequences?"

"It's difficult to say, Miss Eleanor. The fabric between realities is delicate. To create a gateway between realms, the fabric must be torn. And if the fabric is torn, it becomes volatile. It must be monitored . . . looked after. Even guarded."

"You're saying Schrader is guarding the gate?"

"Perhaps."

"Why would he do that?"

"A gate has two purposes. It both opens *and* closes. Guarding it ensures it doesn't remain open too long."

"What happens if it does?"

"As I said, the fabric between realities is delicate. The longer the gateway is open, the more unstable the fabric between realities becomes. If kept open *too* long, the fabric could dissolve, and the dead will exist in our realm permanently."

"But would that be so bad?" Ellie asked, gazing up at her father. Sure, his appearance was less than ideal, but it was certainly better than visiting a gravestone and throwing a flower down on the grass.

"It is an abomination of nature," Renée replied soberly. "To sentence billions of souls to an eternity of aimlessly walking the earth, trapped in their former consciousness, would be the ultimate cruelty, Miss Eleanor. These souls have earned their passage to the other side. Permanently rescinding that passage would not be viewed favorably by the dead."

"And destroying the records would do that?" Ellie asked.

"I cannot be certain of that," Renée replied. "Destroying them may have the opposite effect and close the gate permanently. There's no way to know for sure without trying."

"Which can't be done," Raymond said.

Ellie echoed her father's response.

"Perhaps Mr. Goodwin wasn't trying to destroy the records at all," Renée offered. "Perhaps he was trying to return them to their owner."

"You're saying Schrader wants the records back?"

"It's possible."

Ellie laughed humorlessly. "He's welcome to them."

"He may be unable to collect them himself," Renée replied. "In which case . . ." She gestured to Ellie through the screen. ". . . *you* would have to return them."

"Return them? Return them where?"

"In Egypt, when the tombs of the Pharaohs were robbed, it was believed whoever possessed the stolen artifacts would hold a curse until they were returned to their rightful place. If the artifacts were not returned, the curse would be passed down from generation to generation until the initial insult was rectified."

Ellie looked alarmed. "You're saying we need to return the records to Schrader's *grave*?"

"That is what I'm saying, yes."

"But Schrader wasn't buried with the records," Ellie pointed out. "In the story, the townspeople found them in his house after he disappeared and separated them."

"A small detail in a very large story," Renée said dismissively. "And even if it were true, it wouldn't change my theory. Whether or not he was buried with the records, Schrader still may want them back."

"What if returning them doesn't work?" Ellie asked.

"It may not. But you're playing on Schrader's court, Miss Eleanor. He makes the rules. All you can do is guess what they are and hope you're right."

"*Hope* being the operative word," Raymond muttered under his breath. Ellie chose not to repeat that.

"All that remains now is finding the location of Schrader's grave," Renée said.

"Which shouldn't be a problem for *you*, right?" Ellie said.

"I'm sorry?"

"Dad said you helped him find the records using some kind of ritual."

Renée nodded cautiously. "I did."

"Well, can't you do it again and help us find the grave?"

"I'm sorry, Miss Eleanor," she said softly. A pained expression unfolded across her face. "It doesn't work that way."

"Why not?"

"As I mentioned before, the fabric between realities is delicate. It's also porous. Occasionally, the energy of the spirit world will seep into our own, and when it does, it momentarily alters our perception of reality. Most people experience these leaks of energy as déjà vu, or cold spots in an otherwise warm space. Some even claim to see ghosts. Other people, like myself and my grandmother before me, are able to momentarily harness that energy when it leaks through.

"Schrader's records were forged with that very same energy. That's how I was able to locate them. A *grave,* on the other hand, has no spiritual fingerprint, Miss Eleanor. A grave is simply a construct of the living. When a person dies, the spirit sheds free of its body like a snake, then passes into the realm of the dead. The grave it leaves behind is nothing more than a receptacle for an empty shell.

"And that's what a corpse is, Miss Eleanor. An empty shell, with no spiritual merit or use. I can no more use the energy of the spirit world to find Schrader's grave than I can use it to find my missing pair of Jimmy Choos." She laughed lightly at her own joke.

Ellie did not. "If Schrader's corpse is just an empty shell, what good would bringing the records to his grave do?"

"Just because a grave's power is symbolic doesn't mean the power isn't real. I may not be able to access it, but it exists, and it can be very potent. Schrader may feel that he can't fully achieve peace until his greatest achievement is resting with his earthly body."

"Which brings us back to square one," Ellie said, deflated. "How the hell are we going to find Schrader's grave? That's like searching for a needle in an Earth-sized haystack. I wouldn't even know where to begin."

Just then, the floorboards squeaked behind them.

Ellie and Raymond turned to see Louis Goodwin standing in the doorway, face mangled and jaw misaligned.

He raised his hand sheepishly.

"I may be able to help with that."

FORTY

It was almost 9 P.M. when Charlie and Ana were told they could go home.

They had spent the better part of an hour answering questions about Dale Cernin, and another ten seconds politely shrugging their shoulders when the detective, a stern-voiced but kind-faced woman in her mid-forties, pointed out that the two of them had become something of a death magnet as of late.

It was a fair assessment. Charlie and Ana would have pointed out the same thing had they been on the other side of the table. But since neither of them were present for Raymond's and Dale's suicides, and since Louis Goodwin's death was witnessed by several people—all of whom could vouch that neither Charlie nor Ana had been involved—the detective could do nothing more than draw attention to the weirdness of it all.

Charlie was grateful the grill session was coming to an end. He'd been nursing a little nag of a headache for the last hour that was threatening to become a full-tilt screamer.

As they stood up to leave, the detective pointed to the bruises on Ana's and Charlie's temples.

"How'd you manage those? Electroshock for couples?"

Ana ran her fingers along the side of her face. "I must have gotten it when I fainted," she lied. "I hit the pavement pretty hard. Or so the EMT said."

That part was true. After helping her sit up, the EMT was concerned when he saw how red Ana's cheeks were. He took her temperature, but the thermometer showed a perfectly normal 98.1 degrees.

Ana knew it wasn't a fever. Or even a spike in body heat from the sprinting she'd done. Her skin was holding residual warmth from the room with all of the machines.

Schrader had been in the far corner, just like Charlie had

described, but unlike Charlie, Ana kept her distance. When Schrader lunged for her—chisel in one hand, blood dripping from the other—she was able to pivot and dodge his reach. She turned, and having nowhere else to go, ran back the way she came; back into the hallway with all the doors.

The rotting red carpet under her feet was a blur. Doors flew by her like cels on a film strip. She made tracks for the other end of the hallway, but the more she ran, the more the hallway seemed to stretch out in front of her like pulled taffy. Eventually, her endurance began to expire, and, figuring she'd put an adequate amount of space between her and Schrader, she trotted to a stop, breathing heavily, and peeked over her shoulder.

She'd gone only about fifteen feet.

How is that possible?

Without taking the time to choose, Ana reached for the door on her right and flung it open. She immediately recoiled, shielding her eyes against the glare of a midmorning summer sun.

The first thing she felt was the grass under her feet, thick and lustrous and buoyant. Birds chirped, happy voices floated along the soft breeze, and somewhere nearby, a radio played "Cupid" by Sam Cooke.

She opened her eyes and gasped.

She was outside. In a park, by the look of it. A clean spate of electric-green lawn surrounded her, dotted by the occasional shade-giving tree. To her left, a black '46 Ford trundled by on a street so clean, it looked fake.

The park was sporadically populated, mostly by well-dressed (and neatly pressed) mothers and children. The children hopped and skipped and ran in small bursts as their mothers looked on, speaking in hushed tones to one another while sweating glasses of iced tea and lemonade clinked in their hands.

Ana stepped forward into the past, and, inexplicably, away from any thought of Schrader. A nagging concern tugged at her mind . . . something about Schrader being close . . . but as she strode across the bustling park, her worries seemed to magically dissolve in the daylight. More than anything, she wanted to feel the sunshine on her skin; sunshine that wouldn't be declared dangerous for another thirty years. She wanted to experience a world where rock and roll hadn't even learned to walk yet. She wanted to drink in every polka dot, every swatch of gabardine and rayon, every carefully set hairdo, and every carelessly smoked cigarette.

Two classic cars blaring classics-to-be drove by, and Ana saw a woman step onto the curb. Her hair was down, combed and set into a Mary Tyler Moore bob, but Ana could clearly see that her ears were bleeding. Her gait was smooth but her shoulders were stiff, and it wasn't until she turned her head in Ana's direction that Ana saw she was crying.

The young woman reached the edge of the park and stopped. She stayed there, stiff as a statue and clutching her handbag for nearly a full minute; almost as if she couldn't decide whether or not she wanted to cross the street. Two blocks away, Ana spied a shiny blue Plymouth approaching from the corner of her eye. It lumbered down the street toward the park, engine purring.

With a decisive rise and fall of her shoulders, the woman leaned over and set her handbag on the ground next to her feet. She rose again quickly, running her hands along her coat to iron out the wrinkles, and gazed at the approaching Plymouth with a strange stiffness and an unsettling certainty.

Ana felt her stomach sink as her memory suddenly came back online.

She cried out, begging the woman not to do it, but no one—not the mothers in the park, not the children who hopped and skipped along the grass, and certainly not the woman standing on the curb—heard her.

Then, as if the world were a film, the frame skipped, and Schrader was there.

He stood beside the woman, the tails of his decomposing coat fluttering gently in the breeze, and watched with her as the car approached.

"Leave her alone!" Ana cried, but no sound escaped her throat. If the world were indeed a film, she'd been placed on mute, watching helplessly as the woman prepared to meet her grisly demise.

The Plymouth's engine roared like a waking leviathan. The mothers in the park turned their heads, the children stopped playing, and as the car ate up the ten remaining yards between its front bumper and the edge of the park, Schrader placed his cold, spongy hand on the small of the woman's back, and pushed her gently into the street.

Ana turned away. She couldn't watch. She closed her eyes as the screams from the park, the crunch of metal on bone, and the wail of the tires all faded into silence.

When she opened her eyes, Schrader was directly in front of her. His chapped lips curled into a frightful snarl, eyes burning red as hellfire. The melted skin that filled his ear sockets pulsed a quiet rhythm.

Ana staggered back and collided with a wall. A tattered slip of wallpaper drifted to the floor.

She was back in the hallway.

"Is that what you did to Dale?" she sobbed. "You pushed him off the roof?"

Schrader said nothing. He took another step forward, eyes burning hungrily, ear sockets pulsing angrily.

"What do you *want* from us?" Ana howled, cowering as Schrader got closer. "WHAT DO YOU WANT FROM—"

His moldering hands closed around her head. His fingers probed her skin, and all at once, Ana felt everything. Every memory her mind had ever made suddenly collapsed in on itself like an imploding star. Her senses seared with voices, faces, and sensations. She was both a girl and a woman, watching every experience she'd ever had simultaneously unspool before her.

She screamed, certain her head was seconds away from exploding.

But it didn't.

Schrader released her and everything went quiet. She opened her eyes and saw his face, only now his snarl had disappeared. His expression was eerily calm.

She swiped at him, but missed. He was too far away.

No . . . he was getting smaller.

Because she was falling again.

Falling away into darkness.

Falling away to a place where the pain couldn't reach her anymore.

Ana smiled at the detective and gave the bruise on her temple a casual little tap with her fingers, downplaying the stinging zap of pain she felt when she did it. "Honestly, I could have gotten this anywhere," she lied. "I bruise like a peach."

The detective looked unconvinced. She turned to Charlie. "And what about you? Do you bruise like a peach, too?"

"More like a Bartlett pear," Charlie said, grinning stupidly. He knew better than to crack jokes in a situation like this, especially painfully unfunny jokes, but matching bruises were a hard thing to explain away. He didn't want *that* to be the thing that tripped them up. It had been hard enough answering the questions about Dale while dancing around the Schrader of it all.

Especially considering the fact that Dale had been in the room with them the whole time.

He sat in the empty chair next to the detective, arms crossed casually, and shot them a sympathetic smile from the other side of the table.

"This isn't a joking matter, Mr. Remick," the detective said, then addressed Ana: "When it comes to bruises, I've heard every excuse in the book. And 'bruising like fruit' is a hall-of-famer."

"No one puts their hands on me without my permission," Ana assured her.

"Glad to hear it," the detective said, then stood up and gestured for Charlie and Ana to do the same. Dale stood up, too. "I suppose that's it for now."

"For now?" Ana said, pushing her chair back in. Noticing this, Charlie did the same.

"We may need you to come back in for more questions," the detective replied. "Neither of you are suspected of anything, but as I said, three bodies within two weeks is a little strange." She paused thoughtfully before opening the door. "There may be something connecting the deaths."

"DUN-DUN," Dale said, imitating the *Law & Order* sound effect.

Ana glared at him, then pasted on a smile and shook the detective's hand. "If we think of any reason they could be connected, we'll let you know."

They followed her out the door.

Dale brought up the rear, his head bobbing back and forth on his rubbery neck like a deflated speedball.

Phones rang around the precinct like dogs barking nighttime messages to each other in a quiet neighborhood. Charlie went to the front desk and signed them out while Ana tried not to watch Dale set his neck back into place.

As they turned to leave, the detective called out to Charlie.

He felt a rush of nerves splash across his chest. *This is it,* he thought. *The Columbo "one more thing" moment. She's realized something . . . some inconsistency in Ana's and my story . . . and now we're fucked.*

He turned around, bracing for a pair of handcuffs, and saw a tissue hanging limply from the detective's hand. She stared at him worryingly.

"Your ears are bleeding, Mr. Remick."

FORTY-ONE

Charlie and Ana barely said a word as they drove back to the house.

The same could not be said for Dale.

He was positively chatty, which was strange, since Charlie had always thought of Dale as a foggy day with legs. Now he was like the human equivalent of a scribble. His mind was all over the place, and every thought that occurred to him was a thought he saw fit to speak aloud. He commented on the hues of the traffic lights, the similarity between London's climate and Seattle's, the reason why Sinatra's tenure on Capitol would forever outweigh his years on Reprise, why *The Rocketeer* was an underrated gem of a movie, and the correct way to eat a Pop-Tart (edges first, middle second, and *obviously* untoasted, because who has the time for that?).

He didn't even pause to catch his breath.

But then, Charlie figured, he wouldn't need to.

FORTY-TWO

Raymond was still in his office when he heard Ellie scream.

"Stay here," he told Louis, and dashed out the door. He crossed the length of the hallway in three strides, no longer huffing and puffing as he used to, and skidded into the foyer.

"What happened, sweetheart?"

Ellie's hands gripped her mouth.

Dale stood in the doorway, his rubbery neck bent under the weight of his head. "There now," he soothed, stepping across the foyer on jelly legs and patting Ellie on the back. "It's not as bad as it looks, I promise you."

"Well, that's good," Raymond said, observing Dale's physical condition with an apprehensive grimace. "Because it looks pretty fucking bad."

Dale grabbed a fistful of his own hair and lifted his head up to meet Raymond's blood-puckered face. A dull crunch, like the sound of a thick branch being stepped on, came from his neck. "Speak for yourself, boss."

Raymond stepped forward and pulled Dale into a tight embrace. "I'm so sorry, man. I never meant for any of this to happen. Truly."

"I'm sorry too," Dale replied somberly. "But what's done is done, I guess. No use crying over it now."

"I'm surprised you let them rope you into this mess."

"Peer pressure," Dale said, thinking ruefully of his heroin-riddled days in the London punk scene. "Weak as water, that's me. Probably why Schrader got me first, I reckon."

"You're not weak," Charlie assured him. "It could have been any one of us. For all I know, I may be next on the chopping block." He turned his head to the side and showed off the crusted blood on his earlobes. "See?"

Ellie gasped.

Ana stepped into the light and pushed her hair back, revealing the bruises on her temples. "I'm not far behind you."

Raymond dropped his chin and sighed. "Goddamn it."

"Happened right after Dale jumped," Ana said, letting her hair fall back into place. "I saw his body splayed out on the pavement and then *boom,* I was gone."

"Are you all right?" Ellie asked.

"I'm still a little shaky, but I'll be fine," Ana replied.

"Do you remember anything?" Raymond asked her. "Anything you saw?"

"Just bits and pieces. There was a hallway, and something about a park and an old car, but it's pretty fuzzy now."

"We need to talk about what we're gonna do next," Charlie said impatiently. His head was throbbing badly, and he needed Advil fast. "Ellie's the only one Schrader hasn't marked yet, and I'd like to stop that from happening if we can. We're running out of time. We've already lost Dale. We need a plan."

"As it happens," Raymond said, "I may have one." He looked over his shoulder. "You can come in here now, Louis."

Soft footsteps approached.

Louis Goodwin, shoulders hunched timidly, stepped into the foyer.

Charlie balled his fists, seething. "What in God's name is *he* doing here?"

"Calm down," Raymond said, stepping between them. "He's here to help us."

"The *fuck* he is. He scared Miles and Maisy half to death!"

Louis stared at his own shoes, ashamed. The top of his head, bald and shining under the overhead light, bore a black hole, its edges spattered with still-fresh blood.

"Please . . ." he said, although because his lower jaw was out of alignment, the word came out sounding like *pleashe.* "I'm very sorry . . . I didn't mean to scare them."

Shorry. Shcare.

Louis looked like a dog that had been kicked one too many times. Maybe he actually had been.

"It's all right," Charlie said, and relaxed his stance. "It's just I wasn't expecting to see you, that's all."

Louis tried to smile, but it looked more like an uneven sneer.

Satisfied that cooler heads had prevailed, Raymond placed his hand on Louis's shoulder and addressed the room. "Everyone, I'd like you to meet Louis Goodwin, director of rare antiquities at the Seattle Art Museum."

Ellie glared at the spot where, four days before, she watched Louis fall onto the beverage table and impale his own head on a fireplace poker.

"We've met."

FORTY-THREE

Montana?"

Louis Goodwin nodded. "Yes."

Charlie bit down on his fourth Advil and felt the acrid powder mix with his saliva. They'd barely made a dent in the thunderous pain behind his eyes. "You think Schrader was buried in Montana?"

"I do."

"That does narrow our search down a bit," Ana said, "but Montana isn't exactly . . . you know . . . *small.*"

"When Raymond died, I wanted to find as much information on Ivan Schrader as I could," Louis said. He stood meekly in front of the fireplace, hands clasped at his waist, as if he were applying for a bank loan. "Naturally there wasn't much to find, but I searched the census records, and in 1910, there were three Ivan Schraders listed. Two of them had been born here in the US. One was in his seventies, and had fought for the Union during the Civil War, and the other was a wholesale hardware distributor in Utah."

"Neither of them sound like our man," Ana said.

"The third Schrader, however, *wasn't* a US citizen," Louis continued. "According to a labor register I was able to track down, he'd emigrated from Poland sometime around the turn of the century. He was working as a tracklayer for the Chicago, Milwaukee, and St. Paul Railroad."

Ana's frowned skeptically. "Schrader was a rail worker?"

"It appears so, yes," Louis said.

"You're sure this is the same Ivan Schrader? The composer?"

Raymond broke in. "Unless you were John Philip Sousa, there wasn't much need for composers in early-twentieth-century America. Schrader would have had to take work wherever he could get it."

Louis nodded in agreement. "And, being an immigrant, his options would have been extremely limited."

Ana scowled. "I got news for you, buddy, that hasn't changed much."

Louis shifted awkwardly on his heels. "Quite so." He cleared his throat. "When the lab results came back on the records, there were traces of soil found in the grooves that contained the same chemical compounds found in the soil of the southern Interior Platform of Canada and the northern plains and mountain regions of the United States."

"I assume Montana is somewhere in there?" Ana said.

"It is, Ms. Cortez," Louis replied. "The labor register I found concerned a rail that ran from Great Falls to the Bolero County sawmill near Havre. The whole enterprise was a bit of a self-feeding monster, if you will. Once the rail workers reached the end of the line, the Bolero Mill temporarily hired them to produce the lumber for the next tracks. It worked that way all through the northwest territories."

Over on the davenport, Charlie, whose headache had been playing hell with his ability to concentrate, looked up. "Say that again."

Louis cocked his head to the side. "I'm sorry?"

"The place . . ." Charlie said, closing his eyes. ". . . the name of the mill."

Louis gazed around the room, confused. "The Bolero Mill?"

"Bolero Mill . . ." Charlie muttered, trying his best to ignore the searing pain behind his eyes. "Bolero Mill . . . Bolero Mill . . ."

There was something familiar about that name. Something he'd seen before. Or read before. On a TV show, maybe . . . or a movie, or even a dream he had.

Not Mill, he thought, pushing past the fog of pain. *But something else. Something that rhymes.*

Bill? Twill? Drill? Grill?

No . . .

An image flashed before him.

A sign.

Not a sign in the figurative sense. No, it was an actual, literal *sign.* It was old and made of wood and it stood beneath a stormy gray sky and a hilltop graveyard. A graveyard with tombstones choked by decades of dry growth.

A hilltop graveyard.

Hilltop.

Hill . . .

He opened his eyes.

"Bolero Hill."

He shot to his feet, head thudding in protest, and addressed the room.

"When Schrader grabbed me, I saw something. It was a graveyard. An old one. And there was a sign in front of it. It said Bolero Hill."

Five stunned faces, lit by dancing firelight, stared at him from around the room.

"Are you sure?" Raymond asked gently. "Maybe you're remembering something else from a different—"

"I'm sure, Dad," Charlie said.

At this, the others exchanged glances across the room.

Ana pulled out her phone, typed something into it, then smiled. She held the search results up to the room. "Bolero Hill Cemetery."

The others leaned in to take a look. On her phone was a relatively blank area on Google Maps. Next to the red pin that marked the cemetery was another name.

"Bolero County, Montana," Raymond said, then looked at Louis and grinned. "How about that?"

Ana stuffed her phone in her pocket. "I wonder if the name has any connection to bolero music."

Louis placidly closed his eyes. "Ah. Ravel. Magnificent."

"Cuban love songs," Ana corrected him, smiling. "But Ravel was good, too."

Louis grinned sheepishly, and with some difficulty, seeing as his jaw was bent the wrong way.

FORTY-FOUR

The fire was still crackling cheerfully when Ana and Charlie returned from the garage, shovels in hand. Raymond, Louis, and Dale sat around the coffee table, planning the route to the cemetery. Ellie was over on the far end of the couch, staring quietly out the window. Charlie set down the shovels and walked over to her.

Her skin was pasty-white and clammy. Strands of her hair clung to her cheeks like wet reeds.

"You all right?"

"Fine," she replied, smiling tiredly. "Just a bit of a headache."

"You too, huh?"

"I've probably been sitting next to the fire too long."

Charlie offered her his bottle of Advil but she declined.

"I think I'll just make another pot of chamomile," she said. "That usually helps."

She stood with a grunt and shuffled to the kitchen. Her feet moved like cinder blocks. Charlie watched her go, his heart breaking for her.

Some families are plagued with strokes, diabetes, or heart disease. The Remick siblings got headaches. Real scorchers, too. They didn't happen often, but when they did, they were debilitating, and Charlie often wondered if they'd been subjected to too much music as kids.

All things considered, they had gotten off pretty light. Other than the occasional migraine, the only other malady their family suffered—on both sides—was a bit of arthritis. No heart attacks, no diabetes, no fibromyalgia, no nothing.

Only one of their clan had ever succumbed to cancer. Their mother.

It got her in the stomach first, then spread to her other organs before she even had a chance to head it off with some chemotherapy. Three months later, she was gone.

Joanie Remick might have been defeated, but she did it with class. She pulled in her final breath with a smile on her face and a dandelion in her hair.

And a single request.

For Charlie to go easy on Raymond.

"You two are so alike," she'd said, minutes before the cancer took her. "If you could just find a way to forgive him for what he did, you'd be thick as thieves."

Charlie thought about this as Raymond stood up and went to the kitchen to check on Ellie.

Sometimes he wished he could have complied with his mother's dying request. He really was a harmless man (in all ways except the two ways he'd harmed Charlie the most), but he was dead now, and Charlie couldn't help but wonder how things might have turned out had he forgiven him. If he had just bitten the bullet and made peace with the man, would any of this madness have happened in the first place?

Maybe if he had come home for Christmas, or during the summer—hell, maybe if he'd just *called* his dad once in a while—they wouldn't be sitting here talking about driving nearly eight hundred miles to an old cemetery in Montana and digging up a supernatural composer's grave.

But then again, maybe they would be.

The other part of Charlie, the part that knew who his father truly was, supposed all of this was inevitable.

What Raymond truly was—more than he was a father, husband, or friend—was a collector.

In the end, Schrader's Chord would never have been anything other than irresistible to a man like Raymond. The records were one of a kind. To a Catholic, that would be like drinking the blood of Christ directly from his vein.

Yes, Charlie thought. *This was inevitable.*

Raymond returned from the kitchen, looking somber.

"Is Ellie all right?" Charlie asked. "She's looking a little clammy."

"She had a nightmare earlier. I think she's still a little rattled."

Louis, who'd been poring over the travel plans on the davenport with Dale, asked for everyone's attention.

"If the weather is agreeable, the trip to Bolero County should take between twelve and fourteen hours," he said, tapping the pen on the notepad. "The cemetery is no longer in use, so you shouldn't raise any suspicion by being there, but you'll want to douse your headlights when you're a few miles out. It sits on privately owned land, so the more inconspicuous you are, the better. You'll have to head into Havre to get there, so once you do, take Wildhorse Road north for about thirty minutes until you reach Road 110, then cut in toward Bolero County. Before long, you'll see signs for Bolero Hill. That's where the cemetery is supposed to be."

"And no planes or trains," Raymond added. "We'll have to drive."

Ellie returned, clutching a mug of tea. The steam curled up into the air and licked the underside of her chin.

"You sure we can't fly?" Ana asked. "The more time it takes us to get there, the more opportunities Schrader has to kill us."

"Given Dale's fate, he obviously played the Suicide record," Raymond replied. "Charlie got Murder, and Ellie seems to remember the voice saying Mors Naturalis, which means you got Accidental Death, Ana. It's practically tailor-made for vehicles. Don't you think it'd be better to be in a car when it happens instead of on a plane with hundreds of innocent people?"

Ana thought about how many karma points she'd be docked if she ended up inadvertently killing a planeful of people just because she played a record.

"Guess we're taking a road trip," she said.

"Which reminds me," Raymond added, turning to Charlie. "You should drive. Traditionally, people don't usually get murdered while they're driving."

Charlie smirked. "Tell that to Sonny Corleone."

"I'd offer to take my car," Ana said, "but I don't think it's dependable enough to make the trip. It can barely make it up my driveway, and that's like a two-degree incline."

"We'll take my rental," Charlie said. "I'll call Avis and extend the—" The phone rang and cut him off. It was the landline.

Ana searched the room for it.

"Don't worry about it, champ," Raymond said to her. "The machine'll get it."

After six rings, the answering machine clicked over. A familiar voice drifted throughout the house.

"Charlie," the voice on the answering machine said, *"it's Frank Critzer. Sorry I missed you. I was just calling to see if you're feeling better after that weird business at Shuckers this morning. I talked to the paramedic who showed up after you left and he seemed to think it was food poisoning. I told him I don't know what he thinks food poisoning looks like, but that wasn't it. Anyway, hope you're feeling better. I'm headed out of town tomorrow morning, so if you send me your email address tonight, I'll send you those Forfeiture of Inheritance forms. If not, I can pass your email address along to my office and they can send them to you. Again, no rush, but I thought you'd want to look them over for yourself. Talk soon."*

With a click, the answering machine switched off and Frank's voice was gone.

The room was silent. Outside, a car passed by, and as Charlie listened to the slow *sloosh* of its tires on wet pavement, he suddenly wished he were inside it, spiriting himself away from the house and from his father's eyes, which were now boring holes into the back of his head.

He turned slowly, bracing for impact. "Dad, listen. I—"

"You're refusing your inheritance?" Raymond stood stone-still. His eyes churned like a stormy sky.

"Frank was just letting me know my options, Dad. Any lawyer would do that."

Raymond laughed sharply. "Like any lawyer would do for an ungrateful son, you mean!"

Charlie's Adam's apple jumped. He glanced at Ellie for help, but she had her head down.

Dale stood slowly. "Raymond, I know you're mad, but given everything that—"

"Can it," Raymond spat, then rounded again on his son. "Do you really hate me that much? Was I so fucking terrible to you that you would take my life's work and toss it into the trash like a soiled diaper?"

Charlie stood firm. "Dad, just listen to me—"

"No, you listen to me! Everything you have, you have because of that store. Your mom chose to raise you kids instead of working, and I loved her and supported her for it, but *everything* you had . . . your guitars, your clothes, your first car, this *house,* everything was bought and paid for by records sold in that store. It was my legacy!"

"It's not *my* legacy!" Charlie screamed. His headache, which had subsided a bit, suddenly returned full-force. He closed his eyes and gritted his teeth, careful to keep his voice low. "Yes, I admit it. When I first found out you left me the store, I told Frank I didn't want it. I was blindsided. It had been so long since we'd spoken, I honestly figured you wouldn't leave me anything at all, and when Frank told me the news, I was pissed. It was a knee-jerk reaction."

Raymond crossed his arms. "So you're not going to give it up?"

"I don't know what I'm going to do, Dad. I haven't exactly had a lot of time to think about it, on account of the David fucking Lynch movie I've been living in for the past twenty-four hours. Maybe you could go ask Schrader to reschedule this little freak show so I can have some time to decide what to do with this fucking albatross you slung around my neck."

Raymond shook his head, disgusted. "That store is my life's work, Charlie."

"Don't talk to me like I'm some stranger you just met, Dad. That store wasn't your *life's work.* It was a dusty shithole. A place where you could stroll in around noon and sell used Dylan records to middle-aged burnouts for a dollar fifty a pop. You would have lost the store years ago if Ana hadn't come along and fixed it up, so don't stand there and tell me it was your life's work, okay?"

Ana felt a jolt when she heard her name. Part of her wanted to say *leave me out of this,* but another part of her was grateful that Charlie had acknowledged all the work she'd done. Even if it *had* been used as a barb against Raymond.

"Maybe you're right!" Raymond barked. "Maybe I would have lost the store. But at least I would have gone out on my own terms. I could say, proudly, that I did it *my* way. And that's not nothing, kiddo."

"Listen to you," Charlie seethed. "'Go out on my own terms.' 'I did it my way.' Those are nothing but empty slogans, used by guys like you to make themselves feel better about being failures."

Raymond recoiled, stung.

Ellie took a woozy step forward. She was sweating profusely. "Okay, that's enough. We have more important things to worry about."

"Is that what you think of me?" Raymond said, frowning at Charlie. "You think I'm a failure?"

Charlie's cheeks were bright red now, and his headache was thundering like a set of pistons against his skull. "I *know* you're a failure. Nobody else sees it, but I do. All your charm and charisma were just a cover for your complete ineptitude. You have Mr. Magoo'd your way through life, Dad: narrowly missing every flower pot that came crashing down onto the sidewalk next to you. You have no talent. You have no business acumen. You can't even light a match without burning yourself. You weren't a father. You were a fourth *kid.* A jealous, petulant kid who couldn't stand it if one of us did something well that *you* weren't a part of. Every time Susan aced a test in school, you made sure to let her know where she 'got all her smarts.' That time Ellie had one of her paintings hung in a gallery, you told everyone at the showing that she had a talent for art because you'd forced her to watch so much PBS! And do I even need to mention the incident at Robert Lang Studios? I think the only reason they didn't report you to the police for breaking into the control room was because the remixes you did on my songs were so fucking terrible, they couldn't stop laughing!"

Charlie was on a roll now, and with every new missile he launched his father's way, his headache seemed to hurt less and less. "And I could have looked past all of that," he said, spittle flying from his lips. "*All* of it . . . if you'd just been a good husband to Mom. But you couldn't even manage that! Mom died. Alone and afraid. And where were you when that happened? At a fucking—"

"STOP IT!"

Raymond's words boomed, filling the room, then spiraled into silence like the tail of a thunderclap. The glassware in the armoire rang softly, and the fire seemed to crackle a little softer, whispering like an embarrassed third party, carrying on its conversation in an attempt to politely ignore the very public scene that just unfolded next to it.

No one spoke. No one moved.

Louis studied his own shoes. Dale and Ana exchanged uncomfortable glances. Ellie sat motionless on the couch with her steaming cup of tea, sweat beading across her waxy forehead.

Charlie and Raymond faced each other silently, two gunfighters waiting to see who would draw their pistol next.

The gray clouds in Raymond's eyes boiled. His anger was made all the more intense by the fact that he wasn't breathing. He was unnaturally still, unlike Charlie, whose limbs were shaking badly as fury coursed through his veins like poison. He wanted to scream, wanted to lay into his father again, but the thought of breaking the silence that now hung in the air between them seemed like an unsolvable puzzle. What would he say next? What *could* he say next that would outdo what he'd already said?

No words came to mind.

So, he did the next best thing, and left the room.

He marched into the foyer, reached for his coat, and flung open the front door with such force, the wood produced a loud skeletal rattle. He strode heavily down the lawn, his boots leaving divots in the frosty grass, and fished the car keys out of his pocket.

He needed a cigarette.

He needed a pack of cigarettes.

"I'll tell you what, Dad," he mumbled angrily. "*You* can drive out to that fucking graveyard yourself. This is *your* goddamn mess. *You* can clean it up."

He fumbled with the electronic key fob, slapping away the gigantic plastic AVIS tag that dangled from the ring, and pressed the Unlock button.

The car responded with a dull chirp.

Halfway down the lawn he stopped and gazed thoughtfully at the key in his hand.

He could go. He could leave this whole shitshow behind him if he wanted to. Sea-Tac wasn't that far away.

If Schrader came after him, Schrader came after him.

"At least I'd go out on *my terms*," he said quietly, mocking his father.

Across the street, someone was watching him. Charlie felt it before he saw it. He stopped and shielded his eyes against the glare of the neighboring Christmas lights.

There was a person standing in the Pearsons' rosebushes.

"Hello?"

Charlie's voice didn't sound like his own. It was hoarse from the cold. Or, more likely, from all the shouting he'd just done.

"That you, Mr. Pearson?"

A car approached from the east end of the block. Its high beams spilled across the wet pavement, crept over the rosebushes, and illuminated the face of the man staring at him.

Charlie froze.

Ivan Schrader was screaming at him.

Or, it only *looked* like he was screaming. He made no sound. His mouth hung open in a distended yawn, a black hole on a pale face, and his eyes, wide open and burning red, seemed to scream too.

Charlie felt the key slip from his fingers.

He stared in horror at that silent, screaming face, transfixed; caught in a waking nightmare, and completely unable to move.

Unable to move, that was, until he heard the echoing screech of tires.

When he turned, he saw headlights. They were aimed right at him.

FORTY-FIVE

What in God's name was that?"

Louis Goodwin rushed to the window.

Because it was so dark, it was difficult at first to make sense of the hulking shape of tangled metal and broken glass on the lawn. It looked more like a piece of salvage art than a car wreck: one of those rust-covered, twisted sculptures that had been welded and bent into a form of craftsmanship that Louis had never really understood the appeal of. He scanned the wreck, separating shapes in his head in an attempt to understand the full extent of the damage, then gasped when he saw Charlie's body, sprawled out like a starfish on the damp grass.

"Oh, dear God . . ."

Ellie didn't bother looking out the window. She was already sprinting for the front door, Ana hot on her heels.

Outside, the smell of bent metal stung the air, making their eyes water.

"Holy shit," Ana choked, skidding to a stop and taking in the carnage that lay before her.

A green Subaru Outback, smoldering like a dormant pocket of volcanic soil, had run up onto the lawn. Steam rose from the slits on either side of the hood, and its front two tires (one of which was tilted at an angle) were buried four inches into the grass. A muffled tune, coming from the Subaru's stereo, cut through the silent wreckage. The windows were up, but Ana recognized the song immediately.

It was "Downtown" by Petula Clark. The part with all the horns.

The song was so cheerful, it seemed inappropriate, even antagonistic. Like hearing a laugh track during a medical drama.

Charlie was lying motionless in the grass. Ellie rushed over to him, while Ana took a few exploratory steps toward the wreck. The back of Charlie's rental car peeked out from behind the Subaru. It was completely mangled. Both taillights had been blown out, the remains of which lay strewn along the pavement like shattered pieces of carnival glass. The trunk door had flown off in the crash and was now awkwardly sticking out of a nearby hedgerow.

Ana joined Ellie, who was checking Charlie's body for injuries. She was relieved to see that his eyes were open. "Are you okay?" she said, taking his hand.

He stared up at the night sky, alert, but with an odd, unreadable expression on his face. "Am I . . . am I dead?"

"No," Ana said softly, wiping the hair from his forehead. "No, you're alive."

"Oh," Charlie said, almost casually. "Well, that's good."

"You all right, mate?" Dale asked, kneeling down. Louis stood nervously behind him.

Charlie took a moment to conduct a visual inventory of his body, then said, "I think I twisted my ankle."

Dale smiled. "Considering you were nearly mincemeat, I'd say that's not too bad."

Raymond, meanwhile, went right for the Subaru, his strides long and commanding. "You better hope you have a good fucking lawyer, pal." He had forgotten momentarily that whoever was sitting in the driver's seat wouldn't be able to see or hear him. Nevertheless, he reached for the door and wrenched it open. "That's my fucking boy you almost—"

He paused, right fist hovering in a ready-to-fight position, and stared blankly at the driver's seat.

Ana looked over at him. "What's wrong?"

"There's nobody in the car."

"What?"

"The car's empty."

Ana jogged over and peered through the driver's-side window.

"Downtown" continued to play through the stereo, only there was no one in the car to sing along.

Across the street, a porch light flickered on. Mrs. Pearson, clutching the lapels of her dressing gown, made her way down to her driveway. Her husband, clad in a white T-shirt and boxer shorts, followed her.

"Oh my God!" Mrs. Pearson's dressing gown fluttered in the night breeze, revealing a set of turquoise pajamas underneath. "We heard the crash and didn't know what to think! Is anyone hurt? Do you need me to call 911?"

"There's no need, Mrs. Pearson!" Charlie said, struggling to sit up. "But thank you!"

Mrs. Pearson didn't move. Neither did her husband.

"Had a little accident!" Ana said, gesturing to one of her boots. "Shoelace got caught on the gas pedal! Couldn't stop!"

"You're sure nobody got hurt?" Mrs. Pearson asked, clearly smelling something fishy.

Ana glanced at Charlie. He was clearly still shaken, but otherwise he seemed all right. "Yep! Close call, but everyone's okay."

"Well, praise Jesus, then," Mrs. Pearson said, and Ana couldn't tell if she was serious or not.

"Right," she said. "Jesus." She held up a hand and nodded solemnly. "In his name."

Mrs. Pearson nodded back, then made her way back up her front steps, eyes cast over her shoulder, groggy husband in tow.

Once they were out of sight, Dale offered his hand to Charlie. "Let's get you inside."

He and Louis each took an arm and helped Charlie limp up the front steps.

Ana thought about rushing over to help. He had his arms slung around two dead men. If Mrs. Pearson decided to pull a Gladys Kravitz and watch them through her window, she might call an exorcist when she saw Charlie hopping up the front steps arms splayed out like Jesus on an invisible cross.

It didn't matter. He was nearly inside already, and there were worse things to worry about than a nosy neighbor.

Like the way Ellie was staring quietly up at her bedroom window.

And the way the terror spread across her face when she saw the man staring back at her.

And the way her jaw suddenly began to hurt.

FORTY-SIX

When they stepped back into the house, they did so silently. Perhaps it was because Charlie had missed catastrophe by mere inches and no one knew what to say next, or maybe it was because the bitter words he'd exchanged with his father minutes before still hung in the air like a poisonous vapor trail.

Dale helped Charlie over to the davenport. He collapsed onto the cushions with a squeaky sigh.

Louis gazed forlornly out the window. Charlie's totaled rental car sat near the curb like a crumpled piece of tinfoil. "I sure hope you sprung for the insurance, Mr. Remick," he said softly.

Charlie chuckled humorlessly. Forget the two-hundred-dollar smoking fee. He'd have to pay for the whole car.

When he got back to New York—*if* he got back to New York, that is—he'd have to ditch his apartment and sell off his records. His stomach churned at the idea. His collection had taken a lifetime to curate. He'd also probably have to quit his job.

In the eighties, a hotshot A&R rep could sign Mötley Crüe or Warrant and bankroll the next five years of their life, but this was not the eighties. Thirty percent of his annual income went to taxes, another forty to rent, leaving him to navigate big-city life with one hand tied behind his back and his chin only an inch above the water's surface. The cost of a rental car would sink him. He'd have to find a non-music-related job if he expected to survive the additional monthly payments. It was this thought that nauseated him the most. He'd always shied away from his industry-endowed moniker—he considered it gross and self-important—but, in truth, who *was* he if wasn't the Man with the Magic Ear? What use would his talent be in the tech industry? In finance? In what world would Goldman Sachs benefit from his ability to spot a hitmaking switch from an A-minor chord to an F? And how would he survive an environment that didn't involve music?

Music was his life.

For better or for worse. And if he couldn't paint in its endless spectrum of color, why bother existing at all?

Dale took a seat next to him, head leaning on his own shoulder like an overripe gourd. "You sure you're all right, mate?"

"Physically, yes," he said, massaging his ankle. "Mentally? I don't think so."

Dale chuffed a laugh. "And no fucking wonder! That Subaru that almost hit you was playing 'Downtown.' I'd have shit myself twice if my death was soundtracked by Petula Clark."

"But that's the thing," Charlie said. "The Subaru *didn't* almost hit me. It missed me by nearly fifty feet. If Schrader was trying to kill me, he's a terrible shot."

Ana looked up.

"Yeah," Charlie said. "It was Schrader. I saw him. He was standing across the street."

"Then who was driving the car?"

"Nobody," Raymond said, entering the living room. A sports bandage was in his hand. "That's how it works. After he touches you, you start to see him. And when you see him . . ." He nodded over at the twisted wreckage through the window. ". . . death follows."

"But it didn't work," Charlie said. "I escaped. So what happens now?"

"He tries again," Raymond said flatly. Without asking for permission, he began wrapping his son's ankle. Charlie felt like protesting, but didn't. The bandage was already taking the edge off the pain.

"You can't outrun him," Louis said, staring balefully at the remaining embers in the fireplace. "I tried, believe me. I even got good at it. After five or six times, I figured—or I *hoped*, rather—that he would think I was more trouble than I was worth and just leave me alone." He tapped the bloody hole at the top of his head with his fingers. "Obviously I was mistaken."

"You've bought yourself a little time," Raymond said, putting the finishing touches on Charlie's bandage. "He'll most likely cycle through the others before he comes back around to you."

Charlie was reminded of the movie *Final Destination*. It didn't make him feel better.

"I'm probably next at bat then," Ana said, frowning. "Ellie hasn't had her first run-in with Schrader yet."

Charlie glanced at Ellie, who was standing under the archway that led to the foyer. She was soaked with sweat and her eyes seemed unable to focus on anything for more than a second or two. She swayed drunkenly on her feet, and Charlie was worried she was going to pass out.

"Are you all right, El?" he asked, standing up. A sharp pain shot through his left ankle. He hopped over to his good foot. "You look sick as a dog."

"I saw someone . . ." she said, pausing to take in a pained breath. ". . . in my room."

Raymond ran to her side. "When?"

"When I was outside . . ." she replied, practically wheezing now. ". . . I saw him standing in my window."

Ana turned and sprinted up the stairs.

"My jaw hurts," Ellie whispered. "My back, too. And I . . ." She pulled in another thin wheeze of air. ". . . I can't seem to take a full breath."

"She needs some water," Raymond said, then glanced at Dale. "Would you mind?"

Dale nodded and disappeared into the kitchen.

Louis went to the couch and fluffed up some pillows. "Here," he said, "why don't we have her lie down?"

Charlie and Raymond helped her over to the couch. In their

arms, she felt frail, like a dry twig about to snap. They set her down gently and backed away, not wanting to crowd her.

Ana came clomping back down the stairs in her heavy boots. She shrugged. "I searched every room. There's nobody up there."

Dale returned holding a glass of water. "There you are, darlin'. This should help."

Ellie smiled wanly, thanking him, then brushed back her wet mop of hair and pinned it behind her ears.

On her temples were two dark bruises.

It was Raymond who saw them first.

He gasped, then took her head gently in his hands. "No . . . no, no, no . . ." He tilted her head toward the light, hoping that the bruises were merely shadows he'd mistaken as bruises.

They weren't.

A red tear crawled down his cheek.

"Daddy?" Ellie said, voice cracking. Panic spread across her face and her breathing suddenly became much worse. "What's the matter?"

Ana took a cautious step toward her, as if she were approaching a scared animal. "Ellie, do you remember anything about a hallway? Or a room full of weird machines?"

Ellie immediately understood what Ana was asking, and her own tears began to fall. She got to her feet, swaying unsteadily. "I've got to get out of here, right?" She pulled in a deep, rattling breath. "If he knows I'm here, then—"

Louis reached for her. "Ellie, why don't you sit back down?"

Dale, still holding the glass of water, agreed with him. "There's no need to wear yourself out. Come sit down and have some water. It'll make you feel better."

"I can't . . ." Ellie said, then clutched her chest. She gaped at her brother, eyes wide in alarm. Her skin was a sickly shade of gray. "I . . . can't . . . breathe . . ."

A sudden burst of rage coursed through Charlie. He leapt over the davenport, teetering a little on his bad ankle, and unlatched the black case.

"What are you doing?" Raymond asked.

"What I should have done the minute we listened to these fucking things," he said, throwing open the lid of the case and pulling out one of the records. "I'm gonna destroy them."

"Charlie, *no*," Raymond said, exasperated. "I told you, it can't be done."

Charlie gripped either end of the record tightly in his hands. He widened his stance, as if bracing for an explosion, and said, "Maybe not by you."

He bent the record with such force, it should have immediately snapped in two. Instead, it resisted Charlie's strength. It pushed back, refused to break, and sent a searing pain so powerful through Charlie's ears, he felt as if his head would split in two. He screamed, reapplying force to the record, but it flew from his grip like a Frisbee and landed with a faint wobble on the floor next to Raymond's feet.

Charlie fell to his knees, heart pounding.

Raymond gently—almost reverently—picked the record up and returned it to its case. "I'm sorry, kiddo. They're unbreakable."

His father's words went unheard. Charlie's ears rang terribly, overtaking any sound that tried to get through. He cradled his head in his hands, breathing heavily, and said something to test his hearing.

His voice was practically inaudible, buried beneath two tons of cotton.

Over near the davenport, Louis said something loudly that Charlie couldn't hear.

Which didn't matter. It was clear what he said.

Ivan Schrader was in the room. He stood behind Ellie, his red eyes cooking in their sockets. His cracked lips were drawn back into a furious scowl, revealing a set of decaying teeth.

The room exploded into pandemonium. Raymond and Ana were screaming. Louis and Dale scrambled across the room.

But it was too late.

Schrader threaded his hand under Ellie's arm and buried it into her chest.

She collapsed before anyone could reach her, hitting the floor like a marionette whose strings had just been cut.

Howling like a wild animal, Raymond hurled himself toward Schrader, who vanished into thin air, sending Raymond face-first into the wall.

The others rushed to Ellie's side.

She wasn't moving.

Louis placed his fingers on her wrist, then looked up. A dark shadow crossed his mangled face.

"Somebody call an ambulance."

FORTY-SEVEN

The coffee tasted like scorched turpentine, but at least it was hot.

Ana Cortez closed her eyes and took a long sip from the Styrofoam cup she'd pulled from the dispenser. The pungent sting of the coffee did a good job of washing away the antiseptic, medicinal smell of the waiting room.

It was a busy night by the look of things, and the nurses' station was clearly understaffed. One of the nurses, whose name tag said JOYCE, sat hunched over her keyboard as she typed up the particulars of an elderly man who'd just tottered through the doors with a thunderous cough.

Around the room, Ana heard several similar coughs. Red noses sniffed stereophonically. Puffy, dazed eyes stared vacantly into space, occasionally zigging over to the nurses' station (people hoping their name had been called and they simply hadn't heard it), then zagging over to the TV that had been mounted to the wall.

Ana listened with partial interest as a familiar conversation unfolded on the TV.

"*Forty-two dollars isn't going to break anybody,*" one voice said.

"*Okay, Tom,*" another voice said, a notable squawk in his delivery. "*All right. Here you are, you sign this, you get your money in sixty days.*"

"*Sixty days?*"

"*Well now, that's what you agreed to when you bought your shares . . .*"

"*Tom! Tom!*" another voice cried. "*D'ya get your money?*"

"*No,*" the man named Tom replied.

"*Well I did. Old man Potter will pay fifty cents on the dollar for every share you've got.*"

Then came an uproar of angry voices that cut through the waiting room's quiet symphony of seasonal sickness.

Ana looked up at the TV and watched the remainder of the run on the Bailey Brothers Building and Loan.

She wished she were watching it somewhere else.

It's a Wonderful Life should be watched in a warmly lit room, with a Christmas tree glowing in the corner and a cup of hot cocoa in her lap. Not under the harsh white glare of hospital halogen. She and her mother watched it every year, and judging by the fact that it was already two days till Christmas (and the fact that Gloria Cortez refused to get a DVD player or even a VCR; forget about a subscription to a streaming service), this would be the first year they would miss watching it together.

She stared at her phone, wishing she could call her mother, but it was dead. Had been for almost an hour.

A flutter of panic crossed her heart. If Schrader got his way (and given what had happened to Dale and what was currently happening to Ellie, Ana had every reason to believe he would), she would be dead soon and would never see her mother again.

She checked her watch.

Her mother's house was only a fifteen-minute drive from the hospital. She could easily make it there and back in an hour.

And she would have, if not for the fear of seeing her grandmother the moment she walked through the door.

For years, Gloria campaigned to play host to her own mother, and for years was met with staunch resistance. Andreina Salguero was a proud daughter of Venezuela, had seen Marcos Pérez Jiménez's regime rise to power with her own eyes, and had seen her husband imprisoned for publicly opposing it. Her steadily worsening fibromyalgia, declining eyesight, and occasional bout with atrial fibrillation weren't going to pull her away from her home.

It wasn't until she suffered a thunderclap heart attack while sunning herself on the beach that she was overcome with an urgent need to spend time with her daughter. She called Gloria, arranged a flight, and agreed to a sixth-month stint in Seattle.

Ana was seven years old when her grandmother came to stay.

Andreina was a stern woman, quick to fling judgmental barbs about everything from Ana's fashion choices to her preference for speaking English around the house. She had a craggy, weathered face that frightened her, and a throat so battered by unfiltered cigarettes, every word out of her mouth sounded like the snarl of a possessed raccoon.

Eleven weeks into her stay, she suffered a fatal bout of midnight acid reflux, aspirating a measuring cup's worth of bile and food particles into her lungs and choking to death.

Ana was the one who found her.

She had been sent up to fetch her for breakfast. The curtains were drawn, and Ana wrenched them open, bathing her grandmother's bed in bright sunlight.

She could still remember how her grandmother's face looked that morning. Frozen forever in a shock of horror; eyes open and strained; lips and chin smeared with dried vomit.

It took years—and a lot of therapy—for Ana to defang such a horrible memory, and she wasn't about to voluntarily cast herself in a live-action rerun.

To race across town, only to see her mother bustling about the house while her *abuela* stood hauntingly in the background—her face a rigor mortis freak show as flakes of crusty bile fell from her chin—was too chilling a prospect to entertain.

And that was the problem with houses, Ana supposed. People died in them.

It occurred to her, sitting there in the waiting room and watching George Bailey dole out the entirety of his honeymoon fund to the rancorous citizens of Bedford Falls, that hospitals were no better.

In fact, they were so much worse.

Hospitals were absolutely teeming with dead people.

Thank God she was still in the waiting room.

That wasn't to say the waiting room was completely bereft of dead people. In addition to Dale and Louis, there were quite a few others milling about. The hospital gowns and milky eyes were a dead giveaway.

Pun very much intended, she thought.

The waiting room, however, was nothing compared to what lay beyond it.

When the double doors occasionally opened to let a doctor out or a patient in, Ana would steal a glimpse into the hallway beyond, wishing every time that she hadn't. The halls were positively crawling with the dead, packed like rotting sardines between the walls, shuffling aimlessly, colliding with one another, and uttering quiet cries of confusion and despair.

So many lives lost here, Ana thought grimly. How many had expired within these halls since the place was built?

Whatever the number was, all of them were here, jammed in shoulder to shoulder, like panicked third-class passengers on a sinking ship. Faces rose and fell from view. Thousands of milky eyes searched desperately for a fine and private place in which to spend their unwanted reappearance.

That's what horrified Ana the most.

Had she and the others unknowingly ripped these poor souls away from their eternal sleep? Had they cursed them to walk among the living (and with each other) until their business with Schrader was done?

The double doors swung open again, and Charlie and Raymond appeared, followed by a doctor who was speaking to Charlie in a low voice.

The doctor's face was long and lantern-jawed. His shirt was rumpled around the collar where he'd loosened his tie, and his hand moved in soft, decisive chops as he spoke. Raymond stood next to Charlie, nodding along, even though the doctor couldn't see him.

Ana got close, but was careful to give Charlie and Raymond their space. Dale and Louis joined her. The doctor placed a comforting hand on Charlie's arm and said, "There's no better place she could be than right here." He saw Ana approach, and offered a kind smile.

"Are you two together?" he asked her.

Without clarifying what he meant by *together,* Ana said yes.

That made Charlie smile. It was probably wrong to feel good about that, especially given the circumstances, but he didn't care.

"I'll notify you of any changes," the doctor said. "In the meantime, please try to get some rest."

Charlie promised he would (knowing it was a promise he would have to break), then waved goodbye to the doctor, who disappeared back through the double doors.

"Is she going to be all right?" Dale asked.

"She's stable for now," Charlie replied. "The doctors put her in a medically induced coma."

Louis shook his head sorrowfully. "This is awful. Just awful."

"I still don't understand how she had the bruises," Ana said. "There's no way she wouldn't have remembered getting them. That room with all the machines? Schrader carving into his own bone? It's not exactly an easy memory to forget."

"It must have happened when she was asleep," Raymond said, then, off the others' expressions, said, "When you and Charlie were at the police station after Dale jumped, she looked tired, so I told her to lie down for a nap."

Ana was impressed. "She was actually *able* to sleep? Lucky her."

"She woke up from a bad nightmare, screaming. That must have been when Schrader marked her."

Louis looked horrified. "While she was *asleep*?"

Raymond nodded.

"Can we see her?" Ana asked.

Charlie shrugged. "I don't see why not. There's no listed medical procedure for a Schrader attack, so it's not like they're busy prepping her for surgery."

Behind them, the double doors swung open. Two doctors, deep in conversation, strode out into the waiting room.

Ana glanced tentatively into the hallway beyond. "What's it like through there?"

"Like walking into hell," Charlie replied flatly, then shuffled back toward the double doors. "Come and see for yourself."

FORTY-EIGHT

The dead were everywhere.

They filled every square inch of the hallway, except, of course, for the spaces occupied by the living.

It was a curious thing. Ana expected she'd have to claw through them, like a bathroom-bound concertgoer carving a path through a mosh pit, but it wasn't necessary. With each step, her foot landed on uninhabited linoleum tile. It was as if the living and the dead were magnets whose opposite poles faced each other. If she reached her arm out, they avoided it. When she took a step toward them, they took a step away from her.

"Why are they letting us through?" she asked Raymond quietly, conscious of the fact that her question might be received quizzically by a passing nurse or doctor.

"They know you can see them," he said. "They're frightened."

"How come you aren't?"

"We know *why* you can see us," Raymond said, gesturing to himself, Dale, and Louis. "They don't."

Ana remembered the look of shock on the woman in the bathtub's face when she drew back the shower curtain; the surprise on the face of the boy with the bicycle; the confused expression of the old man sitting in the pharmacy.

"Lots of these people have been dead for years," Dale said, studying the confused and terrified faces as he passed them. "Others for decades. Now they're back, packed ass to ankles, and they don't know why."

As Ana pressed onward, the collective murmur of the dead began to parse itself out. She caught little snippets of voices as she passed.

". . . I need to find my husband . . ."

". . . who won the Mariners-Dodgers game? I held on as long as I could but . . ."

". . . that bastard is gonna pay for what he did to me . . ."

". . . someone needs to feed Bailey. She needs heart worm meds and . . ."

". . . don't believe it, they actually pulled the plug on me . . ."

". . . I shouldn't have taken the ambulance. What a waste of money . . ."

"Hang a left here, Ana."

She didn't hear Charlie. The brief, passing fragments of *vox post mortem* were too compelling to ignore. She'd always loved the concept of famous last words, and while the fragments she was hearing weren't on par with the famous last words of Buddy Rich or Oscar Wilde, they were real; unvarnished and true and utterly human.

"Ana, turn *left*," Charlie said, more forcefully.

She turned and passed through another set of double doors. The others followed closely behind her. Once through, they found themselves in a large square space lined with rooms. Its nucleus was a nurses' station that looked more like a NASA control center than the usual taupe-colored pod of countertops.

Two large LED monitors bipped and beeped as blue EKG lines rose and fell like digital mountain ranges across their screens.

There were fewer dead people milling about, which Ana found odd, seeing as they were in the cardiac wing, but she supposed most people who died of heart attacks did so in the ambulance or on the operating table.

This was where the successes came to recuperate.

Except for Ellie, of course. Her success didn't depend on the doctors. It depended on them.

Charlie pointed to a room bearing the number 142. "She's in there."

One by one, they entered and formed a horseshoe pattern around the foot of Ellie's bed. Like the monitors at the nurses' station, Ellie had her own set of bipping and beeping screens. Plastic tubes crisscrossed her body in wide arcs, some pumping liquid, others not. Cables and wires sewed themselves through her hospital gown. A wheezing sound, like the rasp of dry accordion bellows, came from behind her.

Ana glanced at the tube that had been inserted down Ellie's throat and winced.

She had been intubated.

"I'm not really sure what each machine does," Charlie said, rubbing his eyes until they were red. "But they're keeping her alive, so that's good." His face was drawn and drained of color, and he looked ready to collapse.

The doctors were right. Charlie needed rest. They all did. "What's the prognosis?" Ana asked him.

"I don't know. Nobody knows. The doctors are baffled. They try to hide it, but they are."

"Makes sense," Dale said. "Girl as young as Ellie comes in with heart failure, I'd be baffled too."

Charlie nodded solemnly. "Five cardiologists have looked at her so far. They even called one in who was fast asleep. He still had his pajamas on."

"So it *was* a heart attack, then."

"Not *was*," Charlie said. "*Is.*"

The others stared at him, confused.

"She's still having one," Raymond said, petting his daughter's arm. "It hasn't stopped since we got here."

Ana's jaw dropped. "She's *still* having a heart attack? Like right *now*?"

Raymond nodded.

"We've been here almost four hours!"

"That's why the doctors are so baffled," Charlie replied. "They've performed every test in the book. X-rays, ultrasounds, EKGs. Nobody has any answers. According to the tests, her heart is in perfect condition. Arteries clear; not a single ounce of plaque to be found."

"There wouldn't need to be," Dale said knowingly. "*Mors Naturalis.* She pulled the Natural Death record."

"But she hasn't died yet," Ana pointed out.

"Only because they've got a machine pumping her heart for her," Raymond said. "The moment she's off it, her heart will stop."

Ana's eyes became sharp, focused. "Which means we still have time, right? As long as they've got her hooked up to that machine, Schrader can't collect his four deaths."

Raymond's bloated lips twisted themselves into a despondent frown. He bent low and kissed Ellie's forehead. A shiny drop of red bloomed above her right eye. He bolted upright, horrified and confused, then realized what had happened.

Dale reached for a box of tissues and handed it to Raymond. "Here you go, mate."

Raymond took one and wiped the drop of blood from Ellie's face.

Ana felt her heart break. To see Raymond's pain rendered so literally on his face was too much to bear. She crossed to the other side of Ellie's bed and pulled him into a tight embrace.

"I . . . I can't leave her here like this," Raymond whimpered into Ana's shoulder. "I can't leave her alone."

Louis took a step back and lowered his gaze, feeling suddenly like an intruder. "Such a tragedy when it happens to your child," he said, although he couldn't speak from experience. Shortly after his and Deb's honeymoon, he discovered he couldn't provide the necessary ingredients to make children a reality. Low sperm motility, one doctor said. *No* motility, said another.

As he watched Raymond shed bleeding tears over the body of his dying daughter, he both lamented and was grateful for the fact that he would never get to experience such a profound and unique pain for himself.

He could, however, be of service to someone who did.

"Raymond," he said softly, stepping forward. "I'll stay with her."

Raymond looked up from Ana's shoulder, his cheeks stained red. "No, Louis. I can't ask you to do that."

"Someone should keep an eye on her. Doctors and nurses have

other patients. I don't. They need sleep. I don't. If anything changes, for the good or the bad, I'll be right here next to her when it does."

Charlie pulled his phone from his pocket and handed it to Louis. "The password is 0237."

"Won't you need it?" Louis asked.

"Ana's got a phone," he said, then gestured to Ellie. "If anything changes, good or bad, call her number."

Louis nodded. "I will."

Charlie bent low and gave his sister a gentle hug. The machines surrounding her volleyed arrhythmic beeps. He pinpointed three notes that beeped nearly simultaneously. "D minor," he whispered into her ear, and smiled. "That's pretty dramatic, El."

Ana checked her watch. "If we leave in the next hour, we should reach the cemetery just after sundown. The only problem is, Charlie's car is thrashed and mine isn't strong enough to make the journey. With Schrader gunning for us, we'll need something reliable to drive."

"None of the rental-car companies are open yet," Raymond said. "Not even at the airport."

Charlie threw his arms up in the air. "Oh for chrissakes, Dad!" He turned to Ana and said firmly, "We have a car. Let's go."

Charlie, Ana, and Dale filed out of the room, leaving Raymond alone with Louis and his unconscious daughter. He leaned over and gave Ellie a final kiss on the forehead. "We're gonna get you out of this mess, sweetheart," he whispered. "Just hold on a little longer."

He gave her hand a squeeze, thanked Louis again, and made for the door. The others were waiting for him by the nurses' station.

"My car is up on the fourth level," Ana said. "Ready to make tracks?"

"You and Dale go on ahead," Raymond told her, then placed a hand on Charlie's shoulder. "We'll catch up in a minute."

Ana nodded, then headed for the parking garage. Dale went with her, head bobbing back and forth on his rubbery neck.

When they were out of sight, Raymond nudged Charlie toward a nearby stairwell. "Come with me."

Two minutes and three flights of stairs later, Raymond led Charlie into a different waiting room. A room he hadn't laid eyes on in five years.

Except for the hundreds—literally hundreds—of dead people milling about, nothing had changed. The layout was exactly as he remembered it. Each chair was the same. He knew because, at one point or another, he'd sat in them all. Even the vending machine in the corner was the same. Still out of Cherry Coke.

Even though he knew why he was there, he still forced himself to ask the question.

His father bit his lip, thoughtfully, then said, "It occurred to me that you still haven't asked me my motivation for finding the records."

"I didn't think I had to."

"Why is that?"

"Because it's obvious why you went looking for them," Charlie replied flatly. "You couldn't resist the thrill of the hunt. You never could when a rare record was involved."

"I suppose you're half right," Raymond said. "I couldn't resist, but not because the records were rare. I wanted to find them so I could correct a serious mistake I'd made."

"Oh yeah?" Charlie said, feeling his ears heat up. "And what mistake would that be?"

"*Hi, pumpkin.*"

Charlie felt his limbs freeze.

Standing to his left, dressed in the hospital gown she died in, was his mother.

PART IV

FORTY-NINE

Charlie was in the kitchen when Ana found him.

He was bent low over the open dishwasher, searching for something and clearly not finding it.

Ana stopped in the doorway and drew loose, invisible figure-eights along the countertop with her finger as she watched him. On a different day, she would have done the finger-countertop thing to seem casually sexy, but on that morning, she did it as a way to fill the time until he noticed her presence.

When thirty seconds had passed and he still hadn't noticed her, she started to feel weird and voyeuristic. So she cleared her throat.

"I'm looking for my travel mug," he said, looking up from the dishwasher.

He looked more tired than ever. Thick shadowy bags weighed his eyes down. Ana fought the instinct to tell him he needed sleep (she needed sleep herself; the luggage under her eyes no doubt matched his), but time was not their friend, and such luxuries, no matter how biologically mandatory, were not an option for them, so she pointed to an upturned blue, sparkly number on a wood dish rack. "How about that one?"

"That's my backup mug," Charlie replied, and searched through a row of cabinets over by the window. "There's an old Sub Pop mug around here somewhere. I got it as promo gift during my A&R salad days."

Ana's face brightened a little. "You worked for Sub Pop?"

"'Interned' would be more accurate. I never signed anyone while I was there, but everyone got them as gifts after Wolf Parade's first record came out."

"So the mug is . . . what? Sentimental?"

"In a way." Charlie stood and placed his hands on his hips as he scanned the open cabinets. "I've never signed a band as good as Wolf Parade and that mug has always been sort of a motivational tool. I left it here five years ago and have been meaning to get it back, but I haven't been back home since . . ." He paused. "Well, five years ago."

"Since your mom's funeral."

"Uh-huh," he said, eyes still on the search.

Ana took a step forward, crossing her arms as a way of armoring herself against the awkwardness of the personal question she had no business (but also had no choice in) asking.

"So you really saw your mom back there?"

Charlie's eyes stopped searching. He stared down at the open dishwasher but wasn't really looking at it. "Yeah."

"How did it go?"

He paused, gathering his thoughts, then said:

"It was—"

warm in the chemo ward, just like he remembered it being. The air was thick, but not unpleasantly so, and all around the space, sun-faded motivational posters encouraged him to "Hang In There," and told him that "Good Health is the Greatest Wealth."

The dead that roamed those halls were of the gentlest kind. To them, death had not come as a surprise. Months of chemo and slowly fading hope had prepared them to welcome oblivion with open arms, and as Charlie looked for the second time into the face of his dying mother, he couldn't speak.

She took a small step toward her son. Her frame was withered and frail, just as it had been on the night of the death.

And yet . . .

And yet she appeared strong. Stronger than she ever had been in life.

When she spoke, her voice was exactly as he had remembered it. And as the words "Hello, darling boy" drifted from her lips, Charlie was no longer the man he was. He was the boy he used to be.

He felt his heart collapse under the weight of memory. He was taller than she was. He'd forgotten that. Her eyes had tiny flecks of green in them. He'd forgotten that too. As she spoke, her upper lip tensed up a little, as if she were holding back a laugh, and her right eyebrow was arched a little more than her left, providing her a permanent expression of amused perceptiveness that made it seem she was always in on a joke no one else understood.

Tears flowed freely from Charlie's eyes, and as he opened his mouth to say something to her, he thought—

"It's funny," he said to Ana, slowly. "I spent five years daydreaming about what I'd say to my mom if I got the chance to see her again. I must have run a thousand different conversations a thousand different ways in my head, editing and reediting what I would say. What I would ask. What I would want to know. 'Are you okay? Are you proud of me? Are you angry that your life was cut short? Are you okay that the stories I tell about you are only partly true; that over the years, I've embellished them, filled them in, improved them to the point where I began to believe them myself?' And you know what happened when that chance finally came?"

Ana shook her head.

"My mind went blank." He laughed quietly, from somewhere deep within his throat, then let his eyes finally fix on hers. "All those questions I wanted to know the answers to, all those conversations I'd rehearsed in my head . . . when it came time to say them out loud, suddenly none of it seemed to matter. She was standing there, smiling like she used to . . . smiling like Ellie and Susan smile now . . . and all I wanted to do was look at her."

Ana felt a lump form in her throat.

"I just looked at her," Charlie said. His voice was steady and quiet, almost as if he were talking to himself. "Even though I have pictures and videos of her, somehow—as she was standing there—I realized I'd forgotten what she looked like.

"I knew I only had a few minutes with her. I knew we had to go. And that's why I didn't say anything. If I used those few precious minutes to talk her ear off, I know I would have spent the rest of my life—however long that is—wondering why I didn't just shut up and look at her—and remember her the way a picture never can."

He drew himself up and took in a deep breath.

"So that's what I did."

Ana gazed at him, expressionless. Here was Charlie, having been granted the very wish she hoped could be granted for herself, and he'd wasted it. She waited for her anger to bubble up and explode; for the frustration to burst from her mouth, showering him in well-deserved insults. But the anger never came. Nor did the frustration.

Only more sadness.

"I don't have any videos of my dad," she said, gazing down at the floor. "Just one picture. It sits on the mantel at my mom's house. In it, I'm three years old and I'm sitting on a horse and my dad is standing beside me. We're both wearing cowboy hats. His fit perfectly. I was drowning in mine." She smiled for a moment; then her smile faltered. "I spent so many nights, Charlie . . . so many nights looking at that picture, dreaming of the conversations I could have with him if I got to see him again. What kind of music he liked. What his politics were. If he believed in God . . .

"Thinking of those questions would make me angry. Not at him, but at my mom. Because I was jealous of her. I was jealous that she had so much time with him and I had so little. It wasn't fair. *I* share half his DNA, not her. *I'm* the one who has his smile, not her. And whenever I would ask her about him, I didn't know if I was getting the actual truth or *her* version of the truth."

She looked up at Charlie, lip trembling. "And then I started having these dreams. These nightmares. About the picture of us. The one on the mantel. It was always the same. I would walk downstairs in my pajamas, wanting a drink of water, but before I could reach the kitchen, I would see that picture of me and my dad, only *I* wasn't in it. Neither was the horse. It was just my dad, and he was screaming and pounding against the picture, like it was a window and he was trying to break through. I couldn't hear him, but I knew he was screaming my name. He would pound and pound, and I would stand there, crying, because I knew then that he *hadn't* died. Someone had trapped him in the picture, and he couldn't get out." She paused, taking a breath, then said, "And then I'd wake up, screaming and crying. My mom would rush in and I'd tell her about my dream, and she would just hold me, rocking back and forth, saying, 'It's only a picture . . . it's only a picture . . .' But it wasn't only a picture. Not anymore. I was scared of it. Every time I'd walk into the living room, I'd avert my eyes, because I was terrified that if I saw it, I'd see my dad inside it, pounding and screaming for me to let him out . . ."

A long silence passed between them.

Ana smiled sheepishly. "Sounds pretty stupid, huh?"

Charlie stared at her, not with his eyes but with his entire face. His entire body. His heart beat fast in that moment, but it beat not out of lust or nerves or infatuation. It beat a special rhythm, reserved by the heart for those singular rare moments in a person's life when a true connection is made.

He felt the urge to go to her, to hold her tightly and never let go, to tell her about the Grim Tree and the nightmares that had polluted his own life, when a curious rumbling noise filtered into the kitchen.

"What the hell was that?"

"The Skylark," Charlie replied, gesturing to the garage. "Looks like our ride's ready to roll."

"All right," Ana said, giving him a loving squeeze on the arm, "you keep looking for your mug. I'm gonna see if he needs any help."

She turned and made her way toward the garage.

Charlie smiled warmly, holding the spot on his arm she'd just touched, and watched her go.

But halfway down the hallway, she stopped.

"Forget something?"

No response.

"Ana?"

Nothing.

"Ana, are you all right?"

Suddenly, Ana staggered backward down the hallway, boots clomping like the hooves of a spooked horse. She backed into the kitchen, eyes fixed on the shadowy figure at the end of the hallway.

The figure of Ivan Schrader.

"Ana," Charlie said, reaching for her, "get out of the way. Don't let him—"

Schrader lifted his palm and shoved it forward, forcing a missile of wind toward Ana. It hit her squarely in the chest and lifted her off her feet.

Ana threw her hands out to catch her fall, but it wouldn't have mattered. The open dishwasher door was directly beneath her, its utensil basket filled with knives, all of them blade up.

Charlie panicked.

It was a bed of nails. And she was heading straight for it.

He lunged forward and clamped his arms around her torso.

As they fell, he twisted his body, trying to shield her, and clipped the edge of the dishwasher door with his shoulder, sending a ripple of pain shooting up his neck.

They crashed to the floor with a dull thud, and Ana let loose a sharp yelp.

Charlie rolled to his side, taking his weight off her, then grabbed a knife from the utensil basket and brandished it, casting a terrified glance down the hallway.

Schrader was gone.

He dropped to the floor next to Ana, his heart thudding heavily. He didn't know what he was more frightened of: Schrader or losing her. "Are you all right?"

"I think so," she said, sitting up. She checked her body for injuries, then hissed when she lifted her right arm.

"Jesus, you're bleeding," Charlie said, and reached for a roll of paper towels on the countertop.

"Don't call me Jesus," she joked, smiling crookedly.

He rolled the sleeve of her T-shirt up around her shoulder and assessed the damage. The cut was thin, about four inches long, and ran down the back of her upper arm.

"It's not too bad."

"Think I'll need stitches?" she said, bending her neck to take a look.

Charlie ripped a paper towel from the roll and put pressure on the cut. "No, you'll be fine. It's not deep."

Ana winced. It stung a little.

"Can you stand?" Charlie asked. She nodded, and he helped her to her feet. A flash of red caught their eyes and they shifted their gaze downward.

The culprit of her injury, a bloodstained paring knife, lay on the floor by her feet.

"Look . . ." Charlie said grimly, pointing to the jagged garden of blades sitting in the dishwasher rack. "*Accidental Death*. Two inches to the left and you would have been a pin cushion."

Panic flooded Ana's features. She began to shake. "Charlie, if you hadn't caught me—"

He kissed her then.

And in that moment, everything was okay.

It wasn't a long moment, but in it, Schrader no longer existed. Nor did the deadly knives that nearly impaled her. Nor did the constant fear of death that had taken root in their minds ever since they'd played the records.

Both their lips trembled at first touch. Ana felt a rush of warm giddiness through her chest. Her head felt as if it had been stuffed with gauze, lost in the fog of exhilaration. She pulled Charlie closer to her, felt his eager response and the urgent pressure of his body against hers, and knew he was feeling the same thing.

And then came the sound of a horn.

"Come on!" Raymond's voice cried from the garage. "We're burning daylight here! Let's get a move on!"

Ana pulled her lips from Charlie's, laughing. "It's moments like these," she said, taking his hand and turning toward the hallway, "that I wish life had a studio audience."

FIFTY

The Skylark's engine growled happily along the desolate Seattle streets like a caged animal that had been set free.

For the first time in his life, Charlie sat in the driver's seat. He wished he could lower the top, but seeing as it was forty-two degrees outside (and it would only get colder the farther east they went), he let that wish go.

"Now remember," Raymond said, poking his head forward, clearly unhappy that the back seat had been designated as the dead people's section, "smooth movements, all right? The gas pedal isn't a Super-Fuzz. And the steering wheel responds to an easy touch, so be gentle."

"It's a car, Dad," Charlie said, annoyed. "Not a giant Fabergé egg."

"We're still close enough to the house to turn back if we need to," Ana called back from the front seat. "We sure we have everything? Snacks?"

"Check," Raymond said.

"Water?"

"Check."

"Shovels?"

"Put them in the trunk."

"The records?"

Raymond reached down to the floor and gave the black case a light pat of his hand. "Safe and sound."

"Good," she said, and turned to look out the window.

The world was waking up.

Window shades were drawn open, chimneys were smoking, and as Charlie trundled through the intersection of Westlake Avenue and Mercer Street, Ana gazed yearningly at a Starbucks that had just turned its lights on. She thought about asking Charlie to stop, but flashed to an image of Schrader forcing hot coffee down her throat until she choked to death and kept quiet.

Dale sat with his head leaning against the back window as Charlie weaved his way toward the I-90 bridge. With each turn, he watched the world he'd known for almost thirty years slip past him.

Whether or not their trip to Montana was a success didn't matter. He would not be coming back.

He had been dead for almost fourteen hours, and for the first time since he'd found himself standing next to his own corpse, he felt like it.

Raymond must have sensed the change in Dale, because when he leaned forward and said, "We need to make one more stop," Dale was the only one who didn't look at him like he was insane.

"Dad, we've already wasted enough time," Charlie said. "We're almost at the bridge."

"A few minutes won't make a difference. It's early enough to still beat the traffic to the pass."

"Yeah, but the longer Ana and I are both in this car, we're sitting ducks. He could kill us both right now and be done with it all. We need to put some road behind us."

"Did we forget something?" Ana asked.

"Yes," Raymond said. "Dale doesn't belong here."

"No . . ." Dale said. "It's all right, Raymond. I—"

"If it hadn't been for me, you would have had another thirty years of listening to records ahead of you. I stole those years. Now, I can't give them back, but I *can* give you this." He clapped a hand on Dale's arm. "You've got precious hours left. You should spend them the right way. Not as a fourth wheel on a wild-goose chase across the Pacific Northwest."

Dale stared at him, unsure of how to reply. Raymond turned and faced the front seat. "Go to the store."

The detour added only fifteen minutes to their time, and as far as Raymond was concerned, they were fifteen minutes well spent.

Ana thought so, too.

They stayed only a moment, long enough to make sure Dale got into the store without any trouble. Scads of police tape still crisscrossed the scene, but he made it to the door and tore down the police tape without turning any heads.

Not that there were any heads on the street to turn. Most of the shops on Asterion Avenue didn't open until 9 A.M. They were three hours into the safe zone.

Before he disappeared through the door, Ana rushed onto the sidewalk and pulled Dale into a hug. Since there was no one around to see her embracing thin air, she held on to him for a good ten seconds, sniffling into his shoulder as a hot tear crawled its way down her cheek.

"None of that now, Bangs," he said softly, patting her back. "None of that."

She stood back and wiped her eyes, nodding. "I'm gonna miss you."

"I'm gonna miss you too. But if things ever get to be a bit too heavy, just put on some Eagles. Everybody likes the Eagles."

She smiled, her eyes puffy and red. "Nobody likes the Eagles."

He shrugged. "Same difference."

Somewhere nearby, the canopy of a tree rustled. A string of cheerful tweets and chirps peppered the silent morning air like nimble fingers dancing across the high octave of a piano.

"Well, the birds are up," Dale said. "Time you were off."

Ana gave Dale one last hug, then hopped back in the car.

Through the store windows, she watched him sidle over to the JAZZ bins and run his fingers along the record sleeves. Charlie put the Skylark into drive and pulled away slowly, leaving Ana with the final image of Dale she would ever see.

He picked up a copy of *The Ornette Coleman Trio at the "Golden Circle" Stockholm* Volume 1 and smiled like a man who had come home after a long journey.

Because that's what he was.

Fifteen minutes later, Ana, Charlie, and Raymond crossed the bridge to Mercer Island.

SCOTT LEEDS

Raymond leaned back and watched the choppy water slip past his window. This was his first experience riding in the Skylark's back seat, and despite his initial nervousness in letting Charlie drive, he was enjoying himself. He leaned forward to tell him that, but kept quiet when he saw that Charlie and Ana were holding hands.

He turned back to the window and smiled.

Outside, the sun burned a thin line over the horizon, cutting a path to what would soon be a brilliant blue sky.

It was going to be a clear day.

FIFTY-ONE

They were four hours into the trip, and the Skylark was still driving like a dream.

Unlike modern cars, which were so smooth they hardly felt as if they were being driven at all, the '53 Buick rumbled and vibrated as if it were powered by jet fuel. Each action felt substantial, each turn of the wheel a cooperative negotiation between the car and its driver. The weight of it, the length of it, felt regal. Charlie and the Skylark had bonded, and as he pulled into the Chevron station in Cheney, it was with considerable reluctance that he got out of the car.

He filled the tank and did his best to ignore the steady *whoosh* of the gas nozzle. His bladder ached fiercely, but early on in the trip, he and Ana had made an agreement not to use public restrooms alone. Technically, they *could* go together, but doing so at a crowded gas station was pretty conspicuous, and they wanted to keep their profile low. And besides, public restrooms were the perfect place for a murder or a fatal accident to occur.

Charlie topped off the Skylark's tank, gazed longingly at the sign in the Chevron station's window that read RESTROOMS ARE FOR CUSTOMERS ONLY, then got back in the car.

As they eased back onto I-90, Ana leaned forward and twisted the dial on the Skylark's radio. A clunky aftermarket cassette player had been installed in the console, which had no doubt obliterated the value of the car. None of them had any cassette tapes, so the only musical entertainment they got came courtesy of the radio waves.

Passing through Cheney meant there were more stations to choose from, and after a few minutes of twisting the needle through a jungle of Christmas tunes and pop-country hits, Ana found a crackly but listenable presentation of the Velvet Underground's

"Pale Blue Eyes" on the low end of the dial. Lou's voice whispered through the Skylark's speakers, asking whoever was listening to linger on, and Ana leaned her head against the window and watched the jagged tree line slip by.

When the song ended, the cool, languid lilt of "Pale Blue Eyes" was blown apart by an obnoxious station ID, ripping Ana from her moment of zen. She sat up as an elastic-voiced DJ announced the close of the hour.

She checked her phone, which, thanks to Charlie's last-minute dash back into the house to get a charger, now had power. She glanced at the missed-call notifications. There were five of them. All from her mother.

Ana bit her lip.

"Call her," Raymond's voice said from the back.

"I don't know what I would say," she said, staring at her phone as if it were an alien object. "She still thinks I'm coming home for Christmas."

"It doesn't matter what you say. You can read her the nutritional facts on a jar of jam if you want to. Just hearing your voice will do her good. It'll do you good, too."

"I don't know . . ."

"You may not have another chance after today, kiddo. Call her."

Ana considered this, then asked Charlie if he would pull over.

He checked his watch. It was almost 11 A.M.

"The days are short, Ana. I want to get as much road behind us as possible before it gets dark. Can't you just call her while we're driving?"

Ana held her phone and gazed at him pleadingly.

Charlie knew what she wanted. She wanted privacy. A moment to herself in which she could say her possible final words to her mother without anyone else listening in.

"Just stay in view," he told her, easing the Skylark onto the washboard shoulder of the highway. "Don't wander off into the woods where we can't see you."

She promised she would.

Fifteen minutes passed and Ana was still pacing along the tree line with her phone to her ear. She was about twenty feet from the car, and well out of earshot, but Charlie could see from her expression that she was relieved to be talking to her mother.

Above her head was a battered freeway sign, shuddering against the frigid wind.

SPOKANE 11
PONDEROSA FALLS 42
MISSOULA 213

"Going through Spokane will get us there quicker," Raymond said from the back seat, "but if we go through the Falls, you won't have to tangle with Lookout Pass, which is no joke this time of year."

"I'd rather stay on I-90, Dad," Charlie said. "The plows rarely hit Highway 2 and this car doesn't have four-wheel drive."

"Of course," Raymond said, then added, "I was just thinking about how much you loved the Falls when you were a kid. It'd be fun to see the place again."

Charlie gazed up at the sign that said PONDEROSA FALLS 42 and felt a momentary pang of nostalgia.

Between the late eighties and early nineties, the Remick family spent their summers at a rented cabin on the Pend Oreille River, a small tributary that ran through Washington State's best-kept secret (at least, according to the postcards): Ponderosa Falls.

Seattle and Spokane were the two big dogs in Washington; cities that stretched for miles, peppered end to end with shopping malls, supermarkets, and multiplexes. Ponderosa Falls, on the other hand, was perennially ten years away from its first shopping mall and only had one supermarket and one movie theater to lay claim to, the latter of which desperately needed (and would most likely never receive) a thorough renovation. The four blocks surrounding the little single-screener constituted what residents of the Falls called "downtown," a term that would seem laughable to a city dweller, but to Charlie and his family, they were a magical four blocks. To anyone walking through downtown Ponderosa Falls, they were as close to time travel as they would ever get. The colorful postwar shopfronts and squeaky-clean atmosphere were an anachronistic perk the bigger cities couldn't offer, and because the town's location was so laughably inconvenient, no major industry would go near it. It would most likely stay that way forever.

Or, at least, Charlie hoped it would.

Before he had become too cool for such things, his summers in Ponderosa Falls were the highlight of his year. He'd even made friends there. There was Mattie and his little brother Josh, the kings of the uphill wheelie; and Cristina DiPaulo, a bookish brunette with a sprinkle of freckles across the bridge of her nose. And the giver of his first kiss.

And his second kiss.

And every kiss he would be given between the ages of ten and fourteen.

He wondered if Cristina DiPaulo still lived in the Falls, and if she did, he wondered what she looked like.

And if she was still a good kisser.

"Ready to go?"

Ana opened the passenger door and Charlie averted his eyes, half wondering if Cristina DiPaulo's face (and her puckered lips) were still imprinted on his irises. "How was your mom?" he asked.

"Worried. She knows something's wrong, but I told her I loved her and missed her and that things are kinda nuts right now and I had to go."

"Which is technically the truth," Charlie said, shrugging.

"I also told her I'd see her soon." She bowed her head. "Which isn't the truth."

Raymond placed a hand on her shoulder. "It still could be, kiddo."

Charlie turned the key and the Skylark rumbled to life. "Your Love" by the Outfield came crackling through the radio speakers, and Charlie flipped on the turn signal. He double-checked that Ana was buckled in, then pulled the wheel to the left and hit the gas.

A barbaric roar filled the car as an eighteen-wheeler screamed past them, missing the Skylark by half an inch. Charlie laid into the brakes and pulled the wheel the other way, tires shuddering as he skidded back onto the shoulder. Up ahead, the semi's taillights flashed angrily and its horn blared.

ALBERTSONS, the back of the big white cab said. IT'S YOUR STORE! Nobody spoke.

The still-clicking turn signal played counterpoint to the Outfield's "Your Love."

Charlie reached over and switched the radio off. His heart was thudding.

"Was that Schrader?" he asked shakily. "Or am I just an idiot who didn't check his mirror?"

"Either way, that was a close call," Raymond said. "This is a long trip, and it's easy to get lulled into a false sense of security. We can't get complacent. We need to keep our eyes peeled. All of us."

Ana nodded. Charlie did, too.

And so they drove, chasing the night, eyes open and searching.

FIFTY-TWO

Not long after they passed through Missoula, the snow began to fall.

First it came in barely noticeable wisps, then in heavy curtains. Fat flakes fell from the sky like tiny paratroopers laying siege to the Skylark's windshield. Charlie put the wipers on full blast, but seeing as every part of the car was era-accurate (except for the cassette deck), it took every ounce of the wipers' midcentury strength to keep the flakes from building up.

The sky grew dark above them, and Charlie snuck a peak at his watch. It was just after 2 P.M.

In a fair world they would have had two good hours of sunlight left, but if the snow didn't let up—and there was no reason to think it would—they had seen the last of the clear sky until tomorrow morning.

All they had to do was make it to tomorrow morning.

"Wanna try the radio again?" he asked Ana. They'd had spotty reception since they'd left the pass and had driven the last fifty miles in silence.

She nodded and switched it on. Immediately, they were met with an overproduced pop-country tune about big trucks and dirt roads and star-spangled freedom.

Charlie made a face. "Can we find something else?"

"The pickin's are kinda slim out here, man," she replied, and twisted the tuner knob again. There was a blush of crackle and another song appeared, just as overproduced as the country jam but not as America-obsessed.

A disinterested voice half sang, half spoke through the speakers as a jagged trap beat fuzzed and popped beneath it.

> *Baby, give it up.*
> *I'ma love you like a pup.*

Try and tell me it ain't true.
I'ma stick to you like glue.

Charlie knew the song. More than knew it. He was there the day it was born. He signed its birth certificate and loosed it onto the world.

He gritted his teeth, bracing for impact.

Ana shrugged. "It's either shit-country or shit-pop," she said. "At least until we get closer to civilization. Take your pick."

From the back seat came a soft chuckle.

Charlie glared into the rearview mirror. "Don't fucking start with me, Dad."

"What's going on?" Ana asked warily.

Raymond leaned forward and propped his elbows on the front seat. A satisfied grin spread across his face. "That 'shit-pop' we're currently enjoying? You can thank your driver for that."

Ana stared at Charlie. An open-mouthed smile lit up her face. "*Trey Bae?* He's one of *yours*?"

Charlie grimaced.

"The Polaris in his galaxy of stars," Raymond said, grinning impishly.

Ana shook her head slowly. "*Jesus,* man."

"I'm not proud of it," Charlie said.

"'Baby give it up, I'ma love you like a *pup*'?" she said, chuckling. "That's the best rhyme he could come up with?"

"Look, no one said he was Paul Simon, okay?"

"And who gave him that name? A group of fifty-somethings that *just* discovered BuzzFeed?"

"That was his name when I found him." Charlie gripped the steering wheel so tightly, his knuckles burned white. He hadn't slept in almost thirty-six hours and the threat of death waited for him around every corner. The last thing he needed added to his woes was embarrassment. It was a caustic ingredient hovering precariously above an already volatile mixture.

"And *where* did you find him again?" Raymond asked, grinning smugly. "The Roxy? The Avalon?"

Charlie seethed. "Knock it off, Dad."

Ana's smile disappeared. She threw eyes at Raymond, signaling him to back off, but it was too late. He went in for the kill.

"YouTube!" he cried, throwing his head back and releasing a laugh from both barrels. He turned to Ana, his milky eyes frothing. "Can you believe that? *The Man with the Magic Ear*"—each syllable had thorns as he said them—"never even had to leave the bathroom to find his meal ticket. How'd you find ol' Trey Bae, Charlie? Sandwiched between videos of screaming goats and dipshits who unbox Amazon packages?" He laughed again thunderously. "You might be the first A&R man to discover their next signee while sitting on the toilet!"

Charlie's eyes were thin blades. "Dad, I'm not gonna tell you again."

"Raymond, stop," Ana said.

But Raymond was on a roll. He knew exactly which buttons to push to get a rise out of his son, and as far as he was concerned, Charlie deserved it.

"You know," he said, his voice booming now, "I was okay with it when you left the store to go work in A&R. I thought, 'Hell, maybe he'll help to stave off the river of shit by adding some good artists to the mix and stop the next generation of music listeners from becoming a bunch of garbage-addled philistines.' But then you go and sign a bunch of fucking YouTube influencers, and lo and behold, it turns out my son isn't the cure . . . he's the cancer!"

"Knock it *off*, Dad!"

"I suppose I should blame your mother for that," Raymond said, shaking his head. "She was always too supportive of you."

Charlie's hands began to shake. A blind fury coursed through him, rendering him unable to reply. It was all he could do to keep the car steady.

"She never pushed you," Raymond said. "She saw the talent in you, but she didn't know how to mold it. She just blindly celebrated everything you did, no matter how boneheaded it was. And you know what you did? You treated her like a saint! But not me. I *knew* you could do better; I *pushed* you to do better; and I was crucified for it!"

With that, Charlie slammed on the brakes.

The back of the Skylark whipped to the left, throwing the car into a sliding one-eighty. The brake pedal shuddered under Charlie's foot, groaning as it steadied itself against the fresh coat of powder.

Snowflakes swirled around them as the car vibrated quietly on the side of the highway.

Ana looked up to ask if everyone was all right, but Charlie had already rounded on his father. His face was stone solid, all angles in the shadow of the fading light.

"Remember what I said to you back at the house? Before that car almost ran me down?"

"Jesus fucking Christ, Charlie!" Raymond howled. "You could have killed us!"

"DO YOU REMEMBER WHAT I SAID?"

"Yes!" Raymond shouted back. "You said I was a terrible father!"

"Wrong! I said you were a terrible husband!"

"Oh, *excuse* me. I guess I got my insults crossed. What's the fucking difference?"

"The difference is, you already knew you were a terrible father, but you actually *thought* you were a good husband. *That's* the difference."

"I *was* a good husband!" Raymond barked. A hurricane had formed behind his eyes. "I loved your mother more than anything in the world!"

Charlie laughed derisively. "Is that right?"

"Yes!"

"*Is that right?*"

"Yes! And when she got sick, I moved heaven and earth to make sure she was as comfortable as she could be! To be as *loved* as she could possibly be! I was heartbroken, Charlie! I could barely breathe I was so distraught!"

"AND YET THAT DIDN'T STOP YOU FROM FUCKING ANOTHER WOMAN!"

Silence fell on the car like a lead blanket.

Time had slowed to a stop, and Ana watched, breathlessly, as Raymond and Charlie faced each other like warring chess pieces.

At some point, the left-turn signal had been turned on. Its cheerful cadence encroached on the stillness of the moment like a rude houseguest, refusing to leave.

The anger on Raymond's face quickly eroded into an expression of confused horror. His voice broke as he said, "Charlie . . . how could you possibly think I would ever cheat on your mother?"

Charlie's eyes remained unblinking. "Dan called me on the night Mom died. He told me about the Sonics game."

"Who the hell is Dan?"

Charlie was in no mood to remind his father that Dan Gilroy was one of his childhood best friends. It wasn't a relevant detail. "The night Mom died, you were at a Sonics game."

"Yes," Raymond said flatly. "I was."

"He saw you," Charlie said. "Dan. He saw you holding hands with some brunette woman. I told him it was probably just Susan or Ellie, but he said it wasn't. He was sure of it. He said she was older, your age, and attractive. That she looked Hispanic. I remember all your friends, Dad. You didn't know anyone who fit that description."

Raymond closed his eyes and sighed. "Charlie . . ."

"Do you deny it?"

"No," Raymond said. He opened his eyes. There was a clearness to them that hadn't existed until now. They were still gray, still lacking the humanity of pupils, but in them Charlie saw a brief flash of life. "I wasn't having an affair, kiddo."

"Bullshit."

"It's the truth. She was just a friend."

Charlie shook his head. "I already told you, Dad, you don't have any friends that fit that description."

"It was Gloria."

Charlie blinked. For five years, he'd held an image in his head of his father snuggling up to some woman—smiling at her and stealing kisses from her in the stands as the Sonics scrambled across the court below—while his mother was dying in a hospital bed. He never saw the woman's face in his thoughts. He *certainly* never thought about her name. In his mind, she was just some anonymous trollop who'd unknowingly played a starring role in the worst night of Charlie's life.

"Who . . . who the fuck is Gloria?"

"My mom."

He turned and saw Ana, her face tense in the glow of the snow light.

"Shortly after your mom got sick," Raymond said, "I hired Ana. Her mother, being something of a traditionalist, wanted to meet her daughter's employer, so your mother and I invited Gloria and Ana over for dinner. That's when I learned that Ana had lost her father to cancer when she was just a young girl. Gloria never remarried, and because of that, she felt abandoned by her friends who still were."

"It happens a lot to widows and widowers," Ana said.

"So we made our dinners a monthly tradition. And since Gloria knew what we were going through, she became a shoulder to lean on. For me and your mom.

"She also knew the value of getting out of the house for a while," Raymond added. "Of taking our minds off of the inevitable. So she invited your mom and I to a Sonics game to help distract us for a bit. We wanted to go, but it would have worn your mom out too much, so we stayed home. After that, the chemo got more intense, and we stayed home permanently. Ana and Dale watched after the store while I did everything I could to make sure your mom was looked after—that she didn't have a care in the world she didn't need—and when things took a turn for the worse, and your mom couldn't stay at the house anymore, I stayed with her at the hospital. The staff was nice enough to look the other way for the first couple of days, but they have strict a visitation policy, and after a while, it became unsustainable for me to be there. So I went home.

"I felt helpless, Charlie. Unable to save the woman I loved; unable to understand why the doctors couldn't; and after a while, I kind of just shut down.

"And so . . ." Raymond raised a finger to emphasize his next words. ". . . it was your *mother* who called Gloria. *She* was the one who told her to drag me, kicking and screaming, if necessary, out of the house. So yes, I went to that Sonics game."

Raymond's eyes glassed over red. He shook his head slowly. "Why . . . *why* didn't you say anything to me?"

Charlie stared into the middle distance. "I didn't say anything to anyone. I made a promise to myself that no one would never know. Not even Ellie or Susan."

"But there was nothing *to* know," Raymond said.

A thick fog rolled through Charlie's mind. He was at a loss as to what to say next.

Raymond sighed and sat back in his seat, shoulders slumped. "All these years, I thought you were still mad at me because of the recording-studio thing. Which, on some level, I could almost understand. But the fact that you thought I was some trashy womanizer . . ." He shook his head again. ". . . that really hurts, kiddo."

Snow swirled gently around the car. Charlie watched the flakes stick to the windshield without really looking at them. He felt as if his memory were a printing press, and someone had just pulled a lever and brought the spinning drums to a screeching halt.

The last five years of his life had been suddenly stained by a false narrative. Every ounce of anger and betrayal he'd felt toward his father, every bullshit reason he'd given for not coming home to visit, was now invalid.

Regret was too small a word to describe what he was feeling. *Shame* was too small a word. He looked up at the rearview mirror and met his father's eyes with his own. How was it possible that he could have been so wrong?

From the back seat, Raymond grabbed Charlie's shoulder and gave it a gentle squeeze. "I went to the game because I had already said my goodbyes. I'd said a thousand of them at that point. Anything else I could have said to your mother would have used up strength she didn't have . . . and energy I had no business in taking."

He let his son's shoulder go.

"Do you understand?"

Charlie shut his eyes and pictured his mother, standing in the hospital that morning. He took stock of all the things he'd made a point to remember. The way her upper lip flared out when she smiled at him. The way the light hit the one crooked tooth she never wanted to fix. The way she favored her left leg when she stood. The way her hands looked. The way her shoulders sloped. The way she lifted her chin at an angle to see him clearly.

He remembered all the things he wouldn't have been able to remember had he spent his time with her talking.

And then opened his eyes. "I understand, Dad."

FIFTY-THREE

Ana had been driving only twenty minutes before she looked over and saw Charlie, fast asleep. He'd been bleary-eyed for the last three hours of the trip, occasionally drifting over the freeway's rumble strips, and both Ana and Raymond were worried that he would fall asleep at the wheel and run them off the road, essentially doing Schrader's job for him. And so, after a significant amount of coaxing, he begrudgingly agreed to switch places. As long as both she and Raymond promised not to let him fall asleep.

Twenty minutes after Ana took the wheel, he was snoring like a buzz saw, and neither she nor Raymond had the heart to stick to their promise.

The snow continued to fall steadily. Heavy flakes had turned into heavier ones, and Ana searched for a weather report on the radio. She scrubbed up and down the AM dial, hoping for good news, but the reports out of Missoula, Billings, and Great Falls all said the same thing: uninterrupted snowfall all through the night. To all the little boys and girls around western Montana hoping for a white Christmas, this would be welcome news. To the three people in the 1953 Buick Skylark, it was nothing more than another obstruction their grueling quest didn't need.

To her right, a large sign crawled past announcing the town of LINCOLN: 39 MI. The gas and food signs posted beneath it had faded after years of sun exposure.

Ana glanced at the fuel gauge. They had half a tank.

That was more than enough gas to get them to Lincoln. It would probably be enough to get to Great Falls, now that she thought about it, but they'd most likely be running on fumes when they got there, and that wasn't a chance worth taking. Especially in this snow.

She switched the radio over to the FM band and searched for

some tunes to occupy the time. The only stations within range were playing Christmas music.

That was all right. Christmas music wasn't bad.

She turned the dial slowly. The needle slid past alternating bursts of yuletide tunes and hiccupping static.

"Sleigh Ride" by the Ronettes.

Not bad.

"Mary's Boy Child" by Boney M.

Good, but not the right vibe.

"Grandma Got Run Over by a Reindeer" by Elmo & Patsy.

Never.

"Merry Xmas Everybody" by Slade.

Better.

"Fairytale of New York" by the Pogues.

That was the one.

Ana cranked the volume a bit. From the back seat, Raymond nodded in approval.

"Good choice, kiddo."

Ana sang along to the part about the boys in the NYPD choir and laid into the gas pedal, releasing a thick plume of gray smoke from the tailpipe. The falling snowflakes charged her windshield, changed direction right before impact, and whipped up into the sky above them.

Up ahead, a pair of headlights flashed twice before zooming past.

"That's weird," she called back to Raymond. "Why would they do that? My headlights are on."

"It might be deer. Or a speed trap. You may wanna slow down."

She eased the Skylark's engine down to a low growl and kept her eyes peeled.

About five hundred yards ahead, the highway curved slightly to the right and ducked under a quarter-mile stretch of tunnel. Standing next to the opening was a family of deer. Ana brought the

Skylark to a crawl and gave the horn two brisk blasts with the palm of her hand.

The deer—a mother and three fawns—watched, unmoving, as the car eased past them and disappeared into the tunnel.

Ana gripped the wheel, moving her hands studiously to ten and two, and felt a flutter in her chest as she fixed her gaze on the unfolding darkness ahead of her. As a kid, she loved going through tunnels. Other than birthday parties and water fountains, tunnels were one of the few places it was socially acceptable for someone to make a public wish.

This time was no different.

Please let us make it through, she pleaded wordlessly. Her eyes searched the shadows for signs of Schrader. *Please let us make it through.*

When they made it to the other side, a heavy gust of wind nearly pulled the car across the highway's dividing line. She righted the car with a more forceful jerk than she intended, waking Charlie with a start.

"Everything all right?" he said dozily.

She assured him it was, and told him to go back to sleep.

The snow swirled angrily now. The wind whistled through the seams of the Skylark's ragtop, and the trees on either side of the highway were bending drunkenly to one side.

Ana reached over and switched the stereo from FM back to AM. She twisted the dial, hoping to find an updated weather report, but was met with nothing but static. She heard Raymond say something, but missed it in her search for a clear reception.

After a few more minutes of twisting the dial, she hit pay dirt. A staticky voice rose from the pulsating fuzz.

"*. . . have been delayed, making it difficult for holiday travelers. Nancy Rousseau, a spokesperson for Sea-Tac, spoke with KING-5 early today and apologized for the inconvenience, assuring every traveler that once the fog lifts, planes will start getting back in the air. Those inland, however, may not be so lucky . . .*"

Ana frowned.

"This is a Seattle report," she said, although Raymond didn't seem to hear her. "How are we getting this all the way out here?"

She cranked the volume.

". . . meteorologists are seeing what looks to be the beginnings of a superstorm, bringing with it thirty-to-forty-mile-an-hour winds which could be seen in western Montana as soon as midnight tonight."

"Thank God we'll be through this shit before midnight, right?" she said over her shoulder.

Again, Raymond didn't respond.

"Several parts of the state have already seen heavy snowfall, resulting in low visibility and dangerous driving conditions. One accident has already been reported. A 1953 Buick Skylark was found not long ago on the shoulder of Highway 200, just outside Lincoln . . ."

Ana's heart skipped a beat. She glanced nervously at the rearview mirror.

Raymond was smiling at her.

". . . paramedics arrived on the scene, but because the vehicle was totaled, they were unable to access the passengers. Local police have identified the driver of the vehicle as Ana Cortez of Seattle, and the passenger as Charles Remick of . . ."

Ana nearly choked on her own breath. She glanced again at the rearview mirror.

Raymond was no longer smiling at her.

Ivan Schrader was.

Ana screamed. She tried to hit the brakes, but an invisible hand forced her foot onto the gas pedal. The Skylark's engine roared as it lurched forward, its headlights sweeping the glistening pavement. Gritting her teeth, Ana tried to pull the wheel to the right, but it was locked in place. The car had become a bullet, set on a straight path. Panicking, she switched on the Skylark's high beams and hoped to see open road in front of her.

Her heart sank.

Up ahead, like a ghost appearing from a wall of fog, was a large truck pulling a long white trailer.

The volume knob on the radio turned itself to the right, maxing out its own volume.

"... *Officer Grant Sims of the Montana State Police was first on the scene. He was reported as saying the accident could have been avoided if the stupid bitch had just impaled herself on the dishwasher knives like she was supposed to ...*"

Ana shrieked and turned off the radio. The Skylark gobbled the freeway up hungrily, gaining speed every second. Ahead of her, the truck flashed its taillights, warning her to back off.

Ana responded by laying on the Skylark's horn. It blared weakly in the wind. She gripped the steering wheel and threw all her weight to one side, but still the wheel wouldn't budge. She couldn't stop. She couldn't even slow down. Her foot was welded to the gas pedal with invisible steel.

"Charlie!" she cried. "Charlie, wake up!"

She turned to Charlie and slapped him on the arm, crying, "Charlie! Charlie, wake up!" but he didn't move. He continued sleeping peacefully, slumped in the passenger seat.

As each second passed, the space between the truck and the Skylark was getting smaller and smaller. Ana let go of the wheel and grabbed her thighs. She begged them to move, *ordered* them to move, but her legs were no longer her own to control.

Only ten feet separated them now, and the Skylark's headlights flared across the back of the truck's trailer, illuminating the scene in front of her.

Ana looked up.

Standing on top of the trailer was Ivan Schrader. His coattails flapped wildly in the wind. He gazed down at her, every one of his rotten teeth bared in a wicked smile.

"NO!" Ana bellowed, tearing at her leg and begging her foot to release itself from the gas pedal.

Schrader, enveloped in a cloud of gray exhaust and swirling snowflakes, wiggled his spongy fingers like a cartoon villain and

laughed into the wind. Neither the speed of the trailer nor the occasional bump of its tires seemed to have any effect on his ability
to remain upright. He leaned over and pulled at one of the safety
straps that secured the trailer's back gate. The strap split in half with
a *thwip,* almost as if Schrader's hand were sharp as a blade, and
fluttered along both sides of the trailer. Delighted, he cackled again.
His throaty voice threaded itself into the howl of the wind like a
rumble of thunder, and Ana was forced to clap her hands around
her head to keep her eardrums from rupturing.

Wiggling his fingers again, Schrader bent low over the edge of
the trailer.

"No . . ." Ana said, although she couldn't hear herself say it.

With a flourish of his wrist, Schrader reached for the tailgate pin
and pulled it free.

The tailgate shuddered momentarily; then, with a metallic
groan of its hinges, the door dropped to the pavement, sending up
a shower of sparks as it was dragged along the highway.

The trailer was full of horses.

"Jesus Christ . . ." Ana croaked.

Schrader cackled with delight as the horses whinnied and stumbled nervously along the inside of the trailer, terrified of the now
unobstructed view of the highway behind them.

"Please . . ." Ana sobbed. "Please don't . . ."

Schrader stood up, his ponytail fluttering like a kite tail, and
turned to face the front of the truck. He raised his right hand above
his head, as if collecting the wind in an invisible jar, then closed his
fist with a snap.

A quarter of a mile up the road, a sixty-foot pine tree pulled
itself from the ground and hovered in midair, roots splayed like the
legs of a petrified octopus, then floated from its place in the tree line
over to the freeway.

"Charlie . . ." Ana pleaded, tears streaming from her eyes. She
clawed at his jacket and shook him violently. "*Please . . .*"

Schrader brought his arm down like a conductor, and the float-ing tree slammed onto the road fifty feet in front of them, splitting the pavement into broken pieces.

Ana heard the squeal and monstrous hiss of the trailer-truck's air brakes, but it was too late. The truck ate up the road in a flash, and its front tires collided with the fallen tree before its driver could turn the wheel.

The cab ascended into the air like a whale breaching the surface of the water. Inside the trailer, the horses, eyes wild and white with terror, seemed to float in a momentary stasis. Their hooves flailed about, reaching desperately for the bottom of the trailer, as gravity defied them.

As the cab of the truck began its descent, Ana held her breath, turned her head to the side, and braced for impact.

"ANA, GET DOWN!"

A hand grabbed her neck and pulled her down into the cush-ioned vinyl.

The Skylark's tires screamed along the pavement as a deafening explosion of broken glass, ripped fabric, twisted metal, and the ter-rified screams of horses came from every direction. The invisible vise that had kept her foot glued to the gas pedal released itself. On instinct, Ana reached for the brake with her right hand and pushed. Above her, a shadow passed, blocking out the light of the moon, and a tornado of hair and hooves flew past her ears. The car skidded to a shuddering stop and sent a horse tumbling onto the pavement behind them, bucking and kicking as it went. The car's canvas con-vertible roof went with it, tearing free and sliding along the concrete until it eventually disappeared into the shadows.

Ahead of them, three horses rolled from the trailer and went bouncing along the pavement, sending up clouds of snow with each impact. The largest of them ricocheted off the Skylark's left headlight, shattering it, and went spinning into the road next to Ana's door. The other two tried—and failed—to get themselves up on their hooves.

They were tumbling at too high a velocity to control their trajectory. The second horse slid into the ditch on the shoulder of the highway and collided with a tree trunk. The third skidded away into the shadows and out of sight.

For what seemed like a full minute, no one in the car moved.

The Skylark's engine idled softly. Its red taillights cut hazy beams through the curtain of peacefully falling snowflakes.

With trembling hands, Ana grabbed hold of the steering wheel and pulled herself up. She looked around, unable to contemplate her surroundings at first, then shivered as a snowflake landed on the back of her neck.

To her left, the largest horse stirred slightly. Its snout swayed back and forth as a gurgling whine spilled from its throat. Its body, bent and broken from the impact, trembled in the glare of the Skylark's headlights. Its blood-caked hair glistened like black oil, and one of its hooves—Ana couldn't see which—twitched and jerked, smacking the Skylark's front bumper.

Forty yards behind them, lying on the pavement like a fallen gladiator, was the Skylark's ragtop, its metal frame twisted and mangled. Lying next to it was the horse that had rolled over the top of them.

"Oh my God!" a voice nearby cried. "Oh Jesus Christ, are you all right?"

A man in weathered coveralls and a soiled baseball cap jogged through the twin blades of the Skylark's headlights. His face, all jowls and covered in gray stubble, was ghostly pale. He stared down at the mangled bodies of his horses and hiccupped, bringing his hand to his mouth.

"Oh, Jesus, Jesus . . . fuckin' Jesus," he muttered, falling to his knees and petting one of the horses with a quivering hand. Inside the trailer, two more horses—luckier than the others—snorted nervously. The driver looked up, ashen-faced, then hobbled over to the Skylark. "I . . . I don't know what happened," he muttered shakily.

"I swear . . . this tree just came outta nowhere and fell onto the road . . . I didn't even have a second to . . . oh Jesus God . . . my horses . . ."

Ana pawed blindly at her forehead and felt warm blood on her fingers.

Charlie gave his shoulder a delicate prod with his hand. He was bleeding, too. "I think I got clipped by a hoof."

The truck driver removed his baseball cap and wiped his brow with his sleeve. "Oh thank Jesus you're all right. I thought you were goners."

"We should be," Ana breathed, then looked knowingly at Charlie. "We really should be."

"You two just stay put now," the driver said, stumbling back to his truck. "I'm gonna call an ambulance and get the two of ya checked out."

Charlie slid back in his seat and exhaled heavily. "I can't fucking believe we survived that."

Raymond leaned forward and grabbed Ana's and Charlie's shoulders. "Are you two all right?"

"I think I pissed my pants," Charlie said, lightly prodding his shoulder with his fingers, "but other than that, I'm okay."

"Ana, is anything broken?"

"Probably," she said. "I'm too freaked out to notice, though." She shivered as the wind blew a cluster of snowflakes onto her face. The Skylark was now a permanent open-top. "It was him, by the way," she said. "Schrader. He did this."

Charlie nodded heavily. "When you began to speed up, Dad and I tried to get you to stop, but you couldn't hear us. Or wouldn't hear us."

"There was a weather report. On the radio. It told me what was going to happen. Did you hear that?"

Charlie reached over and switched on the radio. The Pogues were wrapping up "Fairytale of New York."

Ana closed her eyes. Of course. There had been no weather report. The radio hadn't even been switched from FM to AM.

"Listen, if you're both all right, we should get going," Raymond said.

Charlie whirled around to face the back seat, wincing at the pain in his shoulder. "Dad, look around for Chrissake. It looks like we were just dropped into fucking Gettysburg. We can't just up and—"

"Yes," Raymond said firmly, but not unkindly. "We can. We have to."

Ana snuck a glance at the rearview mirror. The horse that had taken off the top of the Skylark was splayed out on the road behind them. Its nostrils shot jets of fog into the air above it as it struggled for breath. She shuddered and looked away. "God, that one's still alive."

"It's awful, I know," Raymond said. "But if we don't get going, it'll get a lot worse."

"Fair point," Charlie said. "Schrader could come back at any moment."

"Schrader, yes," Raymond conceded, "but if those horses aren't dead yet, they will be soon, and I don't think any of us want to wait around to see what that horror show will look like."

The image of bewildered, mangled, undead horses walking around on broken legs and surveying their own corpses flitted through Ana's mind. She quickly unbuckled what was left of her seat belt and nodded to Charlie.

"You're driving."

The man in the coveralls finished placing his call into 911, then hopped back onto the pavement. He paused to dab his eyes with a handkerchief, mourning the three horses he'd lost, but was grateful the two kids in the fancy hot rod hadn't been killed. That night, he would pray his way through the rosary at least two times before he allowed himself to sleep.

If he *could* sleep, that was.

He pulled two flares from the truck's emergency kit and ignited one. The tip spat to life with steady orange fire. He needed to mark the other horse down the road. God forbid anyone hit the poor thing a second time.

He wound his way around the truck, flare burning brightly in his hand, as the Skylark, minus a roof and sporting a busted headlight, blew past him, making tracks in the freshly laid snow.

FIFTY-FOUR

On the surface, the town of Lincoln, Montana, appeared to be less of a town and more of a strip of road where the minimal requirements of a civilization had been sneezed out, erected, and left to languish on their own. Only when someone was driving through on their way to somewhere else did the little town roust itself from slumber and dust itself off.

But it was charming, in the way a town that was little more than a pit stop could be. It had everything a weary traveler needed: a gas station, a motel, and a smattering of restaurants (including the little ice-cream shop with its antique Coca-Cola signs and scrubbed white tile that, during the summer, promised passersby the small-town-American comfort of a cool treat on a hot day).

Even in the dark, as the frigid wind swirled through the unintended open-top that was now the Skylark, Charlie couldn't stop his mouth from watering at the idea of an ice-cream cone. It was a momentary respite from the direness of their situation, a flash to some Bradburyian daydream from the pages of *Dandelion Wine*, and as he eased the battered car into the one-and-only gas station on Lincoln's Main Street, he felt his stomach growl hungrily.

Ana felt it too. Charlie went to top off the tank, limping as he did so, and she cast a mournful glance at the Cenex station's half-lit convenience store. "I don't think I can stomach a pack of Corn Nuts. I want real food." She turned around and gazed at Raymond, the only one out of the three of them who wasn't freezing his ass off or hungry. "I know we said no stops, but I don't think I'm gonna make it much further if I don't eat something." Her teeth were chattering. She tried to hide it, but Raymond could hear it in her voice. They had pushed beyond the boundary of the snowfall, which was a godsend considering they no longer had a roof, but her hair and clothes were wet. Charlie's, too. They weren't soaked, and thank

God for that, but if they were going to make it to Havre without freezing to death, they needed to get dry.

"It's an hour and a half to Great Falls," Raymond said, looking doubtfully up and down Main Street. There seemed to be only one restaurant open. It stood ominously alone, surrounded (*no, choked,* Raymond thought) by a copse of imposing trees. "You'll have a lot more choices there."

"I don't think I can make it that long," Ana said, her clattering teeth punctuating every syllable. Her cheeks had taken on a worrying blue hue.

"What do you think, kiddo?" Raymond said, turning to his son, who was shivering violently as he held the gas nozzle.

"I think Schrader would be pretty p-pissed if we let hypothermia g-get us before *he* did," he said with a pained smile. "Also . . ." He nodded to the lone restaurant surrounded by trees. ". . . that looks like the s-sort of place that has pie."

"And hot coffee," Ana added, closing her eyes and purring.

Raymond smiled.

"Maybe that'll be just the thing to keep you two out of the bowels of the Black Lodge."

FIFTY-FIVE

Lambkins of Lincoln, whose name implied a culinary celebrity befitting a dimly lit, mahogany-lined steakhouse, turned out to be just the ticket for two hungry people with chattering teeth.

There was a small countertop in the back—flanked by dueling Coke and Pepsi machines—that gave way to the kitchen, where a symphony of sizzle and steam was in full swing. Wood-paneled walls glowed serenely under gentle halos of light cast by a series of hanging lamps, and on one side of the restaurant, spanning the entire wall, was a faded mural, hand-painted by the look of it, depicting a cozy scene on the bend of the Little Blackfoot River, which flowed about five miles west of Lincoln.

The restaurant was quiet. There were only five cars in the parking lot (including the battered Skylark) and by the look of it, their owners were all present and accounted for. Two old-timers sat at the counter, talking quietly over two plates that had been licked clean. A pair of brown, bell-shaped coffee mugs steamed lazily beside them. In the back corner, an off-the-clock postman was wolfing down a chicken potpie and ignoring the advice of the woman behind the counter, who called over to him with a motherly warning to "slow down and let your gut catch up, Clark." The woman, whose apron was cinched loosely around her considerable waist, turned and peered over a pair of bejeweled reading glasses when she heard the bell above the door tinkle.

"Holy Moses!"

She placed her pair of readers, which were fastened to a braided strap around her neck, on her ample bosom and shimmied around the counter.

"You two look frozen! What'd you do, *walk* here from Great Falls?" The other patrons turned and stared at Charlie and Ana.

"We had a little car trouble," Charlie said sheepishly, suddenly aware of all the eyes on him.

"I'll say," the woman said, studying the fresh wounds (and not so fresh bruises) on their faces. "You two look like you took a tumble in a cement mixer."

"Is the kitchen still serving?" Ana asked. She didn't care that anyone was staring. The warmth of the restaurant (both the temperature and atmosphere) was already working its magic. She slipped off her leather jacket and moaned blissfully at the immediate thawing effect it had.

The woman—whose name was Pat, according to her name tag—fluttered around them like a fussy cartoon fairy godmother and took their jackets. "As long as the lights are on, the kitchen's serving," she said. "Now take a seat, the both of you. Anywhere you like. But if you'll take my advice, you'll park yourselves in the booth over by the jukebox. It sits directly under the vent. You two'll be dry in no time."

Charlie and Ana happily obliged.

The volume on the juke was set so low, neither of them noticed it was on until they sat down. As they slid into opposite sides of the booth, they were welcomed by the reedy croon of Jim Croce.

As he perused the menu, Charlie hummed a few bars of "I Got a Name," then said, "Too bad Dad didn't come in with us. He loves this song."

Raymond had elected to stay outside with the car, and more importantly, the records. He was fairly confident that the people of Lincoln wouldn't be prone to thievery, but they had come too far and endured too much to chance it. And anyway, he was happy to let Charlie and Ana have a moment together alone.

"You don't want to look?" Charlie said, gesturing to Ana's menu.

"I'm gonna have a western omelet with hash browns and the blackest cup of coffee they have," she said.

She figured she didn't have to look at the menu to know a place like Lambkins of Lincoln did each of these things perfectly.

And as it turned out, her theory was correct.

"You want extra cheese on that omelet, sweetheart?" Pat said after bringing them a steaming carafe of coffee and two brown mugs.

"Please."

"How about you, handsome?"

Charlie ordered a chicken fried steak and two slices of pumpkin pie. He figured any restaurant that kept a seasonal specialty permanently on their menu must be pretty proud of the recipe.

"Good choice," Pat said, scribbling down the order and heading for the kitchen. "I'll bring a third slice for you, honey," she said to Ana over her shoulder. "You can afford it."

Ana smiled and thanked her.

On the jukebox, Jim Croce took a bow and made way for Rod Stewart and his song about handbags and glad rags.

"So do people really call you the Man with the Magic Ear?" Ana asked, sipping her coffee.

Charlie, who'd been fiddling with a small container of creamer, dropped it on the table with a thud. "Please don't ever call me that."

Ana grinned. "Why? Does it bother you?"

"No," he said, sarcastically. "I love it. I hope they etch it onto my tombstone."

"Oh, I'm sorry, Man with the Magic Ear," she said, pouting. "I didn't know it bothered you so much."

"*Hey*," Charlie said, brandishing a plastic straw, "if you don't stop right now, I swear to God, I'll sing 'Cotton Eye Joe' at the top of my lungs and it'll be stuck in your head for two days."

Ana crossed her arms smugly. "I'll see your 'Cotton Eye Joe' and raise you the Kars4Kids jingle. I'm more than happy to fall on my sword and fuck us both with that one."

"Oof," Charlie said, grimacing. "Bad form, old man."

Ana laughed. "Look, if it really does bother you, you don't have to talk about it. It just seems weird for you to have a nickname like that. You don't seem the type."

"Trust me, I'm not," Charlie said, absently rolling the straw between his fingers. "It started as a joke. My mentor, Jennifer Graham, made it up to embarrass me. She even had a plaque made and glued it to my door. It took a crowbar to pry it off."

Ana rolled her eyes. "She sounds lovely."

"She's actually great," Charlie said. "And if it had been something that stayed between us . . . you know, a joke between friends . . . it would've been fine. But this other guy I work with, Luke, put it in a press release, and then *Billboard* picked it up."

"Uh-oh."

"Front page. My goofy Sony headshot beneath the headline MAN WITH THE MAGIC EAR SIGNS YOUTUBE SENSATION."

Ana winced. "Trey Bae, I presume?"

"I was fucking horrified," Charlie said. "Not that I'd signed Trey Bae—he's got a good voice and a great ear for melody, no matter what my dad says—but because that stupid fucking nickname put a target on my back. Suddenly *everyone* was calling me that. And not in the friendly teasing way Jennifer did. They said it with venom. All of a sudden, everyone around me wanted me to fail . . . to fall face-first into a puddle of hubris . . . and you know what? I couldn't blame them. If I'd heard about some asshole in the industry with a nickname like that, I'd want them to fail too."

"It can't have been all bad," Ana reasoned. "Trey Bae sold, like, a billion records, so the nickname may have been self-absorbed and ridiculous, but it was accurate."

"That's what Jennifer kept telling me. And the *Billboard* article *did* help business. But Dad was furious when he saw it. He called my office and said, 'I didn't raise you to lay a crown on your own head, kiddo.'"

"It's so crazy," Ana said, shaking her head. "A week ago, I never would have believed Raymond said something like that. I've known him for seven years, and I never once saw him be cruel."

"Knowing someone at work isn't the same as knowing someone at home," Charlie said darkly.

Ana held her hands up. "Believe me, that's a truth women know all too well, it's just . . ." She paused, considering how to proceed, then said, ". . . after what Dale told me about him pushing you into a record deal that you didn't want, and the whole flying secretly around the world to find those records thing . . . I'm starting to think I never really knew him. Not truly. And that makes me sad."

Charlie reached across the table for her hand. "You *do* know him," he said. "You got to know the good side of him, and that makes you lucky."

"But it's not real," she said, frowning.

"Sure it is. *You* bring it out of him, like my mom and sisters did. I, unfortunately, bring out the bad side."

"But why? You two are so alike."

"When Dad was young, way before he had the record store, he was a musician; a street-corner guitar player, with tip bucket and everything. He mostly played singer-songwriter stuff, like Jackson Browne and Steve Goodman, but he was pretty good. He could even pull a crowd. That's actually how he met my mom."

Ana smiled. "He told me that story once."

"Did he tell you the part where he would sneak his own songs in between covers?"

Ana's smile faltered a little. "No, he didn't mention that."

Charlie sighed. "Dad figured if he could slip an original in alongside 'These Days' or 'Girl from the North Country,' it would validate him as a songwriter and he could take his place among the greats."

Ana leaned back warily. "I feel like there's a 'but' coming on . . ."

"*But* . . . his songs weren't any good," Charlie said. "When he'd play them, the crowd would either start talking among themselves or leave entirely."

"Ouch."

"He wasn't fazed, of course. My mom always stuck around and listened, and that was enough validation to get him through the rough patches.

"But a few years went by, and no labels were biting, so he and my mom pooled all their money together and Dad recorded an album. He called it *Songs for Joanie*."

Ana's jaw dropped. "He made a record?"

Charlie nodded. "He sent a bunch of copies to radio stations around the Northwest, hoping they'd play them, and a few even did, but only because my mom would call in and disguise her voice as different people asking them to play it."

Ana shook her head, astonished. "I can't believe he never told me any of this."

"He wouldn't have," Charlie said, his tone suddenly serious. "He never even told *me*. My mom did. And even then, she swore me to secrecy. Ellie and Susan don't even know."

"What made her break her silence?"

"The incident in the studio. When Dad broke in and changed my mixes."

"Why then?" Ana said.

"She wanted to help me understand *why* Dad did what he did," Charlie said. He stirred his coffee. "He was a good guitar player. He could have easily made a living as a studio musician or a pickup player if he wanted to. But he wanted to write his *own* songs. The problem is, he couldn't write a song to save his life. He just didn't have it in him. So when he saw that his son could write a pretty good melody, he figured fate had given him a second bite at the apple. The only problem was, I didn't want anybody to hear what I wrote, so he had to force me into the spotlight." He picked at his fingernail thoughtfully for a moment, then said, "It was embarrassing, Ana. Watching him in the control room, giving the musicians notes, giving me songwriting tips. The engineers couldn't stand him. Nobody could. It would have been one thing if he knew what he was talking about, but he sounded like a fool. And eventually I had to kick him out of there."

Ana sat back in her seat, eyes trained on her coffee mug. "And your relationship never recovered."

"We were never as close as we *were*, but we did our best to put it behind us. But then Mom got sick and things got tense again. And after I found out he was cheating on her—"

"*Wasn't* cheating on her," Ana interjected forcefully. "My mom's a proper lady."

"After I *thought* he was cheating on her, the anger kind of spiraled, on both sides, and we never got the chance to patch things up."

There was a clink of plateware to their left, and Pat sidled up to their table, arms expertly balancing two plates. "Hope you two got your eatin' pants on!"

Ana's omelet steamed like a busted radiator. The oil on Charlie's chicken fried steak was still bubbling. They thanked Pat and dug in, both of them eating faster than they'd intended.

"So," Ana said, mouth full, "supposing we survive this shit, what's the Man with the Magic Ear gonna give us next? Another Trey Bae? Maybe a girl group?"

"Listen, lady," Charlie said, stabbing his fork at her. "It's not all Trey Baes, all right? I signed, like, ten bands this year. I've got another one coming down the pike. Their new record's gonna be amazing."

"Ooh . . . do tell."

"Well, they've got to change their name."

Ana grinned. "Say it."

"It's pretty lame."

"*Say it.*"

Charlie sighed. "The Mightier Ducks."

Ana's lips ballooned, stifling a laugh, but failed to contain the bite of omelet she'd been working on. A yellow blur shot across the table, landing directly in the corner of Charlie's left eye.

He wiped the rubbery bit of egg away with his finger, then smeared it on his napkin.

Ana howled with laughter, turning the heads of the two old-timers at the counter. "I'm so sorry," she said, hiccupping and covering her mouth.

"I told you they need to change their name."

"Who do they sound like?" Ana said, swallowing her bite of omelet.

"A bit of Cloud Nothings . . ." Charlie mused. "Kind of Strokes-y, but not overtly so."

"Okay, kind of a weird combo," Ana said, nodding as she speared another section of omelet with her fork. "But I could get behind that. And you said the record's good?"

"It's going to be. They've got a single called 'Olivia Quinn' that'll sell like the dickens."

"Who's Olivia Quinn?"

"No idea."

"But it's a good song?"

"*Great* song. Like I said, it'll sell like the dickens."

"Uh-huh. And do the dickens sell a lot?"

"Like hotcakes."

"You sound pretty self-assured there, Charles," Ana said, taking another bite. "What if it flops?"

"It won't."

"But what if it does?"

"It won't. The verses are forgettable but short enough that it won't matter, and the chorus uses the one-six-four-five model."

Ana swallowed. "I'm sorry?"

"It's a chord progression that's pleasing to the ears," Charlie said, laughing. "Not as overused as the Magic Four is now, but it was in the fifties. Now it's used for retro charm, and that's good news for the Mightier Ducks, because it'll ensure their record sells."

Ana put her fork down. "What the hell is the Magic Fo—"

CRRRAAAAHHHHKKK . . .

Ana and Charlie both jumped. To their left, Pat was outside the window, scraping icicles off the underside of the restaurant's roof. The bejeweled reading glasses around her neck swung like a sparkly pendulum as she dragged an ice pick back and forth along the eave. She threw Charlie and Ana a bubbly wave. "Sorry about the noise! If I don't scrape 'em off, they get so big that they fuse to the ground!" She raked the ice pick cartoonishly through the air. "Scrape scrape!" she cooed, giggling.

Ana and Charlie smiled and waved back, then turned to each other and laughed. They both knew the night was far from over, and that delaying their mission was as dangerous as it was selfish (after all, poor Ellie was still lying in that hospital bed), but they also knew that whatever warmth they siphoned from Lambkins would have to last them through the night.

And so they sipped their coffee, got dry, and continued to talk.

"You were saying something about the Magic Four," Ana said.

Charlie nodded. "So the Magic Four isn't a group of specific chords; it's a specific order of chords. And by order, I mean—"

"I know what chord progressions are, Charlie," she said. "Do you know how many times I've had to listen to some prog-rock know-it-all with a shitty Ibanez strapped to their back wax poetic about chord progressions while they shopped for Yes records?"

Charlie thought carefully before answering. "Lots of times?"

"Even more than that."

"That sounds awful."

"It is. Now continue."

"The Magic Four is probably the most famous chord progression in Western music. Most often, it's called the one-five-six-four. For example, if you wanted to play the Magic Four in C major, it would be C–G–A–F. If you wanted to play it in E, it would be E–B–C-sharp–A."

Ana sipped her coffee slowly, careful not to break eye contact. "This is making me really hot, Charles."

Charlie laughed. "I know, normally I would save the sexy stuff for the third date—you know, to really clinch the *deal*—but we're on a bit of a time crunch, so you're getting it now."

Ana's cheeks flushed pink. "Then keep talking."

"Basically the Magic Four is a surefire way to make a hit. Hundreds of songs use it."

"You're not just jaded?"

"Oh, I'm definitely jaded, but that doesn't make it any less true."

Ana shrugged. "So it's cheating, then."

"It's not cheating if you make it your own," Charlie reasoned. "The Magic Four is like an egg. There are a thousand ways to cook it. Some good, some bad. If you cook it good, you look like a genius. If you cook it bad, you look lazy."

"So give me some examples."

"There are too many to count."

"Just a few, then."

"'When I Come Around' and 'Take On Me.'"

Ana nodded. "Both stellar. And I wouldn't call them similar."

"Exactly," Charlie said. "If you do it right, it's barely noticeable."

"What else?"

"'Beast of Burden,' 'Let It Be,' 'Hide and Seek,' 'Glycerine,' 'So Lonely,' and basically every pop punk song ever."

"Wow."

"The list goes on for miles."

"And the Mightier Ducks aren't doing that?"

"No, they're using a different progression. Equally as earwormy but not as overused these days, so it seems fresh."

"Jesus, man," Ana said, shaking her head, "if I thought about music the way you do, I don't think I'd want to listen to it anymore."

Charlie shrugged. "It's not so bad."

"But it's not just that chord stuff," she said. "It's everything. Like the way you could pick out certain notes. Remember when you heard the siren at El Camino?"

"C-sharp," Charlie said, nodding.

"That's fucking nuts! Doesn't it ever get tiring?"

"Of course it does. But at least I found a way to get paid for it so I won't go insane." He paused for a moment, smiling thoughtfully, then said, "I don't want that to sound ungrateful. I actually love my job. And I love signing bands. It's like giving someone a winning lottery ticket. All the stoicism, all the posturing, all the apathetic musician bullshit disappears for a few days, and you get to see true excitement on their faces. And you feel excited with them."

Ana smiled, too. "Well, nickname or no nickname, you do have a magic ear, Charlie. That's a gift."

Having never gotten the hang of accepting a compliment gracefully, Charlie shifted uncomfortably in his seat. And although she'd never say it out loud, Ana enjoyed watching him squirm. She reached across the table and took his hand. He recoiled briefly, feeling a throb of pain in his shoulder where the horse had clipped him, then smiled and gave her hand a gentle squeeze.

They stared out the window at the dark crop of woods beyond the parking lot (an unobstructed view now, thanks to Pat's chipper icicle massacre), and stirred their coffee.

"Do you think this plan's gonna work?" Ana said, her expression suddenly worried. "Bringing the records to Schrader's grave?"

"I don't know," Charlie said, staring vacantly at the remaining crumbs on his plate. "It's just a hunch, but it's better than doing nothing, I guess."

"Well, if it doesn't work and we die," Ana said, raising her mug, "then I'm glad I finally got to know you. And if it does and we live, then I'll get to hear the Mightier Ducks for myself and find out if you're full of shit or not."

Charlie grinned. "I'd say that's worth fighting for." They clinked mugs and drank.

After gulping down the lukewarm remains of his coffee, Charlie stood up and said, "I'm gonna run to the bathroom real quick. After that, let's head out."

Ana, whose mouth was already full with a generous helping of pumpkin pie, gave him a thumbs-up.

FIFTY-SIX

The stinging smell of fresh urinal cakes tickled Charlie's nose.

The bathroom, a simple double-stall job, flickered in and out of view thanks to a restless halogen bulb that had been bolted to the ceiling. Above the sink, the nozzle of a powdered soap dispenser had crusted over like a calcified battery terminal. In the corner, holding court over a patch of missing floor tiles, was a yellow bucket in which a seemingly hundred-year-old mop lay marinating in a soup of brown water.

The urinal, which had been installed in such a way that it was too low for adults but too high for children, was dry. Taped on its backsplash was a piece of paper that read OUT OF ORDER.

That was fine. Charlie rarely used urinals anyway. They had a way of making even civilized men momentarily forget how to use their remarkably user-friendly appendages. What should otherwise be a simple point-and-shoot procedure often became a spirited game of Just Aim It In This General Vicinity. Bonus points if you hit the floor. Double bonus if you spray the wall.

From the outside, the twin stalls seemed to be in working order. He made for the one closest to the door and pushed the handle, only to be denied. It rattled a little under the force of his grip.

"Sorry," he muttered. His voice produced a cold echo that rang against the tile. "Didn't realize someone else was in here."

He tried the other stall, pushing gentler this time, and it swung open.

The toilet was in fairly good condition. Most importantly, it was clean. He unzipped his fly and unloaded his coffee, casting a quick glance beneath the neighboring stall.

There were no feet.

Probably out of order too, he thought. Foot traffic probably wasn't very heavy around these parts, so a single working stall was all that was really needed.

When he finished urinating, he zipped up and checked the toilet seat for splashes. Not a one.

See? he thought ruefully. *How hard is that?*

He goosed the handle with his foot then turned and reached for the knob on the stall door, but stopped when he noticed something move in his peripheral vision. He ducked low and peeked through the space between the stall door and the support panel.

Nothing.

Then, the flick of a shadow.

Fuck, he thought to himself. *I broke the rule. Don't go anywhere alone.*

"Anyone in here?" he said, hoping to sound casual, but knew immediately that he sounded frightened. When no response came he went for the knob again, only to stop himself a second time.

Better check first. Better to be safe.

He took a long, quiet breath, then stood on the tips of his toes and peeked over the top edge of the stall.

Ivan Schrader was in the bathroom with him.

He stood facing the sink, and though his back was to Charlie, the mirror caught the reflection of his twisted snarl and graying teeth.

"Shit!" Charlie hissed, then ducked down. His heart was beating so fast, it felt as if it would leap from his throat and hop away. *You played the murder record,* he told himself. *He can't murder you if there's no one else in here.*

A plan began to take shape in his head. It wasn't a complicated one. It involved a quick sprint to the door followed by an immediate cooldown to ensure no one at the restaurant turned their heads. Then, once he and Ana made it to the parking lot, another quick sprint to the Skylark.

He took a series of quick breaths, psyching himself up.

And then something else in the room moved.

Under the neighboring stall, a pair of feet descended to the floor.

The two old-timers at the counter were the first ones to look up when the screaming started.

The one on the left turned toward the bathroom. An unlit cigarette was perched in the crook of his mouth. "The *hell* was that?"

Ana blew past him, boots skidding along the floor.

"Wait a minute, young lady, it might be dangerous—" the old man said, reaching after her, but Ana was already at the bathroom door.

She kicked it open, sending the door rattling on its hinges, and gasped.

In the far corner of the bathroom, Pat the waitress had Charlie pinned up against the wall, both hands clamped tightly around his throat.

"Charlie!"

Ana dove for Pat's torso and grabbed two fistfuls of flesh beneath the woman's sweatshirt. She tried to pull her off of Charlie, but she was too heavy.

A sneer stretched across Pat's lips. She turned her head and glared at Ana with two bloodred eyes. Ana widened her stance, ready to pull again, but was immediately thrown across the bathroom, boots sqeaking along the tile. She slammed into the urinal with a sharp crack and collapsed to the ground. Bits of porcelain rained down on her head.

Charlie struggled to breathe. He clawed at Pat's hands, spat in her face, kicked at her legs—anything to force her off him, but Pat merely grinned, red eyes burning. Using what little space he had, Charlie reared his leg back and kneed her in the stomach. She staggered backward on her heels, gasping for air.

Something landed with a dull clatter on the floor next to her.

Charlie looked down and saw the ice pick she'd been using to rake the icicles off the roof.

The two old-timers piled into the bathroom, followed by the cook, a bull of a man in a white stained apron.

"Christ, Patricia," the old man with the unlit cigarette said. "What the hell are you doin'?"

The cook reached for Pat, but, like Ana, was immediately thrown back through the air by an invisible force. He careened into the left stall door, blasting it off its hinges, and landed headfirst into the rim of the toilet. His body sank to the ground. Streaks of blood crisscrossed his face. He was out cold.

"Bill!" the man with the cigarette cried. He stared at the unconscious cook and turned to Pat, horrified. "The hell did you do to him?"

But Pat didn't answer. She wrapped her hands once again around Charlie's throat, stared hard into his eyes, and opened her mouth to speak. Only, it wasn't Pat's voice that came out. It was deep and distant, as if her voice were coming from the bottom of a well.

"*Cross the banded thicket and scale the hill,*" she said, the voice rattling her vocal cords. "*Play the chord of the dead. The trees will show you how . . .*"

Pat released her grip on Charlie's neck and staggered back on her heels. The red in her eyes disappeared, replaced by two dazed pupils. Loose tendrils of saliva dripped from her slack lips onto her apron. She stared absently into the distance, and said, "I . . . I don't know what . . ."

And then she collapsed to the ground.

Charlie turned to Ana, breathing heavily. "Did you get all that?"

Ana nodded shakily. "I think so." She grabbed the ice pick and stuffed it into her pocket. "Can you walk?"

Charlie said he could, and the two of them made their way to the door, where the two old-timers stood, speechless, as they surveyed the aftermath of the scene before them. The one with the cigarette perched in his lips looked from Pat's body to Charlie, stupefied, and said, "What happened, son?"

"Call an ambulance," Charlie replied in a hoarse voice.

The two men looked at each other.

"Gonna be tough to explain this," the one without the cigarette said, rubbing his forehead. "Pat's a good woman. Never harmed so much as a fly. Hell, I ain't ever heard her raise her voice."

"I won't press charges," Charlie said. He took note of the offended faces staring back at him, as if pressing charges were even an option on the table, and said, "What I mean to say is, Pat's gonna be fine. This was a one-time thing. I can't tell you how I know that, but I do. Just trust me."

As they fled the restaurant, Ana made a quick detour to a nearby coatrack and filched two heavy Carhartt parkas and a pair of hunter's caps.

"If we survive, we'll return them," she said, tossing Charlie a cap and a parka.

Out in the parking lot, Raymond was lying in the back seat of the Skylark, enjoying the view of the stars. When he heard approaching footsteps, he sat up.

Ana and Charlie climbed into the car with a heavy sigh.

"Where'd you get the duds?" he asked them. When they didn't answer, he said, "Did something happen in there?"

The two of them exchanged weary smiles.

It was three hours to Havre, and Charlie and Ana had just the story to fill the time.

FIFTY-SEVEN

There was cold, and then there was this.

Everything hurt. To blink was to do so under protest. To breathe was to welcome unending rhythmic pain. Every muscle burned under tension, every bone felt brittle to the point of breaking.

They were past the point of shivering, past the point of chattering teeth. There was only the cold and nothing else, and as the sign that read WELCOME TO HAVRE crawled past them, it did so without fanfare.

"Which road do we take?" Charlie cried into the wind. His voice was no longer his own. It seemed to come from someone else in the car; someone else who could feel the scrape of the words across his throat.

Ana reached into her pocket and pulled out the note Louis Goodwin had written them. "Wildhorse Road," she called back, straining to read Louis's handwriting in the dark. "Take it north for thirty minutes, then hang a left on Road 110 toward Bolero County. We follow that road until we see signs for Bolero Hill." She pulled out her phone and opened Google Maps. "Looks like we're getting close."

"And remember what Pat said," Charlie replied, then corrected himself. "Or, *possessed* Pat, I guess. We have to cross through a banded thicket, whatever the hell that is. . . ."

"She also said we have to play the chord," Ana said. "But how the hell are we supposed to do that? We didn't bring any turntables with us."

"You heard her," Charlie said, then smiled thinly. "The trees will show us how. . . ." His mind flashed to the Grim Tree. He laughed, but under the howl of the wind, no one heard it.

"Something's been bugging me," she said as the wind whipped at her hair. "Schrader could have killed you back there but he didn't."

"You noticed that, too, huh?"

"I mean, he basically gave you step-by-step instructions for what to do when we get to the cemetery."

"I guess that means we're on the right path."

"Or that he's setting a trap and we're walking right into it."

Charlie looked at Ana. Her face was stone.

In the back seat, Raymond lay across the cushion and chose to look at the stars rather than take part in the conversation unfolding up front. Guilt was crashing over him in suffocating waves, and he didn't have the strength to stare into the faces of the two people he'd doomed.

If only the dead couldn't feel guilt, he thought.

This far north, the stars burned without obstruction. There were so many of them, the sky appeared tactile, like a black shim had been stretched over the glass dome of the atmosphere and stippled with thousands of pinpricks to let the starlight through. Raymond named the constellations he knew and counted the ones he didn't, trying to distract himself from the plan they'd spent nearly twelve hours and eight hundred miles barreling toward.

If the plan didn't work, and Raymond didn't want to focus on the odds, he would not only be responsible for their suffering, he would be guilty of instilling them with false hope.

And was there anything more irresponsible than that?

"From all of us at KOJM, we wish you a Merry Christmas."

Raymond sat up. The car was now going slow enough that the radio could be heard over the wind.

"Here with their classic, 'Merry Christmas, Darling,' are the Carpenters."

In the dark, Havre slipped by quickly. Little houses with glowing windows floated past them. The trees inside—a Douglas fir here, a blue spruce there—stood like gentle sentries, all twinkling and merry and bright.

Ana turned the volume up. Karen Carpenter's voice, slipping silkily through the Skylark's frozen speakers, did what nothing else could. It warmed her. It warmed Charlie, too. And for a brief moment, they allowed themselves to celebrate Christmas the way it should be celebrated: with flushed cheeks and genuine smiles.

Charlie's only wish was that Havre were bigger. He could have spent eternity cruising by the illuminated homes and admiring the lights (some hung with care, some not) as Karen Carpenter sang about the greeting cards having all been sent.

But Havre, like "Merry Christmas, Darling," didn't last.

He watched the town recede in his rearview mirror. It got smaller as they crossed the train tracks; it dimmed as the Milk River passed beneath them, and finally, as they turned left on Fifth Street and continued onto Wildhorse Road, it disappeared entirely.

Once again, they were in darkness.

"I just thought of something," Ana shouted as Charlie brought the Skylark back up to highway speed. "Will we even be able to dig in this cold weather? The soil is probably rock hard."

"We'll take it in stages," Raymond shouted back. "We'll dig for a bit, drop the records in the grave, and if it doesn't work, we'll just keep digging."

"How will be know if it works?"

"I suppose we'll know if I'm still here," Raymond said, then, off Ana's confused expression: "If the curse is broken, the two of you shouldn't be able to see me anymore."

Ana nodded silently, then turned back around.

Wildhorse Road stretched out before them. The wooded, sloping cocoon of western Montana was a hundred miles gone. Sprawling flatland surrounded them in every direction.

"Doesn't really seem like the kind of area you'd name a place 'Bolero Hill,'" Ana said, looking around doubtfully. "It looks like Kansas out here."

"The rockier terrain is west of us," Charlie said. "When we take a left on 110, we'll probably see it."

They drove on, slowing a bit as they passed Fresno Road, then watched carefully for the road signs.

This far out, they were not well marked.

"Road 80!" Ana shouted into the wind. Charlie looked to his right. The sign was so small, he was surprised Ana had seen it. It didn't help that it had been installed nearly forty feet off the shoulder of the road.

"Road 90!"

Then, a minute later, "Road 100!"

Charlie brought the Skylark down to a near crawl as they approached the next sign. This one, unlike the others, was placed on the left side of the road. Its post was bent at the middle, no doubt the result of a careless driver. The sign appeared to be leaning over, as if readying itself to be sick.

RD 110
BOLERO COUNTY

The Skylark shuddered as its tires turned left onto the unpaved road. A pale cloud of dust flew up behind it, choking off the view in the rearview mirror.

Raymond wanted to warn his son against potholes but kept his mouth shut. Charlie was doing a good job. Unpaved roads always sound a hundred times worse than the actual damage they do to a car, and when it came to the Skylark, further damage was now laughable. His pride and joy had been reduced to a doo-wop version of a demolition derby car.

They rumbled along for nearly fifteen minutes like that, leaving a trail of gray-brown dust behind them, the tires trembling and hopping over the hardpack.

Ana consulted Louis's notes. "It should be to our right," she said, reading. "He said there would be signs for it."

Charlie brought the car to a creeping stop. "Look."

Fifty yards ahead of them, Road 110 came to an end. There was no right or left turn, no smaller road beyond. It just ended.

A plume of dust engulfed them, surrounding the car in a hazy cloud. Ana and Charlie buried their faces into the hoods of their parkas and coughed. Raymond, who had no need of his lungs, exited the car and walked to the edge of the road.

"I think we made it," he said, his voice floating through the cloud of dust. Charlie and Ana waved their hands to clear the air.

Half a mile from where they were standing, looming in the darkness like a sleeping dragon and silhouetted against the moonlight, was a perfectly shaped hill, surrounded by a protective ring of dense trees.

Charlie looked at Ana. "The banded thicket."

"Pop the trunk and get the shovels," she said. "I'll grab the records."

Keys in hand, Charlie went to the back of the Skylark and unlocked the trunk. It was bent from the accident with the horse, and resisted opening for a moment, but after a little effort, he was able to lift the tailgate.

"Raymond!" he heard Ana's voice say. "Don't go too far. We don't want to lose you."

"Just taking a look around," Raymond called back, his voice distant.

Charlie reached for the shovels, but because the trunk had been warped from the accident, they were wedged tightly against a battered cardboard box. He grabbed the wooden handles and pulled, feeling the shovels give a little, but the box was too full. He searched for something sharp, but there was nothing else in the trunk except a half-empty bottle of motor oil and a stack of order forms for the Cuckoo's Nest.

His patience waning, Charlie took hold of one of the box's corners and pulled, tearing a long gash along one side of the cardboard. It came open like a shark's belly, spilling its contents all over the trunk with a rolling clatter.

Charlie bent low and inspected the contents of the box.

They were his tapes.

"Raymond!" Ana cried nearby. "I'm serious! Stay around the headlights so you don't get lost!"

Hands trembling, Charlie sifted through the avalanche of cassettes.

They were all there; all present and accounted for, labeled with black Sharpie in his teenage scrawl. He turned one of them over and read the track list.

1. *Alice*
2. *Sea Legs*
3. *Ghost Parade*
4. *Wolf Guard*
5. *Bad Chorus*
6. *Untitled IV*
7. *The Skeleton Dance*
8. *Sea Legs*
9. *Okay Chorus*
10. *Good Chorus*
11. *Untitled XI*

He laughed giddily, releasing a wispy cloud of breath.

He hadn't thought about these songs in years. A few of them he couldn't even remember writing.

He flipped a few more tapes over and read the track lists, heart racing.

Two emotions went to war inside him. He was furious that his father had pulled the tapes out of the trash, especially since throwing them away had been such a dramatic gesture, but another part of him was so happy, he felt as if he might faint.

And then he heard Ellie's voice in his head.

"He started spending hours in the garage. He'd go in there after breakfast and only come out when dinner was ready . . ."

"I snuck in there once, just to see what he was doing, and he was sitting in the driver's seat, listening to the radio."

No, Charlie thought. Not the radio.

He was using the cassette deck.

A loud crack came from his right, and Charlie slammed the trunk closed.

Twenty feet beyond the side of the road, his father tilted his shoulders to keep himself from falling.

"Are you all right?" Ana asked. She held the black case that contained the records tightly to her chest.

"Fine," Raymond replied. "Just tripped on something." He bent low to inspect what his toe had caught, figuring he would find a jagged rock or a twisted knot of dry brush.

What he found instead was a sign.

The wood was gray and nearly rotted through with age, but the print on its gnarled face was still legible.

BOLERO HILL.

He turned to Ana and Charlie.

"Well, we definitely came to the right place."

FIFTY-EIGHT

As with most large things first seen from a distance, the closer you get to them, the less they're able to retain their shape.

Overhead, the clouds seemed to be gathering around the crest of the hill, as if they were an audience taking their seats before showtime. The dense crop of trees that circled the base of the hill ("the banded thicket," possessed Pat had called it) was so thick that only the smallest blush of moonlight had been allowed through.

Ana and Charlie struggled to see where they were going, zigzagging drunkenly over the shadowy terrain.

Raymond, whose lifeless eyes seemed immune to the complications of the dark, led the way, pausing every now and then to ensure Charlie and Ana didn't snag their feet on a protruding branch or trip on the tangled undergrowth, which, to the confusion of them all, felt swampier than any ground in northern Montana had a right to feel. The mud squelched under their weight as they walked.

Charlie carried his shovel in his right hand, using the handle as a walking stick. Ana kept the pointed end of her shovel in front of her like a lance, warning any unseen beasties dwelling in the woods to keep their distance. Raymond was in charge of the black case. He clutched it protectively, careful not to jostle it too much as he walked. Even though its contents were fixed to be buried, protecting records was, for him, instinctual behavior. Cursed or not, rare vinyl was rare vinyl.

Behind him, Ana gazed skyward and studied the claustrophobic pattern of the treetops. The whole atmosphere seemed so otherworldly, so out of place, that each of them (Raymond included) wondered momentarily if they hadn't fallen asleep and were dreaming it all up.

Dream or not, the swampy darkness of the trees was preferable to the flatlands they'd just come from. For one thing, it was quiet.

Ever since the roof had been torn off the Skylark, their ears had been ruthlessly abused by the crushing roar of the wind. Now the only sound they heard was the occasional snap of a twig or the soft sucking sounds their feet made as they trod along the muddy undergrowth.

"I see a break in the tree line up ahead," Raymond announced, quickening his pace.

Forty yards to the north, the moonlight fanned across a sparse row of trees, cutting itself into hazy shafts. Raymond stepped through the break in the tree line and paused. "There's a path up here!" he said, perching a foot upon a fallen log as if he were Sir Edmund Hillary surveying an unmapped route up Everest.

Charlie stumbled into the clearing and followed the path upward with his eyes. The side of the hill was steep—very steep, and covered in long grass, tangled weeds, and jagged rocks. He planted his shovel into the dirt and rested on the handle, breathing heavily. His shoulder throbbed fiercely, and he wondered if, when it came time to do it, he would even be able to dig.

Behind him, Ana hopped over a large root and jogged into the clearing. "Shit," she said, gazing up at the hill in front of them. "It didn't look this steep back at the car."

"At least we won't be bushwackin'," Raymond said, pointing at a narrow, sloping line of weather-beaten stone steps. "They must have put those in to make carrying the caskets up the hill less of a chore."

"But why go to the trouble of putting a graveyard up there at all?" Ana said, eyes fixed on the hill's summit. "Seems like a weird place to bury bodies."

"*Weird* is kind of our thing now, Ana," Charlie said, smiling wearily.

Raymond readjusted his grip on the black case and placed a foot on the first stone step. "They say the way out is through. For us, I suppose it's up." He hoisted himself onto the second step and began climbing.

Ana followed, shovel slung over her shoulder like a hobo's bindle.

The pulsing pain in Charlie's shoulder echoed his thudding heartbeat. He took a step forward, ready to bring up the tail end, then paused when he felt the hair on the back of his neck stir.

Someone was watching them.

Charlie scanned the hill. Other than Ana and his father, both of whom were already twenty feet up the steps, he saw no one.

Because he's behind me.

He didn't need to see Ivan Schrader to know he was there. He could feel those terrible red eyes boring into his back.

Let him watch, he thought defiantly. He speared the dirt with the tip of his shovel, leaned his weight on the handle, and propelled himself forward.

Up they went, one by one like marching ants, to the top of Bolero Hill.

FIFTY-NINE

It almost didn't look real.

Something out of an old Max Fleischer cartoon, perhaps, or a Universal monster movie from the thirties.

The gravestones were spaced across the summit like pegs on a cribbage board, forming what appeared to be a large, loosely drawn spiral. Some sat upright, others jutted to the left, the rest to the right. The base of each stone sat neatly in the ground, flanked by wispy tufts of grass and overgrown weeds. The names closest to where they stood on the edge of the summit were legible, but only just. Time had worn away the dates and any descriptors down to shallow indents. What might have read DEVOTED HUSBAND at one point was now a smattering of wind-blasted glyphs.

Eyeballing it, Ana estimated the summit to be no more than fifty yards across. She watched with mild amusement as a thin blanket of fog rolled across the ground. "Surprised there isn't a tattered windmill up here too," she muttered. The whole scene was so eerily on the nose, she half expected the ghost of James Whale to pop up from behind a cracked tombstone and yell "Cut!" through a bullhorn. "This is the place Schrader showed you?" she asked Charlie.

Charlie nodded. Unlike Ana, he was not amused.

Two dozen gnarled trees circled the perimeter of the summit like skeletal watchmen, ready to reach out and snatch anyone who got too close to the sleeping dead. Four more trees, smaller and lighter than the ones at the perimeter, stood at the center of the graveyard. Charlie stared at them with a sickening sense of unease. They looked like four old crones, huddled together, frozen in time, waiting to be reanimated.

Waiting for him.

He shivered. All of those nights he'd lain awake as a boy, terrified and staring out his window at the Grim Tree, came rushing back to him. Only now, there were multiple Grim Trees. It was as if he'd stumbled into a nest of them. Any minute now, they would pull themselves from the soil and charge at him, their roots skittering along the ground like twisted spider legs.

For a split second, Charlie considered making a run for it. And he might have, if not for the voice saying his name.

"Charlie . . ."

Raymond placed a gentle hand on his son's back. "Come on, kiddo," he said, smiling. "Let's finish this."

Charlie nodded. He gripped the handle of his shovel and stepped forward.

Ana had already begun the task of checking the tombstones. With each step, fog sighed beneath her boots. She bent low, shovel tucked under one arm, and used her phone light to illuminate the eroded names. "Darcy . . ." she read aloud, sweeping the light across the faded epitaph. ". . . or maybe it's Dashiell . . ." She stood upright and recalibrated her mind. "Doesn't matter. It's not who we're looking for."

She moved on to the neighboring stone and repeated the process.

THOMAS COOPER.

And the next.

JAMES GREY.

And the next.

MARTIN something.

When her light swept across the next stone, she visibly flinched.

"Find something?" Raymond said, looking up from a nearby stone.

"False alarm," she replied. "It said ISAAC. My eyes got ahead of my brain." She moved her light to the neighboring tombstone, read the name BURGESS ROWE, then moved on, silently lamenting the fact that names like *Burgess* were no longer in vogue.

Up in the sky, the clouds continued to swirl slowly, forming a perfect circle above them. In the center, the moon glowed like a hazy iris, watching their actions with hungry anticipation.

What few leaves remained on the trees shuddered as a soft wind swirled through the graveyard.

And yet . . . it wasn't cold.

Somehow, the summit of the hill seemed to be sheltered from the frigid Montana weather, almost as if it were protected by a giant glass dome. An absurd thought crossed Ana's mind: of being trapped in a large snow globe, and any minute, a colossal hand would pick it up and shake it, sending her tumbling up into the sky.

Charlie also noticed the strange atmosphere. To see the rolling fog, the ashen trees, the gray grass, he would have expected a wet cold.

But it wasn't *any* kind of cold.

It wasn't warm, either.

It was no weather at all. Even the wind had no temperature. It was merely a tactile sensation, room-temperature breath that licked the skin without cooling or heating it. Feeling a sudden nagging impulse, he walked to the edge of the hill and scanned the horizon.

It took him a minute to find it, and he had to squint his eyes to see it, but it was still there.

Half a mile away, waiting at the end of Road 110 like an obedient dog, was the Skylark.

Still there.

He looked down at his hands, felt the throbbing pain in his left shoulder, and reassured himself that, like the car, he was still here, too.

Still in Montana.

And yet, it was easy to doubt. The circle of trees at the foot of the hill were dense enough, dark enough, *strange* enough, that Charlie would have had no trouble believing they'd passed through a portal of some kind, some passageway that opened onto a place with no weather and looked like something from the set of *Frankenstein*.

How many others had stumbled upon this place? he wondered.

It wasn't so far out of the way that it couldn't be found. After all, a road had brought them here. A man-made road made by men with eyes; eyes that could very easily see Bolero Hill in the distance.

Maybe that's why the road ends so abruptly, he thought. Maybe the men who made it didn't dare pave any closer.

Maybe the hill stopped them.

And yet, there were the gravestones. Forty or so, he guessed. Someone had to have put them here. Someone had to have lugged the bodies up the hill and buried them. It seemed like such a strange, futile effort to go to such trouble when there were thousands, literally thousands, of perfectly good acres surrounding them, none of which required climbing.

So why *this* hill, then? What made these dead people so special that they needed to be buried all the way up here?

"Charlie."

Ana was next to him. Her phone light trembled in her hand, illuminating the underside of her chin. "You need to see this."

Charlie followed her to the center of the hilltop—kicking up fog as they went—where a small outcropping of tombstones waited for them. Raymond was already there. His face was still, yet Charlie could see the slightest trace of anger behind his cloudy eyes.

"What wrong, Dad?"

Like the Ghost of Christmas Yet to Come, his father gave no reply, and instead pointed to a row of tombstones in front of them.

Charlie reached down and brushed his hand along the stone next to him. It was smooth, and gleamed in the moonlight. Unliked the ragged, timeworn stones on the outer perimeter of the hilltop, these stones appeared to be new. Installed recently.

There were six of them, all in a line. The three on the left were blank. The three on the right were not. He moved his light slowly across the faces of the tombstones and nearly choked when he reached the fourth. He bent low, reading the name etched into the polished stone.

RAYMOND REMICK.

Charlie felt his throat close up. "Oh my God . . ."

Raymond took his son's wrist and guided the light to the stone next to it.

LOUIS GOODWIN.

And to the following stone.

DALE CERNIN.

"Oh my God," Charlie said again. He crawled to his left and swept his light back over the three blank tombstones. They gleamed menacingly in the gray haze of the moonlight, their unetched faces polished to a mirrorlike finish. "That means . . ."

Ana nodded solemnly. "You, me, and Ellie."

Charlie felt a racking sob escape his throat as his own distorted reflection stared back at him from the blank tombstone. "This was all pointless," he said quietly. "The moment we listened to those fucking records, our tombstones were made. There was never any escaping this."

"You don't know that," Ana said, wiping away the burning tears that flooded her eyes.

"We're fucked," Charlie said flatly. "That's it. Fucked."

"No," she said, and took his hand in hers. "There still might be a way. There *has* to be a way."

"We might as well just go ahead and knock on Schrader's grave right now and get it over with."

"*Charlie . . .*"

"Only we can't, because Schrader's grave isn't fucking here! It's a dead end! He's probably somewhere out there laughing at us right now!" Charlie sprang to his feet and cupped his hands around his mouth. "We're right here, you moldy old fop! Sitting ducks with nowhere to go!"

"*Charlie . . .*"

"So just kill us now, 'cause I'm not gonna sit here like an asshole waiting for it to happen!"

"*CHARLIE!*"

Ana and Charlie turned to see Raymond standing at the center of the graveyard, studying the four smaller trees that stood in a square. They were equidistant from each other, like four pips on the side of a die, and unlike the other trees on the hill, they were dead. Their branches held no leaves, and their ashy white bark seemed to cast a dull glow.

"Come look at this."

They shuffled over to Raymond, who took a step back and pointed to the gnarled trunk of the tree nearest him.

Carved into the trunk were the words *Mors Voluntaria.*

"They're all here," Raymond said, directing them to the other three trees. "Look."

Charlie aimed his light at the three other trees. Sure enough, they each bore their own set of carved words.

Mors Accidente
Mors Occidendum
Mors Naturalis

"The trees will show you how," Ana said, echoing Pat's cryptic words, and ran her fingers across the bark of the tree nearest her. Its branches jutted out at odd angles, like a blizzard of bent bones, but only one branch pointed perfectly downward.

"Look at the tip," Raymond said.

Ana moved her light.

The end of the branch had been chiseled down to a thin, fine point.

Sharp as a needle.

She double-checked the inscription on the tree's trunk then held her hand out to Raymond. "Hand me the Suicide record. *Voluntaria.*"

Nodding, Raymond opened the case.

"Ana, wait," Charlie said. "Even if the tree *could* play the record, are we sure that's what we should be doing? You said it yourself: Schrader *wanted* us to find this place. It might be a trap."

"There are three blank tombstones over there," Ana said, taking the record from Raymond and balancing it on her palms like a delicate plate. "And any minute now, our names—yours, mine, and Ellie's—will be on them. If this is a trap, we've already fallen into it. So, if we're fucked, why not be fucked all the way?"

She approached the needle-tipped branch slowly, searching for a turntable on which to place the record, but there was none. There was only a needle-sharp branch that pointed downward. She supposed she could lift the record up to the needle and turn it herself, but that seemed too clumsy a procedure for what was clearly an elegant, albeit absurd, operation.

She was about to say she was open to suggestions, when, as if on cue, the record flew out of her hands and hovered in midair, a foot below the needle-sharp branch.

Ana jumped back. Slowly, the floating record began to spin. Only, it wasn't spinning clockwise. It was spinning counterclockwise. "It's gonna play backwards," she said.

The three of them watched the spinning record rise through the air and make contact with the pointed end of the branch, which sank itself into the groove with precision.

Immediately, a low, distant hum stirred the fog along the soil. Ana rushed back to join Raymond and Charlie, who were searching for the source of the sound.

"Where's it coming from?" Ana said, looking around.

"Everywhere," Charlie said, and turned to the next tree. "Hand me the next record. *Accidente.*"

Raymond bent down and reached for the case and watched it suddenly topple onto its side. Beneath them, the ground rose and fell like a sighing lung.

One by one, the remaining records pulled themselves from the foamcore and drifted along the breeze to their respective trees.

The moment they made contact with their needle-branches, the ground shifted from a slow pulse to a violent tremble.

"Hold on!" Raymond cried, and leaned his weight against a mossy tombstone.

Ana forced her shovel into the ground and tightened her grip. Charlie, having nothing nearby on which to steady himself, lost his footing and fell, landing on his wounded shoulder.

All around them, the tombstones shook, crumbling and spitting shards of decades-old rock. The blanket of ground fog swirled and licked the air, and up in the sky, the clouds roiled furiously.

Charlie slid over to the tree marked *Occidendum* and planted his back up against its trunk. Little stones danced along the ground near his feet like bits of fossil on the mesh of a shaking sieve.

Raymond pointed to the center of the graveyard. "Look!"

The fog swirled away from the ground like a wispy tornado, revealing a stretch of rich black soil. Soil that had seemingly been unspoiled by time. The sky above seemed to inhale, then, in a blinding flash of light, sent a streak of lightning that hammered the black soil. Immediately, the soil began to undulate in a series of thick, dizzying waves. The fog was thick now, pulsing and shifting direction through the air, seemingly in rhythm with the rolling soil. It swirled around the stretch of soil like a shroud, concealing something that was rising up through the earth. It rumbled and growled like an approaching beast, and with a deafening blast, it breached the soil like a giant fist, spraying a shock wave of black dirt through the air.

Ana and Charlie, fearing a second blast, shielded their heads.

But there was no second blast.

Everything went silent then.

The trembling ground was still. The quaking tombstones hushed themselves. The four records dropped to the ground, motionless and cockeyed at the bases of their corresponding trees.

Arms shaking, Ana lowered her hands.

The towering shroud of fog sighed to the ground like a delicate bolt of sheer cloth, revealing the object that had pushed itself out of the ground.

Standing at the top of a newly formed crater was a large, upright monolith, nearly ten feet in height. Like the unmarked tombstones, its surface was smooth, like polished glass, and slate gray. But unlike the three unmarked tombstones, it bore a name, etched cleanly on the surface in sharp, beveled letters.

Ana didn't need a flashlight to read it. None of them did.

The name practically glowed in the moonlight.

Nursing his wounded shoulder, Charlie stumbled to the edge of the crater and peered down.

He laughed humorlessly.

"I guess we didn't need the shovels."

SIXTY

There was no coffin.

Ivan Schrader's body was nothing more than a blackened skeleton, calcified by years of decomposition. His clothes, which were only slightly more intact than the rest of him, hung over his bones like tattered rags, ready to disintegrate into dust at the slightest touch.

Most disturbing of all, though, was the way his bones had been strangled by tree roots. They coiled themselves around his arms and legs and through his rib cage, binding him to his grave.

"Listen, Dad," Charlie said, who couldn't help but continue to stare at Schrader's moldering corpse, "if this works, and you disappear, I just want you to know—"

"CHARLIE!"

He turned and saw Ana staring up into the air.

Fifteen feet above her, suspended in midair, was Raymond.

His arms hung limply at his sides, and his eyes, no longer milky gray, were now stark white. His salt-and-pepper shock of hair moved fluidly, as if he were underwater, and Charlie was suddenly reminded of a line from *A Christmas Carol,* where Dickens described Marley's ghost as being provided an infernal atmosphere of its own.

Charlie and Ana leapt into the air, reaching for his legs, as if they were children trying to retrieve a balloon that had begun to float away.

"He's too high," Charlie said, wheeling around. "We need to find something to stand on. A tree stump or a broken tombstone."

"The case!" Ana cried, and stumbled over to the spot where the it had last been, but the ground was too obscured by fog to see. She bent low, pulling the fog away with her arms like a swimmer performing the breaststroke, but it was no use. The fog merely swirled back on itself, obscuring even more of her vision. "I can't find it," she said in a panic, and began plunging her hands into the fog at all angles, hoping she'd make contact with the case.

Charlie took fifteen paces back and gave it a running start, leaping into the air with all the strength his legs could provide, but he was still about four feet off.

He collapsed to the ground and coughed into the fog so loudly, he initially didn't hear the raking sound of laughter to his right. He pulled himself to his feet and saw Ana. Her face was frozen in fear.

Standing beside the glistening monolith that bore his name was Ivan Schrader.

Without thinking, Charlie lunged forward and swiped at Schrader with closed fists. The composer didn't even flinch. Charlie's hands passed right through him. With every swing, Schrader's eyes burned as he laughed harder.

"Let him go!"

"Here!" Ana said, running from one tree to the next and gathering up the records, "this is what you wanted, right?" She fanned them out in her hands like playing cards. "We're giving them back to you, look!"

Schrader's laughter fizzled away. He stared at the records with an expression neither Charlie nor Ana could read. For a moment, he appeared to be lost in the midst of a memory. The red in his eyes briefly faded, and Ana saw her moment.

She tossed the four records into the grave as gently as she could. They clattered and bounced along Schrader's skeleton, settling into the loose soil surrounding it.

Charlie and Ana waited for something to happen. A glowing light, perhaps, or, even more absurdly, a confetti cannon that announced their successful completion of the task. Something that would signify their victory. Something that announced that they had done what no one else could do. They had beaten the game and returned Schrader's Chord to its rightful owner.

But none of that happened.

The records merely sat there in the dirt, leaning against a decomposing corpse.

Once again, Schrader's eyes burned red, and his lips curled into a smile.

It didn't work.

A white-hot fury coursed through Charlie's veins. They had come all this way, escaped every attempt made on their lives thus far. Surely that had to be worth something. Surely no one else had ever gone to so much trouble to reverse what they had done.

He wanted to scream, wanted to cry, wanted to tear Schrader to pieces, but before he could do any of that, Schrader's smiling lips drew to a close, shrouding his two ghastly rows of rotting teeth, and a voice behind Charlie spoke.

"Charlie Remick . . ."

He spun around and saw Ana with her face lowered, chin toward the ground. "You have traveled a great distance," she said in a deep voice that was not her own. "You have seen sights not afforded the living . . . of existence beyond the veil of oblivion." She looked up at him and smiled. From the corner of his eye, Charlie saw the four records rise from the grave. They moved smoothly through air, as if on an invisible conveyor belt, and stacked themselves neatly into Ana's outstretched hand. She gazed at them with a sinister curiosity. "Were these sights troubling to you? Or, in seeing them, did you find salvation?"

Charlie rounded on Schrader. "Let her go."

A stale, wrenching snicker that crackled like fire came from deep within Ana's throat.

"Why are you doing this?" Charlie asked. "What do you want?"

"Ahhhh . . ." Ana said, and the grin on her face vanished. Long strands of black saliva dripped from her lips and painted her chin. "Why tell you when it would be so much more effective to show you?"

Schrader—the *real* Schrader—watched with delight as Ana, acting as his avatar, lunged at Charlie.

She was so quick, Charlie barely saw her move. Her free hand struck his chest, forcing the air out of his lungs, and by the time he could comprehend what had happened, he was already falling.

His back felt the impact first, followed by the sound of brittle cracks, like a tire rolling over dry twigs. It took a moment to shake the dizziness out of his head, but as his eyes adjusted to his new surroundings, he saw that he'd fallen into Schrader's grave.

And worse than that . . . he'd landed on his corpse.

Every part of him ached. He was no longer able to distinguish between the pain in his shoulder and the pain he felt everywhere else. With a grunt, he planted his knee in the dirt and tried to push himself to his feet, but quickly lost his balance. He put his palms out to catch himself, felt his right hand connect with Schrader's skull, and

his trembling fingertips, covered in blood, reached for a circular pin

Charlie wrenched his hand away from Schrader's skull.

His eyes darted around, taking in his surroundings.

Black dirt . . . violent sky . . . rotting corpse. He was back in the grave. Back on Bolero Hill.

He rubbed his right hand, staring at the skull as if it were radioactive, and caught the faintest whiff of ozone.

I was there, he thought. *In the room with the stifling heat and the strange machinery . . . only, the machinery looked different. It was more organized, more purposeful.*

It had four spidering arms.

Charlie stared fervently at Schrader's bones. He wanted to see it again. *Had* to see it again. This wasn't like the last time he'd been in that room. This was different. He wouldn't have to see Schrader this time.

Because now he could *be* Schrader.

Charlie reached out and touched the skull again.

pulled the circular pin, releasing a hush of air.

The machine's arms readied themselves for the drop. Around him, the four records spun, each bell of the gramophone ready to give voice to the key.

Because he'd found it. He'd found the key.

Oh God! What horrible things had he done to find it? What unforgivable sins had he committed in the name of discovery? He would burn in hell for what he'd done, he was quite certain of it, and he would deserve nothing less. He had become a bringer of death; brought sorrow to families he'd known, pain to those he didn't. In his devotion, he had become a monster, obsessed and righteous as all monsters are; but now he was standing at the gates of absolution, not for those he'd harmed in his efforts to find them, but for the woman who waited for him . . . waited beyond their twisted, goblin bars.

He would have her back. He would correct his mistakes.

All those years spent ignoring her quiet cries of pain, all those times he brushed her aside to chase the elusive glissando, the coda, the augmented sixth, the col legno battuto . . .

He would hear her now. He would bask in the beauty of her voice. And when hell came for him, her song would play in his memory for all eternity, and the righteousness that was once his would now belong to those he'd wronged.

And that was good.

That would be just.

His fingertips, bleeding and trembling, either from pain or from nerves, gripped the circular pin. With his other hand he pulled the lever and released the spidering arms to the drop.

The needles, made of the finest cactus quill, buried themselves into the wax . . .

. . . and the chord played.

The key turned.

And the gates were opened.

The dead rose around him, one by one. He had expected this. They would speak to him, admonish him for what he'd done to them, and he would listen. They deserved that much. But they would have to wait.

All in good time.

First, he had to collect his prize.

He knelt to the floor, ignoring the pain of the wood on his knees, and watched for her. She would be there soon, and when she arrived, he would present himself as her one true love; because he was now . . . he always had been . . . and she would know it was true when she saw what he'd done to find her . . . and only then would he . . .

. . . and . . .

. . . then would . . .

. . . and only then . . .

. . . would he . . . No.

No, this isn't right. Something has gone wrong.

The chord was louder now, the key harsher. It rang terribly, its sound coming from beyond the bells of the gramophones. It had surpassed the bells, vanquished them, and was now flowing freely along the molecules. Oh God! What is happening?

The sound was no longer a sound. The sound was everything. Every scream, every cry of despair, every tearstained wail of pain. It boiled the very marrow in his bones, rang his head like a cathedral bell.

GONG! GONG! GONG!

Oh stop this madness!

Close the gate!

Close the gate and I'll bury the key, I swear! I'll destroy it!

He rushed to the gramophone nearest him, tried to pull the record from its platter, but it wouldn't budge.

And then the air entered the room.

It moved freely, as if propelled by a nearby storm, only there were no windows through which it could enter.

It brought with it a scent, sweet and perfumed, and made his stomach turn. He closed his eyes tightly against it, hoping to expel the odor from his senses, but opened them again when he heard the bellow of a distant horn.

Or was it, instead, the lonely wail of a suffering leviathan?

He took in his surroundings and felt his head go giddy.

He was no longer at home.

He had moved—or had been moved, more likely—to somewhere new. A place so grand, and so dark, and so large, he felt his breath catch in his throat.

Soundless blue flames burned in an endless row of sconces. They licked the polished stone walls and threw dancing sapphire sprites across the gleaming floor.

He got to his feet and inspected his surroundings, nose still tickled by the perfume. The space was cavernous, held upright by colossal columns that rose so high, they disappeared into the dense shadows above. He took a step forward, then another, his feet singing a crisp song on the marble, and wondered vaguely how long it would take to build a room of this size.

As he walked, his eyes adjusted to the darkness. The walls on which the sconces hung were built of endless rows of black, mirrored tile. Each tile was precisely laid next to the other, separated only by a thin line of red grout.

Blood, *he expected, and frowned.* How uncivilized.

Once again, the distant horn blew. He turned on his heel, hoping to locate its origin, and felt his heart drop when he saw her.

"Ivan . . ."

She was there! In the room!

He had found her.

She floated behind a column, her skin a spectral white, feet only an inch or so off the ground, and called to him.

"My love!" he cried, stumbling after her, but his feet slipped along the polished floor. He collapsed to his knees, reaching for her, but she floated away.

He watched her pale form recede into the shadows.

"No! Please! Stay! Stay with me!"

Another voice answered him.

"You have been observed," it said, its tone velvety, its timbre that of a soft autumn breeze, "and so charged."

Schrader's eyes fell upon the center of the room where three thrones now stood.

They were somehow both immense and not. Their architecture was rigidly geometric; the seats, backs, and armrests were all perfectly square and made of black stone, which, like the walls of the chamber, had been polished to a mirrorlike shine.

Upon the thrones sat three identical figures, all of equal height.

Gazing upon this unholy tribunal, Schrader recoiled, frightened.

Their anatomy appeared human, or, at least, it did at first. They were nude, with waxy black skin that gleamed like polished ebony, their eyes the milky white of pearl; their muscled arms hung low and rested upon their pointed knees. Their taloned fingers clicked like castanets, and their hair, glisteningly black and threaded with silver streaks, fell in loose curls over their bony shoulders.

"We have, once again, seen with our own eyes," the one in the middle said, "the folly of your kind."

As it spoke, the sweet perfume filled the room, and Schrader realized, nauseatingly, that the scent was not a perfume at all, but the odor of its breath.

"Are you . . ." Schrader began, quaking at the sight of the three. "What are you?"

"Custodians," the one on the left said. Its voice was much higher than its counterpart's; breathy and melodic, almost as if it were singing. "Tasked with protecting the sanctity of this realm."

Schrader gazed around the chamber. "And which realm is this? Hell?"

"Hell is a construct of man," it replied dismissively. "As is heaven."

"What is it then? Where have you brought me?"

Upon hearing this, the three throned figures laughed.

"Brought *you?*" the one in the middle said, amused. "You stepped into this realm with open eyes, did you not? You created a key and opened an unsanctioned gateway, did you not?"

"It was a cleverly made key at that," the figure on the left added. It waved its taloned fingers with a flourish, and produced Schrader's records from thin air. They hovered above the polished floor, rotating as if in an invisible display case.

The figure on the right gestured to Schrader's bloody forearm, the skin of which had been flayed open, revealing the scraped bone underneath. "You have bound yourself to the key . . . forged it with your own organic material."

Schrader gazed down at the festering wound on his arm. "I had to," he said quietly. "It was the only way it would work."

"And work it did," the figure on the right said, nodding. "You have succeeded. And now you must be charged for your success."

Schrader took a step backward. "Charged with what? I have committed no crime."

Again, the figures laughed.

"On the contrary," the figure replied silkily. "To open an unsanctioned gate between the realm of the living and the realm of the dead is an abomination of nature. It is an action that must be punished."

Schrader held up his hands. They were trembling. "I meant no offense. Please believe me. I only wanted to . . ." His voice drifted into silence as he searched for the words.

The figure in the center moved its head at this, blinking its waxen lids over its pearl eyes. "Wanted to what?"

"It's my wife," Schrader said quietly. "She died."

The figure nodded. "We are aware."

"I only wanted to see her again. To speak to her. To hear her voice."

"And in doing so," the figure on the left said, lunging forward angrily and raising its breathy voice, "you have defiled the laws of nature with your pride!"

Its voice boomed in the space, bringing Schrader to his knees. He shook badly, gazing at the throned figures through glassy eyes. "Please . . . I didn't know . . ."

"Nevertheless," said the figure on the right, calmly, "your transgression must be seen to accordingly."

In the distance, the horn bellowed again, and the three figures stood. The one in the middle stepped forward, while the others bowed their heads.

"You have contaminated the natural way of things. As such, you will now act as custodian and steward of your created abomination, enforcing its laws and ensuring it remains untampered with."

"Please . . ." Schrader cried, his head buried in his hands. "I made a mistake . . ."

"Once the gateway has been opened, the only way to close it again is through payment of death."

Schrader looked up from his hands, eyes bleary. "But the gateway is open now.*"*

"It is," the figure acknowledged. "And its first closing shall be administered by the death of its creator. Fitting, is it not?"

"No!" Schrader cried, falling prostrate to the floor. "Please! There has to be another way."

"As long as the key exists," the figure went on, "you will act as its keeper. If the gateway should come to be opened again, you will enforce on its opener the same sentence we have passed on you."

Schrader raised his head and gazed at the four floating records between them.

As long as the key exists . . .

The records. That meant they could be destroyed.

He could end this. He could put paid to this unholy sentence right now.

His eyes burned red, and with an animalistic shriek, he launched himself through the air, reaching for the records, and pulled one of them from its orbit.

Holding the record tightly in his grip, he collapsed to the ground and tried to snap it in half.

One of the figures, Schrader couldn't know which, laughed cruelly.

"Fool. You believe you could escape your punishment that easily?"

Immediately, every cell in Schrader's body ripped itself apart. The bitter sting of death coursed through his nostrils and flayed his tongue. The air crashed against his eardrums like waves along the side of a ship, splitting its boards and flooding its keel. His nerves thrummed like the strings of a harp, sending him into a fetal crouch. He shook like a leaf, wanting to cover his ears, but the fear of doing more damage than had already been done kept his hands clenched at his stomach.

His eardrums could take no more! They rattled and shook and ached to burst.

From deep within them, something escaped. He felt it pulled from his ears like a drain unclogged.

It floated upon the air, this substance from his ears, and split itself into four wispy clouds of blue energy. Each cloud slipped through space and penetrated one of the four records, soaking itself into the wax.

He screamed louder then.

He screamed and screamed until the pain reached such a pitch, and finally . . . Relief.

His head broke apart.

The world was quiet again. Oh! Sweet silence!

And yet . . . the silence had its own sound. The sound of rushing water far beneath the ground; a humming wash that circled the pipes in his head, over and over again, unable to flush itself out.

He stood, then, on feet that would barely hold him, and opened his eyes.

She was there, reaching for him, dressed in the white she died in. She smiled, greeting him, as the three throned figures looked on. Schrader fell again to his knees, whimpering, bowing before her superiority, and reached for her. She opened her mouth to speak. . . .

"Yes! Oh God! Yes, please speak, angel! Speak before they damn me further. . . ."

Her eyes, a gray soup of death, held him gently. Her lips, still plump, parted. But she had no voice.

Only the thunderous wash of rushing water.

"Speak louder, angel!" he begged, and as he said it, realized his own voice had gone, too. Lost beneath the thunderous rush.

This clamoring nothingness.

She spoke again, and as her lips parted and met again to form the words, his realization became a poison in his mouth.

He was

. . . deaf."

Charlie released his grip on the skull. He shot to his feet and gazed at Schrader's corpse with the careful observance of a man standing next to live dynamite. He turned, peering over the edge of the grave, and saw his father fall to the ground like a pile of laundry. Raymond sat up, shaking his head, and took in his surroundings.

Ana, whose body Schrader had now vacated, was lying motionless at the foot of the *Accidente* tree. The records were still in her hand. Above her, the branches of the tree shuddered under the weight of the wind, and for a moment, Charlie thought he saw her stir.

He wanted to go to her, to help her, but first things first. "Dad, he's deaf!" he cried from inside the grave. "They made him deaf!"

Raymond, still bewildered by what had happened, searched for his son but couldn't see him. "Charlie?"

"He's deaf!"

"Who's deaf?"

"Schrader! They punished him because he—"

A sudden wave of vertigo crashed over Charlie, forcing his knees to go limp. The world blinked in and out of existence as if reality were short-circuiting, and before he could say another word, he was gone again.

Somewhere far off, the horn blew.

Charlie stood on the edge of Nothing, eyes watering as the blare of the horn echoed endlessly across the wretched wasteland.

"I've been here before," he heard himself say, and cowered against the howl of the blowing wind.

No, it wasn't wind.

It was voices. Thousands of wailing voices, sailing past his ears as they hid from the call of the horn.

"I've been here before," he said again, and turned, suddenly aware he was not alone.

Schrader was standing behind him. Only, now, he appeared normal. Healthy. Alive, even. His hair was brushed neatly back over his head and tied off into a small pigtail. His clothes hung nearly on his frame; the tails of his coat bloused pleasantly across his shins. His goatee was well manicured, and his cheeks were no longer paper-thin and stretched over bone, but plump and full.

His eyes, no longer burning red, stared at Charlie feverishly.

"I was here when I first played the records," Charlie said.

Schrader nodded.

"Why did you bring me here?"

No response.

"What is this place?" Charlie asked.

Again, Schrader didn't respond.

Charlie growled angrily. He marched up to Schrader, fists clenched at his sides, and howled, "WHAT DO YOU WANT?"

Schrader smiled, raised his hands, and clapped them on either side of Charlie's head.

A fire burned brightly, throwing swirling shadows along the wall. An olive-skinned man, dressed head to toe in tennis whites, stood in the center of a large, splendid room. Four gramophones surrounded him. He clutched a brass funnel in his right hand.

Seeing Charlie enter, he said in a French accent:

"For ages, I have waited to reclaim what was taken from me."

The man shoved the funnel down his throat and tipped a bottle of poison into it.

Charlie gasped, shielding his eyes against a blast of bright sunlight. When he lowered his hand, he was standing on a street corner in front of a park. A crying woman with bleeding ears turned to him.

"And for ages, I have been disappointed."

The woman stepped into the street and collided with an oncoming Plymouth.

The world turned, and Charlie was back at his house. It was his father's wake.

Louis Goodwin hovered over the railing as the guests below looked up in horror.

"Then I found you, Charlie Remick," Louis said, and went tumbling over the railing.

The wind tousled Charlie's hair. Below him, he saw a blush of swirling red and blue lights. He was on the roof of the Cuckoo's Nest.

Dale Cernin stood, feet half off the edge of the building. He turned and looked at Charlie, his Yorkshire accent soft on the night breeze.

"Destroy the records, and lock the gate forever," Dale said, then leapt off the roof and into the sea of screams below.

The hiss of brakes came from behind him. Charlie looked and saw a mail truck pull up to the house on Wabash Street. He was standing in the backyard. A chill crept down his arms, and Charlie turned, knowing with dread what he was about to see.

Raymond was up in the Grim Tree, sitting casually on a branch as his feet dangled below him. A noose hung loosely around his neck. He smiled, staring down at Charlie, and said:

"You can end this now, Charlie. You can be free of me. Of death." *He reached up and tightened the noose around his neck. "Destroy the records. Sacrifice that which you hold most dear. Give it to me, and I will leave you in peace."*

Charlie felt his bowels turn to water. He finally understood what was being asked of him. He stepped back and stared up at his father through astonished eyes.

No, he told himself.

Not his father.

Schrader.

"You want me to . . . give you my hearing?"

Raymond smiled. "A gift for a gift."

Charlie shook his head. "No. There has to be another way."

Raymond's smile vanished, leaving in its place a snarl. "There is no other way."

"But why me?"

Raymond's eyes, hungry and yearning, burrowed into his own. "Because when music plays, you hear it, Charlie Remick."

"So?" Charlie barked. "Everybody hears music!"

"No . . ." Raymond said, in a voice that was no longer his own. "Others listen *to music. You* hear *it." His threw himself from the branch and dangled from the tree, his throat squeezed by the strength of the noose. "It's a simple exchange, Charlie. Give me back what was taken from me or . . ."*

Charlie saw Ana, sprawled out on the cemetery soil.

". . . I will take . . ."

He saw Ellie, motionless in her hospital bed.

". . . everything . . ."

He saw his own body, beaten and bloodied on the ground.

". . . from you . . ."

Charlie opened his eyes.

He was once again back in the grave.

At least, he thought he was. The world around him was spinning furiously, and with every beat of his heart, his eyes sent a pulse of movement through the air.

His chest heaved, and he coughed. A viscous thread of saliva streaked across his lower lip.

He felt strange.

Very strange.

Something foreign was coursing through his body. It was electric, and bitter—like the stinging, coppery taste of a battery terminal— only it wasn't a taste. It was everything. It was in his muscles and in his veins. It was the pulp between his teeth.

"Dad!" He shut his eyes tightly against the spinning world. "Ana!"

Raymond's face appeared over the opening of the grave. "Thank God you're all right! I thought you might have—"

He immediately fell silent, his face a rigid mask of horrified confusion.

"Oh God . . . Charlie, no . . ."

Charlie opened his mouth to speak, then stammered as his limbs shook uncontrollably. The battery-terminal sensation was stronger now. It pulsed through him in violent waves, and it wasn't until he saw the fear on his father's face that he realized something had gone terribly wrong.

He looked down at his hands.

His fingers were his own, and then they weren't. Clean skin gave way to festering, spongy flesh and then changed back again. Thin cords of pale light slithered between his fingers and around his wrists, coiling and twisting like electric snakes. One second, the sleeve of his jacket was the rough-hewn canvas of the parka Ana had stolen from the restaurant; the next, it was the tattered sleeve of a festering frock coat.

A distant cry escaped his lips.

Ana's face appeared next to Raymond's at the lip of the grave. When she saw Charlie, she gasped.

He was oscillating between his own form and the form of Ivan Schrader.

He could feel his identity slipping away, pulled into the darkness behind Schrader's eyes.

He looked up, eyes burning hungrily, and reached for the records in Ana's hands. *"Give them to me!"*

Ana recoiled, pulling the records out of sight. Charlie/Schrader lunged for her, his hands clawing furiously at the soil in front of her feet.

Raymond grabbed his wrist, and his eyes rolled back white. His lips tensed, his neck bulged, and his legs gave way.

Charlie/Schrader yowled like a rabid dog and pulled Raymond's limp body into the grave. It landed with a dull thump next to Schrader's bones.

Leaping back out of the grave, Charlie/Schrader landed like a cat on the ground above, legs hunched low, chapped lips drooling. His eyes, wild and searching, fixed on Ana, who had taken refuge behind a battered tombstone. "Give me the records!" he barked.

"What did you do to Charlie?" she called back, crying.

"GIVE THEM TO ME!"

The fog by Ana's feet began to swirl. Dark shadows swept over the grass, chasing themselves in wide circles. She traced the path of the shadows and looked up into the sky.

A furious storm was brewing. Clouds clashed and rumbled above her, twisting and ripping themselves apart, firing faint blooms of electric energy that lit up the sky like a switchboard.

With a flourish of his fingers, Charlie/Schrader closed his fist and brought it down through the air like a hammer.

A blinding flash of light etched a jagged branch across Ana's corneas. She dove to the side just in time to see the bolt of lightning strike the tombstone. It exploded on impact, peppering her face with jagged shards of stone. Head spinning and ears ringing, Ana stumbled away, the records clutched tightly in her arms.

Watching her path with quiet resolve, Charlie/Schrader pumped his fist through the air a second time.

Twenty feet away, inside the grave, Raymond got to his feet. He shook his head, dazed, and searched for a way to pull himself out.

Ana dashed for the *Naturalis* tree but skidded to a stop as the second bolt of lightning streaked past her face. The tree went up in a flash of fire, sending a shower of sparks onto Ana's head. Its branches, now black as coal, sizzled. Its gnarled trunk smoldered.

"GIVE ME THE RECORDS, GIRL!" Charlie/Schrader howled.

She cowered, trembling, as the clouds above her reloaded the chamber, and clutched the records with all the strength she could muster. "Why . . . ?" she said, sobbing. "What do you want?"

"Ana . . ." a voice said, wearily.

She turned her head and saw Raymond, swaying on his feet near the open grave. His eyes, heavy and tired, bored into her own.

"Give him the records. . . ."

Ana sobbed again.

"Do it, kiddo. It's the only way. . . ."

Charlie/Schrader's lips curled into a hungry grin as Ana's shoulders fell, surrendering. Exhausted and limping, she stumbled over to him, the records clattering loosely in her left hand. He lowered his arm, calming the clouds above him. On either side of his head, his melted ear sockets pulsed. His eyes burned with the fire of victory. He reached for the records . . . yearned for them.

"*There's a good girl. Hand them over.*"

"If you can still hear me, Charlie," Ana said, reaching into her right pocket, "I'm so sorry about this." With one swift motion, Ana opened her left hand, letting the records fall to the ground, and struck out with her right, driving the ice pick deep into the wound on Charlie's shoulder.

Charlie/Schrader whipped his head back and released an ear-shredding howl. He collapsed to his knees, chest heaving, and tore the ice pick from his flesh. It fell to the ground, painting a streak of red along the dirt.

The two bodies—Schrader's and Charlie's—oscillated quickly now, strobing back and forth so rapidly that both of their faces were practically a blur.

"*daaaaa . . .*"

The sound came out as a rapid vibration, as if the word he'd been trying to form had passed through the wings of a hummingbird.

"*Daaa*aad . . ."

Raymond crawled over to him. "I'm here," he said quietly. "I'm here, Charlie."

"The records . . ."

It was Charlie's voice. He was fighting through it. He was pushing past Schrader. The oscillations were even faster now, and Schrader was merely a faint spectral image.

"The records, Dad . . . I need to destroy them. . . ."

"I know," Raymond replied softly. "I know you do, kiddo."

Ana shook her head. "I don't understand. . . ."

"When I touched him, I saw," Raymond replied. "I saw what needed to be done."

The thin cords of light around Charlie/Schrader's fingers crackled like the energy around a Tesla coil. He reached again for the records.

"Ana . . ." Charlie wheezed. "Now."

Ana bit her lip, hoping she was making the right decision, and handed Charlie the records.

Without speaking—speaking would use up too much energy—he gripped the stack of records on both sides and forced them into a bend.

A searing pain shot through his head with such force, he immediately released his tension on the records.

Yes . . . Schrader's voice said from somewhere deep within him. *That's it. . . . Give it another try . . .*

Charlie gazed up at the roiling sky above, and was suddenly aware of the warmth oozing down both sides of his neck. He didn't need a mirror to know what was happening.

His ears were bleeding.

Badly.

Gripping the records harder this time, he forced them into another bend. His eardrums burst like two blisters, spraying thick slings of blood in both directions.

Ana cried out and reached for him, but Raymond held her back. "Charlie, stop this," she pleaded, fighting against Raymond's grip. "You already tried breaking them back at the house. It didn't work."

"Too slow this way . . ." Charlie/Schrader said calmly. His voice was distant now, soaked in reverb. It seemed to be coming from everywhere.

". . . the ice pick . . ."

Raymond stared solemnly at Charlie, his noose-warped face

flickering between bright light and pale shadow, cast from the beams of light that circled his son's hands. Knowing what had to be done, he grabbed the ice pick from the dirt and passed it to what remained of his son.

Charlie/Schrader turned the object slowly in his hand, gazing dreamily at the bloodstained point.

"I found the tapes, Dad."

Raymond's eyes, cloudy with death, once again became glassy and red. He laughed sweetly. "I probably should have told you."

"Thank you for saving them."

A bloody tear crawled down Raymond's cheek. "They're your best work, Charlie. Your very best." He wiped the tear away, leaving a blurry red streak on his chin, and smiled. "*You* were mine. I know that now."

Charlie smiled back and lowered himself to his knees. Schrader's face phased in and out so rapidly, it was barely visible now, and it was Charlie's eyes and Charlie's eyes alone that telegraphed the certainty of his actions. With the reverence of a priest, he placed the stack of records onto the soil and stared at them for a moment, as if saying a silent goodbye.

He wondered momentarily if it was Schrader who was saying goodbye, or if it was him.

He supposed it was both of them.

Ice pick in hand, he took a deep breath. His mind flooded itself with thoughts of what he'd be giving up. The new music he'd never hear. The old music he'd never get to hear again. The sound of a live band, or an orchestra, or a squelching amp when a guitar feeds back, or the clatter of a dropped drumstick, or an elevator ding, or the roar of a crowd at a ballpark, or a turn signal; or the sound of a crashing wave, or a field full of crickets on summer night, or the lash of rain against a window, or the cry of trick-or-treaters at his door; or the sound of a dog barking, of a roller coaster plunging, of a group of waiters singing him happy birthday, of Ellie and Susan giving him hell in that way only sisters can, of Ana and her laugh . . .

Raymond placed his hand on Charlie's shoulder, and Charlie smiled. For the first time since he'd pulled Raymond's animated corpse down from the Grim Tree, his father's skin was warm. It spread along his shoulder and spilled across his chest, filled his lungs and his heart with light, and as he looked over his shoulder to say goodbye to his father, he saw something else new.

Raymond's tears were clear.

With a final squeeze of the ice pick's handle, Charlie raised his hand into the air and plunged the chiseled tip into the stack of records.

SIXTY-ONE

He could feel the scrape of his screams up his throat, but he could not hear them.

The pain in his head was only an echo, and as it thundered into the distance and died into nothing, he forced his muscles to relax.

His senses, or what remained of his senses, came online one by one. Touch came first. His fingertips swept the soft carpet of grass on either side of him. Tiny, granular flecks of dirt worked their way into the grooves of his fingerprints and sent a wave of shivers up his arms. Taste came next, and the dirty-penny tang of blood on his taste buds, which, in turn, activated his sense of smell.

Sight followed, and it came slowly.

His eyes registered light first—the moon still shined brightly, and with each blink, the edges of its crescent shape became sharper. Shadow followed, and then everything in between.

Everything in between.

Yes.

He was sitting both at the bottom of the grave *and* on the grass. The world had been split into transparent animation cels—one containing the dark outlines, the other containing the painted color—stacked askew, creating a blur of realities.

The grass soaked the seat of his jeans with frigid dew. From the side of his eye, he saw Ana Cortez come stumbling toward him. To his right, he watched two lovers—separated by time and grisly circumstance—reconnect.

The three throned figures, with their pearled eyes and waxy skin, stepped to the side as Ivan Schrader fell into his wife's arms.

And as her lips moved, he could hear her.

But Charlie couldn't. His senses continued to fill themselves with the sights and smells and tastes of the night, and, as the transparencies slid together, a clear picture was finally formed.

He took a deep breath but couldn't hear it. He reached for his father's hand and grabbed his own shoulder.

It wasn't there.

Raymond was gone, and with him, the gravestones, the skeletal army of trees, Ivan Schrader, the throned figures, and Bolero Hill itself.

He got to his feet, shivering violently at the sudden cold, and took in his surroundings. He searched for Bolero Hill, but there was nothing but flatland on all sides, stretching into an infinite horizon.

There was only him . . .

. . . and someone else.

Ana ran toward him, waving a rectangle of light that glowed brightly in her hand. Her lips moved frantically, forming words and phrases Charlie ached to hear, but the only sound his ears could register was the sound of his own heartbeat.

He felt a rush of sadness then, knowing what he'd given up. But as Ana knelt beside him and showed him her phone, he knew what he'd gained.

It was a text from Ellie.

Just woke up in the hospital!! Where is everybody?

SIXTY-TWO

There were voices in the room.

He could feel them.

He remained still, feeling curiously omniscient as the vibrations tickled what was left of his eardrums and breathed along the fine hairs of his skin. He sat up, head swimming and packed with fog, and searched drunkenly for the ghosts that had woken him.

His eyes landed on a plastic bracelet around his wrist. He blinked, clearing the haze, and read the words GREAT FALLS CLINIC HOSPITAL.

Underneath that: REMICK, CHARLES.

A stocky woman in pink nurse's scrubs shuffled into the room. She checked an array of monitors to his left, picked up a clipboard, then shot him a warm smile.

How are you feeling?

That's what she *would* say if he'd been able to hear her. Instead, she spoke to someone else in the room. Charlie traced her eyeline and landed on the two familiar faces next to the window.

"Hi," Charlie said clumsily, feeling his voice bounce around his skull. Except for the feel of it on his tongue, he had no way of knowing whether or not he'd formed the word correctly. He said it again, "Hi," and became suddenly aware that he was opening his mouth too wide.

Ellie rushed to the side of his bed and wrapped her arms around him.

He grunted, or, at least, he thought he grunted, and Ellie stood up, grinning guiltily. Her lips formed the word *Sorry.*

Charlie felt for his shoulder. It was buried under a clean braid of white bandages. Ellie slowly mouthed the words *How are you feeling?*

"Drunk!" Charlie shouted, very aware of the newly uncoordinated relationship between his lips and his tongue. "Did you guys slip some tequila into the IV bag?"

Ellie laughed. "Pain meds," she said, and when it was clear Charlie couldn't understand her, enunciated cartoonishly: "PAIN MEDS. From your SURGERY."

"Surgery?" Charlie said, but knew it sounded like *Soogewy?* He blushed.

Ellie laid a hand on his good shoulder. "You're doing GREAT."

Ana floated up alongside Ellie. Charlie's heart leapt when he saw her face up close. She held a whiteboard in her hands. On its surface, scrawled in green marker, were the words *Your shoulder was infected.*

Charlie closed his eyes and sighed. How long had it been since the accident with the horses? It felt like a lifetime ago.

"How long . . ." Charlie sounded out, but Ellie had already beaten him to it. Scribbling on her own whiteboard, she wrote: *You've been here for 2 days.*

He breathed the thought through his mind. Two days. Considering what they'd accomplished in one, that *was* a lifetime ago. Charlie opened his mouth to sound out another word, but changed his mind and instead reached for a whiteboard. Ellie handed him hers.

He wrote: *Schrader?*

Ana replied: *Gone.*

Charlie wrote: *You sure?*

Ana replied: *We're in a hospital. If we could still see dead people, we would know it.*

Charlie considered this. It was a fair point. He wrote: *The Skylark?*

Ana replied: *Towed to Seattle.*

Charlie nodded. That was good. Repairing the damage to his father's car would put him significantly out of pocket, but he didn't care. The Skylark had been their chariot through the fires of hell, and no matter the cost, it would live to see another day.

The only thought that mattered at that moment, the only idea that seemed to bring him any sense of hope for his own future, was the image of him, Ellie, and Ana barreling along I-90 in the Skylark as the summer sun nipped at the back tires.

He smiled at the thought, then wrote: *When can we leave?*

Ana replied: *Tomorrow morning. We have plane tickets.*

The nurse, who Charlie had forgotten was still there, took out her own whiteboard.

Charlie laughed. There was something absurdly comical about a room full of people talking via the written word. He felt as if he'd woken up and found himself living through some bizarre twist on *The Newlywed Game.*

His eye was drawn to a series of sudden flashes of white light in the far corner of the room.

The TV was on.

He watched with an amused frown of disgust as the commercial for Kars4Kids played on the screen. Five fresh-faced kids dressed in black and pink bobbed and swayed while they pretended to play the insufferable earworm of a jingle on their instruments.

He smiled, scribbling on his whiteboard, and nodded at the TV. *Maybe being deaf isn't so bad after all.*

Ana grinned and smacked him on the leg.

The Dr will check on you in 1 hour, the nurse wrote, then, after a brisk erasing motion with the side of her hand, followed it up with: *for now, try to get some sleep.*

Ellie turned to the nurse and asked her something, but Charlie couldn't tell what it was. Due to his years spent in loud venues, he thought he'd become fairly proficient at lip-reading, but now that doing so was a necessity, it seemed impossible. If only people spoke like movie stars from the thirties, he thought, where enunciation was its own form of acting, but modern people slurred too much.

He sat up with a struggle—ignoring Ellie's hand on his shoulder that urged him to relax—and asked for water. The nurse handed him a Styrofoam cup. He drank deeply, savoring the cool rush down his throat, and asked for more. The nurse wrote: *In a while. Take it slow after surgery.*

She said something else to Ellie and Ana, then left with a smile.

When she was gone, Charlie turned his head and faced the window. Outside, the snow fell lightly. The pale yellow light that traced the horizon told him the sun would burn through the clouds soon enough, and he wanted to be awake when he saw it.

He leaned back into his pillow, anticipating the sun's return, and realized something that hadn't occurred to him until that moment.

He'd been there two days. It was Christmas.

He turned and looked at the two women standing at his bedside. He felt their warmth; breathed steadily knowing they were there; then lifted his whiteboard and scribbled a message.

You'll stay with me?

They promised him they would.

He didn't need a whiteboard to understand that.

EPILOGUE

It wasn't even 11 A.M. yet.

Charlie checked the weather app on his phone. Eighty-six degrees and rising. By noon, it would be in the nineties. Above him, the sun sat high, a blazing coin in a sea of blue. He could feel his skin cooking. There were no clouds that morning, and, if the weather app was telling the truth, there wouldn't be any for the foreseeable future, either.

The pavement was cooking, too. He could smell it.

People always say that when one sense goes, the others grow more powerful, but as of yet, his senses of taste, touch, and sight hadn't gotten the memo. His sense of smell, however, had become almost superhuman.

He still struggled to forget the disastrous Fourth of July weekend when Ana and Ellie had dragged him to the local fairground. The sweet summer scents of the midway—sawdust and cow shit, cotton candy and corn dogs, elephant ears and hush puppies—were so overpowering, Charlie was certain his sinuses would explode. He went home that night and stuffed two cotton balls soaked in Vicks up his nose just to eradicate the sickly sweet concoction from his memory.

On more than one occasion, he'd lie awake in his bed, pleading with whatever cosmic being that might be listening that he would be more than happy to give up his sense of smell in exchange for getting his hearing back.

Thankfully, as time went on, the sleepless nights filled with fitful pleas to the gods began to dwindle. He still had them now and then, but, as with any new obstruction, there were tricks to cope. When any scent became too strong, he simply breathed through his mouth. When a new record came out that he ached to hear, he simply hummed a tune he knew by heart in his head.

And he knew a lot of them.

He took a final drag of his cigarette and flung it into the sand-filled bucket next to the curb. It was too hot to smoke, and anyway, he promised himself he would quit soon. Just as long as he didn't have to define the word "soon."

He weaved his way back through the steady stream of sidewalk shoppers, all dressed for the weather in a way that he wasn't, but Charlie had never felt comfortable in shorts. Every year he bought a pair, figuring *Hunter S. Thompson wore them and I can too,* and every year they lay forgotten in the back of his closet, tag still attached, until it was too cold to wear them.

At the end of the block, he saw a hand wave at him.

Dustin the UPS guy (another full-grown man in shorts, Charlie observed) held out a clipboard and smiled. On more than one occasion, Charlie had seen Dustin take an extended midday break at the south end of the block, and on more than one occasion, Charlie offered him a cigarette while he did so. Dustin didn't know sign language, but Charlie had become a fairly decent lip-reader over the last eight months, and every time Dustin took the cigarette, he said the same thing.

"Okay, but this is my last one."

As long as I don't have to define "soon," I won't ask you to define "last," Charlie thought.

Today, however, Dustin was all business. He waited, hands pleasantly propped on his hips as Charlie signed the delivery slip, then took the clipboard with a practiced flick of his wrist, gave Charlie a little salute, and hopped into the big brown truck he'd parallel-parked, with surgical precision, between a Mercedes and a Lexus.

Charlie watched Dustin pull away, wishing he could have heard the UPS truck's engine roar (he could hardly believe he missed such mundane, everyday sounds), then turned on his heel and made for the door, feeling his skin yearn for air-conditioning.

As always, Dustin had left the day's shipment stacked along the north wall of his father's office.

His office, now.

He moseyed over to the boxes, checked for dings or tears (of which there were none), and stopped when he saw a smaller package sitting on top of the stack.

He read the name on the return label.

J. Graham.

Heart fluttering a little, Charlie opened the box. Inside, placed on top of the bubble paper that concealed its contents, was a note.

Charlie,
I don't care what happened to you, you're still The Man with the Magic Ear. Enjoy the spoils of your labor, Ye O Mighty One!
They were your finest find. No doubt about it.

Backstage passes for life,
Jennifer Graham

Charlie smiled and set the note aside. He removed the contents of the box and tore away the bubble paper.

In his hands were ten copies of the Mightier Ducks' first album. Only now they were the Ducks.

Charlie laughed. He supposed it was better than the old name, but not by much.

He pulled one of the records from its sleeve and placed it on a nearby turntable. With his left hand, he cranked the volume on the amplifier, and with his right, he laid his palm down on the subwoofer.

The needle dropped into the groove, four seconds of silence passed, and the song began.

Charlie could feel it. Every hit of the kick drum, every slap of the snare. Every chug of the rhythm guitar, every squeal of the lead. The bass thundered along, hammering a string of quarter notes during the verse, and then, when the chorus kicked in, it began to swing.

Charlie closed his eyes and smiled.

They had made "Olivia Quinn" track one.

After two verses, three choruses, and a mercifully quick bridge, the song ended. Charlie sat still, right hand resting on the subwoofer, and drank in the vibrations between tracks. Quiet, to him, was no longer what quiet was to other people. The song might have ended, but he could feel the silence humming beneath the skin of his fingers, under the ball of his palm.

He leaned over to reset the needle so he could feel the song again, then jumped when he felt a tap on his shoulder.

Ana Cortez glared at him impatiently.

"What?" Charlie felt himself say.

Ana signed something to him, but she was too quick. Charlie only caught *"office"* and *"waiting."* He picked up his phone, ignoring Ana's exasperated expression of protest, and typed into a speech app. When he was done, he held up his phone and pressed Play.

A robotic voice said, *"I'm having a moment here. Do you mind?"*

Slowly, Ana signed *Stop using that fucking thing. We spent four months in ASL classes with you so you don't have to sound like HAL 9000.*

Charlie grinned impishly and began typing the words *I'm sorry, Dave,* but Ana snatched his phone away and stuffed it into a drawer.

Sign language is faster. Use it.

Defeated, Charlie fingerspelled the words *Yes, boss.*

Both she and Ellie had been much faster studies than he had been, and had even begun speaking to each other in sign when Charlie wasn't around, simply because they could. Until he went deaf, he had always thought of himself as a good arguer, but good arguing takes speed, and until he buckled down and practiced sign language two hours a day like he'd promised, he was going to lose every argument he stumbled into.

Ana motioned for him to stand. *Come on, we're ready.*

Charlie signed *Okay* and watched Ana flit out of the office.

Before following her out, he opened one of the larger boxes

Dustin had delivered. Stacked neatly inside were fifty freshly shrink-wrapped vinyl records. He pulled one out and stared at the cover.

A twenty-five-year-old Raymond stared back at him, his eyes deep and soulful, his helmet of mahogany hair draped wispily over his thick sideburns. The right corner of his lips kicked up a bit, hinting at a smile.

Charlie ran his fingers along the embossed album title.

Songs for Joanie.

He flipped the record over. Stamped on the lower right was the name of his new boutique label: *Cuckoo's Nest Records.*

He'd had a thousand copies printed.

Ana popped her head back through the door and tapped her watch.

Downstairs, Ellie was behind the register, bagging a stack of jazz records for Harold Meehan. When she saw Ana and Charlie descending the grand staircase, her eyes went wide. She hopped up and down, clapping lightly.

Harold grinned when he saw Charlie and signed *Can I get a discount?*

Charlie laughed and gave him a thumbs-up. It was the only phrase Harold had learned so far, and he'd gotten a lot of mileage out of it.

With a little squeal that even Charlie seemed to hear, Ellie made her way to the front door and pushed her way through, skipping out onto the sidewalk. Ana and Charlie followed, but before they went through, Charlie turned to Ana and signed, *Are you sure you're okay with this?*

Ana pantomimed a big sigh. *It was* my *idea, dummy.*

Well, just so you know, you are *family*, Charlie signed back. He leaned over and kissed her cheek.

Ana took his hand and gave it a squeeze.

Once they were all outside and situated properly, Ellie called up to the two contractors standing on ladders, shielding her eyes from the harsh glare of the sunlight. "Hey, guys! Are you ready?"

The contractor on the left nodded. "Whenever you are."

Ellie gave them the thumbs-up, and the contractors unclipped a large sheet of brown paper and let it fall to the pavement.

Charlie, Ana, and Ellie smiled as they gazed up at the shiny new sign.

REMICK RECORDS
Family-Owned

ACKNOWLEDGMENTS

Thank you:

To my editors, Kristin Temple and Claire Eddy. Your expertise, professionalism, encouragement, enthusiasm, and kindness helped shape this story into what it is, and I'm so grateful to you. To the team at Tor/Nightfire: Esther Kim, Ariana Carpentieri, Jocelyn Bright, Jessica Katz, Jacqueline Huber-Rodriguez, Susan Walsh, Rafal Gibek, and Valeria Castorena. The fact that so many incredible people dedicated their time and talent to something I typed into a computer is still astonishing to me.

To JL Stermer, my agent and friend: for your constant, unwavering support over the years, endless laughter, constant good advice, and all-around awesomess. I'm so lucky I met you. None of this would have happened if you hadn't taken a chance on me.

To my Los Angeles, New York, and Seattle friends: Jimmy and Amanda Page, Luke and Courtney Forand, Jim Donohue, Marjon Rahimian and Erik Paulsson, John Green, Jessica and Brent Qualls, Lizzy Rolando, Natalia Wolff, Scott Spiegel, Sara Bordo, Kathy Pak, and Melissa Walker-Scott.

To Liz Keenan: for the lunches at the Irvington and the strolls afterward. You're the coolest and you know it.

To Manal Aboudafir: the Céline to my Jesse. Let's take the corner booth at Bemelmans Bar.

To the family Cartagena: CC, Loli, Joana, and Tito, for always treating my sister and me like family, and for your friendship and generosity, which has meant the world to the both of us. Every time I say goodbye to one of you, I can't wait until I see you again.

To Genesis Rodriguez: there simply isn't enough space here to list the ways your friendship has made my life better. Whole sections of this book wouldn't exist if we'd never met.

To Russell Scott: for being my daily partner in crime and for sharing in my medically unsafe obsession with book collecting. And for everything else. Cheers, Redberry.

To Martin Kearney-Fischer: my oldest friend. For always being there to feed my obsession with aviation, for never letting your arms get tired, and always making sure there's a high-quality fire extinguisher . . . right in the kitchen.

To Seth Nicholas Johnson: the conversation started over twenty years ago and hasn't lost an ounce of steam in all that time. You are the Frasier to my Niles, or, depending on the day and situation, the Niles to my Frasier. Either way, it's always a blast.

To Richard Scott Leeds: my uncle and namesake—thank you for *Super Castlevania IV,* wandering the aisles of Video Unlimited with me when I was a kid, and for always being there.

To Janine Leeds: for being the best little sister a fella could ask for. You've got the warmest, kindest heart, and you make everyone you meet feel special and unique and seen. Lowfat Paris, Neens.

To Dad: the first voracious reader I ever knew. I wish you could have read this one. I think you would have liked it. And thanks for the Peter Benchley books. I still have them.

And to Mom: who, when I was boy and you read the last line of a book to me, never said no when I asked you to read it again, who never told me to hurry up when I was in the middle of my third hour at the library, who never balked when I told you I wanted to be a writer when I grew up, and who always believed in me, especially when I didn't believe in myself. You radiate light and kindness and love and positivity, you laugh in the face of adversity, you never despair, and, let's be honest, you're just a hoot to be around. I hope I made you proud, Mom.